madman on the water

Kenner McQuaid

NOTICES

It is the Constitution of the United States itself that explicitly empowers Congress to enact laws concerning copyright protection of literary works. The Copyright Act of 1976 and its subsequent amendments, as interpreted by the courts of the United States, provides copyright protection for authors the minute that pen is put to paper or a finger strikes a computer key- regardless of whether or not the work has been registered with the U.S. Copyright Office. The author exclusively is able to exercise the 'bundle of rights' contained in the Act, including distribution rights. Any acts of infringement committed with respect to this work will be addressed in the federal court having proper personal jurisdiction over the defendant(s).

DISCLAIMER: This book is not intended to provide any legal advice. The author assumes no liability for any reliance by any person upon any of the legal questions and/or scenarios discussed fictitiously herein. Always consult with an independent, licensed attorney in your jurisdiction for legal advice specific to the facts of your particular situation.

Front Cover: *Princeton Harbor after Storm*, 2008.07.09
Rear Cover: *Sunrise on 10th Street*, 2008.08.22

Photos Used by Permission.

For Brian
I received the call just an hour ago that you had killed yourself. We always joked that you'd be buried in that damn black & white shirt you wore six days out of seven. And you were! I just didn't ever think it would be this week, brother. May you rest in peace and laughter forever.

Your pal,

Chips
2/27/08 3:14 p.m.

P.S. You won't fucking believe this, but the Phillies actually won the World Series.

NOTE

My name is Patrick McShea, and I've always considered myself to be a very flawed person due to my Irish Catholic upbringing. This was compounded by my experience with clinical major depression while in law school. I dictated this journal during the summer of 2010 at the suggestion of my psychiatrist, Dr. Karlis. I began to transcribe it, unaltered, at my friend Harry Trimble's vacation home in Angel Bay, NJ using an ancient laptop that employed a handcrank to power itself up. I was often under the influence of various medications, gorgeous sunsets and illicit intoxicants when I had my digital voice recorder in my hand. A look directly into a man's mind reveals varying degrees of shadow and light. When listening back to my own voice on the recordings, I was stricken with the reality that mine has been filled with dark, dark shadows for many, many years. It is, at times, disturbing.

PATRICK ALYOSISUS McSHEA, ESQ.
SEPTEMBER 23, 2010

Preface

It was shortly before noon when I finally decided that it was time to get the gun. Nothing outrageous had caused me to leave my insanely cluttered desk and walk out of the office on that cold March morning. I was simply fed up with leading the pathetic lifestyle of a working class law school failure. I never planned to be 32 years old and desperately broke while sleeping on the couch in my parents' Northeast Philadelphia basement like I was some sort of tortured artist still trying to find myself. I worked upwards of 60 hours per week at some hole-in-the-wall insurance defense firm earning a whopping salary of $49,750. It was my third job in three years. I got fired from the first two. My student loan debt was approximately $90,000 with interest mounting daily. My checking account balance stood at $727.46. There was neither a savings account in my name nor any retirement fund to speak of. I hadn't made a payment on my maxed-out credit card in six months. I needed $3,700 in dental work and the firm offered no dental insurance. My blue '95 Honda Civic EX had 154,256 miles on its odometer and looked like it had spent three years in service in Afghanistan. My poor mother had bone cancer. Payday was still 11 days away. Bankruptcy wasn't even an option for me. I had researched the issue myself, and it's harder to get student loans discharged in bankruptcy than it is to walk the 239,000 miles to the moon. Smothering in an economic quicksand with no help on the way, I had finally realized that any further struggle with its slippery grains was simply in vain. I accepted that it was just my time.

I didn't bother to tell my bitch of a secretary that I was leaving the office for good. My scheduled two o'clock settlement conference at City Hall with Judge D'Orazio no longer held any importance. I took some morbid delight in knowing that Janice would be going crazy looking for me after fielding the screaming phone call from His Honor's Chambers that would threaten thousands of dollars in sanctions against my hellhole firm for my non-appearance. She would be yelling and bitching and stomping around the office in her big black boots, calling out for me and cursing with each crushing step on the drab office carpet. I couldn't give a fuck about Judge D'Orazio or my conference or my client. I'd already be dead.

That entire week had seen the city fall into the grasp of a deep, painful, unrelenting freeze that carried enough of winter's brutality to kill. I took the cold personally, like almost everything else in those days. The remarkably bitter weather aside, the day had been like any other. At 9:35 a.m., I arrived in my 16th floor office inside the Reddington Bank Building, a bland, squat, aging office tower which was just off Market Street, the main thoroughfare that cuts east-west across Center City Philadelphia between the Schuylkill and Delaware Rivers. It was low rent office space perfect for the low-rent law firm that employed me. Like most of the other offices occupied by the junior associates, I worked in a cave painted in a dull battleship gray color with no molding and no window. My role was to defend minor car accident cases and slip-and-fall lawsuits for massive insurance companies with tens of billions of dollars in assets. There could be nothing more boring or more mindless. I spent my days pouring over one-page police reports, chiropractic records, auto repair estimates, senseless graphs on EMG study reports, and pages and pages and pages of computerized office notes taken by an insurance adjuster who didn't have a fucking clue as to how to properly evaluate the merits of an auto accident claim. Occasionally, I would spend a couple of hours preparing for a deposition so that I could pose such riveting questions as, "Sir, is it your testimony under oath here today that the light was *green* when you entered the intersection at 6th and Westmoreland?" or "Ma'am, did you see a yellow warning cone in place *before* you walked down Aisle 5?" Watching industrial-grade paint dry would have been a 100% improvement over this job. It probably paid better, too.

I hadn't been fully awake in five years. Three hours of uninterrupted sleep on my parents' basement couch was a minor miracle, no matter how much dope I smoked in the breezeway or how many of my mother's pain or sleeping pills I had stolen. I had fallen into the same miserable pattern day after day, night after night, week after week, month after month, year after year. Get to bed around 11 o'clock on Sunday night. Maybe pop a few pills, maybe not. I'd drift off around 12:45 after lying down at 11. Wake up around 3 a.m. My thoughts, all of my 133,000 simultaneous thoughts, would constantly charge through my brain from the nothingness, ensuring that I would never, ever get a full nights' rest:

[die die die die die i need to die so this will fucking END! $995 per month for the next twenty years just for the student loans! how the fuck will i ever be able to afford a house before i'm 45? at this rate i will be out of mom and dad's basement by 2014. *that's four more fucking years!* who will be calling my mother tomorrow while i am at work? mother sick and weakened the phone rings ring ring ring ring it rings all day from morning till night. does patrick mcshea live there? yes he does he's my son. please tell your son to call us ma'am as soon as he is able or there will be serious consequences. what consequences? i have no cash no credit no assets no hope no dreams i am crushed under the weight of desire of imminent DEATH. my god lauren taylor had the nicest legs in the entire law school universe or any universe for that matter. how could i ever have deserved them? so toned so golden so smooth the target of my ever-perverted fantasies and always insatiable lust. her lips were so soft so red so wet so painful to touch only once that it's almost better that i never did at all.

you were so right to move to boston with that dorky accountant you met during happy hour lauren! a $155,000 big firm salary plus bonuses is not too shabby you and your perfectly toned mind and calves were destined for it.   can i get myself out to california? impossible. not even enough money for gas! homelessness would be worse than this basement despite the better weather in san francisco. how 'bout indiana? the cost of living is much cheaper. just work at the supermarket and rent a shitty college town apartment. student loan people would never find me. lawyer? not me no siree bob i'm just a guy who is down on his luck and needs a job. skip's my name how do you do sir? everyone is so friendly here in the hoosier state. that's right hoosier hospitality is no accident i saw the sign on the highway that's why i came down here from canada. no i don't have a social security number yet because i'm canadian of course but as soon as you put me to work i will start getting that all straightened out kind sir.   fourth grade thrown into a dumpster by georgie inammorato felt so small walking home stinking like garbage.   mom yells at me because i'm home late and my shirt is stained with who the hell knows what. how is this my fault you fucking bitch i am the smallest kid at school. i can't believe that i am so flat fucking broke that i can't maintain my own teeth like someone living in a trailer park on welfare who dropped out of school in fifth grade. ignorance is total bliss. stomach churns and churns with acid and bile and utter hopelessness. wonder what my kim is doing these days? i know she's not on the couch in her parents' basement or in my parents' basement either. just like i know that i fucked that pretty south korean pussy a thousand times and never got sick of her frenzied voice moaning my name in ecstasy. i fucking hate myself. i am weak i am worthless i should burn i should die in ways that no one should ever die because i took a gift and squandered it. i fucked up so many classes with c's and c-minuses. such a fucking dope! professor brady you bastard you told me what a brilliant legal mind i had when you were piss drunk then stuck me with a d+ and said not to worry about it? easy for you to say you fucking balding bearded prick! daddy sent you to yale and you have tenure making over $155,000 per year and tax shelters and investment properties. i have NOTHING and need to interview with law firms with a D+ BLAZING on my transcript that screams PATRICK A. MCSHEA IS A STONE FUCKING IDIOT. TO AN AUTO DEFENSE FIRM MAKING 40K FOR YOU ASSHOLE GOOD LUCK PAYING OFF THOSE STUDENT LOANS HAHAHAHAHAHAHAHAHAHAHA i should have gotten a gun and walked up to your office on the third floor next to the fire escape and pulled the fucking trigger so that i could have the last laugh as a bullet flies into your pompous ivy league skull. no i would shoot your leg first so i could see the horror on your face and laugh because yale man now knows he is going to die very prematurely very painfully instead of spending 20 more years teaching civil procedure to soulless perky-titted twenty three year-olds wearing glasses with thick frames and tight sweaters that always sit in the front row and stare up at you vigorously tapping away at their laptops for 80 minutes without blinking. already 3:45 a.m. it hurts my chest is empty and burning i want to wither away and die i have nothing after twenty years of schooling. could i catch a break at some point before i climb the ben franklin bridge? i would look out toward the thousands and thousands of lights in the office towers where people are earning real money and living life but oh not me i have offended some unknown unseen deity who has brought curses upon my very soul! so cold so cold so fucking bitter cold as i stare down into the turgid blackened water of the dirty delaware river. i have to piss now. the water looks so far below me i will be dead long before i touch it. but what if i live? i won't. i jump i fall i scream it is too late for anything else my bitter heart stops. i hit the frozen water lifeless i'm DEAD. hello does anyone care? who will come to the funeral? who will be the most upset. i don't feel like getting up to take a piss 4:07 a.m. toilet is over ten steps away much too far for my tired legs. did i get the carpets cleaned? i will next week can you hand me some brussel sprouts in the meantime for my fishbowl? the fish love to eat the brussel sprouts and rutabagas and duckworms. wait! i don't own any fish. i had a tank at iowa in my bedroom because the sorority girls would love to get stoned and watch the neon tetras swim back and forth for hours. i am semi-dreaming senselessly. am i finally drifting off again? its 5:25 shit almost time to get up i finally slumber]

Alarm goes off at 7. My entire body aches. Roll over and hit sleep. Alarm goes off at 7:09. Hit sleep again. I'm angry. So fucking angry. And tired. Alarm goes off at 7:18. Hit sleep again. Alarm goes off at 7:27. Turn off the alarm. Lie on the couch for ten more minutes wondering how many more months I will last working at my latest horrible, low-paying legal gig as I hear my dad make his tea upstairs. He's had the same job as a high school teacher for over 30 years. I finally get up from the couch to walk into the bathroom and stand over the toilet for a few minutes because I hate my life so much that I literally feel sick about it. I haven't had a drink in eleven years, but I vomit repeatedly like an alcoholic with a raging hangover struggling to maintain a job just to keep a roof over his head. Run in and out of the shower. In the car by 8:20 after saying goodbye to Mom. She asks why I'm running so late. Interstate 95 is a parking lot. Sit in traffic for almost an hour. Get into my office by 9:35 a.m. Turn on my computer. Check the local news. Check my work e-mail. Dozens of reminders pop up about cases I've forgotten about or am completely ignoring. I continue to ignore them by first checking my personal e-mail. Twenty new messages, 15 of which are spam, 3 of which are stupid chain e-mails from girls who will never fuck me and the remaining two are from friends I never bother to see anymore. I think about which pointless work assignment I should begin first. This becomes a twenty minute project inside my scrambled egg brain. I finally open Word Perfect and begin to make revisions to the last of yesterday's lame assignments. Check my e-mail again, even though there couldn't possibly be any new messages except for crap. Read all of the local and national news websites. It's 11:00 a.m. by now and I've done absolutely nothing. Would I work harder if I had a better job with better pay? Or am I now just a lazy fuck at my core? Walk down to the kitchen for my third cup of water this morning. I drank the first, then drank only half of the second before dumping the rest into the plant that's dying on the top of the bookshelf. Piss. Get back to working on something. The phone rings. It's the partner. He wants to know if I finished a draft of the motion response in the *Hardy* case that he assigned me last week. Of course I hadn't. I had completely forgotten about it. It has to be filed with the court tomorrow. "I'll have it finished up in about an hour," I say. That will keep him off my back for a bit while I throw something together and hand it to Janice for preparing the numerous unnecessary forms to be attached to it for filing, which will cause her to bitch endlessly because she'll have to get off the phone with her sister and do actual work. Partner calls again. I'm so tired. "Did you finish the Interrogatories *Robeson?*" he asks. "They're due tomorrow, too." I desperately try to recall the *Robeson* case. Is it a car accident? A slip and fall? A two-bit products liability suit?

I pull up the electronic file. It's a car accident case. Interrogatories are the biggest pain in the ass. The attorney for the allegedly injured plaintiff sends out 109 typewritten, single-spaced questions with subparts for my client to answer, all because he hit the plaintiff's car in a Wal-Mart parking lot while traveling 5 miles an hour and allegedly caused 'significant and permanent' injuries to the guy's neck and back. Only my client can tell me when the last time he had an eye exam before the accident or whether he had changed his windshield wiper blades in the past 90 days- not that any of that shit really matters, anyway. But it's billable hours. In small-time cases, sending out 109 Interrogatories is only designed to punish you into settling. It never works. We just roll up our sleeves and bill. "Did you send the Robesons a certified letter asking them to contact you about the Interrogatories?" the partner wants to know. Yes. They signed for it, then ignored it like every other motor vehicle accident client does. Did I go out to their house and try to chase them down like I am their parole officer instead of their lawyer? No. Did I drop my drawers and take a dump all over the file? I should have. The irony might have been considered high art in some quarters, since the one Redweld holding the file materials was the legal equivalent of a steaming pile of shit. Every case that I was assigned was a steaming pile of shit. And, with some talented attorneys with more seniority somehow working at this low-budget defense mill, every file that I worked for the next couple of years would be as enthralling as cleaning up afterbirth. "What about the Interrogatories in *Miller?*" Partner asks. Client didn't respond to my calls for those draft answers, either, but I assure Partner that I'm on it.

I first fumble through the *Robeson* file and find the client's phone number. I'm so distracted by self-hatred that I have to dial three times to get a 10-digit number right. Phone rings twelve times. No answering machine. No voicemail. No luck. Seven years of school for *this?* 'This' goes on all day, every day, for months and months at a time. I forget about a deadline, placate the partner somehow and instead rely on my natural abilities to throw something together last minute between staring at the computer screen for hours and wondering how I'm going to escape this life. I can't, of course. There's too many student loans and I'm not qualified to do anything else except litigate car accident cases. I haven't touched a real legal file in years. If I somehow scored an interview with a real law firm with a real litigation practice, I wouldn't have a clue anymore. I'm strictly slip/fall, red light/green light, all day, every day. I try to make up the time that I waste staring blankly like a zombie at my computer screen all day once the clock hits 7:00 p.m., when everybody else is finally gone and there are no phones ringing or secretaries from South Philly endlessly chatterboxing about the latest brute from the pipefitter's union that they're fucking. Do about an hour and a half of real work somehow, some way in addition to whatever I managed to get done during the preceding ten and a half hours. Make some contact with the clients that never, ever return my calls. Leave the office at 8:30 p.m. or so. No traffic, home by 8:55. Microwave the dinner that Mom saved for me and inhale it. Go down to the basement. Strum my old guitar for about 20 minutes or so. Sit back and rest my eyes for a few minutes, only to fall asleep for almost an hour. Wake up in a daze. Surf the net for a bit, usually wasting my time searching through online porn to find pictures of naked women that sort of resemble my own friends and former classmates. Back lying on the couch by 11:00 p.m. Stare blankly at the white ceiling. I've memorized every detail of the tiles directly above where my head sits on the couch. Turn the light out next to the couch. Fall asleep around 12:15. Wake up again between 3 and 4 a.m. Back to sleep around 6. Repeat. By Thursday, I can't physically get out of bed when the alarm goes off because I've only had sixteen or so hours of staggered sleep over four days. Leave work early on Thursday and Friday- by 6:30 p.m., at the latest- even though I've legitimately billed only 4 of the 9 hours I need to for each day. I spend the rest of my time staring blankly at the computer monitor watching the screensaver move back and forth and back and forth and up and down.

It puts me ten billable hours behind for the week. Forty for the month. Over four hundred for the year. I can't even inflate my time because the cases I'm assigned are so simple. No one could ever believe that I spent 15 hours reviewing a car accident file when only $10,000 at most is at issue. I feel like the village idiot. Stay in the basement Friday night. I'm too tired to go out. Mom's concerned that I don't seem to see my friends much. I no longer take any weekend road trips or short flights to visit my fraternity brothers that are spread out along the Eastern seaboard. I don't even walk the six blocks to see my neighborhood high school buddies anymore. Wake up around 1 p.m. on Saturday. Go the office for a few hours. Do nothing Saturday night and all day Sunday except to sleep and dread work on Monday. This wasn't living. It was Hell. I'd need a job making at least $90K to have any kind of quality of life. Attorneys with no law review, no grades, three bad or unknown firms on their resume and two 'involuntary terminations' don't make the leap from making dogshit to almost a hundred grand. It wasn't going to happen. I had no choice but to waive the white flag.

* * *

The scenery along I-95 North is typical of any aging Rust Belt city- abandoned warehouses, burned-out buildings, highway ramps that lead to nowhere, and a constantly dreary winter-gray sky that allows only the slimmest margin of sunlight to reach the pockmarked surface. The few factories that are still operating constantly spew thick, chemical-laced smog from their exhaust towers, covering the entire stretch of highway with the oddly sweet smell of pollution. I reached the Allegheny Avenue exit in less than 10 minutes, just as the car interior began to warm to a comfortable temperature. Allegheny and the streets surrounding it aren't known to anyone unless you are a Philadelphia native or are forced to do business in the area. Its path eventually leads to a crumbling, decrepit neighborhood that is akin to an urban Appalachia, housing a forgotten Caucasian underclass completely isolated from mainstream society despite existing only twenty minutes from the Liberty Bell and the hundreds of thousands of tourists that visit each year from all over the planet. It was the kind of place where the frustrated neighborhood boys that can't get into the pants of the neighborhood girls during the hot, boring summer nights entertain themselves by throwing stray cats in front of the trains. The main artery, Kensington Avenue, is no longer the busy commercial strip running through the working class rowhouse neighborhood that was broadcast to the entire free world in *Rocky*. Now there was little of anything save closed-down factories and boarded-up storefronts, the streets infected by pale-skinned prostitutes and other vermin that started working the corners at 8:00 a.m. hoping to service the longshoremen coming off the night shift.

They were joined by a bunch of zoned-out wraiths desperately stumbling around in the trash underneath the elevated rail tracks, mumbling to themselves and reaching under their tattered coats to scratch the skin raw on their arms and chest and backs while desperately in pursuit of their next fix. It was their sole obsession in life. They searched for scrap to sell, loose change to pocket and elderly persons to rob with the unrelenting zeal of Admiral Halsey chasing the Japanese carrier fleet across the Pacific. Every junkie from Houston to Omaha to Johnson City and points further north somehow knew that the cheapest, most powerful smack on the East Coast could be had on these streets. The names of the locals in the police district blotter that had gotten busted for soliciting prostitutes, scoring drugs and the usual urban mischief were joined by others from equally godforsaken places across the United States who should have had no knowledge that this slice of earthly shit even exists. My battered car, Pennsylvania tags and white skin allowed me to blend-in enough with the filth to protect me from the watchful eye of the law for a time. Every cop in the district knew that there was no reason for someone from Virginia or Delaware or New York to pass through these streets unless they were looking for drugs or a quick ten dollar BJ, and few blacks lived in the neighborhood. I couldn't have trusted myself if this had been a warm summer night and some diseased seventeen year-old was offering herself on the cheap. I was so far gone from my former life as an Iowa frat brat mingling with adorable sorority girls in a riverside mansion that five minutes in the mouth of a ragged-looking underage junkie with hepatitis or gonorrhea or anything else picked up while working this squalor would have been far too tempting.

I moved across several intersections, driving slowly through the neighborhood in search of a drug so potent that it might kill me alone if I somehow lost the guts to pull the trigger. The cold had forced most of the street peddlers to take cover inside the abandoned rowhomes that dot each block like rotting teeth in the dark mouth of the city. The repeat customers would know where to look; I was a first-timer with no fucking clue. Finding little action along the main drag, I turned up and down and up and down the random side streets, the trash on their sidewalks blowing around in circles while the elevated screeched and rattled noisily against the cold steel above. A hooded figure slipped out from a small brick rowhome standing alone with vacant lots on either side. He looked up and down the street with his hands in his thick, black sweatshirt like he was waiting for somebody or something. I had found my man.

* * *

I drove my old Honda back onto Kensington Avenue and suddenly veered off into a garbage-strewn, pothole-filled sideway underneath the onramp back onto I-95 North. I came to a stop and turned off the ignition. I took a few seconds to stare straight ahead through my grimy, cracked windshield. I thought of nothing. This was the most profound moment of my entire life and I approached it with all the gravity and urgency of walking down to the corner to buy a newspaper. I exhaled deeply, opened the center console and pushed past a bunch of folded, old paystubs, wrinkled gum wrappers and various ATM receipts showing food stamp-eligible account balances as I searched for my cheap, metal, violet-colored pipe. The eerie, tremolo-drenched sound of Tommy James and the Shondells was playing on the oldies station as I sparked my lighter and heard the soft crackling of the grass and powder igniting. The tar immediately flared, snapping and burning a brief, bright blue. I softly inhaled from my piece. My first taste of the white dragon was a total disappointment. I expected to see swirling stars and be immediately thrust forth into a drug-induced orgasm that would absolutely blow my brain apart neuron by neuron, cell by cell. Instead, I felt nothing aside from the dull, tranquil haze brought on by the pot smoke. The natural, woodsy flavor of my grass was totally fucked up by the chemicals and cutting agents creating an awful, unholy taste in my mouth. I took a second hit, then another. And another. And another. Still nothing. The clock on my console said 1:57. It was always about 15 minutes fast because I was always late for everything. My cell phone was off. Janice was probably already storming around the office while wondering where the fuck I was. What a cunt.

I next reached for the firearm. It was lighter than I expected. Now I had to figure out how to load the fucking thing and finish the job for good [rush is intense! intense! intense! reality melts away i need to vomit no i'm just excited! it's a good sick so euphoric what a powdery thrill! what a fantastic feeling! i float i fly i'm no longer cold where am i? who am i? who fucking cares? *i* don't. i relax. i lean back. drop the gun on my lap. what a high what an incredible fucking high! much better than sex!!! lasts longer and no criminally insane megabitch to deal with afterward. i gag going higher and higher what a wonderful life i dry heave but i'm so fucking wasted who the fuck cares it blasts through my veins and arteries and capillaries and burns into my brain through rapid bolts of angelfire. it don't matter if i have nothing if i have this sweet deadly powder with me! a flash of neutron bombs in my synapses and cells before the rush drains from my body. i am calm i am serene i am finally at peace. i am a lawyer with a gun smoking heroin and it is no stranger than puddles forming in the rain. curses! curses! screaming yelling bloody murder my high is being fucked up! how dare you interrupt my lone moment of ecstasy! get the fuck out of the car get the fuck out! hands up! hands up! the door next to me opens i fall, fall like a bag of rocks onto the cold ground but feel like feathers what is happening? i struggle to get up i stumble i fall i stand where are my glasses? i am face to face with death from another man's gun]

Officer Liam Thompson stood across from me with profoundly disturbed look upon his face that was atypical for a third-generation cop that had patrolled these bad streets for close to a decade. But Liam happened to be both a police officer and my first cousin. I began to vomit violently. As Liam radioed for an ambulance, I thought I heard the soft flutter of the wings of my guardian angel pass through the gray, freezing cold of winter on its way toward a much better place. I envied that angel, like I envied all the dead. I did nothing but throw up all over myself for the next two hundred and forty minutes.

Wednesday, May 26, 2010

5:57 p.m.

I have mixed feelings about my cousin Liam saving my life. It seems like I'm caught in the proverbial deep, black hole and I'm trying to dig myself out with only a plastic spork. It's now been revealed that I suffered from clinical major depression that was allowed to fester for five full years because I somehow failed, or simply refused to recognize, that I was mentally ill. That represents hundreds of sleepless nights, three lost jobs, some very bad women, and hundreds of thousands of fucking dollars that was left on the table when I graduated from Villanova Law School with a 2.62 GPA instead of the modest but respectable 3.45 I held at the end of my first year. The biggest kick in the balls is that much of this was ultimately preventable with earlier treatment, which provides a constant source of blame that I cast generously upon myself at all hours of the day. I can't help but assign blame. I'm still a lawyer, after all, and whenever something bad or unfortunate happens it's never an accident; it is *always* because somebody fucked up, and that person has to pay the price for their grave misdeeds.

There are many issues in my life that need to be addressed and remedied, but only one may have a relatively quick fix. That's my social life. The other issues, like my desperate financial situation and failed career, have no short-term solutions and will have to be evaluated over a number of years. I haven't accepted that yet. Constant financial distress is a difficult pill to swallow, especially for someone in a 'profession' where money is thrown around obscenely and is the sole motivation behind every decision made by everybody with respect to everything. This is because lawyers are rarely content with what they have. There is always someone or some firm that has more money or bigger clients than you do, and lawyers and their massive egos simply find this intolerable. The headlines of the daily legal publications are constantly ablaze with the latest eight-figure verdicts, the newest raises in associate salaries, and increases in profits per partner for mega law firms that garner almost a billion per year in revenue.

The good news has slowed since Wall Street collapsed into its own filth, but there is still no shortage of disputes to feed the shit machine that is the modern practice of law. For me personally, these front page reports are a constant reminder that I am a legal outsider trying to climb Jacob's unconquerable ladder to a heaven of stability and fortune and success. *All* lawyers are trying to climb a ladder of some sort to greater financial and professional recognition, but very few ever find themselves satisfied with their progress. Often, they're so bogged down in the haze of discovery, motions, stock acquisition agreements, more discovery, more motions, billable hour

1

benchmarks, inhuman partners and drugs and alcohol and depression that they don't realize they've lost their grip on the sacred ladder until they've already hit the ground hard. It's not that the strong survive and the weak are cast aside in the law; the reality is that usually only the sociopathic survive. And for what purpose? Who the fuck knows. My own belief is that the practice of law is often a refuge for many people that lack a soul and don't have anything better to do with their lives. Many lawyers would disagree with that sentiment, but that's only because they're too pompous or blind to admit the pathetic truth about themselves. Instead, they hide behind their accolades, bank accounts and lawyerly notions of superiority until they realize one day that everything else they've ever had- friends, spouses, children- are long, long gone.

I think about all of these things constantly when I drive. The Garden State Parkway is the latest thoroughfare that I'm polluting with my Honda. It is a long, green but very boring highway that stretches 172.4 miles from Exit 0 at Cape May in the south to the New York state line just past Montvale, NJ on the northern end. I don't always think about my life and the law when I'm on the road, though. Just as often, I think about my car. It has certainly seen better days and I'm not sure how much time it has left. It's stressful. I know there's a lot of rust in the frame and its various constituent parts, but since I can't see it I don't waste any time worrying about it. There are other things that I can appreciate. The transmission sometimes struggles mightily to get from third to fourth gear. The motor in the passenger's side window is broken, the mirror on the driver's side (the third, I might add) is fastened to the door by duct tape, and the vehicle's weather sealing has broken down in various places leading to a constant smell of mildew in the interior. As an added bonus, the Check Engine light is constantly aglow. The windshield's cracked, too, but the crack isn't propagating. It's not a car one would expect to see a 'lawyer' driving. But the piece of shit starts every time I turn the key. It gets me places. I couldn't ever pick up a date in it, but I haven't had any reason to be concerned about that for quite some time.

I think about my futility with women when I drive, too. I'm not afraid to admit that I almost dread having regular interactions with women again. I'm just a shell of the guy I was as an undergrad at the University of Iowa or during the four carefree post-college, pre-law school years when I had only $28,000 in student loan debt and dated a med student with an ass that would have brought nations to war in another epoch. This is a dangerous time for me. My ego is fragile, and my confidence is nil. There is no question that women can sniff out the scent of desperation within minutes of meeting you. For most, it's a repellent. Less scrupulous women sense the slow death of your manly soul and circle like vultures, hungering for your attention (and

2

your wallet) but refusing to provide any affection in return. Equally desperate women view you as an opportunity to score the always-elusive boyfriend by latching onto you in the hope of sharing their misery through constant, unreasonable demands on your time. This is complemented by guaranteed weekly mental meltdowns over the state of your 'relationship.' With any luck, I'll just step in shit one night about five minutes before last call and all of my over-thinking regarding women can just stop.

My psychiatrist, Dr. Karlis, was just as concerned about the lack of intimacy in my life as he was the other deficiencies that were destroying me. This proves that he is a very wise man, because the simple truth is this: although the little peach pills that I pop every day have stabilized my body and mind somewhat, I will never be able to move forward completely without experiencing the prolonged high that comes from falling into the arms of a pretty woman with soft lips and an alcohol-flavored tongue. By my own estimation, I haven't had sex in 398 days. Sex used to be a semi-regular occurrence for me. It no longer is, obviously. The last woman that was dumb enough to sleep with me was my high school megacrush Brigit O'Brien after she broke our 14-year silence by finding me on facebook. I hadn't seen Brigit in over a decade, and the demanding mistress called 'time' was not very kind to her. I think it was the scars from her C-sections that were the straws that really broke the camel's back, though. That's about when Britney Spears became completely unattractive to me. It's too odd to see scars from childbirth on a sex symbol. It's even odder to see them on your best friend from high school. Sex that is unfulfilling due to a lack of attraction can sometimes be just as bad as no sex. That's why I cut Brigit off. To me, it was just as frustrating to be sleeping with a formerly hot but now overweight, divorced mother of 2 as it was to be alone. You feel bad about yourself when you're alone. You also feel bad about yourself when the best you can get isn't good enough to please you. My lingering Irish Catholic guilt wouldn't allow me to use Brigit any longer. It's far easier to just cut the other human out of the picture rather than complicate things any further. I didn't know at the time, of course, that my only other option would be a 398 day drought.

My phone begins to vibrate, and since there are no other cars on the road I fumble through the pocket of my $19.99 Old Navy khaki shorts to retrieve it:

New Message: Maria Napoli
5/26/10 6:06 p.m.
Enjoy ur summer and RELAX. U need it patrick.
Call me if u ever need 2.

Message to: Maria Napoli
5/26/10 6:07 p.m.
Thanks! I will def stay in touch.

3

Maria Napoli was my best female friend from law school. She's personally responsible for my graduation from Villanova Law. By my 3L year, she could tell something was seriously wrong with me even though I was bathed in some mixture of ignorance and denial myself. I had picked up a very bad habit of missing Taxation of Partnerships & Corporations during my final semester, which was offered on Monday and Thursday at 8:30 a.m. The partners at the firm where I was clerking had 'suggested' that I take that bear of a class before ultimately deciding in March of my 3L year not to hire me on the day my offer letter was to be tendered. Once that little incident happened, I *never* slept. There was no way I could make it to class without being fashionably late or skipping it all together. Sometimes I wouldn't even bother with my 11:00 a.m. class, either. Maria would always find me on the days I skipped lecture to lead me into an empty classroom to go over her notes with her. I had no business background, and Subchapter K of the Internal Revenue Code was the biggest mess that I ever had the misfortune to study. If she hadn't taken the time to do that, there's no question I would have failed the exam and not graduated in May. I probably would have been pushed over the edge to suicide given the way I was already feeling.

Maria even came to my parents' house twice in order to force me to go over material with her at the kitchen table. My mother adored her. I liked to pretend that Maria didn't have a gigantic crush on me, but she did. I didn't find her physically attractive at all, even though I have been saddled with a permanent unrequited lust for almost every woman that has dark hair, dark eyes and a last name that ends in a vowel. I tried. She never pushed the issue with me. I refuse to enumerate what I found unattractive about Maria because I think the world of her as a person. I even considered kissing her once but just as soon thought the better of it. I knew that I couldn't be happy with her because of the lack of physical attraction. I couldn't lead on a close friend. It felt rotten to be on the other end of one of those deals, though. I guess they can suck whether you're in the role of the denied or the denier, if you have developed a conscience somewhat.

Since I skipped my law school graduation, I couldn't thank Maria in person for all of her effort in keeping me above water during my final, torturous semester. Before I snuck out of my parents' house to get high, I had a dozen roses delivered to her at the ceremony even though it left me with only $79.00 in the bank. The card read, *'Thanks for the B+ in biz tax. You're going to be wildly successful. Love, Patrick.'* I didn't see Maria again until the Pennsylvania bar exam in late July, and we didn't have much of a chance to talk. You don't linger after any of the three examination days. You just get the fuck out of there as soon as possible. I was so

4

beaten after taking the New Jersey bar on Day Three of the testing that I fell asleep on Route 1 driving home and woke up in a different lane. Maria was concerned that I didn't look well. I assured her that I was fine, even though I wasn't. No one wants to be burdened with the truth. She eventually met a social worker at the public defender's office where she worked and is now happily married with a baby boy. She knows I'm under psychiatric care, but I spared Maria most of the details of my meltdown. I couldn't completely hide everything from her. It never made sense to her that someone she once called a 'brilliant' law student while grossly intoxicated was always employed by shitty firms and out of work every eight months or so. It didn't make sense to me, either. But it does now, thanks to Dr. Karlis.

My car continues sputtering toward GSP Exit 15, which will lead me to Angel Bay, NJ. I've only been there twice, and I was too young to recall any of it now. I may have been conceived there, but I'm not a member of a family where anything of that sort would be discussed. My specific destination today is 728 St. Michael's Drive, which is an aging, barf-orange duplex located at the foot of the Seventh Street Bridge along St. Michael's Sound. I've never been there in person, but I've seen enough pictures to know that it is one of the most hideous-looking homes in a resort town that is flush with coin. The property was purchased as an investment seven years ago by Harry Trimble, a former industrial dishwasher salesman who now makes a killing peddling the cryostats that house the liquid helium and superconducting magnets used in higher-end MRI machines. He doesn't care about the appearance of the house. His plan is to demolish the place when the market improves to build a vacation dream palace for his soon-to-be-wife Marie. Harry's not one to throw good money after bad. He once said that he wouldn't paint the exterior unless the Cape May County Sheriff showed up heavily armed and with a court order. He then reconsidered and said he'd rather be shot. I can appreciate that. I feel the same way about my car.

I can't actually say that I know Harry too well except for a few brief social interactions over the years and some obnoxious e-mails that he's sent me over the past three weeks. I know that he's a good egg, though. One of my fraternity brothers would accompany him on monthly trips to Las Vegas during their single years. Brother Steve demanded that Harry let me stay in his house in Angel Bay rent-free this summer as settlement for a dispute over $2,000 that somehow involved gambling winnings and hookers. Steve's sole concession was that I would be declared House Bitch, which meant that I would help maintain Harry's dilapidated heap during the week when I am the sole occupant of the abode. The hope is that I'll be able to relax somewhat and integrate myself back into regular society in some way. I have no idea what to expect from my summer residence. It will be a marked improvement from my parents' basement just on the basis of central air alone. For now, Harry has given House Bitch a number of assignments via a lengthy e-mail entitled 'The Calm before the Storm.' The Storm represents Friday's initial invasion of the seven renters that will hastily descend upon 728 on weekends after escaping 40-60 hours of Work Hell in Philadelphia. All of them have some kind of personal connection to Harry. Their migration will continue back and forth until Labor Day, when the leaves turn and the shore towns empty so that people can get blind drunk in asphalt parking lots before Eagles games to forget the fact that the team perpetually wins, yet will always fail to deliver the City a Super Bowl because of the unrelenting arrogance of the organization and their not-yet-successful methods.

I'm eager to meet some new people, but it's sometimes awkward because I don't drink alcohol. It's not because I find it morally objectionable or went to rehab. A severe case of irritable bowel syndrome forces me to avoid the substance in all of its forms. I do smoke marijuana, however, and I plan to smoke a great deal of it this summer. I have to. I feel stress the very instant that my eyes open each morning, and it does not abate. I plan to be pretty much high all day now that I'm away from the parents except when I'm behind the wheel of an automobile. I declined the opportunity to be prescribed any kind of tranquilizer. Given the choice, I'm fine with being merely dependent upon marijuana rather than addicted to Xanax. I don't want to hear any stories about people who get 'addicted' to pot. It's like being 'addicted' to sex. You can stop. You just don't. I know a lot of people who smoke a lot of marijuana and I've never witnessed anyone vomiting violently and repeatedly, going into convulsions, or seeing little, black, non-existent bugs crawling all over their skin because they didn't smoke weed for two days. Anecdotal evidence in the form of telling me any story that begins with, *'In college, I knew this one guy who smoked a lot of pot and...'* will not be accepted as proof and isn't going to convince me that weed is addictive. I drink six cans of 7UP a day, every day. It doesn't mean I'm addicted. It just means I like it. I could stop if I had to, but I don't have to, so I won't.

I turn off the GSP at Exit 15 and find myself on a narrow, elevated causeway that cuts through a forest of green marshlands intersected by a maze of inland channels and waterways that reflect the large, puffy white clouds hanging in the late spring sky. A vast sound appears to the left of the roadway, with rows and columns of old, sleepy bungalows and bright, airy mansions surrounding its banks. The road gradually grades to near sea level as I enter the town itself. Though less than 90 minutes away, I'm certainly not in Philadelphia anymore. This looks more like California on the East Coast. Though traffic on the streets is sparse, my Shitmobile immediately announces me as an outsider. Every car on the road here is a well-maintained, late-model import driven by people of varying ages that are far more successful at their chosen professions than I am. Or, they are just wealthy because got their money the old fashioned way: they inherited it. I reach 728 only five minutes after entering town. Harry's house is easily spotted. The weather-beaten exterior stands out among the new constructions and modest bungalows purchased for $6,000 during the Sixties that are now retirement residences for the grandparents and represent a goldmine for their children and grandchildren. The lot next to Harry's sold for $2.1 million when the real estate market peaked several years ago. Harry, who will never be accused of being stupid (at least while sober), picked up his house with a now bought-out partner for a modest $385,000. I know this because I looked up the deed online while bored one day. That's what unemployed nerds do sometimes.

I pull into the side driveway to walk my bags and guitar toward the sliding glass door of the property's lower unit. It's unlocked, as it has been since last September. Crime, I understand, is so minimal in Angel Bay that people have been hauled off to jail for failing to pay jaywalking citations. In Philadelphia, no one bothers to arrest anyone unless you threaten the President or kill a cop. There's two bedrooms in the downstairs place, which has white sheetrock walls and is sparsely furnished and decorated. There's evidence of water damage on the ceiling and the walls; the carpet is a faded, frat house beige that contains a rainbow of oddly-shaped stains courtesy of various assorted spilled drinks and spilled bodily fluids. There is one electronic relic of note present: an original ICE bubble hockey table featuring the USA vs. USSR, the latter in the classic red and white trim uniforms with 'CCCP' across the front. I haven't seen one of these in at least 15 years. I can't help but put my bags down to investigate. A raucous recorded cheer and an organ cadence erupts from the machine as soon as it is plugged into the wall. It makes me feel like I'm in seventh grade and at the local arcade again. That's not a bad feeling. I had a lot less to worry about then, even if it didn't seem like it at the time.

My assigned bedroom is located down the hall on the far left and is known as the Board Room. The white-painted, paper thin door is adorned with a red, white and blue bumper sticker from the American Cannabis Society that reads, 'Thank You for Pot Smoking.' The room itself is a medium-sized square that contains the following elements: two sets of bunk beds stolen over a decade ago from a dorm at Drexel University, a queen sized bed, a white wicker end table with a single drawer and a lamp atop it, a closet, and a broken clock with its hands Superglued to be permanently set at 4:20. The walls are covered with a mixture of bare sheetrock and white-painted plywood paneling that is straight out of 1976. My bags and old guitar placed away, I text both Harry and my mom to inform them of my arrival before walking to a nearby nameless deli in search of food.

9:02 p.m.

You first realize that you're getting high when you're able to look into the cloud of discharged smoke to see the individual lines and quills and gray-white wisps in the misty haze of marijuana dancing and swirling in slow motion before dispersing upward into the air innocuous. I'm at that point now. Tonight is the first time that I have witnessed a truly spectacular sunset in years. In Philadelphia, the sun sets on the Schuylkill River side of the city and the final moments of its descent are obscured by a maze of buildings, rail lines and the traffic zipping along America's most un-drivable highway, Interstate 76. The sky is sometimes colorful, but you're robbed of the grandeur of the fiery ball disappearing into the horizon unless you're viewing the event from a skyscraper. While in law school, the solid albeit little-known law firm where I clerked was housed on the 41st floor of a relatively new office building. On the winter days when sun would be setting in the 5 o'clock hour, I'd walk to the mahogany-paneled west conference room to view the scene from the giant panoramic windows looking over the edge of Center City, the Art Museum and out to the nearby suburbs. Although there were still plenty of railroad tracks and other eyesores in view, there was an undeniable majesty to the soft orange glow of the low winter sun reflecting off the pristine glass facades of the postmodern skyscrapers, the icy waters of the Schuylkill, and the thousands of cars filled with non-lawyers slowly traveling the twisted maze of ramps and highways leading in and out of the fractured metropolis. I would take a few minutes to think about things, confident that I was going to make something of myself and that my living in parents' basement was a temporary sacrifice that would soon be a thing of the past. Maybe I'd be able to throw my parents some coin to ease their burden a bit, even. This was four years ago. I'm still in their basement. I still have no coin.

While a skyscraper provides a very unique vantage point to view the setting sun, it couldn't ever match what I've just witnessed. The fifty-foot wide channel at the rear of Harry's property, which is lined by houses and boats of every size and shape and color, curls to the left and opens into a watery expanse that reflects the crawling remnant clouds and the purples and reds and yellows and deep blues of the painted sky above. Such a landscape often calls for genuine Skywalker moments of reflection and introspection, but I have nothing profound to contemplate. The call of destiny is strangely mute for someone with a law degree who is supposed to be entering his prime earning years. I simply stare into the sky and listen to the faint sound of windchimes drifting from a vacant property somewhere across the channel. I'm smart enough to know that I'm not on the cusp of greatness in any way. I have no success to savor, hold no career goals that are remotely realistic, and I'm not about to assume a powerful, individual mastery of any known art or craft that will satisfy my inner soul. No carefully planned life changes are imminent, such as an engagement or pregnancy or the purchase of a home. In fact, I'm almost terrified of what the future may hold for me financially, mentally and emotionally. I can't say that I've lost everything, though. I had nothing to begin with. I hoped that becoming a lawyer would change that. I was dead wrong. My short-term goal is to get high while trying to renew my passport to the warm, blinding oasis between a woman's thighs; my long-term goal is to get a job so that I can live in my own apartment with a fucking bedroom door. Both of these goals appear equally daunting and unobtainable. As hundreds of stars begin to assert themselves brightly against the twilight, the constant sharp, itchy pricks from several species of small insects force me back inside 728 for the night.

Thursday, May 27, 2010

9:06 a.m.

The e-mail in my hand reads as follows:

Dear Bitch:

This is the list of what must be done by the end of the day on Thursday so it's all finished before the assholes start arriving. You should be able to knock all this shit out in one day if you use half a brain and dont waste time getting high and searching for kiddie porn on my internet connection. Save the receipts for anything you buy but buy generic. We dont need name brand shit to clean a fucking toilet if you know what I mean. Buy some gloves or whatever you might need to do these things but dont buy an entire fucking radiation suit on my dime.

1.   vacuum the carpets and wash the floors in the kitchen and bathroom. i don't think the floors were washed after we went down and trashed the place on new years.

2.   ditto the sheets and towels. they are probably pretty dirty and filled with spunk.

3.   clear the fridge of anything left over from last summer or new years and clean it. this thing is old as fuck and im trying to get one last summer out of it. you may have to defrost the freezer with elbow grease. yeah, its that old and i think i accidentally left it on after new year's.

4.   make sure the garbage disposal is clear

5.   clean and scrub the toilet and shower. that toilet has seen better days. it always smells like puke.

6.   clear and clean the outside showers and make sure they are in good working order. if you don't get the outside showers working you will see the biggest explosion of bitch dynamite when the girls are all crying and fighting over who gets next on the one inside shower downstairs.

7.   stock the fridge with beer, soda, water, beer and pick up a bottle of stoli o, one of stoli razz, a bottle of Jack and some spiced rum. the girls will demand that bubble gum vodka shit. just don't let anybody see you carrying it into my house.

8.   get batteries for the remote

9.   take the kayaks, life vests & paddles out of the shed and clean them off

Marie and I have a wedding and will be down in a couple of weeks. You don't need to do anything in the upstairs unit. That's Blotto's job. The rest of the idiots know you will be there and that you smoke weed. It's really unacceptable to them if you don't. Call if any problems.

Harry

p.s. dont park your piece of shit car in my driveway. it will scare the neighbors and bring down my property value.

It appears that I have a full day ahead of me. Lawyers typically don't like taking orders from regular people, but my humble roots as the son of a Catholic school teacher and a homemaker have prevented me from ever getting too big for my britches. But I'm still a man, so I find the performance of any household chores to be annoying unless I get pretty stoned first. Any stoner knows that a little weed can suddenly turn even the biggest slob into a domestic cleaning machine. Doing the dishes seems much more interesting when your stoned, focused mind can't ruminate on how completely boring the task at hand is. So instead of being a mope, you chug along like cleaning those dishes is second only to peace in the Middle East in the grand scheme of our world's affairs. I grab the Ziploc bag holding my last couple of buds and some shake from a stale quarter of Northeast Philly dirt weed that I picked up over a month ago. This dirt weed is the same as regular marijuana, except it's cheaper and it sucks. Filled with seeds and large stems, it is best characterized as unemployment weed. I take a minute to pack my small, cheap, violet-colored pipe that I used on the day I tried to kill myself. It gives me the chills every time I look at it, but I'm too cheap and too broke to spend $15 to replace it. Actually, it's more than that. It serves as a reminder for me that only two months ago I was blasting heroin with a gun on my lap. Presumably, there's nowhere for me to go but up. Only time will tell.

My bowl packed, I reach into my pockets and realize that I don't have any flare. There are few things more annoying than having the excitement of the start a long-awaited trip being quashed by finding out that you have to stop and get gas first. A thorough search of both the upstairs and downstairs units yields neither my lighter, any lighter, nor matches. I'm forced to return to the nearby deli, which has no actual name but instead has a cartoon cow saying, 'Moo! Moo!' hanging on the pediment over the doorway. I pick up two very ugly lighters. One is yellow with purple polka dots, and the other is a shimmering, sparkling pink. People are much less likely to pocket and walk away with a hideous-looking lighter, and every dime I spend these days counts. I also order a turkey sandwich and grab a few other things for lunch so that I won't have to make another trip later. The streets are practically vacant as I walk back toward Harry's. There's a view of the water from almost anywhere. It's a much better setting than the sweltering basement on Revere Street. The town is so nice that I almost feel like I'm walking through a movie set. There's no graffiti, no angry car horns constantly sounding off, no trash littering the streets and no one begging for change on the corner. The best part is the smell of the salt air. It's very subtle, but very soothing. Legend has it that these saltine breezes compel women to remove their panties 50% faster than they normally would. Being blind drunk probably contributes as well.

Back at the house, I place my sandwich and soda into the refrigerator until lunch. I take this opportunity to look inside the freezer for the first time. It's a fucking igloo. There appears to be a bottle of vodka and a pint of ice cream trapped inside like some million year-old mastodon bones. I prop the door open and turn toward the sweeping, mopping and vacuuming portion of my list while the ice softens itself up.

12:17 p.m.

I just inhaled my turkey sandwich and the ice in the freezer needs a bit more melting. The next task for House Bitch is to clean the two outside showers and place them into a useable condition. What sounds like such a simple chore proves to be more of a challenge than I anticipated. It's not because I'm stoned. I find that the ground is covered by a thick, slick, green mold worthy of a smelly, stagnant swamp in some part of the world serviced by the Peace Corps. Even my untrained eye can spot at least three additional species of mold in various colors growing on the wooden walls, including what appears to be the dreaded *stachybotrys chartarum*. I first dispose of the various items in Shower #1 that remain from last summer. This includes two small, mashed bars of colored soap, a discarded pink razor, a screwdriver, a crushed can of diet root beer(?), a hemostat, a rusted container of shaving cream that screams 'tetanus booster' and a small dead bird. There is also a gold key that I place into my pocket in case it might be of some importance. The hemostat, which is presumably made of stainless steel, looks to be salvageable and I put it aside for its intended use as a roach clip. I next turn on the hose in order to perform an initial spray-down of the facilities. Water is flowing from the spigot, but nothing is shooting out from the hose nozzle. This is because someone at some time saw it fit to cut the hose in half.

1:07 p.m.

I return from my walk to the local hardware store and now have a working hose. My spray-down accomplishes nothing. The spoiled shower mold stands down and refuses to give up its posh digs. Good ol' fashioned elbow grease is a necessity. Though my hands are occupied, my mind is not. A man's unoccupied mind will inevitably turn to women, although it's not always fantasy. Often I'll wax philosophically in my own head as part of a vain attempt to explain and justify my great and many failures with the opposite sex. Right now, I'm thinking about my old friend Lori DiDominico while I scrub. I will never have an ounce of sympathy for any man who scores Italian pussy easily. I've always been in awe of Italian girls with dark hair, dark eyes and dark legs. If you have a last name that ends in a vowel like Ambrosini, DiMartino, or Cacciola then there's a decent chance that I'm going to be hopelessly attracted to you. It's *always* a fruitless endeavor.

Many of Philadelphia's law firms are staffed with authentic, hardcore Italian-American secretaries from South Philly that have at least one grandparent who still speaks the native tongue and cooks the seven fishes on Christmas Eve. They call a 'picture' a 'pitcher' and use words like 'skeeve.' I don't even bother with conversation other than the typical courtesies. All of these girls require that you carry a union card in order to date them. When they were little girls, Daddy came home from working at the refineries off I-76 and scooped them up into a pair of hands covered by raw skin with the feel of 40-grit sandpaper. That's their frame of reference for what a man *really* is. They are *not* going to date a lawyer with soft hands who works behind a desk all day. They don't even consider us to be real men. They get all done-up for work and wear short skirts with heels into the office, but it's not for the lawyers. They need to impress the lunch pail guys they see on the bus or train on their way to and from work. They make sure to re-apply their make-up before going out to grab lunch so they look just exactly perfect when they walk by the construction sites filled with union tradesmen. Some of us professionals refer to these guys as 'South Philly Doctors' because every Maria, Tina and Gina from Two Street to South Broad affords a union electrician with a severe alcohol problem the same amount of high esteem that regular society would bestow upon a renowned orthopedic surgeon who performs surgeries on poor children for free. It's those high union wages earned by rough hands that these girls are chasing. When the secretaries run out of the building at 5 o'clock, they don't give the young lawyers a second thought except when they make fun of us, motherfuck us, or if one of their friends suddenly needs legal advice about getting a divorce from Frankie or Joey. The Italian girls from my Northeast Philly neighborhood weren't much different. Even the ones that went away to Penn State would only date cops or firemen if they returned to the neighborhood after graduation. It wasn't much of a surprise. Their fathers were all cops and firemen, too. If you weren't, you couldn't ever be a real man in their eyes.

Some of the Italian girls from the more affluent suburbs would be more open-minded about their dating choices, since their white collar fathers generally looked upon the union guys with distain. But the good-looking ones always had unlimited options. In the end, it's always the women that get to pick. Pussy is not a democracy; it's a dictatorship. It never hurts for a guy to be good-looking or clever or a good flirt, but it's never the man's choice in the end. If you're just a regular guy like me, you usually have little say about who you date. You can pick out as many prospects as you want, but it makes no difference unless someone picks you back. My friend Lori was an Ivy Leaguer, so she didn't dismiss me out of hand as a complete tool even though she was of Italian decent and depressingly hot. The last time I saw her was almost five

13

fucking years ago, when Lori's beautiful olive-toned body was clothed only in a pair of black socks pulled up to her knees. I've yet to fully recover from that night. If there was some instrument by which I could send a probe to the West Coast that would explore Lori's fertile mind and unravel every last strand of each beautiful helix in her feminine DNA, I'm sure I'd discover that she's never fully recovered, either. Our last kiss was halted by Lori pushing me out the door because she was sobbing uncontrollably. Whether this was because she realized she loved me as much as her fiancé or simply pitied me remains unclear; I never had the chance to ask her. I never would, either. I'm just glad she threw me out of her friend's apartment when she did. I was about to crack apart myself.

Speaking of things that are cracked apart, the hot water handle in this shower has seen much better days. It'll have to be replaced. A quick turn cuts my hand and also reveals a small leak in the hot water pipe. After also taking inventory of the damage to Shower #2, I'm forced again return to the hardware store for additional supplies. It would have made sense to inspect both showers before my initial trip to the store for a new hose, but these things are much less obvious when you're completely fucking wasted. I'm fine with that. It's small, small price to pay for being so relaxed and so high that my many failings, save those with women, are at least dismissed temporarily from my overburdened mind.

2:15 p.m.

Pick, pick, pick, pick, pick. Chip, chip, chip, chip, chip. Defrosting the freezer by hand is the current project, and I'm working very carefully as I attempt to release a half-full bottle of Grey Goose from its icy tomb. I know from my Irish Catholic upbringing that if there's someone who wants to get drunk in Africa right now, it would automatically be a grave sin to waste it. Personally, I'm glad that I can't drink. Alcohol leads to anger, anger leads to violence, and violence leads to jail. There's no question that with my mental illness I'd be dead or in prison if I could partake. I hear the glass door in the living room suddenly slide open. A very large white male with a short Mohawk and giant shades covering his eyes enters the property. He looks like one of those dudes who could literally kill me with just one punch, even though he's at least an inch shorter than I am. He's massive. "I'm Dizzy," the dude says way too intensely. "I live down the street for the summer. You must be Harry's FNG."

"I am," I say as we shake. He has a grip of iron. "Patrick."

"When are the rest of the assholes going to be here?"

"Tomorrow."

"Tell them that I'm meeting up with the white owl in A.C. if anyone's interested. Probably not, though. This house is a bunch of pussies. You guys just drink beer and smoke weed and think that's entertainment. You kayak?"

"No, but I'd like to give it a try sometime."

"Good. I'm always looking for a second paddle. Be out on your dock at 7:45 tomorrow morning. Later!" The large man runs abruptly out of the house and disappears into a silver Mercedes with the engine already running. He screeches out of the driveway, racing off to parts unknown.

9:56 p.m.

Women are like fish. Men always obsess about the ones that got away and love to tell stories about them. It's true that guy talk is usually dominated by a general discussion about who we've screwed, who we're currently screwing, who we wish we were really screwing instead, and theories on why we aren't screwing them. They'll be some purely speculative stuff, such as which girl in your circle of friends might taste the best or which one has the dirtiest mouth in bed. Someone will always chime in with a blowjob story involving deep throat or the way his ex-girlfriend used to do this cool thing with his balls. And then, something in the conversation will jar someone to lower his head and recall with great regret the story of the big fish that got away or never was really on the line at all. The rest of the men in the room will listen in a respectful silence like the speaker is talking about somebody who has died. Others will be prompted to tell their own tales, after which even the manliest dudes will smoke another bowl, do another shot, or blast one last line of coke up their nose in order to blunt the feelings that arose from everything that was just said.

I dwell upon my own fish stories as I find myself alone and stoned while lying on a couch in a strange place with a guitar that now has a broken D string. I often think of my ex-girlfriend Kim when I'm in a strange place, whether it's a hotel room in an unfamiliar town, or on a plane, or while driving a long, empty highway cutting across a landscape to nowhere. I always felt completely safe when her pretty head was lying on my chest. 'Safe' is the best word I can use to describe it. I didn't have a care in the world when we were together. Anything short of nuclear war could not have troubled me when I was locked inside her slender arms, and the prospects of anyone ever using a $140,000,000 warhead to take out Iowa City, IA were remarkably dim.

I first met Kim thirteen(!) years ago in the foyer of my fraternity house during a particularly raucous sorority mixer that involved a stocked ice cream bar set up in the dining room. There were 5-gallon tubs of at least a dozen flavors, with a large table at the end filled with all kinds of toppings and syrups and sauces and hard liquors. By midnight, the bottles of hard liquor were emptied and most of the brothers and sisters were using scoops of ice cream and the various toppings and syrups and sauces as projectiles. Just before all that madness started in earnest, I spied the very pretty, kind-looking South Korean girl that I'd been eyeing-up all night standing alone in the foyer. She wore a short blue & brown themed plaid skirt and a tight brown sweater stretched over some surprisingly shapely breasts. It didn't end there. The most critical feature of all, her legs, were very defined and covered by a pair of eye-catching patterned brown tights. I approached.

"Did you have Music Appreciation with Professor Dix last semester?" I asked.

"After two hours of staring at me, that's the best line you could come up with?" was her reply.

"Sorry. They call me Shit."

"Shit? *Who* calls you Shit?"

"Everybody, really...it's short for Shitsniffer."

"Pledge name?"

"No. I was raised by baboons."

"O-*kay*. Where's your funny accent from, Shit?"

"Northeast Philly. Yours?"

"Rochester."

Upstate New York, I learned over the years, is God's Country for low-maintenance, down-to-earth women with good looks and a soul. I also breathed a mental sigh of relief that she didn't automatically blurt out 'Adrian!' when I mentioned that I was from Philadelphia. That gets so fucking annoying. This girl might be a keeper, I thought.

"Can I have a name?" I asked.

"Kim," she said. "And I did have that class last semester. You always sat near the back with the pretty red-haired girl and that guy who looked like he showered, like, once or twice a month." The guy who showered once or twice a month was close by, rolling around on the floor with two screaming girls that he was mercilessly attacking with a bottle of chocolate syrup.

"You weren't about to leave this Mensa meeting, were you, Kim?"

"I was hoping that you'd finally get the guts to come over to talk to me and that you'd be semi-intelligent. So far, you're one for two, Shit."

"One for three gets you into the Hall of Fame."

"The Hall of Fame under my skirt has *much* higher standards."

"I usually have a problem meeting standards. Any kind of standards. Most standards, really."

"Do you have any pot?"

"Obviously..."

"Maybe we can go upstairs and talk about that, then."

That's how eighteen months of ecstasy began. Very attractive women are so much more accommodating with their time when they actually have an interest in you. That doesn't happen often enough. Getting into Kim's Hall of Fame proved to be a bit harder than I first thought, though. We sat on my bed and got stoned and talked for three hours about our favorite things and hopes for the future, which when you're 20 amounts to an absolutely misinformed nothing. We both wound up at the University of Iowa because we were running away from home. When you grow up in the Northeast United States like we did, you can't possibly imagine a place more distant on so many levels than Iowa City. Kim was running from her super-strict upbringing at the hands of first-generation Asian immigrants; I was running from a particularly virulent strain of Irish Catholicism. She was such a good conversationalist that my growing curiosity with the space between her thighs and the sound of her sex voice wasn't distracting or annoying. I normally find these pre-kiss conversations to be a painful event because I become very preoccupied with what the girl might taste like under her jeans or her skirt. It's not that I'm a scumbag. I'm just a man, and men are attracted to women on a level that no woman could ever completely understand. Kim, ironically, was drawn to me because she said that I 'always looked so fucking happy and friendly.' Of course, I was happy then. I lived in a mansion on the banks of the Iowa River with 30 troublemakers and a chef. Even as the years continue to pass and I'm separated by distance from my former home, I can think of nothing that could be better than those days.

The more I talked to Kim that first night, the more I realized that she was very intelligent and very sweet. The time passed quickly before we started habitually yawning and decided to hit the sack. Kim wouldn't even let me kiss her that first night despite being a somewhat aggressive flirt. I'm usually not too keen on sharing a bed with someone who won't kiss me unless the girl is already a very, very close friend or somebody's sister. My first instinct is to push the freeloader onto the floor and rightfully claim my entire bed for myself again. But when Kim put her head on my shoulder and placed her left leg across my body, I didn't even care that I was getting blanked. It just felt right for her to be there. She was the only thing I thought about for seven long days until I saw her again. I was even more attracted to Kim the next time she visited, and she wasn't even wearing a skirt or anything sexy or revealing. It was one of those moments when you think to yourself, *'Holy shit! I can't believe this girl is here to see me.'* She was simply that pretty. My roomie was somewhere in Nebraska for a long weekend related to hunting, fishing, bird watching, or something

17

equally uninteresting, so Kim & I popped *Clerks* into the VCR and got stoned after we (more precisely, she) had a few beers with the boys and some stragglers downstairs.

I finally hooked up Kim that night, but we didn't have sex for six weeks. That seemed like an eternity, especially in college. There was a reason for this, though. Although Kim always presented as shy, classy and reserved girl in public (at least when sober), a switch went on in her brain as soon as the bedroom door was locked. Fortunately for me, it was the 'whore' switch. Sex was her only release from the lingering resentment over the rigors of her high school years and the stress of maintaining her 3.98 GPA as a double major in finance and biology. Kim's passion for dirty sex was her way of taking secret revenge on her father for being a total bastard for 18 years. She approached it with the same intensity and serious mind that she would anything else in her life. Kim couldn't sleep with me until she felt that we had developed a bond that was sufficient and sincere enough that she could feel comfortable completely letting herself go. Truthfully, she was so talented and enthusiastic in bed that it was borderline disturbing. I didn't complain. Once we fully bonded, she was willing to do anything at all to please me. An outstanding role player, Kim had no qualms about bringing her authentic Catholic school uniform from St. Lucy's Preparatory School for Girls to campus for a visit to Principal McShea's office, which was located on the second floor of my fraternity house. Kim would sit on the edge of my bed in her red plaid skirt, white blouse, red vest and her red knee socks, with a look of guilt on her face as she uncomfortably twisted her black and white saddle shoes along the wooden floor. When pressed, Kim would part her legs and slowly lift her skirt over her tender thighs to reveal that she was sent to my office for the very serious infraction of not wearing underwear in class. Since such an egregious violation of the dress code carried the penalty of expulsion, Kim would be willing to do *anything* to avoid her parents finding out. You haven't even *seen* pussy until you've had a South Korean girl. It's comparable to the best offerings of the prettiest girls anywhere on Earth. The only tragedy was that I was too young and inexperienced at 20 to fully appreciate it at the time. Some of the best sex, however, was when we wouldn't say a word and just listened to each other breathe and moan. I remember those nights just as well.

It isn't just the other-worldly sex that makes me constantly reminisce about my favorite college girlfriend, though: in my 32 years, she's truly the only girl I've ever loved. There was never more than five minutes of bullshit during the entirety of the relationship. We could have sex for hours or do nothing at all for hours; I was fully content with her mere presence alone. It was humbling at times, even. She was one of those women that you could stare at for days and never get tired of looking at her. I didn't even have a desire to be with anyone else. There was no reason to. I found it liberating to experience complete emotional and physical contentment with another. There was no sexual frustration of any kind, no 'what ifs' or bitterness about other girls past and present, and no thoughts that maybe there was someone else 'better' out there for me. I saved a lot of time by not having to think about things like that, and I poured that extra time into much more important stuff like our relationship, hanging out with fraternity brothers from all over the country that I might never see again after graduation, and my own studies. You can sit in a library for hours when you don't have to worry about where your next blowjob is coming from and don't have to concoct some ridiculous plot or flirt endlessly to get it. If I could have half the time back that I've spent fruitlessly trying to get women into bed, I'd be well on my way to being President of the United States right now.

I haven't felt the way that I felt with Kim with any other woman, before or since. We only separated because I wanted to return to Philly after graduation and she had been accepted to Stanford to pursue graduate studies in economics. Like most college students, I was flat broke by graduation and my parents vowed to cut me off the second I was handed my diploma. I couldn't have moved to a place like Palo Alto even if I wanted to. Breaking up seemed like the right thing for us to do at the time and we lost touch soon afterward. You could legitimately 'lose touch' with someone only 12 years ago. There was no text messaging. There was no facebook. E-mail was still a nascent form of communication accessed via a dial-up connection and wasn't yet widely used. Not everyone had cell phones, which had only recently evolved from the 'car phone.' I think that I kinda lost touch with Kim on purpose. I knew that every nerd in her graduate program would be trying to make her Hall of Fame, and she was living in a legendary college town that was down the road from one of America's greatest and most vibrant cities. It would only be a matter of time before I became an afterthought. I didn't want to be around for the awkwardness of calling her apartment and having some strange dude answer the phone. There aren't many girls like Kim in a cold, blue collar, parochial place like Philadelphia. I knew that I would have a much, much harder time replacing her than she would have replacing me. That's true for all good-looking women, I guess. I was definitely far too young at 21 to get married, but I was also far too young to recognize that the connection that I made with Kim was such an incredibly rare life occurrence. Over a decade later, I still think of her every time I listen to Dylan's 'Girl from the North Country.' Sometimes, when the haunting, reverb-kissed voice of Johnny Cash takes the second verse of this acoustic ode to a lost love from upstate New York, a melancholy mood and marijuana with the proper concentration of THC will instantly moisten my eyes.

19

My thoughts of Kim and her pretty, kind face are interrupted by the sudden opening of the sliding glass door to my right. A life form in a tight, dark blue mini-dress stumbles into the living room. This raven-haired vixen can't weigh much north of a buck. I immediately glance down at her feet. It's not that I particularly like feet; I didn't even realize that women had them until I was 30. Often, they are gross. But if I can tolerate a woman's feet, then I'm assured that I could be 100% attracted to her physically. This new arrival, who is wearing a pair of slinky black stripper shoes to compliment her short dress, is a firm 'pass.' Nerves set in. This is my first interaction with a female in months that isn't a blood relative or one of my buddy's wives.

"Is something wrong with you?" the woman asks with some hesitation, probably because I'm staring through her like she's some sort of sexual alien.

"You have pretty eyes," is my stoned, creepy reply from my reclined position on the couch. Game isn't my thing these days.

"What are you, sleeping?"

"Relaxing."

"I'm Kirsten," she says somewhat sternly and impatiently.

"Patrick."

"Is anyone else around tonight? When are they getting here? What are you doing?"

"I'm still relaxing."

"Do you have anything to drink? Beer? Liquor?"

"I just stocked the fridge this afternoon. Help yourself."

Kirsten walks her very sexy body over to the kitchen. Her heels clap against the tile floor the way that only high heels do. I haven't heard that sound in a private residence in so long. Kirsten yanks open the refrigerator door with some serious gusto for someone so slight. I'm able to ascertain two things from our brief encounter: that she's already pretty drunk, and that she'd probably be a very adventurous girl in bed. She's best described as 'dirty hot.' I think it's the small, dark eyes.

"You only have beer?" Kirsten asks as she stares into the fridge. "Is there anything else? How 'bout vodka?"

"Vodka's in the freezer. Mixers on the counter."

"I don't see any cranberry juice."

"It's on top of the toilet."

"Seriously?"

"No. We don't have any."

"Dork," she says before offering an exasperated sigh. "Is there ice?"

20

"Ice would be in the freezer with the vodka."

"I know where it *is*," Kirsten replies with far too much attitude. "I was asking if you *have any*."

Various sounds coming from the kitchen indicate that the woman is starting to make herself a drink of some kind. Her task completed, she returns to the living room and makes herself comfortable on the second couch arranged perpendicular to mine. "How come you're not drinking?" she asks like something is very seriously wrong with me.

"I don't drink."

"You must be real frickin' fun at parties," she replies dismissively. Kirsten and I aren't exactly hitting it off here.

"You smoke, Kirsten?"

"No. I hate that shit. It's so bad for your lungs! I'll do some coke if you got it, though."

"Can't help you there."

"How do you know Harry, weakness?"

"Mutual friend. You?"

"He's friends with my *asshole* ex-boyfriend," Kirsten spits. "I have to pee. Don't steal my drink."

"It's safe, Kirsten."

"That's right. You're the freak who doesn't drink alcohol."

As this intrusion walks from the room, I take the opportunity to retrieve my phone from my pocket.

Message to: Harry Trimble
5/27/10 10:08 p.m.
Showers in good shape. Anything
i need 2 know abt this kirsten girl?

The toilet soon flushes. There is a delay of approximately one minute before Kirsten returns to the living room, presumably because she is staring at her dirty hot self in the mirror to find flaws in her appearance that no man will ever notice given her dress and her legs and her shoes and her eyes and the permanent 'fuck me' look on her somewhat intense but intriguing face. Kirsten returns and seats herself back onto the couch.

"Your drink is still safe," I report.

"No roofies?"

"I'm fresh out," I reply with mock disappointment. Kirsten lifts her butt from the couch cushion so that she can pull her dress down to mid-thigh. Content that she's no longer providing me a free show, she reaches for her all-important drink and makes herself comfortable once again. I feel excitement rush through my chest just from watching Kirsten cross her trim legs in my presence. She does have pretty feet, too. My stoned eyes follow the thin line of black leather that passes at a slight angle just beneath her red-painted toes before I slowly trace the slight curve of her arch toward the y-strap that wraps tightly around the tanned skin above her right ankle.

"Do you smoke?" Kirsten asks, suddenly jarring my mind back to Planet Earth.

"Haven't we discussed this?"

"I'm talking about cigarettes, ass."

"I've never smoked anything that can kill you," I lie.

"Funny," Kirsten replies as she digs through her...I don't even know what you would call it. It doesn't look like a purse and it's not large enough to qualify as a 'bag.' But it holds things like driver's licenses and lipstick and loose change. Kirsten grabs a Parliament Light and infects the room with its noxious stank. Feeling out of place with neither a drink nor cigarette, I take my violet pipe and a lighter from the nearby coffee table into my hands.

"You're not going to smoke that stuff in front of me, are you?" asks the drunkard.

"Yup."

"It smells funny."

"I think you do, too, Kirsten."

"You're *so* clever."

"Thanks," is my equally sarcastic response.

New Message: Harry Trimble
5/27/10 10:13 p.m.
run 4 the hills and hide ur car

I ask Harry for clarification, but he never responds.

"Who ya texting with?" Kirsten demands to know.

"My mother."

"You're a mamma's boy, aren't you? You look like one."

"You're so pleasant."

"What's the ring on your finger?"

"My class ring from the University of Iowa."

"And you still wear it? How old are you? Why'd you go to school all the way out *there?*"

"Why not?"

"I went to Penn State," Kirsten informs me. "We always beat you guys in football. Not that I was ever sober enough to remember any of the games..."

"What'd you study at Penn State?"

"Psychology," she says. "Umm...do you want to walk down the street to the bar? I'm kinda getting bored with you."

"I think I'm just going to relax on the couch for the night."

"Don't be such a fucking wus," Kirsten snaps as she stands on her heels. "Come to the bar with me." Despite Harry's warning, I allow her to grab me by the hand and lead me out of the house.

10:37 p.m.

I find myself seated at the bar of a large but mellow establishment off Seventh Street & St. Michael's Drive called the Crow's Nest next to my new, drunk pal Kirsten. Her looks alone make me nervous, but this learned fear of women that I've developed over the past five years is tempered by the knowledge that I'm apparently on a bar date with one hundred pounds of insanity. Of anyone, I should know insanity when I see it. Only 60 days ago, it was me. A young bartender approaches.

"The usual?" he asks to my companion.

"I guess that means I should bend over," she replies with a laugh.

"And you, sir."

"I'll have a 7UP or a Sprite."

Kirsten rolls her eyes as the barkeep begins to preparing our beverages, then starts another conversation with me.

"So tell me what you do for a living, mama's boy."

"I'm between jobs right now," I reply, which is the universal euphuism that men use for 'broke and unemployed' when talking a woman that they might want to fuck later.

"What *were* you doing?" Kirsten asks like I'm on a job interview of some sort.

"I'm an attorney."

"Oh!" Kirsten exclaims, as if it's something special to be a lawyer. It's typical, and it always makes me uncomfortable. It's not because I'll usually be peppered with inane questions about moving violations, DUI scenarios, or mortgages that I have little interest in answering. It's because I'm instantly saddled with expectations that I can't ever meet. If I tell any woman under 25 that I'm an attorney, half of them will look at the streaks of gray in my salt 'n pepper hair and immediately ask what kind of car I drive. A battered blue '95 Honda Civic EX with over 160,000 miles on the odometer isn't the answer they're looking for. That simply doesn't compute. Kirsten must be over 25, because she doesn't ask about my car. Instead, she renders me a word receptacle for the next twenty minutes while bitching about what an asshole her nameless ex is. The entire thing boils down to the fact that he dumped her two months ago for no reason and that he never returned her calls and texts promptly. Neither of these complaints registers as very offensive behavior with me, but Kirsten characterizes her ex the way that historians would describe a dictator. Ruthless. Calculating. Relationship challenged. A cold-blooded murderer. She drowns her sorrow after recalling the horrors of this relationship with two shots of Patron Ultimat, the latter of which mostly drips down her chin.

"I'm having a little trouble swallowing right now," she laughs.

"You just became a *lot* less desirable, Kirsten."

"I give *awesome* blowjobs," she claims in her defense. "It's definitely all in the hand technique, anyway." I'm always skeptical of anyone who finds it necessary to advertise their own competencies. It usually means that you're really not good at something but too dumb or drunk to recognize it. The reality is, though, that Kirsten looks like she could suck a golf ball through a garden hose with her large, shiny, pink lips. I'm intrigued. "I have to pee again," she announces. Kirsten struts off to the restroom on her pair of wonderful legs. Harry's scouting report screams for the exercise of caution here despite my current streak of sexual futility. My suspicions begin to be confirmed as she stomps red-faced out of the ladies' room several minutes later and returns to her barstool with a thud.

"Melissa fucking Mitchell!" she exclaims.

"Who?"

"My fucking ex from last summer cheated on me with that *slut*. And then dumped me for her! Ugh! I can't even go to the bathroom without having to run into these *whores*."

"Whores have to piss, too, ya know," offers the mellow barkeep.

"She's not even that good-looking," Kirsten bitches. "I don't know what the fuck my ex's problem was."

A petite brunette with long, brown hair in a little black dress and heels exits the ladies' room. She's a total head-turner. I haven't had a woman that pretty in bed in five years. If this is the girl that is 'not even that good-looking' then Kirsten needs an immediate appointment with a first-class optometrist. "Whore!" she yelps across the bar to this beauty. Every eye in the Crow's Nest is now lasered onto Kirsten and I. "You fucking slut!" is her next yelp.

"Knock it off," orders our bartender sharply. "She's a customer just like you are."

Ms. Mitchell approaches a much taller gentleman who apparently is Kirsten's ex-ex-boyfriend in question and reaches to give him a kiss on the cheek. This sends Kirsten into a frenzy. She charges from her barstool like a bull seeing red, knocking it onto the floor in the process with a thunderous thud easily heard over Carrie Underwood's 'Before He Cheats' coming from the bar's speakers. She makes a drunken, psychotic beeline straight toward the couple. Seizing a full pitcher of beer from another patron's table, Kirsten launches it clear across the room at the pair while shrieking at the top of her lungs about the fact that Melissa now sucks the same penis that apparently once spent some quality time in Kirsten's anus. "So tell me how my ass tastes, bitch!!!" are Kirsten's last words to the pretty brunette before the bouncers, who were expecting an uneventful weeknight shift, eagerly charge toward the madness. I'm so embarrassed at this point that I'm ready to attempt suicide again. I toss $50 onto the bar and rush toward the exit, fleeing into the cool Angel Bay night in terror.

Friday, May 28, 2010

"The only people for me are the mad ones, the ones who are mad to live, mad to talk, mad to be saved, desirous of everything at the same time, the ones who never yawn or say a commonplace thing, but burn, burn, burn, like fabulous yellow roman candles exploding like spiders across the stars and in the middle you see the blue centerlight pop and everybody goes 'Awww!'"

-Jack Kerouac

7:45 a.m.

I'm standing on the backyard dock wearing a life vest wrapped tightly around my torso when Dizzy rolls up in a large, green, two-person kayak. I must look like a fucking tool. He confirms my suspicion. "Relax, Chief," the large man chuckles as I'm about to climb aboard the craft. "You can ditch the vest. You may very well die today, but it won't be because of anything on this trip. We're not going out into the ocean."

"Where we goin'?"

"First, we're going to paddle into the marsh to photograph an osprey nest. It's not really the nest itself that I'm interested in. The females are probably just incubating right now, and I don't want to bother Mom. I want to see what the male is up to. Then, we'll go out to the Old Wharf to photograph some wading birds and various waterfowl. Sound good?"

"Sure," I reply, even though 'photographing various waterfowl' wasn't on my to-do list for today. Dizzy and I begin to paddle out into the vast expanse of water over which the sun spectacularly set the previous evening, prior to my bar date with a woman gone berserk. When we're not talking, the only sounds to be heard are the paddles pushing through the water, the familiar calls of laughing gulls, and strange sounds from other birds and marsh creatures that I've never seen or heard before. Though 'serenity' is a much over-used word, this is it. The fact that I ever practiced law, tried to off myself, or spent a year sexless seems like a groups of far, distant memories from another lifetime in some parallel universe.

"Ever go hunting, man?" the expedition leader asks as a small gray and white bird dive-bombs straight into the water next to our craft with a splash. Dizzy doesn't flinch or even seem to notice.

"I'm a city boy, 'cept for college," I reply as the bird surfaces from the water with a small fish in its beak and flies off. "I fired a rifle once in my life."

"Back in 'Nam?" Dizzy jokes.

"Something like that. It was in grade school in my buddy's backyard in the Poconos."

"My family had a house in the Poconos when I was growing up," Dizzy says as a squadron of distinctive-looking, large, black and white birds with long, bright orange

26

beaks skim past in formation less than five feet from the kayak with their lower mandibles opened into the water. I swear that we are supposed to be in New Jersey. It's possible that we may have passed through a vortex into another continent and I missed it. "My dad was a chemical engineer, and was pretty successful at it," the front paddler continues. "I'm the only total fuck-up in my family. My older sister is an obstetrician and my older brother is a fuckin' flight surgeon on an aircraft carrier. I do coke with strippers and sell donuts."

"I'm the total fuck-up in my family, too," I confess as another splash in the water occurs at 3 o'clock. The same gray-white bird surfaces with another fish in its beak and gobbles it up like candy before again flying off.

"Are you the youngest?" Dizzy asks.

"Oldest."

"I was the accident baby," he says. "My sister is 13 years older and my brother, 16."

"I think most of us are accidents, man."

"I haven't had any accidents myself, fortunately. Especially with some of the trash I sleep with sometimes when I'm fucked-up. Geez...they would need to build more prisons just for my kids alone. But this is why I asked about your hunting experience: There is little difference between the nature photography I'm doing today and hunting for game. The end result is different, but our methods are exactly the same. Once we have displayed great patience and spent countless hours stalking and studying and becoming one with our subject, the culmination of all of our hours and weeks and months of groundwork ends in but a single second using a single finger. For the photographer, it's the click of the shutter; for the hunter, it's the pull of the trigger. I've been behind both the camera and the gun during my lifetime. And the only gun I have any desire to fire going forward is the one inside my pants."

"How's that goin'?" I ask as Dizzy pauses to grab a beer from the cooler aboard at 7:51 a.m. precisely. Men can always find common ground by talking about pussy and trading fish stories.

"Pretty well," he says after a lengthy gulp. "*Too* well, even. I have a lot goin' on between my six donut shops and my photography."

"You own the shops?"

"Are you fucking kidding me? You think I stand behind a register all day with a paper hat asking how many packs of sugar some asshole wants with his coffee?"

"My bad. So how does owning six donut shops make you a fuck-up?"

"It does when your siblings are doctors and very proper and mature. I mean, my brother's a fucking Rear Admiral. Plus, it was all my dad's doing. He bought two of them right before he got MS. He said he wanted something to do when he retired from being an engineer, but the truth was that he was totally hooking me up because he knew I didn't have the attention span to finish college or do something in my life that would pay me enough to survive. So once I got kicked out of college, he had me up at 4:30 a.m. every morning to make the donuts. I fuckin' hated it. Then he died and handed them both off to me. Now I have six. But my dick is nothin' but trouble, man. In fact, I spend more time running from the girls that are chasing *me,* rather than chasing women of my own. Take two nights ago, for example. It's a Monday night, it's raining, and I'm totally stoned but I'm sitting in my condo back in Philly bored out of my fucking mind and counting down the seconds until I can get onto the water here with my camera."

Dizzy pauses to take another gulp of beer as our winged escort dives to capture and swallow fish number three. I think the bird's just showing off at this point. "Now listen to me, McShea," Dizzy continues after swallowing, "there is *nothing* more dangerous when you're stoned and you're bored than having a cell phone in your hand filled with the phone numbers of a bunch of 18 to 22 year-old employees that want to fuck you. I'm 36. *That* could lead to a lawsuit, I'm sure. Does anyone underwrite sexual harassment insurance for small businesses? See if you can find that out for me, Esquire. So I text this one chick Shelly because she's hot and blonde with this tight, tight little ass that you'd have to see to really believe. And I *know* she wants to fuck me. So I shoot out a harmless text like, *'Did we sell a lot of blueberry cremes?'* just to open a dialog because that was my Donut of the Day. Two seconds later, she texts back, *'Can u get me pot?'* Now, where the *fuck* do you get the idea to text your boss for pot in response to a work-related question? I never bring pot into my stores. I may be stoned when I stop over, but I don't even *mention* drugs in front of my employees. So I tell 'er that her request is inappropriate and illegal, but I didn't say it exactly like that because that's way too many letters to type. I get distracted easily. And she texts back, *'what if i want other things frm u'* so right then I know I can nail 'er. And it's Monday, and I'm stoned, so I pick Shelly up at her stepmom's dump in South Philly near 22nd & Hell and fuck the shit out of her back at my place in Olde City. And then I'm thinking, *'If she's dumb enough to ask her boss for pot, then what the fuck is she doing at the register all day?'* But now I fucked her, so even if her receipts are all fucked up or there's funny business then I can't do anything about it. And the sex wasn't even good, which is a real kick in the nuts because Shelly looks *great* naked. So I wanted to get fucked, but I got totally *screwed* instead. And now she's blowin' up my phone left and right for Round Two and better hours, which I *have* to give her now. Sometimes sex just isn't worth it. I never would have said that

28

in my twenties. I've found that a man's balls are both his best friend and his worst enemy. They're much, much more trouble than my fuckin' coke habit. I can just put down the coke if I have to. My balls ain't goin' anywhere. Sometimes I feel like-"

Dizzy suddenly cuts himself off, stopping his stroke and signaling silence. I instantly lurch forward, dropping my paddle and losing my balance before falling into the frigid water with a splash. When I surface, the cold becomes the least of my concerns. A brown behemoth of a bird with a wingspan of no less than five feet is swooping toward me while screeching like something from a bad science fiction movie. I have no idea what the fuck I am supposed to do. Dizzy offers no guidance. He is too busy fumbling through his equipment bag to attach a large, white lens to his camera that would look much more appropriate on an NFL sideline or a Southern California beach while documenting celebrity cellulite. I duck back under the water in hopes that the bird will pass without trying to eat my eyes out from my head. I surface ten seconds later, gasping for breath while desperately treading water.

"You didn't tell me we were photographing a fucking pterodactyl today!" I manage to yell as I shiver in the cold waters of the sound.

"It's an osprey, dude," Dizzy replies rather calmly.

I was under the impression, for some reason, that an osprey was more like a sparrow than a creature with a wingspan as large as the average human female is tall.

"A *sparrow?*" Dizzy says incredulously as I reveal my ignorance concerning all things ornithology. "Why the fuck would we paddle all the way out here to take pictures of a fuckin' sparrow? Now here he comes again! Stay above water in case he's hungry and goes diving for a fish."

The large raptor is staring down Dizzy directly with its yellow, beady eyes of hate as it circles our kayak at a high rate of speed. I can feel the wind from the bird's wings flapping as it passes directly behind me, screeching and squawking and hissing the entire time. "Marvelous!" Dizzy exclaims. "The fucker's looking right into my lens! This is *fantastic!* This is exactly why I ditch Philly every summer."

"Are we going to *live?*"

"Relax, Chester," Dizzy replies after the angry bird departs and his camera finishes firing off like a machine gun. "I do *all* of my homework. Ospreys only actually attack humans 5% of the time. *Humans* attack humans more often than that. Ospreys are a lot like the women in my life. Very beautiful, but they just like to flap their wings and make a lot of noise with their empty threats. Then they leave. And in the end, it gets them nothing yet leaves me with a bunch of great pictures that I can show my friends and tell lies about. Now climb back aboard! Let's head out to the Old Wharf and get nice and fucked up along the way."

29

"How long's it take?" I ask after removing myself from the near-freezing water.

"Why?" Dizzy asks as he throws me an old towel with some large, yellow and black stains of some sort on it. I don't hesitate to use it. The May water is *that* cold. "You got somewhere else to be?" he wonders aloud. "A date? Job interview? Diarrhea?"

"None of the above today."

"Then what's the difference? It's just time. You're on the water. You're in the sun. You're with nature. Time ceases to have any meaning at all. There's nothing more relaxing. Who the fuck is going to bother you out *here?*"

"The ospreys, apparently."

Dizzy chuckles as we again begin to paddle. "What would you rather deal with?" he asks. "A male osprey telling you to stay the fuck away from the nest he's building for his future osprey family, or some annoying girl blowing up your phone *all...fucking...day* because she talked to someone at some club who heard through her cousin's sister's uncle's brother that you went to the mall with your ex six weeks ago to buy her all kinds of lingerie before you took her home and had copious amounts of unprotected butt sex. That's much more annoying to deal with."

"True."

"That happens to me a lot. Girls yappin', I mean. Anyway, the Old Wharf is about forty minutes away in smooth water with two paddlers. We'll stop at a sandbar about halfway and smoke some weed, if that's okay with you."

I indicate my assent to this plan and we move onward under a low but burning sun, escorted by a band of birds issuing shrill tweets in between their dives for breakfast.

8:52 a.m.

The marsh opens, and a small, ancient fishing pier flanked by a row of abandoned, dilapidated wooden buildings appears along the muddy banks of the sound. A line of double-crested cormorants sits along the worn rooftops, drying their outstretched, brown-feathered wings under the blazing sun. A dozen wading birds and other feathered beings are feeding along the shoreline near the pier: great egrets, great blue herons, a little blue heron, male and female mallards, and a half-dozen of Dizzy's favorite bird, the smaller but pugnacious snowy egret. A black-crowned night heron with glowing red eyes stands watch over the entire scene from an elevated position in the marsh. Except for the ducks, I've never seen any of these things before. I'm just listening to Dizzy chatter. My role here is to maneuver him to get close enough to shoot the birds as they feed without alerting the sentry heron and scaring them off.

"Are any of these birds going to attack us?" I have to ask.

"Attack? No. You should be more concerned about getting shat upon. These birds are skittish, man. Skittish! So you need to slow your roll on that paddle, Chief. In fact, let's take a final smoke break before I get all *Nat Geo* on these motherfuckers." We stop the kayak and begin slowly begin drifting with the current toward the edge of the marsh. I take a toke of the Tupelo Honey we have on board and pass the bowl back to Dizzy before helping myself to a banana. The bowl passed between the two of us and my supply of potassium replenished, I shift into slow gear and softly stroke my paddle through the sound's waters with a determined, stoned focus.

"Now listen," says Dizzy, "you have to try to get closer to the birds, but you can't make it *obvious* that you're trying to get closer to the birds. They don't like that. So pretend that we're just a regular husband and wife leisurely paddling through the sound together while on vacation..."

"Am I the wife?"

"I guess you're the wife. You're the skinny one, right?"

"If I'm paddling, why do I have to be the wife?"

"Just fucking paddle casually, okay?"

"I'm paddling casually. Hopefully, they'll deactivate the deflector shield around the forest moon."

"Which movie was that from?" Dizzy asks in reply.

"The third one."

"Of the *first* three, right? The real ones. From when we were both kids?"

"Yeah."

"When they built that new Death Star."

"Correct."

I position the kayak about ten yards away from shore, parallel to the line of feeding birds. Half of the herons and most of the egrets immediately lift their wide wings and scatter to another part of the marsh. "I told ya, man!" says Dizzy as he readies his equipment. "But that's okay. I'm going to lock in on this great egret right near the pier. He's too focused on breakfast to care about us right now. He's probably stoned, too. This entire fucking town is, except the old ladies. They're just addicted to nicotine instead."

I look toward the tall, long-necked, yellow-beaked bird with dazzling white feathers slowly stalking the waters in search of prey. Neither ungainly nor awkward, this elegant bird gracefully walks by lifting its long black legs with large, four-toed feet from the water. It stops suddenly. The bird lowers its long neck, its yellow eyes flush forward, and the yellow spear that serves as its beak positions itself directly above the

31

surface of the sound. It waits. And it waits. Several seconds pass. The bird strikes! In an instant, its beak enters the water with a splash. When it emerges, a large blue claw crab has been impaled. Dizzy, giddy with excitement, is firing off his camera as fast as it will allow. The egret shakes the crab free from its beak, then flips it into the air with a deft flick upward. The bird now catches the crab, shaking it violently back and forth until the claws separate from its body. A seagull intervenes, trying to steal the crab from the clutches of the egret. It will not relinquish its prize. It engages the gull, then extends its wings and flaps itself two feet closer toward us. The gull flies off and does what gulls do best, which is to shit all over the place. We're fortunately spared. The egret lifts its head and finally swallows its meal, shell and all, which now takes the form of a pronounced lump as it travels down the bird's long, snake-like neck. Dizzy scrolls through his photographs and seems pleased with the results. "I'll tell ya one thing," he says. "I like crabs as much as the next guy, but that crab has to fucking hurt like hell when it comes out the other end. Probably needed some Old Bay, too."

"Why? We're *in* an old bay."

"That's true," says Dizzy as the bowl is again produced. "There's more seasoning in this very water than in between the legs of every woman in this entire town. And that's saying a lot."

12:17 p.m.

I received a mild sunburn but survived my virgin expedition into the Angel Bay marshlands relatively unscathed. I learned a lot of things during Dizzy's varied drunk, stoned and ADHD-afflicted lectures this morning. I know that he has slept with 137 women: 82 white, 8 Hispanic, 9 Asian, 7 black, 14 Italian and 6 Jewish. His favorites are Asian, Italian and Jewish or any combination thereof. The birds that were dive bombing for fish around the kayak are called terns. I am now able to differentiate between a great egret (large-sized, white feathers, black legs, yellow beak) and a snowy egret (medium-sized, white feathers, black legs, black beak) with 100% accuracy. I know that double-crested cormorants and their warm-weathered cousins, the anhinga, stand with their wings out and sun their feathers because they lack the oil on their plumes that would make them waterproof. How any of this newly acquired knowledge will help me to earn money, get laid, or have any practical use at all is unclear.

In the meantime, the assholes have begun arriving at 728. A bubble hockey tournament was held immediately. Playing as Mother Russia, I won my first game by a one-goal margin before getting blown out in the final by a score of 7-3. My increasingly stoned hands put the puck into my own net three times. I'm now one of five males seated on the living room couches while smoking a seemingly endless supply of marihuana cigarettes. The dope is supplied by Alexander Page, a former Class AA catcher turned marketing man for an Independent League team in Surf City. His mother sent it to him from San Francisco via Fed Ex in a large box of cookies containing macadamia nuts. The cookies have also been made available and are delicious. On the far couch is the 6'4" Blotto, a computer programmer for a third-party pension administrator who had a brief stint in camp with the Minnesota Vikings after college. He sits with Peter Sharkey, a functioning alcoholic who sports the largest mop of salt 'n pepper hair that I ever seen on a person with a day job. Though fit, he looks at least three times his stated age of 36. Sitting between Blotto and Sharkey is the fifth male in the room, Baxter, who was rescued from living in an empty lot among piles of tires and rusted appliances in North Philadelphia. A large, gray mutt, he is notable for the black, layered jowls the size of fine drapery hanging from each side of his mouth. He looks to be the largest producer of slobber in the known universe.

"Summer," says Page as if something profound might follow. "It makes me think of only a few things: Harry Kalas, God rest his soul; the Philadelphia Phillies; fresh brews cracking; seagulls squawking; bong water bubbling; and piss drunk blonde girls with big smiles and bigger titties. Anything else is irrelevant in my world until after Labor Day. I don't expect any of you to disagree."

"I would include a few all-nighters with hookers in A.C.," says Sharkey. "Maybe some nose candy and a bottle of Dom, too, in a bi-level suite with a Jacuzzi and elephant tusks coming out of the sides of the headboard on the king-sized bed. Some people live the high life, and some people drink it. I do both. The rest of you commoners can fuckin' suck it."

"I like to go fishing on occasion," adds Blotto with much less flair than Sharkey just mustered. "Other than that, I think we have everything that's great about summer covered. I'd hang myself during the winter if it wasn't for summer in Angel Bay. The only thing stopping me is that I wouldn't know how to tie a good knot for my noose. Or, I'd be married to Trisha. Which would be like being dead, anyway."

Sharkey takes a moment to polish off his beer. "Fishing!" he exclaims after it's killed. "Bah! If I'm drinkin' on a boat, I wanna see some broads. The only lines droppin' should be courtesy of my genius upon some drunk, unsuspecting girl with low self-esteem. Other than that, forget it. It's boring in a bad way."

"What's boring in a good way?" I need to ask.

"Baseball," Sharkey replies and follows it with a high-five to Page. "There's nothing more boring and more relaxing in my old age and physical condition than to

33

watch a game of baseball with a case of beer by my side. You get someone who throws a wicked change-up or curve and I could watch 'im work all day. Someone throws a ball, someone else tries to say 'fuck you' and hit it out of the ballpark. Repetitive, but fascinating and dramatic at times. It's the ultimate reality show. Nothin' like it."

The moment that everyone has been waiting for now arrives. The first female resident of 728 enters, Cindy 'Stinky' Seaver. I can't say that I'm disappointed. She sets the bar high. Stinky is blonde and leggy and pretty with large, precious-looking brown eyes. She is also very pissed off. "I just got arrested over thirty fucking dollars!" she exclaims as she struggles not to cry.

"Didn't take long for the drama to start," says Sharkey as he looks at his watch. Blotto is especially perturbed.

"How many times are we going to have this conversation, Stinky?" he asks, annoyed. "Prostituting yourself on the cheap is no way to go through life, woman! Thirty dollars doesn't go very far these days, anyway. That's a tank'a gas and some pork rinds. I like pork rinds. I could go for some right now, as a matter of fact."

"I always liked Lorna Doones," remarks Page as Stinky stands in the living room with tears now streaming down her face. "That was always my one secret stoner food that I was afraid to admit I liked. What a stupid fucking name for a cookie, man."

"They were named after a character in a British novel published in the nineteenth century," says Blotto using the tone of a cultured professor.

"Thanks, C-3PO," Sharkey replies. "It still doesn't explain why you should name a fucking cookie after any person that's not a female porn star. That's my contention, anyway. Who wants to get me a beer? That sounds like a job for Cindy Seaver."

"Does anybody care about what just happened to me?!?" asks the blonde rather impatiently. No one speaks. "Fine!" she says before stomping toward the kitchen. "I'm going to the fridge and grabbing *one* beer for myself. Fuck the rest of you guys and all of your small, little wee wees."

"I'd like to hear your story, Stinky," says Page. Sharkey rolls his eyes and sticks his own finger down his throat.

"As soon as I got into town today," she begins with a sniffle, "I got pulled over for going 28 in a 25 zone and I was arrested for an outstanding parking ticket from six summers ago! And I even paid the fucking thing, but didn't read the fine print that says you have to pay $30 in court costs, too. Do you realize how much sun time I just lost? It's incalculable."

"That's a pretty good word from a blonde, 'incalculable,'" Page observes.

"I'm surprised you can read, Stinky," says Sharkey with a chuckle. "Is that something special you learned for this summer? What's on tap next? Long division?"

"I'm a good reader," Stinky says proudly while slowly shutting down her faucets. "Even though I'm blonde and *sexy*..." She further emphasizes this last point by shaking her shapely butt back and forth after selecting a beer from the refrigerator.

"Just keep downloading more bikini pictures to your facebook," Sharkey suggests after another toke from a nearby jay. "I was able to cancel all of my internet porn subscriptions after your last trip to Aruba."

"I'm going to ignore that *disgusting* comment for now," Stinky says as she heads for the couches to hand out fresh beers and take a seat with us. "I talk to my *mother* on facebook and you- I'm not even going to go there." She places her little body between Page and I.

"You're the new guy?" she says to me once seated.

"M'mm. Patrick."

"I was hoping you'd be a lot cuter," she informs me, and despite the odd smile on her face I know that she's not kidding.

"Let the man sit for ten minutes before you start chastising him for not being up to your lofty standards," says Sharkey. "Is that other guy out of jail yet?"

"Three months," says Stinky while holding up two fingers. "I just got a letter from his parole officer the other day. Besides, I wouldn't say something like that if I didn't think the new guy is good-looking. Otherwise, that'd be really cruel."

"Hasn't stopped you from being cruel before," Sharkey replies. "Why won't you finally sleep with Page? He's only been drooling over you for four fucking summers."

"Five," Stinky corrects.

"Six," laughs Page. "We met Summer of '04."

"We did? I don't remember..."

"I think that's his point," says Blotto.

"Well, my latest boyfriend is visiting in two weeks!" she says excitedly. "The one that *didn't* go to jail for trying to burn my house down..."

"Can't wait," deadpans Page with a roll of his brown eyes.

"Look at me," Stinky continues as she looks down toward her trim thighs. "I can't stand it. No guy is gonna want to sleep with me if I look this pale all summer, boyfriend or not. I look like a corpse."

"You probably fuck like one, too," says Sharkey after another sip from his bottle. "The only difference is that you're able to get up and be put into a cab afterward."

"Whadda think about Stinky, Baxter?" asks Blotto of his drooling, flatulent canine companion. The dog perks his large ears at the mention of his name, looks at Stinky, sticks out his long, meaty, pink tongue, and yawns.

"See?" says the pretty blonde. "Even the dog isn't interested."

"He's fixed," explains Blotto.

"He's smart," says Sharkey.

"I'm going to put on my new blue bikini and lay out," Stinky announces. "I've had enough of the peanut gallery already.

"It's mutual," Sharkey replies.

"Nice to meet you," says the blonde to me as she rises from the couch.

"Sorry I wasn't cuter," I reply.

My comment gets a nice chuckle from the Board. Stinky blows me a kiss as she disappears down the hallway toward the bedrooms. Baxter hops off the couch and follows her in hopes that she will give him something to eat. It is at this time that I notice he has only three legs.

"He was like that when I found him," Blotto feels compelled to explain.

"I didn't think you ate it or anything," I assure him, quite stoned.

"I'm sure you didn't," he replies. "It's just one of things that we might as well get out of the way, because it's pretty fucking obvious that he has three legs."

"So do I," laughs Sharkey. "Doesn't seem to do me a damn bit 'a good, though."

2:47 p.m.

Dizzy has summoned me to his rental, a large new duplex situated on the sound only three blocks from Harry's dump. I follow the scent of freshly exhaled marijuana to the second floor living area, which is bright and airy with light wooden floors and a deck overlooking the water. Dizzy sits upon the couch pushing a brush through the thick coat of a large, beautiful Bernese mountain dog named Molly. Lionel Ritchie is playing through the Bose speakers hung in each corner of the room. I don't ask why. There is a laptop open with an extra monitor on the table, all of which is surrounded by several empty beer bottles and a jay burning down in an ashtray nearby. The dog takes an interest in the new arrival and walks over to my place on the couch once I am seated. "She's vicious," warns Dizzy. "She'll make that osprey this morning look like Mother Theresa." The dog approaches, sits in front of me, and offers me her paw much like a human would offer a handshake. I take her paw then begin to run my hands through her soft, freshly-brushed fur. She moves forward and plops her big head onto my lap.

"Molly is the best woman that I've ever met, aside from my mother," Dizzy says. "Her love is unconditional. All I do is walk her, feed her, pet her and brush her. She follows me around all day like I'm a hero. Sometimes a man needs to feel like a fucking hero. She'll never turn on me. I don't have to worry about her little insecurities about her thighs or her poor self-esteem. I don't have to constantly hear about her asshole ex-boyfriends that I'm 'just like.' I don't have to deal with that odd bond she still has with her college boyfriend because of the abortion. As long as I meet her basic needs and show her the affection she deserves, I have *noooooooo* problems. The only problem with Molly, in fact, is that every dog is a terrible heartbreak waiting to happen. You *have* to accept that this wonderful presence in your life will predecease you. But Molly is smarter, better behaved and much friendlier than most women, *and* keeps me warm at night. If I want sex, that's why the text message was invented. Man, if we had text messaging in high school or the one year I lasted at Bloomsburg...I don't even want to think about it. I'd be a father ten times over already. Now check this shit out."

Dizzy turns the monitors toward me and pulls up a series of photographs that would look at home on the pages of *National Geographic*. They're large, clear close-ups of various bird species flying, foraging and feeding. In one, the last gasp of a minnow's life is captured as the open-mouthed fish is about to flipped down the long, black spear of a beak on a white-feathered snowy egret. Another photo shows three colorful mallard drakes close-up and frozen in flight amongst some hens, their outspread wings revealing a patch of beautiful iridescent purple-blue feathers that I'd never noticed before. It isn't until the slideshow turns to the infamous osprey that I realize that all of these incredible photographs were taken by Dizzy during our expedition this morning. The angry bird with beady yellow eyes and extended talons looks like it's determined to fly straight out of the screen at us and attack. I had no idea that this is what Dizzy was doing in addition to drinking beer and smoking weed on a warm, sunny day.

"Nothin' like takin' pictures of birds," he says. "I love being out there in the marsh, man. There's always something goin' on out there. And speaking of *birds*..."

An eye-catching, blue-eyed, barefoot, long-haired blonde wearing a black bikini on her very bikini-worthy body enters the room. She's completely flat-chested, but I never cared about breasts. I'm always in search of the perfect combination of a tight ass, tan legs and sexual chemistry. I almost always fail to obtain it. This new arrival is even a 'pass' on the feet test. She's sexy as hell. This is the kind of girl that typically ignores me. "Have you met this whore yet?" Dizzy asks me. "Heather, this is

Patrick." The blonde looks over at me with her pretty blue eyes and gives me a funny stare.

"That's not Patrick," laughs the whore. "That's Woodchuck." *Woodchuck.* The source of this grade school nickname was a massive overbite that required two awkward years in an orthodontic appliance to correct. Consequently, it's not my favorite nickname. And this is a bold statement coming from someone whose pledge name at Iowa was 'Shitsniffer.' "Smile for me," the blonde asks. Noting that my overbite is now cured, the blonde stretches herself over Molly to give me a big kiss on the lips. I have no memory of this woman. "We only went to third grade together before I moved to the 'burbs," she explains. "I was fat in grade school, too. You were like, smart or something, weren't you?"

"I used to be, yeah. I ran out of brains some time in law school."

Dizzy chuckles as he pulls-up another picture of the osprey onto one of his monitors. "At least now we know why you have unbelievably poor self-esteem despite that great body of yours, Heather," he says.

"I have no tits," the blonde replies, ignoring the fact that the rest of her is pretty fucking smashing. Women are so ridiculous about their looks. I doubt the runner-up to the Miss Universe pageant ever sleeps at night because she's simply unable to cope with being only the second-most beautiful woman in the entirety of creation. Heather reveals that her last name is Ball, which confirms that she was indeed fat in grade school. In fact, she was fucking enormous. The only time I ever punched someone without direct provocation was when Dino Morelli was mocking her to tears for having three chins. I suckered him right in his nose and bloodied it. I ran before he could kick my ass. Since he was a dirty white kid that went to public school, I survived because I didn't have to deal with him that often. "I've never forgotten that," says Heather after we recall and laugh about the story. She also jokes about a life-changing incident where I climbed into the choir loft during a third grade Class Mass and gave an impromptu organ performance right after the Gospel. Heather gives me another kiss and leaves to sun herself further on the floating dock outside known as Twat Island. "Maybe we'll make out later, Woodchuck," she says with a smile.

"He can do better," responds Dizzy, which leads the blonde to give him the finger and a disgusted sneer. "Trainwreck," he says to me after the sound of Heather's feet walking down the stairs falls silent. "It's always the hot ones who are crazy because guys like me have fucked with their heads since they were in eighth grade. So once they hit 30, that's 15 years of high-impact brain damage you have to account for. And that's a shame because if you're 33 years old and still look as great as Heather

38

does, you deserve to be happy once in a while instead of drowning in your own constant, self-inflicted misery. But, yeah, I've hit it and definitely would again."

"Why wouldn't you."

"Exactly. We're on the same page here, Woodchuck."

Fuck. 'Woodchuck' is definitely going to stick. It was nice to receive even a small bit of attention from Heather, though. In addition to Heather's attention, I also receive several kisses from Molly before I return to 728.

4:46 p.m.

"Any red-blooded American male who doesn't like this song don't like ice cream *or* pussy," declares Blotto as law while 'Gimmie Shelter' comes through the speakers of his black convertible Beamer. Our destination is Angel Bay Market. "I'm really in the mood for a chocolate donut," he then says. "Not all chocolate. Just the icing. Possibly with sprinkles. Do you call them sprinkles or jimmies?"

"Jimmies. My mom calls them jimmies."

"All of the girls in college called them sprinkles," Blotto says. "I just got into the same bad habit." He passes me shopping list that is basically indecipherable. "This is very good that you're taking this trip with me," he continues. "When we get back to the house with a bunch of cleaning supplies, the girls will get the mistaken impression that you're *domestic*. It gives you somewhat of a free pass for the first couple of times that you act like a drunken imbecile at all hours of the night."

"I don't drink," I offer.

"Why not? Rehab? Angel Bay is a bad place for anyone who went to rehab. We hate quitters around here."

"No rehab. Bad stomach."

"Hmm. Did you ever need to shower so bad that you could smell your own balls? I think that's where I'm at right now."

"Yeah. Mostly in college while I was pledging. A warm shower and clean socks were considered luxuries."

"When I played football in college, a lot of schools would shut off the hot water in the visitors' locker room if you upset them on the road," Blotto says. "I always thought that was kinda petty, like some bitter woman saying, *'You beat us? Fine! But now you won't be getting any hot water out of me. No. Way. So how does that make you feel, huh? Nah-na-na-na-NAH-na! Now don't you ever fucking do that again!'* But think about how much money you save by not drinking. I'd be driving a Ferrari if I didn't drink. We need paper towels. Make sure we get paper towels."

"You put that on the list," I assure him after translating the name of third scribbled item. A beautiful blue C5 Chevrolet Corvette turns onto St. Michael's Drive in front of us. My stomach twists, just like it does every time I see those four telltale taillights on the highway in front of me. The license plate might as well read, 'U FAILED.' I've wanted to drive a Corvette since I was 9, when my mechanic neighbor gave me a ride in a white '74 Stingray that looked like the Mach 5. Twenty-three years and a law degree later, I'm no closer to owning even a very used one. In fact, I'm approximately $90,000 further away from ownership. Blotto untwists my stomach by bringing me out of my pitiful ruminations and back to the current events at 728.

"While I have you here, Woodchuck," he says, "allow me to apologize for having to deal with my ex on Thursday night."

"So *you're* the lucky man..."

"Not exactly," Blotto says with a crooked smile. "Kirsten is the kind of woman that you replace the hairdryer on the sink with a .44 Magnum and just hope for the best. The problem is that the second your penis enters her vagina, you have immediately entered into a permanent contract with a woman possessed by a demon. This demon is a very insecure demon and it feeds on constant attention. You will receive upwards of 60 calls, texts, facebook messages and e-mails per day, and she will fly into a rampage if you fail to respond to any of them within thirty seconds. It doesn't matter if you are at work, on a train, on a plane, in outer space, or find yourself handcuffed in the back of a police car after you fell down drunk in the middle of a sidewalk and shit your own pants. Not that that's ever happened to me, of course. I'm just giving you a very arbitrary but detailed example to explain my point. But anyway, Kirsten's only conclusion when you fail to immediately respond to any of over 6,000,000 potential forms of communication is to assume that you're not responding because you're fucking someone else. Now, how old are you?"

"Thirty-two."

"I wasn't sure if you were in your thirties or not because you still have a full head of hair," Blotto says. "So you know full well that when a man enters his thirties, he sometimes wants to come home on Friday after a long work week and just sit in a big chair with a beer and a joint and not be bothered by anything or anybody. One Friday, I came in from working three days in Tulsa, Oklahoma of all places and I had the worst day of my life in the Montgomery County Courthouse the Monday before I left. But that's another story for another time. So I had the taxi driver stop so that I could pick up a giant rack of ribs on my way home from the airport. I was so hungry, just *starving*, and I couldn't wait to eat those fucking ribs, man. Kirsten is blowing up my phone while I was in the cab and I just didn't feel like dealing with her. That's when I realized that I was done with her. It was such a relief to not have to see her for three days. It's way too stressful to have to provide that level of attention to someone when you have a job and a dog and other things going on in your life, like friends and rec league basketball. My only concern at that time was feeding myself some ribs. Feeding Tearsten's attention demon was not my priority. My phone's almost dead because I forgot to bring my charger to Tulsa, accidentally on purpose, so I just shut it off. I get home and grab Baxter from my neighbor, and he's thrilled to see me. I'm stoned and sitting in my chair with my ribs and the remote and cole slaw and candied yams with Baxter drooling next to me and *Stripes* happens to be on. Can it get any better when you're completely exhausted after a work trip? I think not. Except for adding a blowjob, but only if the girl is going to agree to vacate immediately afterwards so you can eat and watch the movie in peace. And Tearsten would not have let me eat and watch the movie in peace. It would have been, *'Why didn't you call and see if I wanted to order anything, too? Why are we watching this movie? It's old! You've probably already seen it twelve times. Tell me all about your trip. Did they send any girls down there with you? I want to know exactly who was on that trip! That bitch Kelly wasn't traveling with you, was she? Ugh! I hate her! She wouldn't fucking stop staring at you at your Christmas party!'* and all the other horseshit you have to constantly put up with from a hot, miserable, insecure girl. Then she'd start going through my phone, which women somehow feel is a birthright these days. So I have these ribs on my plate, Tearsten is presumably at her house a few blocks away, and the meat is just falling off the bone. I'm in heaven. I hear my storm door open and someone tries to make their way into my house. I knew it was Kirsten, but I was smart enough to lock the door and draw the blinds so she couldn't tell that I had the TV on. She starts banging and yelling and screaming but there's only going to be Hell to pay if I open that fucking door because I've been ignoring every call and text since I was at the airport in Dallas five hours before. I figured she would just give up and go home, or go out to the bars to get loaded and arrested. No such luck. A few minutes later, I hear some sounds coming from the area outside of my kitchen. Baxter starts barking. Then I hear glass breaking and all sorts of noise, and I find Kirsten lying on the kitchen floor bleeding and screaming because she tried to climb in my window but fell right through it. Then Baxter started to attack her. He never really warmed up to Tearsten, to put it mildly. I don't think you can imagine how pissed off I was."

"How long were you guys dating at this point?"

"Two weeks, I think," Blotto replies before sneezing all over his steering wheel. "Actually, it was more like three months. Either way, it was far too early in the relationship to be breaking into someone's home. I wasn't going to deal with this mess, so I grabbed her phone and called for an ambulance. It seemed like a good idea when I was stoned. She was bleeding all over the fucking place and her elbow is swelling to the size of a grapefruit. She definitely needed legitimate medical attention. And she's yelling and screaming the entire time, and Baxter is barking and howling the entire time. So the ambulance shows up, the cops show up while the house still smells like weed, and pretty soon they're asking me questions outside and investigating me for domestic violence. And the more pissed off I got about all this, the more convinced they were that I had done something. I refused to let the cops into my house because they'll smell the weed, which, by the way, was quite dank. Then they threaten to confiscate Baxter. I'm fairly certain that I would have grabbed one of the cops' guns and shot them both if they went anywhere near him. Long story short, someone was interviewing Tearsten at the hospital and must have realized that she was out of her mind, so they finally backed the fuck off. But when I turned my phone on that next morning, I had 68 nasty text messages from her and my voicemail was full. Not to mention that she threw a brick through the windshield of this very car with her good arm. Her entire life revolves around broken glass, it seems. So, needless to say, I was done with her forever after all that. She still calls me constantly, though. No one else has ever put up with her for more than three weeks or so, which is amazing given her great looks. So Tearsten became a little obsessed with me. But the only reason why we made it three months was because I happened to be traveling for work a lot at the time and didn't have to deal with her. I'd be on the road for three days, fuck her for four, then I'd be able to escape back out onto the road again before she got too, too crazy. I can't imagine what she would have done if I cheated on her. You know what?"

"What," I respond dryly.

"We need to buy cups, too. Did I put cups on the list?"

"Affirmative."

"Good. That's good. You can't drink without cups. Well, you can but it really puts the kibosh on the more intoxicating drinking games. I was thinking when I made that shopping list. I must be sober enough to drive."

I must be way too stoned to see the value of that correlation.

5:27 p.m.

Blotto encounters a woman breathing hellfire as soon as we return from Angel Bay Market and enter the upstairs unit with supplies in hand. "Get the *fuck* over here!" the voice shrieks like an irate mother who just discovered a sticky copy of *Girls Who Eat Sperm for Brunch* stuffed underneath the mattress of her sixth-grade son's bed. I can't see the source of this madness as I unload the bags containing cups, laundry detergent, limes, glass cleaner, dryer sheets, paper towels, a chip clip, a dish towel, cranberry juice, a closet pole, carpet cleaner, Doritos, tile cleaner, matches, and a chocolate donut into various cabinets and places in and around the kitchen. Well, not the closet pole. I kind of put that aside and pretend it's no longer my responsibility. I also place the bag containing the donut onto the counter as Blotto inquires further regarding the complaints of this severely pissed off wench with a dirty mouth. Reconsidering, I help myself to the donut and hope that Blotto will forget about it. These are the kinds of things you do when you're way stoned.

"I'll tell you *exactly* what the fucking problem is here," the female voice roars. "The problem is that you and Harry promised Gina and I that the upstairs unit would be spotless if we rented a room this summer. Now go inside that bathroom and take a look at that showerhead. Look at it!"

"I believe that 'Gina and me' would be proper grammar in that instance, Jenna," is Blotto's calm and dignified response.

"Don't fucking tell me what's proper and improper grammar, you twit," seethes the woman. This gives me a chuckle, because I've never heard a guy who is 6'4" be referred to as a 'twit.' Jenna must be some odd, gangly tall chick with big legs. That's what I picture, at least. Stoned and firmly entrenched on a comfortable couch, I have no desire to get up to see what this latest scream machine actually looks like. Blotto continues speaking.

"So your problem, again, Jenna, is..."

"MOLD!" the woman exclaims in the voice of someone receiving a jolt from the electric chair. "How the hell am I supposed to get myself clean when the water has to travel through some ancient colony of fucking fungus before touching my body? If I take a shower in there I'll be dead in a week from who-the-hell-knows-what."

"May I touch your fungus, Jenna?" Blotto queries politely.

"No!" the woman shouts as if it was a serious proposition. "You may *NOT* touch my fungus. Why am I even still speaking with you? Get a brush and whatever else you need to clean up that fucking mold. NOW! And God help you if I need to put the EPA on speed dial this summer because of any more rotten *filth* in this house." Blotto returns to the kitchen to grab some sort of spray cleaner and a brush from underneath the sink after first tripping over the closet pole that I had set upright on the floor. I click on the television in order to get an update on the Phillies game. After a batter grounds out to short to end the inning, I find myself startled by a pair of large brown eyes that are intensely trained upon me like a lioness stalking its prey. Except that this lioness sits about two inches off the floor and has a face covered by snot, with a particularly unnatural-looking accumulation directly upon the surface of its left eyeball. It cautiously approaches and takes a congested sniff of my person before turning to waddle into the middle of the room. I now realize that this certified biological disaster of a dog is beset with a severely inflamed reddened anus that takes up 85% of the surface area on the rear of its body. I follow the path of this creature intently as Blotto receives further cleaning orders from Jenna, who now demands that the closet pole be placed somewhere into her bedroom. Into the closet, I assume.

"You know where this pole's going if you come within four feet of me, Jenna," he laughs.

"You know what, Blotto?"

"What."

"Nevermind," says the woman.

"I hate when girls say that," the man complains. Jenna apparently smacks Blotto in response. "You're a very testy girl, Jenna," he says. "And if you hit me again, I will shove this pole so far up your angry little asshole that it will come out of your mouth and you'll have to taste your own shit. How does that sound to you?"

There is no response. My attention turns back to the little dog on the carpet. After Cole Hamels strikes out the first batter of the new inning with a nasty change-up, the diminutive canine drops to its haunches and extends its left front paw toward the ground. This thing then begins to rotate itself on the carpet in complete circles while its wide, pink tongue gleefully hangs out of its blackened mouth. The dog's velocity increases with each spin. I have no idea what the fuck is going on here with this squat, spinning, crusty, snotty pug beset with the Mother of All Buttholes. "Princess!" Jenna the Bitch calls from the hallway, which brings the ass rotations to a brief halt.

"What the hell is that *thing* doing?" asks Blotto aloud as he walks back into the kitchen for a brew and spots the disobedient, smiling Princess again whirling away on the carpet.

"Princess had an infected anus," Jenna explains. "That's how she scratches her butt when it gets sore. And she's not a 'thing,' Blotto. She's a living, breathing creature with feelings and a soul."

"I have rescued a dog myself," Blotto replies. "But he does not ever spin on the carpet like I've just witnessed. Actually, he couldn't because he has only one front leg. I guess that's what separates Princess from Baxter. Please pardon my ignorance concerning the state of her butthole."

Jenna lets out a frustrated sigh and the bathroom door slams shut. Several now-muted curses and complaints are verbalized, and water begins streaming in the shower. The batter for the Chicago Cubs hits a one-hopper to short. There are no further documented complaints of fungus or old pugs spinning upon the carpet. But

Blotto wonders what happened to his donut. I manage to convince him that he ate it in the car.

9:39 p.m.

Page, Peter Sharkey and I detect the sweet scent of 'girl' emanating into the area from somewhere near our current location in the Board Room. Intrigued, we follow the trail down the hallway into the Slut Room and seat ourselves on the beds to watch the just-showered Mallory get herself ready for the evening. This very intimidating, very womanly thirty-three year-old stands in a pair of painted-on jeans and a black top in front of the room's long, wide mirror hung over the dresser. Her legs are longer than an unemployment line in Detroit. It is time to blow dry and brush her long, dark hair, which is a process that may possibly take twelve hours. I sit in a stoned silence, completely captivated by each stroke of Mallory's brush, each turn of her neck, and each instance when I'm unintentionally teased by the running of Mallory's red-painted fingers through her own damp hair before she completely starts the process over. This entire scene has pushed my intoxicated mind straight back to the feeling of being fifteen again. Sharkey is not as impressed with this display as I am.

"Slut! Slut! Slut!" he exclaims, pounding his almost-empty beer can into his hand for emphasis after every utterance. "The goal was to go 'slut' for your outfit this evening, Mallory. I demand to know what the hell happened. *Jeans?* I came in here to watch you stand around in a pair of *jeans?* You've *got* to be kidding me. Your top's pretty weak, too."

"What do you realistically expect from me, Peter?" questions the brunette as the strokes from her massive brush continue. "I have B-cups. Even with these rubber chicken patty-looking things I shove into my tops, it's tough to look slutty with B-cups unless you expose your entire back or midriff. And I'm not going to do that because I'm not 23 anymore. These also happen to be the tightest jeans I own. I almost needed to grease up my legs and jump into them from the roof. And it's too cool right now for a miniskirt. So, I guess what I'm saying is, give me a fucking break, Peter."

"You sound like a typical woman making a bunch of excuses," says Sharkey dismissively. "I think you're dropping the ball here. You have an opportunity tonight to celebrate your release from relationship prison by getting drunk and running around the Shipwreck like a runway model off her Ritalin. Instead, you go jeans. Suck it. And while you're at it-"

Mallory picks up the nearby hairdryer and smiles to herself before putting it on full blast to drown out Sharkey's voice. His opinion on this matter firmly rebuffed, he takes this opportunity to retrieve a fresh beer from the kitchen. The coast now clear, the small button on the hairdryer is placed back into the 'off' position.

"If only Blotto could see *this* operation," comments Page after a lengthy gulp from a bottle of Corona Light with a lime slice. "That fucker's passed out in his own drool right now."

"I'm pissed at him," Mallory replies. "I don't know why he found it so necessary to throw me into the channel today while I was peacefully sunbathing on the dock. I didn't want my new Phillies hat to get all wet with salt water."

"It's better than being raped," opines Sharkey sincerely as he reenters the room. "He's had his tongue hangin' out for you for three years. And which one of you waste products has infected our refrigerator with Corona Light? *Corona?* Fine. Completely acceptable. Corona *Light?* Just give your rent money back to Harry and call it a season. Please. I won't eat or drink 'light' anything. It's my duty as the most masculine presence in this house."

Mallory launches a look of total disgust on her pretty, brown-eyed face toward Peter following his commentary. She then complains about an unexpected knot in her hair. "How old are you, anyway, Peter?" Mallory asks after this situation is rectified by several powerful strokes of her brush. "You look about 52. And I brought the light beer, by the way."

"Figures," Sharkey replies. "It's always the girls who are hot and skinny that consume 'light' everything even though it doesn't make a bit of fucking difference to their already sexy bodies. But to answer your original question, I am 36. I am living proof of what alcohol, drugs and hookers can do to a man over three decades of abuse. I'm a longitudinal study of what *not* to do to the human body, and I must say that I'm pretty fucking proud of it. It's been totally worth it. I don't need to be in tip top shape to sit in a fucking cube all day and sell mortgages to complete assholes. Not that I'll have a job much longer in this economy..."

Now entering the room is Stinky in a white bathrobe. "Where's your electronic monitoring bracelet, you convict?" Sharkey wants to know.

"Fuck you," she replies with a pleasant smile before quickly ditching her robe. This reveals a beautiful, cellulite-free, most feminine body covered by only a black thong and a matching bra. It's the most undressed I've seen a woman in thirteen months without a $10 cover charge and a two-drink minimum. "Did you hear that Peter jerks off to my facebook pictures, Mallory?" says the blonde as she reaches into the closet and grabs a pair of dark jeans that she attempts to step into.

"I'm not surprised by anything guys do these days," Mallory replies. "That's why I took all of my sexy pics down from my profile."

"Doubt that took long," chuckles Sharkey.

"It's kinda your own fault," says Page to Stinky. "Is it *really* necessary to put yourself on facebook lookin' all tan on a tropical island while making sexy poses in a bikini that's practically made out of dental floss?"

"Sounds like I'm not the only culprit here," Sharkey observes before taking a long swig.

"I look hot in those pictures!" Stinky says in her defense. "I'm just not trying to look hot for *you* people. Please conduct yourself accordingly."

"Please add me as a friend, Stinky," is my request.

"I can do that right now from my iPhone," she replies. "Well, maybe I should put some clothes on first."

"Don't bother, McShea," says Sharkey to me. "Only Hot Dudes facing criminal indictment are allowed to 'admire' her pictures. Anything else is *waaaaaaaaaaaaay* too boring for this fucking mess of a broad."

"Like I'm the only girl on Earth who's ever dated a criminal!" Stinky snaps.

"Of course, you aren't," says Sharkey with a laugh. "Eva Braun ring a bell?"

"Who's Eva Braun?" asks Stinky while trying to put on a pair of skintight jeans. It looks like it's becoming a major project.

"She's an actress, I think," offers Mallory. "She won an Oscar or something for some movie in the 1950's."

"Wasn't she in E.T.?" Stinky asks. "I think she was in E.T." She then falls flat on her face after trying to unsuccessfully untangle the left pant leg of her jeans from the bottom of her foot.

"I would wear flats tonight," Mallory suggests to her fallen roommate. "You're already pretty trashed."

"Bah!" Sharkey exclaims. "Flats? You just need to take care of your gas problem, Stinky. If astronauts can land on the moon and come back to Earth, I'm sure some doctor somewhere knows how to normalize your ass. Soon, I would hope."

"I can't help it if I have a slightly irritable bowel, Peter," Stinky replies as she returns to an upright position. Her jeans finally finish making the long journey up her trim legs and are snapped shut. I decline to announce that Stinky and I have an irritable bowel in common. Speaking about the state of my colon in the company of my new friends would be TMI. She must have a much less severe case than I do if she is already pretty hammered. Stinky grabs a sequined black shirt to place over the top of her body and makes her way to the mirror with a three ton make-up bag, which couldn't possibly be necessary because she already looks pretty good. The bag is not yet opened when Mallory glances over at Stinky when handing her the hairdryer.

"You were planning on wearing a black top, too?" Mallory asks of her mirror mate.

"I don't think all that much 'planning' was involved," Sharkey observes. "In fact, I think we saw the entire thing go down right here. I'll grab the pool, forty pounds of pudding, and we'll settle this whole fucking problem right now."

"You know what?" says Stinky. "I can wear my red top tonight instead."

"Please do," says Sharkey sarcastically. "We can't allow you and Mallory to clash by both wearing black."

The plot now takes an unexpected twist.

"I don't know if I brought my red slut heels with me this weekend," Stinky wonders aloud as she returns to the closet and begins poking around while bent at an angle that her makes her apparently malfunctioning ass look especially enticing. "I was all about coordinating my top and shoe colors tonight! And now my dream is dying right before my very eyes."

"I don't see what the problem is," says Mallory. "Black heels go with almost anything." Stinky's red top is produced from the closet, and all agree that it looks becoming when placed onto her body. Further dispute as to who has the right to wear a black top to Shipwreck this evening is safely averted.

"I'm so excited!" the blonde exclaims as she again takes her spot at the mirror, now in red. "In two weeks, I'll *finally* be having sex again."

"Is that how long it takes for The Clap to clear up?" asks Sharkey following a sip from his bottle. "Spending two weeks with your vagina out-of-commission is really bad for business, Stinky. Prompt, efficient service is what keeps all the customers happy."

"My vagina is *fine*, Peter."

"So it says on bathroom stalls throughout the entire tri-state area," is Page's comment. Then he begins a stoned giggling fit at his own joke, which immediately infects me.

"My boyfriend is *finally* coming in from L.A.," Stinky now explains further. "I am going to ride him like...I dunno. Something you ride hard until your legs really hurt. Like a Big Wheel."

"If I waited over one month for a guy to fly in from the West Coast, I think I'd want a better ride than a Big Wheel," says Mallory as she digs through her bag for some make-up item that cost at least forty bucks, even though she's just as fucking pretty without it. "But apparently my expectations regarding anything related to men or sex are a bit too high these days."

"Boo-hoo," yaps Sharkey. "Sucks to be young, smart and skinny, doesn't it, Mallory?"

"Thirty-three is not young, Peter. For a guy, yes. For a woman, we start going into Red Alert around now. It's completely possible at this point that I'll wind up husbandless with no kids."

Page and I make guy contact, simultaneously rolling our eyes upon hearing such an attractive, sweetly-voiced, sexy woman speculate that she will spend the rest of her life alone in a dried riverbed of childless sexual misery. We both burst out laughing, probably because the two of us just spent the past ten minutes lost in perverted fantasies about Mallory's butt.

"What's so funny?" the woman demands to know as she turns her half made-up face toward us while unscrewing her mascara brush from its case.

"Nothin'," Page replies innocently.

"How do you think *I* feel?" Stinky asks before adding to this installment of 'Hot Chicks with No Self-Esteem,' which will be replayed over a thousand times during the course of the summer. "Not only did my boyfriend move to L.A., but I think my tits got smaller and my ass got bigger over the winter. Isn't aging great? I hate being 30! If this keeps up I'll be finger-banging myself for the rest of my life. I'm not surprised, though. I started getting cellulite in *eighth grade*. I didn't even have breasts yet."

"You were better off with The Clap," opines Sharkey.

"I rode a Big Wheel when I was little," declares Page after first overcoming a lengthy THC-induced brain delay. "I made my mom cut the streamers off, though. Otherwise, the older kids would just rip them off and call you a fag."

"Where'd you grow up that kids ripped the streamers from your Big Wheel?" Stinky asks, sounding horrified.

"Lawrence, Mass," replies Page. "Which is right outside of Boston. Then South Philly, then the suburbs for high school with some of these assholes, then one year at the University of Miami getting drunk and chasing women, and...it's all a mess, really. So the answer to your question was, 'near Boston.' Damn. I am *stoned*."

10:59 p.m.

If it was even possible, additional trouble has walked into my life on a pair of black flip-flops. Her name is Gina Marie D'Amico, a way hot Italian thing who sleeps in one of the upstairs bedrooms with Jenna the Bitch and Princess the Spinning, Butthole-Scratching Pug. The butterflies were instant as soon as I saw Gina Marie, which was pretty fucking stupid and disappointing on my end because my career batting average with hot Italian girls stands at a paltry .062. Gina was raised in the suburbs north of Philadelphia, so I'm not going to be automatically disqualified from dating her despite the fact that her last name ends in a vowel and I have earned two degrees. Unfortunately, she does look like one of those women that would expect you to have a job. She also has a boyfriend whose father owns a Porsche dealership on the Main Line and is worth millions. That's not going to help my cause. But she has laughed at everything that I have said in the last twenty minutes, even when what I said wasn't very funny. Few things attract a man to a woman like their constant laughter during a conversation. Gina doesn't actually 'laugh,' though. It's more of a snorting vocalization worthy of a pig in heat. It's disarming, somewhat. She's clothed in a disappointing combination of a conservative green top and a pair of somewhat loose jeans as we walk to a nearby bar called the Shipwreck aka Trainwreck with Peter Sharkey, Stinky and Page. Her boring bar threads are probably because she's an accountant, which is the world's most boring profession and filled with the world's most boring people. And the next male accountant I encounter in the elevator of a Center City office building that stands over 5'7" will be the first. Sharkey takes issue with Gina's choice of clothing for this evening.

"What's wrong with my outfit?" asks the stunning Italian-American.

"Blah," replies the resident fashion critic. "Can't see your huge tits, can't see your great legs. Throw us a bone, bitch."

"I don't need to throw any of you dogs here a bone. But thank you. What do you do for a living, Patrick?"

"I'm unemployed," I confess enthusiastically. Sometimes it's better to just get that out of the way. The brunette has a very unusual take on the situation.

"You know what?" she asks rhetorically. "I think that unemployment can be *sexy*. It's like, you don't have a job, yet you seem to be fine with it. I think it shows that you have a lot of confidence in yourself and your ability to land a new position."

"I think it shows that he's a jobless bitch with no income," Sharkey opines as we move closer toward the bar. I have no comeback to that. It becomes apparent as to why the Shipwreck had earned the 'Trainwreck' moniker as we move closer toward the establishment. A very attractive blonde in a little black dress and heels is standing smack in the middle of 7th Street, screaming at the top of her sexy lungs while positioned opposite from a very tall, very confused-looking dude. Dude has his hands stretched out in a 'wtf' position and is apparently pleading 'not guilty' to the charges:

"Three FUCKING years, Jason, and you NEVER fucking loved me, did you? DID YOU!!! You're a FUCKING liar! LIAR!!! It's always been about that fucking whore Tracy, hasn't it? HASN'T IT!!! I guess the fact that she sucked your best friend's DICK hasn't changed anything, you fucking prick. I hate you! I fucking HATE YOU!!!"

"It's the first weekend of the summer, for fuck's sake!" yells Sharkey out into the street. "At least wait until July before you start makin' all *that* noise." Paying Sharkey no mind, the blonde begins to administer her man a severe beating with her pocketbook. With each thrust of the oversized bag, at least two or three items fly loose and land hard into the street. It's a cell phone, a tin of mints, and a pair of tweezers on the first swing; a pack of Marlboro Lights, lipstick, and a lighter on the second; and, for the grand finale, the third swing brings a tampon and what Gina at first believes to be red vibrator but is actually a toothbrush holder. Everyone plays up the vibrator angle, though. Sharkey wonders aloud whether the blonde could be so kind as to switch it on and immediately place it into his rectum.

"Must be similar to your model," says Page to Gina. "And that is one lucky machine, I might add."

"I don't *need* a vibrator," Gina snaps in response.

"I don't know what the hell you're talking about, Gina," says Stinky, who is again dressed in black and livin' the dream of a matching shoe/top combination. "We *all* need a vibrator sometimes."

"That's where you're *wrong*, Stinky," says Page. "The only thing a woman ever needs to vibrate is the cell phone of any male non-relative in your address book. It takes five seconds to send a text message. Depending on distance and the need for a shower, and maybe a little stop at CVS to grab some condoms, it might take anywhere from 5 to 65 minutes for an actual living, breathing dude to show up at your front door instead of something that needs batteries or an outlet. Outlets and batteries and masturbation really aren't meant for each other. That's how bad accidents happen. Just give me a warm shower and a bottle of conditioner and I'm all good to go."

"Everything you said is just *way* too complicated," Stinky replies to her suitor. "I always feel like such a whore the next day, too."

The police now arrive to intervene in the street disturbance, drawn to the scene by the stopped cars, honking horns, and the various drivers of the various stopped vehicles calling the blonde a stupid slut. The girl suddenly takes a gratuitous swing at one of the bike cops with her pocketbook and is promptly cuffed to the applause of dozens of passers-by, including Peter Sharkey. "Bread and water for you tonight, bitch!" he yells with glee after a few claps. "Now hand over your panties! It's all part of procedure. Official business. I'll take those shoes, too. Love the shoes. They look like fuckin' death weapons."

"Eww!" says Gina. "I hate her shoes. They're trashy-looking."

"You will be, too, in about three hours," Sharkey replies.

We approach the bar entrance and I'm not even carded. The 'salt' portion of my salt 'n pepper hair must be taking over more than I care to admit. I pay Gina's $10 cover. Nothing says, 'I'm *really* interested in having sex with you later' like paying a girl's cover charge. She offers thanks as if I have imparted a great gift which has touched her through the very depths of her soul, but I'm not convinced she got the real message.

11:33 p.m.

Tearsten suddenly approaches. Her eyes are as red as her short, spectacular dress and matching flip-flops. The place is far too crowded to run away, so I'll have to deal with her. And I'd rather not, because this possessed evil spawn of Eve looks far too tempting. "Why'd you leave me alone at the bar last night, asshole!" she sneers.

"No reason."

"Whatever happened last night was really no big deal."

"Call me old fashioned, but I think throwing a full pitcher of beer at a girl and asking her at the top of your lungs- in public- how your ass tastes on her boyfriend's dick is a pretty big deal."

"Attitude..."

"Whatever, Kirsten."

"If I don't remember something, it didn't happen. Come dance with me."

"I'm meeting someone."

"Who?"

"A girl from law school," I lie. It's a particularly egregious lie, because I'd never date another lawyer. I don't want to come home 10 minutes late from watching a game and be faced with hours of bad attitude and pointed questioning over it. Attorneys are conditioned not to trust anybody, and many of them don't leave their lawyer persona at the office. Combined with the social awkwardness already displayed by most them, attorneys make for brutal 'companions.' Not satisfied with the level of attention I'm providing, Tearsten runs off to harass someone else.

11:57 p.m.

"Do you dance?" Gina asks me after sipping on a fruity-looking concoction that I paid for out of my unemployment funds.

"Kinda," I reply, meaning 'no.'

"Good enough," Gina says as she grabs my hand. While *en route* to the room with the dance floor, she decides to give me an introductory tour of the Shipwreck. I'm convinced that the onramp to I-666 South can be found here. I have not seen such a spectacular collection of women in one place anywhere since my fraternity days. There are possibly thousands of females migrating and trying to mate within the maze of the various bars and rooms of this gigantic watering hole, and at least 70% of them are far above average-looking and far above intoxicated. I'd consider it to be a target-rich environment. Unfortunately, I've never been much of a ladies man at the bars outside of Iowa City. This is the East fucking Coast here, filled with millions of options and millions of dollars. White collar money and blue collar muscle rule the day. If you have both, you're golden. I have neither. So I'm automatically going to be disqualified by 50% of the women here because I'm thin. I'll be disqualified by another 49% because I have no job and no money. The 1% that's left, I ain't finding in this uncontrolled chaos. I was far too spoiled at Iowa than I ever had the right to be.

I'm finally dragged into the Shipwreck's Disco Room to scores of flashing colored lights and sweating women dressed like escorts who won't be able to spell their own names in approximately twenty minutes. I have rhythm from playing the guitar, but I'm too self-conscious to dance without being drunk. Gina probably has the ability to change that. Her friend DJ Buttfuck is spinning tonight. "It's not his real name," she explains in case I had any doubt. The current selection is a classic track over which the voice of Khia raps about her neck, back, pussy and crack. Gina pulls me straight onto the floor and starts to smoothly twist her sexy body in front of me. I feel like I just paid $20 for a table dance. Except that Gina is wearing more clothes and the dance is free. Funny how that works out. She begins to grind her small butt into my crotch suggestively. This is admittedly redundant, because there is no way to un-suggestively grind into someone's crotch while a woman raps in her best Ebonics about receiving oral sex from a thug.

"I want to spy on Stinky," Gina says, nodding toward her left.

"Is that your excuse for pushing your ass into me?"

"Maybe," she replies. "Do you think I have a nice ass?"

"Maybe," I reply in turn.

"It's getting a little big," she says with some concern.

"Shut the fuck up, Gina."

Stinky herself is positively dangerous on the dance floor. She displays more personality and rhythm than many celebrities making millions off their moves. The man with her seems far from impressed, though. He appears to be the stereotypical total asshole that every girl wants to fuck once. He is one of those Hot Dudes with a million dollar body and a ten-cent head who hits the gym six days per week, specifically so that a too-tight shirt can be sported at a Jersey Shore bar all summer long. Standing a shade over 6'3" and wearing a two-sizes-too-small tan shirt and a purple East Carolina cap worn backwards, this douchebag has taken on the appearance of a giant penis. He stares at Stinky with vacant eyes while she smoothly dances all around him. Apparently, he finds the whole thing silly. It's fucking weird.

"That guy is *not* hot," says Gina into my ear as we sway to some freestyle hit from the Eighties that my brother used to constantly play on an old mix tape. I get the chills just from feeling Gina's warm breath against my face as she speaks, and I consider her non-attraction to a total d-bag to be an encouraging sign. "What do you think of Stinky?" she asks me.

"She's really pretty. I'm not her type."

"She picks the *worst* guys."

"Then maybe I *am* her type..."

"I meant, she picks assholes."

"And who doesn't? Nice guys are boring."

"You're not boring..."

"Maybe I'm not such a nice guy."

"No, you are. Half the guys here would already be trying to rip my clothes off right here on the dance floor. So I can tell that you're nice."

"So I've completely screwed-up already?"

"Pretty much," Gina snorts. She continues to dance with me for some time. I grab her slim waist and start massaging her hips, feeling her soft feminine curves in my hands through her too-loose jeans. She immediately excuses herself to go the bathroom. Disappointed, I walk in search of a restroom myself before wandering to find my housemates.

1:39 a.m.

Blotto has convinced two very beautiful and very intoxicated women that he has been selected by NASA to perform a solo test flight to Neptune next month. "I hope to be back before Labor Day," he explains. "But I can't make anyone any guarantees. I suggest that if either of you have any inclination to take me home, that you do so immediately. If not, then I suggest we do more shots. If these are my final days on Earth, I intend to spend them naked and intoxicated. So far, I am executing half of my plan perfectly."

"More shots! More shots!" squeal the women.

Sharkey approaches. "What the fuck is going on here?" he demands to know.

"Blotto is flying solo to Mars," says one of the women. "Or Neptune. One of those places. It's somewhere really far away with no beer."

"I know," Sharkey replies with a grin. "I'm goin' with 'im."

Gina comes up and grabs me by the hand. "Walk me home," she commands as she pulls me toward one of the exits. Her great Italian looks, engaging personality and the salt air blowing off St. Michael's Sound have made me completely forget how fucked up my life actually is right now. Women and a change in scenery definitely have the ability to do that. I note that Gina is doing more stumbling than walking. We're forced to lock arms in order to keep her upright and stable. She'd have two broken ankles already if she was wearing heels. I accuse her of being wasted.

"Am not!" she insists. "I'm just avoiding the alligators that are all over the sidewalk." I fail to see any alligators in our path. "You have to be drunk to see them," Gina explains further. Then she slaps me and gives a hard push with both of her little hands.

"Why so violent, Gina?"

Next is a drunken giggle, a harder slap to my arm, and an even harder push toward a telephone pole.

"Why are you trying to kill me?" I ask of my drunken assailant. "We haven't even made out yet."

"We're *not* hooking up," Gina states, her voice suddenly very, very sober. I must give her a subconscious look of hate, because she goes right on the defensive: "We are not hooking up for several reasons. One, I just met you, like, five hours and sixteen minutes ago. Second, we live in the same house almost every weekend, and you don't *ev-er* shit where you eat. Third, I have a boyfriend that I have been dating for two years. Fourth, I'm not a cheater because all cheaters are scum and deserve to be tortured and fed southern fried rats. And fifth, I'm having my fucking period. Got it?"

"Southern fried rats?"

"I'm drunks," Gina snorts in reply. "I mean, drunk. Intoxicated."

"Is Chas a spy?"

"A spy? No! He's an accountant, too."

"Then how will he know if we hook up?"

"Ugh! That's completely irrelevant."

We arrive at 728. She dismisses me with a kiss to the cheek and heads upstairs, leaving me with that unique, very disappointed feeling in the pit of my stomach.

2:32 a.m.

Blotto and Sharkey return to the Board Room empty-handed. Page is nowhere to be found. We receive a message that he is asleep on a random lawn located somewhere between 728 and the Moo Moo. Stinky and three other hot women stumble into the Board Room demanding weed. Then they all realize simultaneously that they have to pee and immediately stumble right back out. "We just went from heroes to zeros in about four seconds," Blotto observes.

"I'm still a hero," says Sharkey after burping. "Just not in the traditional sense. I'm more like a drunken samurai, except without the samurai powers and a sword." Upon further reflection Sharkey says, "Don't listen to me. I'm drunk. I don't even know what the fuck I'm talking about."

The sound of the girls giggling in the nearby bathroom continues as Blotto begins to pack his personal water pipe, Euripides. He hits it himself before passing the bong to me. I ask Blotto about the girls at the Shipwreck that he was drinking with in celebration of his solo flight to Neptune with Sharkey. "When we walked out of the bar with them," he explains, "we realized that they couldn't walk without serious assistance. *Very* serious assistance. So we figured the smart thing to do was to leave them at their own house and avoid a visit from the Special Victims Unit tomorrow morning. Just because you *can* sleep with somebody, doesn't mean you *should*. But we did get their numbers. I think. I'm not too good with electronics at this time of night, even though I'm an interplanetary space pilot."

The girls return from their group pee in the bathroom. They giggle, drink, smoke, burp and generally make little sense for about six minutes until their phones begin blowing up. They all run out in search of Hot Dudes without bothering to bid us goodbye or goodnight. "Did those girls just smoke our weed, not hook up with any of us, and leave without saying goodbye?" asks Blotto.

"That's pretty much what I saw," says Sharkey. "You may think that you saw something different, but you would definitely be wrong."

"I remember when I used to be cool," Blotto laments before hitting the pipe again.

"When was that?" asks Sharkey skeptically.

"I dunno," Blotto replies after exhaling. "When I used to play football in stadiums filled with 100,000 screaming fans, play in bowl games and have sex with cheerleaders pretty regularly, I guess. Things like that."

"And when was all this happening? Like, 1994? Whatever happened in 1994 isn't exactly going to help your cause now."

"Obviously," says Blotto. "Exhibit A: it's two-thirty in the morning on a holiday weekend and I'm sitting in here with you assholes. And Baxter." Baxter looks up at his master at the mention of his name. One of his mutt eyes is brown and the other one is blue and lazy. The dog returns to a relaxed posture on the queen when he realizes that a treat is not forthcoming.

"So what was it like being in an NFL training camp?" I ask Blotto just to make conversation and relieve the boredom caused by having no attractive women present.

"My buddy who played safety probably summed it up the best," the tall, blonde-haired drunk replies. "If you *really* want to know what it's like to play in the NFL, take a walk to the bottom of your driveway in your street clothes. Stand back 15 yards from the garage door, and then run as fast as you can, and as hard as you can, directly into it- with no pads. That's what it feels like to tackle a veteran NFL running back that just burst through the hole from seven yards deep at full speed. The first time I played special teams in college as a redshirt freshman, I had the privilege of being the wedgebuster. I didn't care. I was young and reckless. Now I'm just reckless, and with my drinking especially. I took out this guy so hard that everything I saw turned green. Everything! It wasn't just the grass. The sky, the fans, the players...all of them were green, and there was a buzzing sound in my skull that sounded like the largest swarm of prehistoric bees that had ever been in one place at one time. I started walking toward the wrong sideline, then realized that *my* uniform was a different shade of green than the ones Virginia Tech was wearing. I didn't even remember playing in the game."

Blotto pauses to consult Euripides before continuing. "I'm going through film with my position coach that Monday," he says after exhaling, "and he's pointing out what I did right and wrong. And I'm like, *'I was on the field on Saturday? When the fuck was that?'* But there I was, plain as day on the film. You can't even imagine what goes on during the course of a game with the violence and trash talking and racial epithets and everything else. There was no internet when I played, so things got pretty intense because no one would find out what you said on the field unless you broke the code and blabbed to a mainstream newspaper. And no one ever did. I once had a linebacker telling me all game, *'You got another thing comin' if you think I'm gonna let a motherfuckin' pale-ass KKK cracker like you into MY end zone. By the way, your white girlfriend loves to visit my daddy in prison and suck his big fat dick.'* This guy was *good*, though, man. Played a few years for the Raiders, I think. I had 2 catches for 6 yards that game. He comes up to me after the game and says, *'Sorry about all that 'cracker' stuff. I saw that you had 112 yards last week vs. Tennessee. Head games, man. Head games. And my dad's really an accountant, by the way.'* I can appreciate that. But with God as my witness, an opposing safety once said to one of my wide receivers, *'You're way down South now, boy, and you ain't one of MY niggers. We do two things to other people's niggers down here: kick their ass on the football field, and hang them in trees off of it.'* But it worked. I got so pissed off at this dude that I later wound up giving him a cheap shot right in front of a ref

57

that pretty much cost us the game. The problem was that my quarterback had completed a 30 yard pass to the opposite side of the field on a play that, as far as I knew, was supposed to be a run to the weak side. So all I read for the next week in the papers was about the 'inexplicable, stupid personal foul by David Bristow that turned a 30 yard gain into 15 and kept the team out of field goal range in the game's waning minutes.' And I'm thinking, *'This dickhead called my wide receiver a nigger with a straight face. If you assholes in the media really knew what went down on the field, maybe you'd shut your fucking mouths once in a while.'* You get into a pile after a fumble and guys are spitting into your facemask, trying to poke your eyes out, biting your fingers, grabbing your junk...it was scary playing football at a high level sometimes, to tell you the truth. But come to think of it, just being alive is pretty scary- especially with some of the women that we're forced to deal with just because we have balls and need to get laid."

Gina suddenly enters in black boy shorts and a red Chase Utley t-shirt. This outfit is much, much hotter than her bar duds, but she'd never believe that. Her olive legs are sweet.

"Finally, a little bit of skin!" Sharkey exclaims.

"I can't sleep," says my new crush as she takes a seat on my bunk next to me.

"Would you like to smoke some of our marijuana and then run out without kissing any of us or even saying goodbye?" Blotto asks her.

"Sure!" she replies eagerly.

"Nice legs," says Blotto as he hands her Euripides.

"I'm pale," Gina declares in response, even though she's at least six shades darker than anyone else in the room.

"You're hot," says Blotto matter-of-factly. "Accept it."

"Thank you," she says with a snort before sparking.

Mallory now enters. Blotto perks up immediately in the presence of his own house crush. "Here to finally profess your love for me?" he asks, his voice filled with both alcohol and hope.

"No," the latest brunette replies sweetly. "Actually, I already have a guy waiting for me in my room."

"Ha!" exclaims Sharkey. "Mallory just sunk *your* battleship, dickwad."

"I can do without the analysis, Peter," is Blotto's response.

"I just wanted to say goodnight to everyone," Mallory says.

"Before your brains get fucked out," Sharkey adds.

"Peter!" is her one-word, sharply toned response.

"I'm not knockin' it, sister," he replies. "I wouldn't mind listening to your ankles talk for a while myself, Mommy Longlegs."

"Nobody is going to be listening to my ankles talking," Mallory says sternly. "Goodnight, everyone. And thanks again for the save on the dance floor tonight, Woodchuck. You're a real team player. He was like, the weirdest guy ever."

"No problem," I reply as Gina starts laughing at the latest mention of my grade school nickname.

"I hope your shoes match your earrings," Sharkey says to Mallory as she exits. She shakes her head with a slight smile on her face as she shuts the door to the Board Room behind her.

"Did she just meet that guy tonight?" asks Gina with some concern present in her voice.

"Only a woman could ask such a stupid, irrelevant question," Sharkey replies. "You and Woodchuck seem to be getting along pretty smashingly...when'd you first meet him, you whore?"

"That's completely different," Gina insists.

"How so?" inquires Blotto.

"Because we're becoming friends and I'm not going to sleep with him," she insists. Both Blotto and Sharkey laugh at my expense. "And Woodchuck paid my cover," Gina adds excitedly.

"Smart work there, Woodchuck," says Sharkey. "Gina clearly owes you a blowjob. Now let's hit the lights and you can start getting to work on that, Snortalufagus."

Gina giggles and tells me to move over so that she can recline in my bunk. Euripides is passed around once again. The lights are turned out. Gina places her warm body next to mine and wraps her slender arms around me. She is snoring in my ear less than a minute later. I don't mind. I'm taking baby steps at this point. I'm just grateful to not have to spend the night alone like I did each time in my parents' basement.

Saturday, May 29, 2010

8:46 a.m.

I find that Gina has already vacated my bunk when I awake. Page enters as I wallow in my pathetic disappointment. He looks to be in much worse shape than I am. Both of his hands are cuffed to a small pink bed tent with a depiction of Sleeping Beauty on it. This begs for an explanation. "Umm...Page," begins Blotto with a completely straight face from the queen, "it appears that you're attached to a pink tent of some sort this morning."

"You're a fucking fag," adds Sharkey before he begins laughing hysterically.

"Do we still have those lock cutters in the shed?" Page asks very bitterly. "Or handcuff keys? I swear that we had a pair of lock cutters around here for some reason."

"You might need to call the A-Team," Blotto suggests. "If you can find them. Not only are they a crack commando unit, but they're still on the run from the government somewhere."

"I remember starting to walk back from the Moo Moo," Page recalls fuzzily, "and I saw Mindy Miller walking somewhere ahead of me. I've always had a thing for Mindy Miller. And like two dozen other girls in Angel Bay, but that's not my point. I saw her walking into this house on the corner of 10th Street with a bunch of other people, so I started walking on the lawn toward the front door. Then I decided that the grass was really soft and it would be a great place to go to sleep for some reason. That's when I first realized that I was no longer wearing any shoes. I don't remember anything after that. So I woke up this morning, handcuffed to this fucking bed tent that my friend Julia uses as a sex fort when she wants to get it on when her roommate's around. But we didn't have sex, she says. Then no one could find the keys to the handcuffs- even though there was no reason for me to be handcuffed to anything last night aside from a jail cell, maybe- and I realized that I had to give birth out of my ass to a giant baby of crap. And there's six chicks in the room laughing at me but nobody really doing anything about it, so finally I said, 'Fuck it' and got up and left. Now I owe her twenty bucks. And I'm still attached to this thing and still have to take a shit."

"Yeah, you're pretty screwed," is Blotto's take as he grabs a recent issue of *Sports Illustrated* from beside the bed and begins to casually leaf through it, laughing the entire time behind its pages. Baxter, who appears to be the jealous type, knocks the magazine from his master's hand and back onto the floor. Then he hops off the bed, takes the magazine into his giant mouth, and removes it to an undisclosed location in the house. He returns a short time later and hops back up onto the queen.

"I swear that somebody put a little something extra in one of my drinks," is the theory offered by Page, who looks very concerned and perplexed about this incident. "I haven't been that fucked-up since the wet cameltoe contest at Spring Break '98."

"I think I was 12 then," I crack, which gives Blotto quite a chuckle. Then I'm forced to reveal that Page and I are the same age.

"Is this woman who took it upon herself to handcuff you to her sex fort actually cute?" asks Sharkey. "I hope that you're not crawling around inside pink tents with some fucking hag."

"She is," says Page. "She's quite a little dish, in fact. Cute little redhead."

"Cute little redhead," repeats Blotto. "Isn't that an oxymoron?"

"They can taste funny if you get a bad one," Sharkey says.

"Is there a reason why you're not smoking marijuana right now?" asks Blotto of Page as he rises from the queen and grabs the necessary implements.

"Umm...because it's 8:56 a.m. and I'm hungover and handcuffed to a tent? And I still have to dump."

"Your point?" says Blotto. "You're a poster child for someone needs a legitimate escape from reality right now."

"I don't have a point," says Page. "My entire life doesn't have a point. I can't even hold Euripides."

"Stop yer cryin', bitchass," chides Sharkey.

Stinky enters, still wearing last night's outfit. "Whose dick did you suck last night?" Sharkey asks immediately.

"Did we camp out last night and I missed it?" she asks with excitement upon seeing Page, evading the question. "I want to camp out on the back yard one night with everyone and make a fishbowl of pot smoke!"

"We did *not* camp out last night," says Page matter-of-factly as his phone begins blowing up with all sorts of texts.

"Someone wants their tent and handcuffs back," Blotto says with a laugh.

"I forget," Stinky says. "Why did I even bother to come in here?"

"Because right now Mallory is in your bedroom on her back, takin' it balls deep," offers Sharkey. Blotto throws an empty glass at him. It misses and shatters against the far wall. No one even acknowledges that it happened.

"Mallory's outside drinking coffee," Stinky reports.

"That was my next guess," Sharkey says.

"Is anybody hungry?" asks the blonde.

"I assume we all will be shortly," says Blotto. "Then I suggest we head to the Marina for breakfast and to scout what some of these women *really* look like when they first wake up in the morning without make-up."

"Little help first?" asks Page.

"Mallory has handcuffs," says Stinky. "The keys might match."

"Mallory...has handcuffs?" asks Blotto.

"M'mm," Stinky replies before retreating to the Slut Room. She returns a short time later. "I can't find them," she reports. "And Mallory isn't outside any longer."

Page stomps toward the bathroom to give birth, though unable to wipe his own ass because he is still handcuffed to a pink Sleeping Beauty tent formerly used as a sex fort.

11:36 a.m.

We return from eating the Marina's entire menu. The food was great, but service was so painfully slow that Blotto politely asked the lovely 17 year-old waitress if a bunch of one-armed cooks had taken over the operation. Page has freed himself from the sex fort but remains handcuffed. Mallory is nowhere to be found and cannot respond to any text messages because she left her phone at the house. Perhaps inspired by Page's plight, Blotto is in a mischievous mood. "Have you formally met Jenna yet, Woodchuck?" he asks me.

"No," I reply. "I just heard her screaming to you about mold."

"She's a fucking bitch," is Sharkey's concise take. "I'd fuck Baxter before that wench. She's so snotty and selfish that I swear she's had her vagina sown shut. It would probably cause her pain to give pleasure to somebody at her own body's expense."

Blotto kindly suggests that I introduce myself to her under the guise that I am an animal control officer. The pretext is that the County has been called by several neighbors concerning a very unsightly pug with leaky bowels and an objectionably prominent anus. "You'll know Jenna when you see her," says Blotto as he struggles to fit me with a two-sizes-too-big blue collared shirt from the closet to make me look more authentic. "She's really not much to look at. This should help keep her attitude in check for a bit." Blotto hands me a clipboard from someone's work bag before I go upstairs to do the deed. Had I not been fueled by six hits from a water pipe filled with the KB, I might have recognized Blotto's plan to be somewhat flawed. Instead, I walk upstairs to the top unit of 728 St. Michael's.

I knock on the door and enter to find a slender woman of long brown hair with golden highlights lying upon the living room couch. Wearing only gray sweat shorts and a tight blue shirt with white stars on it, she is relaxing with her lengthy, toned legs stretched out very comfortably. Her body is straight out of one of my unfulfilled teenage dreams. The woman's olive-toned face is partially obscured by a pair of glasses with thick brown frames and the small yellow highlighter positioned between her full lips. She reads what I immediately recognize to be a legal pleading. This young-looking girl who presents as a semi-intellectual doesn't bother to look up from the page when I enter, which is convenient because it gives me an extra few seconds to stare-up her C-cups. I clear my throat. "I'm looking for Jenna," I announce boldly.

"You've found her," says the couch girl after removing the highlighter from her mouth. "May I ask you a favor?"

"Umm...*sure.*"

"Could I at least have your name before you start eye humping me so aggressively? I feel like I should call the fucking cops."

"I'm Patrick," I reply weakly. "And, I'm with the police. Sort of."

"So what brings you here today to see me, Mr. Policeman?" Jenna asks with much annoyance. "Is that marijuana I smell? And I'd inquire about getting a shirt that fits you a little better..."

"Umm...I received a call from the neighbors next door...uh...I understand that you're the registered owner of a certain pug?"

"Yes."

"And it's also my understanding that this pug is HIV-positive, correct?"

I don't know where the *fuck* that came from. It certainly wasn't part of the script. Jenna removes her glasses to take a better look at this rank stranger, revealing an absolutely stunning pair of pale, ice blue eyes surrounded by the smooth skin on her soft face. She bites down onto the end of her frames as her lovely irises flame right through me with an angry silence. This girl is *beautiful.*

"Which of the juveniles living downstairs told you to say something so *absolutely* fucking stupid to me?" Jenna demands to know after a few seconds of staring like she was trying to hit me with a death ray. Princess herself now waddles into the room and takes a congested sniff of me before somehow leaping onto the couch next to Jenna's feet. The dog turns to face me and sneezes before panting like she's seconds from death.

"Is that the pug in question, ma'am?" I ask, even though this act has already jumped the shark. I don't know what the hell to say at this point. Between Jenna's pure beauty and my own awkwardness, I'm so uncomfortable. Jenna decides to launch her highlighter at me. "Answer my fucking question, dickless," she sneers. "Who told you to come up here?"

"I'm not exactly sure who it was," I reply, unwilling to implicate any of my new weekend housemates.

"Not sure?"

"I'm still getting to know everyone's name downstairs. I'm sorry."

"How do you know Harry?"

"We have a close mutual friend. Can I ask you a more serious question, Jenna?"

"What."

"Is that a pleading in your hand?"

"So you're a paralegal? I'll tell you one thing: you're definitely not much of an actor. Pretty pathetic, if you ask me."

"I didn't ask you. I'm an attorney, actually."

"So which firm was dumb enough to extend you a job offer?"

"I'm...kinda in between jobs right now."

"That's unfortunate," the brunette replies sarcastically and goes back to reading.

"Umm...where do you work, Jenna?"

"Wheat, Winklespect, White, Morgan & Straw," she responds like I should get down upon my knees to pay some form of homage to her legal greatness.

"Is that the same law firm which everyone else in the free world refers to simply as 'Wheat,' Jenna?" I ask just to be a pest. But it's undeniably Philadelphia's top firm. The first-year associates pocket a modest $145,000 plus a handsome year-end bonus. And for many of them, it's the first actual job they've ever had in their young lives. "Where did you go to law school?" I ask to break the tense stare that Jenna continues to provide.

"Pennsylvania," she replies. "How about you, Patrick? New England College of Law? Widener? Mail order outfit somewhere?"

"Villanova," I reply.

"My cousin Maria Napoli went to Villanova," Jenna says, proving once again that Philadelphia and its surrounding suburbs are probably the smallest place on Earth. I choose not to reveal the connection, since Maria knows some details of my condition. There's no need for those worlds to collide. And besides, Jenna is making me feel like a completely stoned idiot. How sneaky of Blotto to bluff that she wasn't one of the prettiest girls in Angel Bay.

"Is Napoli your last name?" I ask in order to confirm the extent of Jenna's Italian ancestry.

"No," she replies. "My last name is Love, for your information. Anything else you need to know? Social security number? My bar identification? Sneaker size?"

"I think I'm good."

"Can you just do me a favor, Patrick, after you toss my highlighter back to me?" the brunette asks after a few more seconds of awkward silence.

"What's that, Jenna?"

"Go kill yourself."

6:17 p.m.

Page was freed after three hours in captivity by the key to Mallory's own handcuffs. She was riding her road bike during this time and the cuffs, for some reason, were in the glove compartment of her car. The frustrated and hungover Page finally took a shower and got so high afterward that he passed out for nearly four hours. My new crush Gina now departs for suburban Philadelphia to attend a cookout hosted by her boyfriend Chas and his family. "It was great meeting you yesterday," she says with a kiss to my cheek. "I'll see you soon. Text me."

12:52 a.m.

A very, very, very sloppy and slightly overweight girl that I recognize from law school stumbles over to Stinky and me while we are people watching inside the Shipwreck. My former classmate flashes me with a wide, drunken smile. "Hi, John!" she says happily as she approaches before forcing a wet, gross, and unsolicited kiss onto my lips. "Good to see you again!"

"I'm not John. I hate John."

"You look like John O'Hollaran."

"My name's Patrick, remember?"

"Patrick, John, whatever...you still have a penis, right?"

Before I can respond, the slob unexpectedly launches her large, drooling tongue into my mouth. She practically rips my lips apart with her overly aggressive kissing technique. I would expect a better kiss from the likes of Baxter. Stinky taps this embarrassing inconvenience on the shoulder. "Excuse me," she says.

"Is something wrong?" the girl replies.

"Actually, there is," my pretty blonde housemate says with a twinkle in her eye. "Woodchuck took my anal virginity this afternoon. So I kinda feel a little uncomfortable with all of this. Not that you're missing anything. He's *really* small." The girl makes a strange face and drifts away. She now starts making out with a portly gentleman leaning against the nearby bar who probably hasn't been laid in as long as I have. He's absolutely thrilled with his sudden piece of good fortune.

"Thanks for the save," I say to my new blonde friend, not revealing that Stinky has really saved me not from this drunken slob, but from myself.

"You're welcome," she says pleasantly. "Now buy me a drink. Or two. Or three. There's three things that I never turn down: a man with rock hard biceps, a free drink and a good sale on shoes or jeans. But don't buy me beer. It really sets my irritable bowel off."

1:36 a.m.

I bought Stinky a shot known as a Yeast Infection per her request. I felt a bit awkward asking the bartender if I could have one. After Stinky downed her drink and went in search of Hot Dudes to endlessly flirt with, a very good-looking girl with dirty blonde hair and big brown doe eyes suddenly approached to my left and ordered a drink as I lingered at the bar with my Sprite. She's very involved with her phone right now. She may be composing the longest text message in the history of Earth. I decide to take a stab here.

"How's the book coming along?" I ask. To my great relief, the pretty girl laughs.

"My friend is having all kinds of ex-boyfriend drama," she explains. "I have to keep texting her to let her know which ex is in which room and talking to which sluts."

"Sounds like a project."

"She gets around. I'm a good girl."

"In a place like this? I don't believe you."

"Shut up. Where's your house at?"

"Seventh & St. Michael's. I live with Harry Trimble."

"Oh, I know Harry," she says pleasantly. "All of the guys in your house are sweethearts! I'm on Tenth off Dune. Can you walk me home after I finish this drink? I'm fucking bombed and my friends are all...well, who knows what the hell they're doing at this point of the night."

"I'm Patrick, by the way."

"I'm not going to tell you my name."

"Why? Do I look like a sex offender?"

"Not at all," the blonde says with a laugh and a very pretty, white-toothed smile. "I just have an annoying name."

"Now I'm curious."

"It's Dharma."

"It's not annoying. It's a pretty name."

"Sure, if it wasn't for that *fucking* TV show. And it's even worse because my last name is 'Gregg.' I can't wait to get married just so I can get my name changed."

The girl downs her drink like a professional after she's finished speaking. She slams the emptied plastic cup on the bar (which tips over spreading ice everywhere across), and we exit the Shipwreck together after approximately seven seconds of interaction. Dharma the Doe-Eyed Dirty Blonde grabs my hand as soon as we exit onto Seventh Street & Dune Drive. "I'm wasted," she relays again.

"That seems to be the common theme around here."

"And like you're sober, Dad."

"Dad? Do I look like I'm in my fifties and about to spank you?"

"My birthday is in two weeks," says the blonde. "How old do you think I'm going to be?"

She looks about 29, so I guess 24.

"Omigod, no!" she says with a smile. "I'm going to be *twenty-eight*. I can't stand it! That's like, two years away from being 30."

"You're really good at math, Dharma."

"Shut up. We're taking a shortcut through this parking lot. It leads right to my house." I'm lead off Dune Drive into a parking lot that serves a bunch of expensive condo units facing Ninth & Dune. As we walk, the drunken blonde is for some reason inspired to lead me to an elevator at the rear of the lot. "Elevators are fun when you're drunk," Dharma giggles as she hits the 'up' button. The doors immediately open and I'm lead inside. In two seconds, the buttons for each of the nine floors are all glowing pink.

"What are we going to do for nine floors, Dharma?"

"We can make out," I'm casually assured. "You were sweet enough to walk me home. And I know *exactly* where to find you later if you try any funny business, Mister." Something must be wrong here. This was too easy. "We can't have sex, though," the blonde qualifies. "I just met you like, two minutes ago."

"Can we go to second base?"

"Maybe," Dharma replies with a grin as I take her little waist into my hands. "It depends on how long it takes us to make it to the ninth floor. I need to know a guy for at *least* five minutes before I let them touch my breasts."

"You're such a prude," I reply as I guide Dharma against the nearest elevator wall.

"Aren't I?" the blonde giggles. "I might as well become a nun."

I decline to make a sexy nun joke. It's time to stop talking. Dharma smells *great*, even after hours sweating at the bar. I haven't had any wonderful womanly curves in my desperate hands for far too long. They settle into her body so perfectly. Dharma's arms become locked around my neck and neither of us hesitates. Her lips are delicious. Very delicious. And soft. And wet. I forgot how great it was to simply kiss a woman who is as sexy as this little gem is. It sounds awkward for a man to admit, but I *love* to simply make out. An attractive woman with wet lips who is a great kisser makes you forget about everything on Earth except how amazing the woman in your arms really is, and how great it would be to go down on her. Just as the excitement moves itself up a notch, Dharma pauses. "Do you like my new shoes?" she asks as the door opens at floor number two. I look down at a pair of very busy-looking, strappy black heels placed on her tanned feet. "They were on sale," she says as I spy a toe ring around Dharma's third toe on her right foot. Toe rings are *so* sexy. Yet, I have no idea why.

"I like your toe ring," I reply.

"It's old," says Dharma as the door shuts and the elevator again begins moving.

"You're sexy."

"I am?" Dharma replies with considerable surprise. I thought it would be obvious. The mirror in her room must add 60 pounds and distort her features to make her look like a Mrs. Potato Head constructed by a special needs child from a set with missing pieces. She instantly launches her tongue down my throat with great fervor in response to my genuine compliment. By the ninth floor, I've pulled down the front of her white halter top and have begun to suckle her soft B-cups. Dharma moans and starts digging her fingernails into the back of my head. I reach under her skirt and massage her left thigh on the way to the front of her panties. "We need to hit the buttons again!" Dharma says as she conveniently tears herself away from me, pulling her top back up in the process. She hits the first floor button only this time. I manage to hit 4, 6 & 7 before the giggling blonde pushes me away from the console. "You've been such a bad boy," she says before putting her arms around my neck again.

"I'm sorry," I say quite insincerely. Dharma pulls me out of the elevator when we reach the first floor again and gives me her number when we arrive at her front door at 131 Tenth Street, whereupon I am dismissed with a quick kiss to the lips.

2:27 a.m.

I arrive in the Board Room, where Sharkey and Page have just finished sharing a post-Shipwreck jay with two very attractive girls who have now abandoned them in search of hotter prey. This, I do not understand. Neither of these guys is unattractive and both have *plenty* of personality. But women don't ever seem satisfied in a candy store like Angel Bay is. After 2 a.m., options begin texting and women's phones start vibrating with enough force to cut steel. It's not easy to keep a woman in one place unless she's *really* into you or her phone battery is dead- but a woman in Angel Bay will never allow that to happen. You might as well just drive back to Philly if you don't have a working phone. I report my first experience in forever with a pretty blonde to the Board with great enthusiasm. I pace excitedly around the room like a high school sophomore describing a maiden sexual experience, gesticulating like a Southern Baptist preacher as I describe the girl's great looks, sexy outfit, and beautifully shaped nipples. I'm quite proud of myself. Sharkey decides to pooh-pooh these events by posing a very valid question:

"How could you let a piss drunk woman take you into an elevator at 2 a.m. and *not* fuck her?"

"It happens," I reply, even though I don't think it ever has.

Page has been sitting in quiet contemplation for the past minute or so. He looks up at me with the stoned, wise, drunken eyes can only come with several summers of experience in Angel Bay. "Was her name Dharma, by any chance?" he asks.

"It was," I admit with hesitation.

Sharkey immediately bursts into a bellowing, cackling laughter.

"We've *all* fallen victim to increased and unmet expectations because of Dharma," Page explains while giggling himself. "Once she kisses a man, she will never talk to him again. She will not talk to you at the Shipwreck. She will not talk to you at parties. She will not talk to you if she sees you at the Moo Moo or on the street. Don't even *think* about texting her. She won't return those, either, and I think each one freaks her out even more. Facebook? Out of the question. My friend request has been pending for almost a year. We have no plausible explanation, other than that she's a fucking nutcase. We thought she might have a long-distance boyfriend but that theory was dismissed by one of her housemates. Shit. How *great* does she look in a skirt? I hooked up with her two summers ago and was flying higher than an X-wing for two weeks before I realized that I'd been totally fucking duped. She's way hot, bro. She's just like a...ghost kisser-er or something."

"You need to learn to expect these kinds of things, McShea," Sharkey says while reclining on his bunk and hitting the 'send' button on his phone for the first of at least a half-dozen times. "Women in, or nearing, their thirties may have as much sanity and brain power at work as my dirty sneakers. In fact, I'd give the sneakers a slight edge. They don't cry and they don't forget to take their Pill. My sneakers do smell bad, though. I really need to invest in some Odor Eaters. And whoever finally makes earplugs that can knock out the sound of that one annoying bird that starts chirping at 4 a.m. and keeps you up for the two hours right before your alarm goes off for work. I have a few grand burning a hole in my pocket right now that's just going to wind up getting raked off a roulette table somewhere up the road if I don't do something with it soon."

4:03 a.m.

In the high of my sleep, I hear a woman screaming, a dog barking, and a male voice yelling about a filthy clam of some sort. I awake to a Board Room with the lights on full blast and the door stuck into the nearby wall via the knob crashing into the sheetrock. The source of this madness is Tearsten, who looks downright fucking sexy albeit completely insane in a pair of pink pajamas bottoms with little kittens on them that are riding up her ass. She's wearing fuzzy bunny slippers, too. She screams for Blotto, who feared this might happen and is stationed at a safe house with a co-worker several blocks away. Baxter is barking back at Tearsten from the queen like a junkyard dog. Unfortunately, he does not attack.

"BLOTTO ISN'T ANSWERING HIS FUCKING PHONE!!!" her attention demon screams from within. "HE SAID HE WOULD BE HERE LATER!!!"

"Shut your vulva, Tearsten!" orders Sharkey from his bunk. He's clearly not pleased. Neither am I. I'm the asshole that's going to have the fix the newest hole in the wall and I hate working with spackle and sheetrock.

"WHY ISN'T HE ANSWERING MY PHONE CALLS!!!"

"He doesn't have to answer your phone calls, you fucking hag!" Sharkey screams back. "You guys are d-u-n done! Finished! Kaput! My advice is, shut the lights off, get the fuck out of here, and jump the fuck off the dock. Try not to let the sharks eat you as you drift out toward the ocean. They get hungry at night."

"HE SAID, HE WOULD BE HERE!!!"

"He's not," says Page matter-of-factly. "Shut the lights out. Leave. Please."

"WHERE THE FUCK IS HE!!! IF HE WENT HOME WITH ANOTHER GIRL I AM GOING TO BURN THIS FUCKING HOUSE DOWN WITH ALL OF YOU ASSHOLES IN IT!!!"

"There's propane on the top deck," says Page. "Good luck with that little project."

Footsteps are heard stomping down the hallway. Dizzy enters, shirtless and sweaty. He grabs a screaming Tearsten and throws her over his shoulder, running out of the room with his brain un-balanced booty. He misses cracking her head on the door frame by about a half-inch.

"You better have an armed guard watching that Mercedes of yours!" Sharkey yells out after Dizzy. "She's the biggest one 'n done on this island!" Sharkey rises from his bunk and removes the door from the wall and locks it shut. The lights are turned off. A quiet high has returned to the Board Room once again and I soon drift off to sleep, dreaming of lips that I will probably never touch again.

Tuesday, June 1, 2010

"You are who your record says you are."

-Coach Bill Parcells

8:17 p.m.

On Sunday, we held a small bar-b-que at 728 during the afternoon and hit the Shipwreck at night. It was only half as crowded, since all of the pretenders trying to fit their entire summer into one holiday weekend had discovered that their livers had signaled surrender by Sunday morning. It's now the work week for regular people, so I'm left alone at the house with only my own mind and a jay of Purple Kush that Page was kind enough to roll for me as a welcome gift before he returned to Philly. There's nothing to do right now but to think. Much of it is a waste, since I'm not exactly qualified to speak on the exact psychological and psychiatric processes that flipped my mind inside out during October 2004. That's when the unwinnable battle with depression started that torpedoed my ability to relate with women and sabotaged my career. I have some theories on why I didn't get the help I needed. I often speculate on whether events in my life that I thought were long buried in the recesses of my mind may have made me vulnerable to attack. The only thing of which I am certain is that my legal career was essentially over before I even began my third year of law school. The law may be the only profession where half of its graduates are deemed unworthy to legitimately practice before they are even handed their degrees. In the law, you are who your GPA says you are. My 2.62 GPA tells a potential employer that I'm a stone fucking idiot. I couldn't disagree with a potential employer with that opinion. The problem, though, is that I'm *not* a stone fucking idiot. Most reputable firms (and even top government jobs) require that you submit a copy of your law school transcript along with your resume. I can't do that, as it will reveal my supposed gross legal ignorance. This limits my job prospects to low-end firms that either chase ambulances or defend the claims made by the allegedly injured assholes, with a salary in the range of $40K-$50K. These types of jobs are known in legal circles as ShitLaw. No one wants to practice ShitLaw. If someone does, they're either devoid of a brain or have some weird, clinical fixation with defending the world from bogus neck-and-back claims in the righteous name of Justice- all while their own bank account and credit rating sinks faster and lower and deeper than the *Titanic* after the iceberg.

I never in a million years expected to fail on such a massive, grand scale. Nobody enters law school and says, 'I'm going to totally fuck up this opportunity so I can make $42K litigating small-time auto accident cases for a bunch of asshole insurance companies.' No law school is ever going to tell you that it's a distinct possibility, either. My fate was sealed when, in the midst of my mental meltdown, I bombed my 2L second semester with a 2.55 GPA. This brought my overall average below a 3.0 for the first time, and neither I nor my GPA would ever recover. I became one of those 'attorneys' with an asterisk next to the bold black script on my diploma that reads *Juris Doctor*. I was a 'lawyer' in name only. It would be *years* before I would be able to earn a salary that would give me any kind of life outside of my parents' basement or I'd touch a file not related to a car accident or a slip and fall case.

My dad has always failed to understand this. He's currently delivering a long-distance lecture from Philadelphia as I sit outside on a deck chair while anxiously twirling the unlit jay between my fingers. Dad is not happy that I am 86 miles away in Angel Bay collecting unemployment for the summer. He wants me pounding the pavement looking for a new job at another auto accident defense mill making $48K. I could handle such a 'job' much better now, but I see no need to dive right back into the pool of filth filled with cervical and lumbar sprain/strain and amorphous conditions like 'thoracic outlet syndrome' and 'segmentary dysfunction' diagnosed by 'doctors' who went to chiropractic school on some island in the South Pacific that is rarely acknowledged outside of college history textbooks with maps depicting World War II naval battles. The ShitLaw experience is further enhanced by other things like the parade of malingering plaintiffs trying unreasonably to squeeze every dime out of their cases because of their allergy to work, moronic insurance adjusters bound by piss poor business models who'd rather spend $15,000 in legal fees than settle a legit claim for $10K, and partners hellbent on increasing billable hours at all costs in the name of profits that I would never personally see. That's not practicing 'law.' It's simply indentured servitude under the guise of time and case management. Dad can't understand this, repeating 'a job is a job' at least six times during his rant, even though he knows full well that working yet another round of ShitLaw won't provide any much-needed beef to my resume or pay enough to get me out of his cold basement while also paying down my student loans.

Dad also likes to forget that I overdosed on heroin and tried to shoot myself three months ago. He's one of those people that places blame on 'the drugs' for everything that has ever happened to me. Once I mistakenly revealed during our only (and fruitless) family counseling session that I'd been using marijuana since college, it automatically became the source of every problem that I ever had in my entire life, including the ones that pre-dated my use of 'the drugs' by up to twenty years. *Reefer Madness*, it was. I thought my legitimate suicide attempt might give me at least *some* leeway before running right back into the grind, but Dad is not very forgiving. There is no rest for the weary in an Irish Catholic household. Christ Himself fell three times on his way to Golgotha but He stood up each time and kept pushing, knowing full well that a hammer and three nails would succeed in staining the rocks and dirt and dust on the Hill of the Skull with every last crimson drop of His most precious blood. Jesus didn't throw down His Cross and run off to a friend's house at the Jersey Shore for the entire summer at the first sign of trouble like I did. And Dad is simply not having it.

The reality is that he doesn't know any better. It's hard not to admire such a hard working man on some level, but it's frustrating that no working class Irish Catholic father will ever accept the legitimacy of psychology or psychiatry. It's all bunk to them. It's greeted with the same mixture of distain and skepticism as astrology, tarot card readers, or opening a 600 page tome of ancient alchemy and using eye of newt in an attempt to turn wood into gold. He's convinced that I need to exercise more and return to attending Mass every Sunday instead of taking meds and spending money I don't have to meet with Dr. Karlis every few weeks. I'm mostly silent as Dad continues to lecture, knowing that I can't explain to him without sounding like a complete smartass that forty push-ups a day and a reading from Paul's Second Letter to the Ephesians isn't going to balance the neurotransmitters in my brain back to normal human levels. Dad doesn't want to hear about serotonin, law school transcripts, internet job searches, or some crackpot shrink making diagnoses that simply don't exist in his mind. I can't really blame him, though. Like many other regular people, he thinks I've been granted superpowers because I have a law degree. I'm supposed to be a Legal Jesus. I just snap my fingers and the guilty go free, the sick are healed, and piles and piles of money suddenly appear all over the place while everyone rolls around and kicks their feet in the air after making snow angels in the $100 bills littering the conference room floor.

People think that a J.D. is a one-way ticket to living the life of a rock star with a briefcase instead of a '58 Les Paul and a stack of Marshalls with enough wattage to power the next launch of the space shuttle. That's because no one ever hears about ShitLaw lawyers like me. Law schools pretend we don't exist. You won't ever see any of us in a movie, on *Dateline,* or read about us in the latest bestseller by John Grisham. There's nothing dramatic or glamorous about representing 'adverse drivers' or defending convenience stores from slip & fall lawsuits concocted by overweight slobs with fibromyalgia that haven't collected any kind of paycheck since they went on disability or SSI or whatever the fuck they've been collecting from the government over the past three decades or so. It's a humiliating way to have to practice 'law.' It's in the best interest of the law schools not named 'Harvard' or 'Yale' to keep ShitLaw a big secret from everyone. People would think twice about dropping $60,000-$120,000 on law school if they knew that 50% of each graduating class is staring at the prospect of working as a drone in a private firm with a starting salary of $50,000 (or less) after graduation. By the time you're making serious coin- and you will eventually unless you get depressed and get fired from three jobs like I did- all of your friends with careers in the private sector will be making the same money that you are (or more) without the student loan burden that you have. Most of them will also be working 10-20 hours per week less. To me, law school doesn't qualify as much of a return on your investment assuming that a trust fund didn't cover your tuition and expenses. That's why the thousands of people that keep matriculating each year at the nation's law schools are largely suckers.

Dad ends our pointless conversation in order to run to the store for my mother, who must have a can of diet soda and a pack of cheese-filled orange crackers before going to bed. She picks up the phone next. My mother was absolutely fucking brutal when I was growing up. We enjoy a great relationship now. The battle with cancer mellowed her out a bit. Her tone is much different than my dad's. More comforting.

"Hello, Patrick."

"Hi, Mom."

"How are you feeling, Son?"

"Horrible."

"Really?"

"No. I'm fine. How are you, Mom?"

"Don't worry about me. Still in remission, thanks to all of the blessed novenas to St. Peregrine. Do you sleep at all?"

"Some nights, yeah. Almost six or seven hours."

"How are the other people?"

"I like 'em. Very friendly, very down to earth. The one girl is Maria Napoli's cousin."

"Small world, isn't it? Is she as nice as Maria?"

"Not exactly. She's the one exception."

"What's Maria doing these days?"

"Married, kid, federal public defender."

"Do you ever regret not dating her?"

"Never," I chuckle.

"You're going to Hell, Son."

"I know. You've been telling me that since I was 7."

"Let's not dwell on the past, Patrick. It doesn't do either of us any good."

"I know, Mom."

"Did you take a walk by the house where I met your father?"

"I did. It's a four-story mansion with Greek columns."

"It was a small yellow house with black shutters thirty-five years ago," Mom says with a laugh. "And where are you again?"

"At 728 St. Michael's. Corner of 7th right next to the bridge."

"There's not an ugly orange house still on that lot, is there?"

"Yes."

"Still? Oh, dear. Even I partied in that dive! Just stay out of trouble. Your father played baseball in high school with the police chief there. They've been close friends for *fifty* years."

"I'll keep that in mind, Mom."

"I love you, Patrick. The day you were born was the happiest day of my life. I pray every night that this will pass."

"Thanks, Mom. I love you, too."

Mom would never Fed Ex me kind grass from San Francisco and doesn't have a dime, but I wouldn't trade her for anyone else in the world right now. I definitely wouldn't mind if she stepped it up and sent me a package of cookies, though.

* * *

Message to: Gina
6/01/10 8:42 p.m.
How was the bbq?

New Message: Gina
6/01/10 8:44 p.m.
bor-ing! lol id rather stab myself in the eye w a fork

Message to: Gina
6/01/10 8:47 p.m.
And how is ur neck back pussy and crack feeling?

New Message: Gina
6/01/10 8:48 p.m.
lol lol lol feeling neglected on that end

Message to: Gina
6/01/10 8:49 p.m.
Chas sounds a little light in the loafers.

New Message: Gina
6/01/10 8:51 p.m.
lol kinda see u sat

Message to: Gina
6/01/10 8:52 p.m.
xoxo lol

New Message: Gina
6/01/10 8:54 p.m.
haha xoxo 2 u 2 woodchuck

Message to: Dharma Gregg
6/01/10 8:56 p.m.
How was ur drive back 2 philly?

Thursday, June 3, 2010

> *I confess to almighty God,*
> *and to you, my brothers and sisters,*
> *that I have sinned through my own fault,*
> *in my thoughts and in my words,*
> *in what I have done, and in what I have failed to do;*
> *and I ask the blessed Mary, ever virgin,*
> *all the angels and saints,*
> *and you, my brothers and sisters,*
> *to pray for me to the Lord our God.*

> *-Confiteor*
> *Mass of the Roman Rite*
> *Roman Catholic Church*

8:37 p.m.

I'm fairly convinced that my upbringing may have played some role in putting me in the position I am right now. I grew up in the strictest of Irish Catholic households with parents indoctrinated via the Baltimore Catechism, and everything I ever did was wrong. It was tough growing up with two parents. My father, a Catholic high school teacher, was usually home from school before I was. When I was younger, I loved the fact that Daddy was home from work by 3 p.m. to play with me. Once I hit school age and could make some of my own choices, it became a burden because there was at least one pair of adult eyes on me at all times until I left home at 17 for college. I was a very precocious, intelligent and vocal kid until third grade or so. I remained intelligent afterward, but I stopped opening my mouth so much and spent most of my time reading to myself and playing with my *Star Wars* action figures. I'd play sports with the neighborhood kids once a week when the organized teams were in off-season. That was about it until eighth grade when I wanted to start socializing with girls, even though it never amounted to much. The Choir Loft Incident was the primary catalyst behind my five-year hibernation between third and eighth grade. My boredom with school and all of the things going on around me sometimes lead me down Mischief Lane when I was younger. One morning in September 1986, our entire third grade class took the ten foot walk from school into St. Raymond's Church for our monthly Class Mass. Church always bored me to tears. There's few things worse than trying to put a seven year-old in an uncomfortable pew for almost an hour. An hour seems like weeks when you're younger. There was no way I was staying in my pew for the entirety of this Mass.

I asked to be excused to use the bathroom at the back of the church as soon as we arrived. My teacher bitched about it, so I told her it was a #2 and it was extremely urgent. I walked toward the back of the church but never went to the bathroom.

78

Instead, I walked up the long flight of stairs to the choir loft and sat up there by myself instead. I stood on the organ bench and looked down toward my homeroom teacher, Ms. Dunberry, who was especially dimwitted. I was too young to know if she had an alcohol problem, but she was always late for work and fell asleep in class at least a dozen times that year. I shouldn't be so harsh. Maybe she was depressed the same way that I was. Ms. Dunberry on that day was too busy gabbing with the other teachers about nothing to notice that I never returned from my trip to 'the bathroom.' I felt like the King of the World sitting in the choir loft all by myself and looking down into the vast expanse of the church and its beautiful stained glass windows depicting the patron saints after which the parishes in the Archdiocese were named. Even though our parish was St. Raymond's, it was the giant stained glass window of St. Patrick that was most prominently displayed on the left wall of the church at the center. He held his mighty staff in one hand, and a depiction of St. Raymond's Church itself in the other as he stood atop a solid rock with snakes crushed underneath his feet. I felt sorry for my pathetic classmates who had to sit in the pews under the watchful eyes of their teachers while I was so free the entire time. The pastor, Monsignor Morrison, exited the sacristy and began to say Mass. That's when I noticed the microphone on the far end of the organ. There was a switch on the handle, which I placed into the 'on' position. It worked. I waited until Father was done reading the Gospel, then removed my orthodontic appliance. I launched into an inspired performance of 'If You're Happy and You Know It' complete with some putrid banging on the organ keys in front of me. This didn't go over too well, especially when half of the kids seated below eagerly clapped their hands after each line. Ms. Dunberry and Sr. Ursula were in the choir loft before I even had a chance to execute an escape back into the pews, which was really impressive since Ms. Dunberry was wearing Clogs and Sr. Ursula was just plain old.

I was walked through the church so that Msgr. Morrison could view the perpetrator, with no less than four girls saying, 'You're in trub-bull...' as I was led past the pews. I was escorted directly to the principal's office. Sr. Helen called my mom and my aunt, who happened to be a nun in the same Order. I remember that my red-faced father had the look of a man with criminally insane tendencies when he tore into the office 40 minutes later with my mom and three year-old little brother in tow. That's when I realized that my little stunt might not have been too entertaining. There was a long session with The Belt. I was suspended from school for a week, which I spent at home with my mom and my brother who ran around the house screaming all day like a madman. He was too young to appreciate how miserable God was going to make his life for the unspeakable crime of acting exactly like every other three year-old in world did, so Mom used more conventional methods of discipline with him. I was different. By the time the week was over, she had convinced me that I was so evil that I had personally driven the nails into the crucified Christ myself. I had embarrassed my entire family to no end. My mom was going to have heart palpations when walking into church on Sunday, she said. I was surely the talk of the entire parish, even though no one outside of the nuns and my parents actually gave a shit. My aunt was angry with me. My grandparents were angry, I was told. You know that you must be in deep shit if your *grandparents* are seriously pissed off at you. God was watching me, and I was promised that He would personally respond to my sacrilegious and disrespectful act when I least expected it. I was terrified.

God did exact his revenge, because he made me grow up on Revere Street. It wasn't that Revere Street was a bad place or that my parents didn't keep the house in great shape. They did. But Revere Street was right next to Crafton Street, and for some reason all of the baddest motherfuckers that St. Raymond's parish had ever seen were clustered onto that block like an unexplained cancer. One of them was Franny the Retard. I think he was 15, but it was impossible to tell visually. He had the mongoloid head and all of the other signs of serious retardation. He appeared sympathetic, but he was a sickening bastard. It wasn't just because he once shat in the middle of Revere Street and started throwing his output at all of the neighborhood girls. One day he cornered me in the breezeway that ran between my parents' house and the neighbors' while a game of Freedom was in full swing. He unexpectedly pushed me up against the brick and stone of the house and mumbled something that I couldn't understand. Actually, I did understand it but it made absolutely no sense. But he repeated it: *wret me see ur dingle.* I laughed. Like I would ever show anyone my dick, especially Franny the Retard. Franny grabbed me and threw me so hard against the wall that all of the air was knocked out of my body. He repeated his demand. "No," I replied, breathless. It would only be a matter of seconds before some of the other kids ran through the breezeway and saved me. Seconds passed. No one appeared. Just as I regained my breath and opened my mouth to yell for help, Franny hit me with a forearm shiver to the jaw that knocked my teeth together and made me woozy. He was three times my size and had dummy strength in spades. I was seeing double. I surrendered. I pulled down my zipper and showed him my penis. He put his big, fat, retarded hand on it, of which I saw two in my dizziness. I struggled further but couldn't escape. The sound of kids laughing and yelling drew close. Franny ran. He couldn't have been that fucking retarded. He knew he was doing something he wasn't supposed to do.

I put myself away and pulled up my zipper. I looked around. To my relief, there were no witnesses. I felt the greatest shame of my young life. *I had just been assaulted by a retard and he touched my wee wee.* I couldn't understand why somebody would do that to me. I just knew that it was all my fault. God had fired the first salvo in His revenge for the Choir Loft Incident, and it was a most crushing blow. I went inside the house. Dad was sitting in his chair reading the *Philadelphia Daily News* and there was a photo of a bloody corpse on the cover from the city's latest Mob hit. He didn't look up from the paper. I ran upstairs before I might have been forced to confess what happened. I closed the door to my bedroom, completely traumatized, and took a nap. I managed to forget about it in a few days. A young mind can be very resilient at times. Then we went to Mass on Sunday. Monsignor Morrison himself exited the sacristy as the celebrant. My mother immediately stiffened in the pew like a firing squad was entering the church and aiming their guns directly at the McShea family. As the congregation was lead in the Confiteor, my mother glared at me for some reason. The words resonated deep within me: *I have sinned through my own fault, in my thoughts and in my words, in what I have done, and in what I have failed to do.* I knew those words described me *exactly*. At the age of 7, I was already a grave sinner. I felt the shame of interrupting Our Lord's Supper with my organ playing all over again. I felt the shame of God's revenge manifested through Franny the Retard. I tried to fight Franny off. But I couldn't. I failed. That was my fault, too, for being so weak. I couldn't believe that I had succumbed to a retarded predator. I should just run out of the church and go straight to Hell right now in order to save God the trouble, I thought. I felt like that every time I heard that fucking prayer until the eighth grade.

Franny the Retard wasn't the only threat sent by God. It was Georgie Inammorato that held the distinction of being the resident dyslexic on Crafton Street. I skipped second grade, while he repeated in twice. We both wound up in third together. I was 7, he was 10. Things like ADD, ADHD and dyslexia didn't exist in 1986, and especially not in Catholic school. But if it did, it would have certainly been seen as a punishment for masturbation rather than a legitimate medical diagnosis. Georgie invariably would take out his frustrations with being unable to read by using his fists on my body. I never knew when he would strike; there was no pattern or predictability to any of his attacks. It could be on the walk from school to home for lunch, the walk home at the end of the school day, or even the walk back to school *from* lunch. The result was always the same: I took a beating, and I was ashamed. When I would get my bath, my mother was horrified that I'd be covered with bruises. I told her it was from playing tackle football or getting hit too many times with a pink

Mylec hockey ball. There was some truth to that, so she bought it. The response was a ban on playing any football, which solved nothing.

Report card time was the worst for me. During the walk home (only the *real* pussies get a ride to and from school), one of the Crafton Street Crew would invariably rip my report card out of my hand or from my school bag, see that it was littered with A's, and then throw it into middle of the oncoming traffic roaring down Levick Street which was a state highway disguised as a residential street. While I waited patiently for the traffic to pass, someone would come up from behind and punch me in the back of the head with all of his might. My mother would scream at me and question why my report cards would often be laden with tire tracks. Was I really so clumsy that I couldn't hold on to my report card or smart enough to put it in my school bag? How could I possibly hand it to my grandmother when it was so dirty? I didn't give a fuck whether my grandmother thought my report card was dirty or not. I thought it was enough to get straight A's in every single subject for six straight years until I started elementary algebra in eighth grade. But it wasn't enough for mom and dad. Nothing ever was. The slightest misstep and I'd turn out like Uncle Robert, who OD'ed on smack and died when I was two. My parents were convinced that Uncle Robert and I were cut from the same cloth for some reason. I had Robert's eyes, everyone said. We shared this light brown/green combination in our irises that changed depending on the lighting and the color of the clothes we were wearing. That's all the evidence my mother needed that I was destined for Skid Row. I'd definitely be shooting up in an alley somewhere until I OD'ed myself if everything I did and said wasn't monitored and scrutinized *ad absurdum*. I never made any missteps, though. And I wound up broken and OD'ed on smack, anyway.

In October of fourth grade, something set Georgie off while we were walking home at the end of the day. I had no idea what it was or what it could have been. He started pummeling me without mercy. I decided not to run. I was finally going to stand my ground. I managed to give him a nice fat lip with a punch to the mouth. I was so pleased with myself that I completely lowered my defenses in order to admire my work, like an NBA showboat who lays down a vicious dunk and is too involved in his own celebration to notice that the opposition now has a fast break opportunity down the other end. Georgie wasn't a typical bully who would just push someone until they finally responded. He punched me so hard back that my ears began to ring. It was time to run. I escaped behind a dumpster next to the pizza joint on the corner. Georgie caught me within seconds. Out of sight of the nearby crossing guard, I was beaten and lifted into the dumpster. Then he shut the metal lid atop of me.

There were mice and rats everywhere in that thing, and it took me a terrifying ten minutes to get out. I was a fucking sweaty, smelly, bleeding mess when I walked into the front door of 6128 Revere Street. My mother exploded. *'What did you do THIS time?'* she screamed. *'How dare you come home late from school when I'm sitting here waiting for you and worried!'* You *should* be worried, you bitch. Your first born son is getting his fucking ass kicked every other day. But I knew that every episode with Georgie or anyone else was surely my own fault, and the wrath of both my parents and God would follow. In an Irish Catholic household, everything that happens to you is *always* your own fault. If I had left for the walk to school in the morning at 7:53 a.m. instead of my customary 7:50, and I happened to be run over while on the sidewalk by a stolen car roaring down Levick Street that was being operated by a stone drunk who was legally blind and had no driver's license, my parents wouldn't ever blame the driver for running me down. I was supposed to leave for school at 7:50 a.m., you see. And if I had left for school at 7:50 like I was supposed to, then I never would have been in the position to be run over by a literally blind drunk with no license flying down the highway in a stolen car. I failed to do what I was supposed to do by leaving for school at 7:53 instead, and when you fail to do what God, parents and country demand *then everything that happens to you is your own fault and you deserve all of the consequences that follow from your deliberate act of gross disobedience.* That's why I never got help when I started feeling depressed during law school. Why should I have? It was clearly all my fault that I was feeling that way and stumbling in the classroom as a result. I was the one who chose to work during school while taking five classes. If I couldn't handle that, I was weak and deserved it because it was a decision that had solely been in my hands alone.

Dad took a bit of a different approach when Mom told him of my latest act of disobedience on Dumpster Day. He thought that I was smart enough not to jump into dirty, rat-infested garbage dumpsters for no reason. I confessed what really had happened. My mom still blamed me. After the infamous Choir Loft Incident, I had lost all credibility with her. I must have done something to set Georgie off, she said, if I was even bothering to tell the truth. Dad told me that I did the right thing by trying to defend myself, and that he would 'speak' with Mr. Inammorato. He walked out of the house toward Crafton Street and was angry enough to kill. I ran out of the house after him while my mom was busy with my little brother. Mr. Inammorato, a disabled steelworker and full-time bookie with ties to the Mob, was a neighborhood legend of 5'8" and 245 pounds of muscle. He was a human fire plug. I had never seen someone so wide in my life. One of his arms weighed more than my entire body. The word around school was that he once punched Lenny McCoy's dad so hard that both of his

83

ankles were broken from falling backward so quickly with such force. And I'd see Mr. McCoy outside the school yard, and he always walked with a cane. I was petrified of Mr. Inammorato. Georgie must have been, too. Dad grew up in a tough neighborhood along the Schuylkill and was no chump by any means, but I didn't see anything good coming out of this.

To my relief, Mr. Inammorato handled the entire episode rather calmly. Georgie and I shook hands and I went home. He beat the fuck out of me the next day again. I couldn't tell my dad. I didn't want him making another visit to the Inammorato house. I just changed some of my habits. I made sure that I was always the last kid out at dismissal then I'd walk some circuitous route home. Mom would bitch and moan that I was late and was convinced that I was somehow up to no good when I was only trying to protect the family from a scumbag dago involved with the criminal underworld. Georgie eventually caught on and would sometimes be waiting for me outside the school doors. I fought this by sneaking out of line and going out another door or by using an emergency exit which set off the fire alarm. That drove the teachers and principal crazy, but I did it at least a half-dozen times and never got caught once. And if I had, so what? Would it have damaged my 'permanent record' that doesn't really exist? I would have been punished no end, but anything in my house was a punishable event anyway.

By the end of fourth grade, I began having severe pain at times after meals. I spent some days in a great deal of pain, and I never understood why. I didn't make the connection that certain foods which I had been eating for years now had the capability to destroy any toilet I sat upon. The pain humbled me, and I turned to my parents for an explanation. They both failed miserably. My dad was convinced that it was all in my head. My mom told me that my pain was God's way of trying to pull me closer to Him and that prayer would bring me relief. Looking back, that was the most stupid fucking thing that my mother could have said to an eight year-old. It wasn't just Georgie Inammorato and the other kids at school that were the problem now. God was out to get me *again!* Except for the Choir Loft Incident, I was living a good life for an eight year-old, I thought. But that incident really was a doozy. My attempts to make amends weren't enough to please God and they certainly weren't enough for my mom given her constant lectures and guilt trips. It made me think that I was somehow flawed. I feared doing anything even slightly wrong going forward. If God made me hurt like hell as punishment for the way I lived my life at age 8, I knew He'd give me cancer or strike me dead if I missed church, ate more cookies than I was supposed to, or someday went past second base.

My parents finally sought medical treatment for me in high school for whatever the hell was ailing me. After a battery of tests, including a rather unwelcome invasion of my colon with several yards of camera and a suction tube, the diagnosis was irritable bowel syndrome. No one takes IBS seriously unless you actually have it. My case was pretty severe and was accented by a ridiculously sensitive manifestation of lactose intolerance that appeared out of fucking nowhere. I was told to avoid the four most important food groups at all costs: alcohol, carbonation, caffeine and nicotine. I'd rather die than drink alcohol with this condition. After only two drinks, I will begin to have alien labor pains in my gut that are followed by prolonged episodes of diarrhea that do not subside until the offending substance is completely expelled from my digestive tract. I've never even finished a bottle of beer. I'd have to sit on a toilet because it would start exiting my body as quickly as it entered. At times, the pain from an episode is unbearable. I usually distract myself by punching the walls or a nearby sink as I sit hopelessly on the toilet while the pain reaches near-agony. Marijuana will eliminate the pain from a mild episode in an instant; a moderate flare-up can also be quieted over time. There is nothing that can be done for the pain of a severe episode short of morphine.

My IBS has been calmer since I began taking my antidepressants. I think it works to slow down my metabolism, which stops my GI tract from going totally haywire. I don't think it's a coincidence that I gained 25 pounds within 3 months of starting my medication. I've never experienced that kind of weight gain in my entire life. Things have even calmed to a point where I can drink an entire can of 7UP or Sprite with no aftereffects whatsoever. I'd been drinking only water and Gatorade for over 15 years, which was pretty boring. Not as boring as a year without sex, but nothing on Earth could ever be that boring except living in a cloistered convent with no cable.

No doctor could ever explain why my GI tract decided to stop working properly at times. One might be tempted to cite a change in body chemistry, but I know the real reason. The constant stress of my stomach churning with worry about the fallout from the Choir Loft Incident, Franny the Retard, and having to deal with Georgie on the walk home every day destroyed its ability to function properly. I don't need medical school to figure that out. No one could ever tell me otherwise.

Franny the Retard wound up dying only a few months after the assault. My mom told me that I should say a prayer for his poor soul. I promised that I would, but it took me eight years. I last saw Georgie Inammorato only several months ago at St. Raymond's twenty-year reunion. He was the first person that I encountered when I walked into the old auditorium, which was much smaller than I had remembered.

Georgie greeted me warmly with an aggressive manhug and relayed that he was a successful ironworker with a pretty wife and two kids. He laughed when I mentioned that I was an attorney; it was his second guess after 'astronaut,' he said. I don't harbor any ill feelings or bitterness toward him whatsoever now. It couldn't have been any easier to be the functionally illiterate D-student with a criminal for a father than it was to be the small kid that was bullied. I couldn't ever deny, though, that it was certainly Georgie that planted the first seeds of self-hatred and repressed anger within me, and that's part of the reason why I'm sitting where I am right now with nothing. But I actually should have thanked him for making me such a worried mess. If I was able to tolerate alcohol while mentally ill- and my mental meltdown may very well have happened even if Georgie never existed- I have no doubt that I would be dead or in jail right now. And given the great anger and emotional instability that I developed while struggling to understand what was happening to my mind, it would certainly be for something most serious, like murder or rape. Or both. So thanks, Georgie. If you hadn't been dyslexic or I had grown up in a different section of St. Raymond's Parish, I might be on death row right now instead of watching yet another spectacular sunset from Harry's back yard.

* * *

> *New Message: Gina*
> *6/03/10 8:36 p.m.*
> *hey what r u doing im really bored*

> *Message to: Gina*
> *6/03/10 8:39 p.m.*
> *I got real high to blunt my feelings of personal inadequacy.*

> *New Message: Gina*
> *6/03/10 8:41 p.m.*
> *lol is that ur excuse?*

> *Message to: Gina*
> *6/03/10 8:45 p.m.*
> *I want 2 treat u like a rental property.*

> *New Message: Peter Sharkey*
> *6/03/10 8:46 p.m.*
> *yo bitch. did i leave my laptop down there?*
> *i have no access to porn. my cable provider doesnt carry cinemax.*

> *New Message: Gina*
> *6/03/10 8:50 p.m.*
> *lol lol lol behave woodchuck!*

Message to: Gina
6/03/10 8:50 p.m.
Zero chance of that.

Message to: Peter Sharkey
6/03/10 8:57 p.m.
There is a black laptop that says ray dominguez.

New Message: Peter Sharkey
6/03/10 8:59 p.m.
thats my real name. keep up the good work.
check out the bank statements folder. hint:
it aint my bank statements.

New Message: Gina
6/03/10 9:02 p.m.
lol im going 2 bed

Message to: Gina
6/03/10 9:03 p.m.
Now whos being boring?

New Message: Gina
6/03/10 9:04 p.m.
some of us work 4 a living woodchuck.
u can think abt my awesome sexy body
to entertain urself lol

Message to: Gina
6/03/09 9:05 p.m.
I usually do.

New Message: Gina
6/03/10 9:06 p.m.
haha just keep ur hands above the covers lol

Message to: Gina
6/03/10 9:06 p.m.
No chance of that either.

New Message: Gina
6/03/10 9:07 p.m.
gross

Message to: Gina
6/03/10 9:08 p.m.
Goodnight gina.

New Message: Gina
6/03/10 9:08 p.m.
goodnight woodchuck

Message to: Dharma Gregg
6/03/10 9:12 p.m.
Hey. How is ur work week going?

Tuesday, June 8, 2010

5:45 a.m.

The weekend was fun, but devoid of any significant excitement or entertainment since neither Gina, Jenna the Bitch, Peter Sharkey, Blotto, or Dharma appeared in Angel Bay. I spent most of my time smoking marijuana with the cool-as-ice Page and fruitlessly flirting with women while wholly unable to communicate using standard spoken English. Dizzy and I now board his kayak less than 15 minutes after sunrise. Today is one of those rare days where the low tide coincides with sunrise or sunset. These are the perfect conditions for bird photography, Dizzy explains. Not only do the wading birds he loves to shoot forage at low tide because they need to stand upright in the water while they hunt, but they prefer to do so early in the morning and late in the evening. The warm, golden light on their white or blue feathers in this 'magic hour' is the added bonus. We're mostly silent for the first twenty minutes of our trip to the Old Wharf. Neither of us is fully awake yet. I just concentrate on paddling through the still waters of the sound with a mind that is experiencing a rare moment of contentment and clarity. The breeze over the water is crisp at this early hour. I don't know why the cool morning air is always described as 'crisp,' but I can't think of another word that could describe the quality of the air any better than that. Dizzy finally speaks after paddling in silence.

"Did I ever tell you about Magdalena?" he asks.

"Is that a person or a town?" I reply, shaking myself out of my early morning brain fog.

"It's both," Dizzy explains. "It's not just the name of my beautiful ex, it's also a small town in New Mexico right under a range of mountains there. Her dad was in the Army and stationed in Albuquerque. He was Italian. Well, he still is, I guess. Her mother was originally from South Korea. How do like *that* combination?"

I'm too speechless to even reply. It's the best pussy I've had, combined with the best pussy I really haven't. That will give me something to dream about during my down time.

"So her parents were out on a drive one Sunday and heading back to base about two weeks before her mom was due," Dizzy continues after cracking open a bottle of water, "and she suddenly started getting contractions just as they were passing through Magdalena on U.S. 60 there. So that's how she got her name. Magdalena Regina Giordano. She was *beautiful*, man. Absolutely fucking beautiful. When guys are talking about pussy, I think anybody who hasn't had a South Korean girl just needs to butt their way out of the conversation and let the real vaginal connoisseurs speak their truth. And with the other half of Maggie being Italian, you

88

not only have a *great* cook but you're talking about the finest, nicest piece of pussy that this world has ever seen. She had these small, small, little lips that were perfectly tan on the outside, and perfectly pink on the inside. This thing was a work of *art*, man. She would never let me photograph it, though, even in a tasteful sense. She was the only woman that used to constantly make me feel insecure because I found her so fucking attractive. She looked awesome. And I'm not just saying that because she was *my* girlfriend. I'm saying it because it's the fucking truth."

"So the problem was..."

"Once she moved in, everything was her way or the highway, man. I just couldn't adjust. *No more Angel Bay! You're selling your boat! We're moving because I just found out your ex lives in the condo down the hall! I know you fucked the manager of your store on 20th Street!* and all of this other shit. Plus, she was just simply miserable like every other woman is miserable. She was an accountant, so some nights during tax season she wouldn't get home until 10, 11, or even after midnight sometimes. And she would be so pissed off if she walked in at 11 p.m. and I was sitting on the couch smoking a joint and watching TV. I'd have her dinner in the fridge, I might even have a hot bath ready for her, but she was *so* fucking pissed off that she was at work to 11 o'clock when I was just sittin' on the couch chillin' and watching the tube or going through my photographs. She took everything personally. Like it's my fault that I have my own businesses that practically run themselves because I overpay people to manage them, like my high school buddies and single moms whose only other option is standing on the street corner sucking dick to make that kind of money. At the time, I had three stores and was turning over $100,000 a year in profit. For *years*. So she looks at all of my financials- without me asking her to, by the way- and she's like, '*You're overpaying your management. You could be bringing home $37,000 more per year if you simply paid market rate for their services. You would have more working capital, you could open a new store, you could be building for our future together, blah, blah, blah, blah, blah.*' So I said some bullshit about wanting to employ a more conservative growth strategy in light of the current economic indicators. I just remember that when I said it, I couldn't believe how intelligent I sounded. I was fucking *wrecked* on coke. I slipped up sometimes. So anyway, she bought it for a little while. I couldn't tell her the truth and be like, '*I'm fine with making $100,000 per year and working 15 hours a week while I take photographs and get high all day.*' She'd flip. She thought that if I was making $100K working 15 hours, then I should work 50 and make a half-million. But donuts and my businesses aren't my passion. Photography is. And I sell enough of my work now to cover the cost of *all* my equipment and trips. My shops are just a means to an end, ya know? Maggie refused to understand that or compromise. She had *no* patience, man. Zero. Everything had to be done *now*. Now I own six shops, work 20 hours and make about a quarter-mil per year."

I almost lose my breakfast. I went to law school when I could have made $250,000 hawking donuts? *Donuts? Fucking donuts?*

"But Maggie was so completely, totally impatient that she couldn't wait for that," Dizzy continues after polishing off his water. "And she *still* wouldn't have been happy with me only working 20 hours. She also saw my camera as the other woman. I just wanted to live my life the way I lived it before I met her, minus the strippers and coke. Those, I was willing to concede. It got so bad that she used to take it personally if I was tired and she was awake and vice versa. That's when you know it's fucking over."

"Why'd you even let it last that long?"

"Because I fucking loved her, man. Every night, even if we were arguing to the death about something incredibly stupid and irrelevant, as soon as she curled up to me and put her head on my chest, everything felt safe. I knew that the woman next to me was loyal and was a good person and would be a good mother someday. We just couldn't get along. Do you know what I'm talkin' about, or do you think I'm nuts?"

"I know exactly what you're talking about. I think you're nuts, anyway, though."

"Well, I *am* nuts. Like Chinese chicken salad. But blame Tearsten for making me think about this entire mess. That fucking bitch was blowing up my phone all night on Saturday. All night! She's always blowin' it up and sending me messages like, *'I want 2 lick every inch of that rock hard body of urs stud.'* So sometimes you take a bite at the worm, even though you *know* that there's a hook attached. I knew I'd find the psychopath at your place stalking Blotto, so I got all banged-up and carried her back to my joint again. She went straight on her back. So late on Sunday afternoon, she unexpectedly shows up at my place with her bags and tells me that she's staying over because she has flex time and isn't going into work the next day until noon. Now, I did *not* invite her over. I had plans for a week already to meet this girl on the Atlantic City Bikini Team that I fuck every few weeks or so."

"I'm jealous."

"You should be. I'll show you the photo shoot I did for her when we get back on land. So anyway, I tell Cuntlips that I already have plans to go to A.C. for the night. And she's like, *'What time are we leaving?'* So I'm like, *'There's no 'we' here, Kirsten. I'm going to A.C. by myself.'* So she flips the fuck out and starts her shit and all her screaming, saying things like, *'Why did you fuck me again on Saturday night if you* didn't want to be with me? Do you think I'm just a whore? Do you think I'm just some cheap slut that goes around every weekend fucking everybody in town?' And I'm like, 'Well, yeah. I do.' I mean, I just don't understand it. She tells me she wants to fuck, I do it, and then she's yelling at me for doing exactly what she asked me to do in the first place. When will she *finally* understand that a dick doesn't necessarily carry a commitment with it? Then the repair bill for the windshield she cracked on my Mercedes in her rage was over $300. I sent it to 'er, but I'm not holding my breath on payment. The only positive was that the girl from A.C. had to drive here to see me instead."

"Why do you even bother with Tearsten in the first place?"

"You'd agree she's fucking gorgeous, right?"

"Agreed."

"Sometimes the devil you know is better than the devil you don't know, you know? See, Maggie wasn't *really* crazy. She was just an only child of divorced parents, so without having siblings around she never learned the skills of compromise or sharing. Then there's the inevitable problem of her going apeshit when 100% of my attention isn't directed toward her at all times. Her expectation was that I would provide the 'perfect' family that she never had. Kirsten's just nucking futz sometimes."

"Wasn't pulling in $100,000 per year enough for her?"

"For Maggie? No. It wasn't just the money that was the issue, though. In her view, I wasn't working hard enough. Period. She grew up with that super-strict Asian mother where if you don't work 1,000 hours per week then you might as well rid the Earth of your lazy self. It was a character flaw in Maggie's eyes. She never shut up about it once she moved into my place and realized the way my schedule *really* worked. So sometimes I'm glad I left her, sometimes I wish I didn't. She had some great qualities that you don't find in a lot of people, and she was so fucking kind and beautiful when we were getting along. Sometimes, I just want to freebase and get so fucking high that I can pretend she never really existed at all. And, in fact, sometimes I do."

1:06 p.m.

To: *PMcShea77@junkmail.com*
From: *jawilliamsoniii@decesq.com*
Subject: Resume

Dear Mr. McShea:

We have reviewed your resume and other materials which you provided to us electronically. Perhaps you were ill-informed regarding the services that DEC

Attorney Search provides for the legal community. We specialize in placing both new and experienced attorneys into positions within the nation's most well-known and most competitive firms. The materials you provided do not reflect the kind of credentials required for placement with such firms. Quite frankly, DEC Attorney Search would lose credibility with its clients if we recommended you for the opportunities available with these employers.

We regret that we cannot help you at this time. Should your credentials somehow become more desirable, or should you know of someone that could better utilize our services, do not hesitate to contact DEC Attorney Search in the future.

Sincerely,
Jonathan A. Williamson III, Esquire

Wednesday, June 9, 2010

> *4:37 a.m.*
>
> Nightmares.

They are constant and unrelenting. I'm scared half the death to go to sleep sometimes, even though sleep provides a necessary escape from my reality. Some of my nightmares are admittedly commonplace, but their constant reoccurrence places them on par with the more disturbing visions that haunt my sleep. At least six nights a month, I dream that all of my teeth have fallen out. Less frequent but incredibly stress-inducing are the occasions when I dream that both my law degree and undergrad diploma will be revoked because further review of my high school transcripts revealed that I never actually passed French III or Trigonometry. I must take a comprehensive examination on both subjects in 24 hours; failure means that I no longer even have the equivalent of a GED for my resume. I grab a trigonometry text and cower in fear at the first sight of a parabola. I quickly realize that I have absolutely no shot to pass. The stress I feel during these dreams is palpable. I awake alone, the sheets soaked with sweat, my chest tightened and I'm unable to breathe properly because I know I can't afford to replace the teeth I just lost or recover economically from all of my educational credentials becoming even more worthless than they already are.

The other one-off visions are profoundly disturbing and seemingly boundless in their degree of severity and depravity. Consider the following: my own mother has morphed into a demon whose sole mission is to capture me and drag me into the Abyss for eternal torture; I am kidnapped by a sadistic, schizophrenic cannibal who screams bloody hell about me not fixing the driver's side seatbelt in his '72 Gremlin before having me cook my younger sister in an oven and eat her from the feet up; or, my gentle, kindly, elderly next-door neighbor forces me to sodomize him or he will tell my father that I played doctor with his great niece before I raped her with the barrel of a hunting rifle.

This morning's nightmare was that I was running down a busy Market Street during the lunch hour in order to avoid an angry mob that was chasing me. I was dressed in a $1,000 suit that I've never owned while carrying a briefcase that I've never used. I was sweating profusely and breathing heavily as I ran and ran and ran as fast as I could. I bumped into an elderly, gray-haired white woman who was walking with a cane, knocking her to the ground and breaking her hip. I continued to run. I had to. The angry mob was closing quickly. Pedestrians of all kinds were screaming and yelling, pointing to the poor old woman that I had just injured. Out of breath and out of will, I slowed my pace. The angry mob behind me, consisting of

93

well-dressed law partners and several of my law professors, knocked me to the ground and reached into my pockets to steal my wallet. They took all of my cash, my law license, and went to the nearest ATM to withdrawal what little money I had in my checking account. They divided the meager spoils as the police arrived to deliver a beating before arresting me. Taken to a holding cell at the nearest district, I was repeatedly stomped by my cellmates while the cops watched and laughed. Battered and bleeding in my own mind, I finally awake and walk out to one of the living room couches to continue sleeping until Dizzy arrives for another early morning kayak run.

Thursday, June 10, 2010

8:26 p.m.

My last girlfriend that I'd publically admit to dating was Vanessa Albrecht aka Vanessa the Annoyer. This was quite some time ago. Over seven *long* years, in fact. I met her during my pre-law school, pre-depression years when I was living in Manayunk, a mixed working class/yuppie rowhome neighborhood situated in the northwest corner of Philadelphia along the Schuylkill River. Life was pretty good then. I had a decent job as a juvenile probation officer and lived with a fraternity brother originally from the East Coast and an old high school buddy. My student loan burden from undergrad was only $28,000 thanks to a mixture of parental support and scholarships. I took my LSAT stoned and scored a 159, which put me in the 89th percentile. It wasn't great, but it was good enough. I always studied high and did pretty well with the practice tests, so I thought it wise to leave my methods unchanged for the real thing. I was accepted to the Villanova day law program and the Temple night program, and the hardest part of law school is getting in. I had options. Life was good. I was filled with great hope for the first time since I left the endless fields of corn and soybeans surrounding Iowa City to return home.

Vanessa lived directly across the street from me during my last two years in the 'Yunk. She was a med student who was originally from Utica and did undergrad at Syracuse, so she wasn't automatically put-off by my slight build and the white collar appearance that was the bane of the native Philadelphia girls. Vanessa said that she used to watch me playing Wiffle ball with the little kids on the street while she would sit in her bedroom reviewing her notes from class. She thought that was cute. I had no idea that she was interested in me until she showed up piss drunk at my house one Saturday night about 3 a.m. and shoved her tongue down my throat about ten seconds after I answered the door. It wasn't that she was suddenly overcome by my manliness. She was just loaded and had no social skills.

I'd be lying if I didn't admit that I thought Vanessa was very hot as soon as I met her. She just wasn't my speed at all. If I could have my choice of women, I would always pick a sweet Italian or Asian girl with dark hair and brown eyes who looked great in a skirt. Vanessa was of German descent, had blonde hair, blue eyes, and I don't think I'd describe her as 'sweet.' She certainly had a soul, but she sometimes displayed an unfeminine edge and chain smoked Marlboro Lights like cigarettes were slated to become contraband in a week's time. But Vanessa had a great ass, so all of my other criteria kinda fell by the wayside about four seconds into that first kiss. This ass really was the stuff of legend, and it remained the same exact size and tight shape throughout the duration of our nine month relationship. (While men would call such a prize a 'stripper's ass,' women tend to refer to such 'undefined' asses derogatively as 'ten year-old boy asses' in a weak, jealous attempt to make men feel that pursuit of such fine booty somehow makes them a closet homosexual pedophile.) So even though Vanessa wasn't my type at all, I never had an issue with her looks. On that basis alone, she was far, far out of my league. It was the other things that were the problem. Aside from her annoying smoking habit, Vanessa had a propensity to talk too much. Way too much. Her favorite sounds were the rattle of an ATM spitting out hundred dollar bills from my account (I had a job then) and the sound of her own voice. The endless dinners at restaurants that only served dishes which guaranteed me three days of diarrhea were bad enough. But whenever I got tired of talking and became quiet, Vanessa would henpeck me about everything- the old shirt that I was wearing while relaxing on my own couch on a random weekday, the small hole in my sock, or why I was twenty minutes late walking across the street to her place last Tuesday.

My roommates eventually banned her from the property during sporting events because she was such a distraction. *'Who's winning?'* she would ask every six seconds, as if the score wasn't displayed right on the fucking television. I'd point out that the score was on the screen, but she claimed that she couldn't correlate the score to the logos or colors of the participants. She couldn't have really been that fucking stupid when she was maintaining a solid B+ average at a reputable medical school like Temple. I think it brought her pleasure to annoy me and this provided her a distraction from her studies. Fortunately, Vanessa's other distraction was sucking my cock. There was no question that we could click in the bedroom at times. She once performed fellatio upon me 16 days in a row, a personal record which will likely stand forever. And these were porno-quality blowjobs, not disinterested half-efforts from a rank, drunken amateur who was wishing she was in bed with someone else. I've had far too many of those. I always did Vanessa the favor first. Twice, sometimes. Often, I would lick and sniff her ass like a rabid dog. All of these oral delights we shared between us didn't matter in the end, though. She was still fucking annoying, and became so even in the bedroom as time wore on.

Vanessa had this odd fixation with having to be totally naked in bed. This sounds like something that would be welcome, but it was completely weird. One night in late March 2003 I took her out and got her completely wasted after dinner, which was usually a mistake because two drinks would make her talk twice as much as normal. This increased exponentially with each drink, so by drink #5 there wasn't even enough oxygen left in the area for me to breathe. Drinking made Vanessa incredibly horny, though. She was wearing a black sweater, a black & white patterned skirt and these super-sexy black boots that came up to just below her knees. She looked outstanding, as she usually did. It's an incredibly exciting feeling to have access to the body of someone that's very attractive. Vanessa might have been a pest, but sometimes she made me feel like I was 17 again and girls were this new, exciting thing. You can't put a price on that. I was eager to get her back to my place and go down on her for days.

Unfortunately, Vanessa ran into someone from medical school as we were leaving the brew pub so I had to suffer impatiently through 85 minutes of watching Vanessa and her classmate chew each other's ears off while I had a raging boner in my pants. Even worse, the classmate's boyfriend was boring as fuck and we could find no common ground to spark a conversation. His primary interest was foreign films, and I confess to being a raging philistine when comes to foreign films and literature. The Sixers were getting pasted, so I turned away from the televisions and passed the time by admiring Vanessa. She did look great in a skirt. I loved her thighs, and I could never get over the fact that an ass like that was *mine*. Her skin and blue eyes looked so nice in the soft lighting of the bar. And her lips! Those soft, pink lips could do some wonderful things. Vanessa actually enjoyed giving head, which is the entire trick to a spectacular blowjob. She was a great kisser, too, when she wasn't yapping too much. But it was the boots that really got me that night. The black leather wrapped so nicely around her calves. Vanessa would definitely be getting it from behind.

I finally got Vanessa into my bedroom and was so excited to start removing her clothes. I was standing behind her, so I first reached for the little zipper in the middle of the back of her skirt. It slid to the floor. There was only a small black thong covering Vanessa's tiny little ass. I dropped to my knees. I took each side of her thong into two of my fingers and gently pulled it from around her thin waist. It made a slow trip down her thighs and over her sexy black boots. Vanessa did the heavy lifting by taking off her bra and sweater. After hours of waiting to taste her and fuck her, I was finally about to deliver oral sex from behind. Just as I was about to kiss the back of her left thigh, Vanessa launched herself onto a seated position on my bed. She immediately stuck one of her boots in my face, hitting me on the chin. "Take my boots off," she ordered.

"I...wanted you to keep them on."

"Why," she replied impatiently.

"Because you look very sexy in them."

"Take them off, Patrick."

"Could you just-"

"No. I've told you this before. When I'm in bed, I need to be totally naked. I don't know why that's so difficult for you to understand."

"I can't understand it because…"

"We're not filming a porno here, Patrick. We take off our shoes and socks in bed. So unzip my boots. Now."

"You're really killing the mood, Vanessa…"

"Maybe you can date your friend Lori down the street, then. I'm sure she'd dress like a whore in bed if you asked her to. You guys spend enough time making eyes at each other…"

"Lori has nothing to do with this. I've been waiting the entire night to-"

"I'm not listening to you."

"You need to go home, Vanessa."

"You are fucking *impossible* to get along with, Patrick."

Vanessa the Annoyer got dressed and took off in a huff. What a buzzkill *that* entire event was. I'll never understand it. I was the one who was raised Irish Catholic and was supposed to have all of the weird, unexplainable sexual hang-ups. I was incredibly disappointed, but I dusted myself off and went out to meet my roommates at the bars and had an okay time.

The misadventures in the bedroom with Vanessa didn't end. Despite the fact that Vanessa would cum 9 out of the 10 times that I went down on her, she became obsessed with having orgasms during sex. She rarely did. I don't think a lack of female orgasm during intercourse reflects negatively on a man's abilities. For a woman, orgasm can be as much a psychological event as a physiological response. You sometimes have to coax it out of them. It's difficult to play the role of sex coach while also performing physically, especially if you really don't give a shit whether the girl cums or not. Vanessa had to have everything just exactly perfect and we were rarely on the same page. She had to be on top at a certain angle for a certain time at a certain pace, and I had to be talking to her the entire time with my words becoming increasingly dirty commensurate with whatever gear her hips happened to find themselves in. I guessed wrong a lot, often throwing out an ill-timed c-word when a *'You look so fucking hot naked on top of me'* would have been much more appropriate. The lighting had to be perfect. Day orgasms were impossible. Night orgasms were, too. Candlelight worked sometimes. The temperature also had to be right. There was a lot of throwing covers off, putting covers back on, and leaning forward to adjust the thermostat on the wall above the left side of her headboard. She also had that dreaded habit whereby a woman will sometimes push the forehead portion of her skull against yours with all her might when she's on top and things are getting particularly intense for her. That fucking hurts. I can't tell you why it doesn't hurt the woman just as much. All I know is that it fucking kills me and it screams 'rookie.' It was bad. I'm sure there was some hot stud out there that she would have found mega-attractive and it wouldn't have been such a project. I wasn't a hot stud, and felt no guilt about it. Vanessa picked *me*, after all.

I was pretty relieved when Vanessa grabbed a medical residency at a respected children's hospital near San Francisco. Had she stayed in Philly, I would have been held hostage by her ass (and eventually, her salary) despite the fact that she drove me fucking crazy. It's nearly impossible for a regular guy to throw away the ego trip and opportunities for pure sexual satisfaction that come with having a woman naked in his bed that's way out of his league. It's like giving up a steady diet of filet mignon and caviar when the alternative is trying to satisfy your insatiable appetite by fending for yourself against thousands and thousands of other savages with more knowledge and better weapons than you have. No one wants to be stuck eating fucking grass and leaves when filet mignon is being put on the table every night, even if the person serving it can be difficult. Vanessa came back to visit some friends a few times during my first year of law school and we had sex in a Center City hotel room on two occasions. We lost touch, but she found me on facebook last year. She's married with a kid, and still looks great. Her husband is a dorky-looking neurologist that makes me look like a Mr. Universe contestant by comparison. There was no way that he could say 'no' to that ass, either. I'm glad she's happy. She's lucky that she didn't wind up with me. All things considered, though, I'd take another night with Vanessa in a heartbeat. I've been eating grass and leaves for many years now. It's been incredibly difficult to digest after gorging at some of the decadent feasts to which I had the privilege of being invited in the past. As I stare into an endless willow sky of pinkish clouds and feel the comfort of a cool breeze blowing off the sound, all of those nights with Vanessa and Kim and those Iowa farm girls seem so long ago and far, far away.

Saturday, June 12, 2010

2:04 p.m.

Gina D'Amico sent me 129 text messages over the past two weeks and called me on Thursday while she was getting a pedicure somewhere in Center City. I've been invited to join Gina and Jenna Love for their secret pow-wow on the roof of 728, where they escape to sun themselves in order to avoid things such as the watchful eyes of Harry and the Board, launched water balloons, Dizzy's cameras, and other assorted juvenile mischief and shenanigans on which everyone prides themselves after having to act like work stiffs all week. Gina smiles brightly at me after I complete my climb through the attic skylight and arrive on the roof of the house. Her black bikini-clad, tanning, already-spoken-for body looks so absolutely inviting while reclining in her beach chair. Jenna appears to be an even a greater prize as she lay on her stomach with her bikini top undone while reviewing a legal brief. Her olive-toned skin is perfect. Even the soles of her feet are unblemished. She's a genetic freak. Her too-tight behind is covered only by a thin oval of pink fabric that immediately gets my attention. "What took you so long to get up here, Woodchuck?" Gina wants to know.

"Board meeting," I explain while trying to stumble stoned into the spot between Gina and Jenna's positions. Gina catches my staring at the BigLaw lawyer's tempting butt and giggles. I place a Rutgers beach towel that I found in a closet between the two nymphs and lie down to relax.

"Do you need suntan lotion?" Gina asks. "I have some. It's only SPF 4, though."

"I found some downstairs. SPF Irish, I'm wearing."

"I need your advice on something," Gina says to me.

"Dump him."

"It's a legal paper, silly," she replies. "My friend Jenna is 'too busy' to look at it for me."

"I'm not 'too busy', Gina," spits the high-strung hottie. "I just said I'd take a look at it later, okay? I have plenty of my own work to do. I have to bring work with me or I can't come down here every other Saturday or I can't make plans with Michael on Sunday night."

Gina sticks out her tongue in Jenna's direction as she begins to root through her beach bag for a document that I wouldn't ever volunteer to read if I didn't want to firmly place Gina's ever-darkening legs on my shoulders and pound her into the next universe.

"How was your shower today, Jenna?" I ask simply to make conversation as Gina engages in a veritable archeological dig into her bag.

"I didn't shower yet today," she replies unpleasantly. "That was a stupid fucking question."

"I just want to ensure that there's no more threats from any ancient colonies of fucking fungus."

"I have no idea what the hell you're talking about," Jenna snips. She sees it fit to empty some of contents of her water bottle onto my face. I can't believe she's related to my friend Maria from law school, who has 100% of Jenna's brains, 10% of Jenna's looks but only 1% of the attitude. Gina, somehow oblivious to the water attack, hands me a stapled, three-page document entitled "Non-Compete and Non-Disclosure Agreement." It's sure to be an exciting read. I remove my $5.00 shades to begin a scan and translation of the legal blabber on the first page. I give Gina a brief run-down of my knowledge on restrictive covenants, which is buried somewhere deep in the recesses of my brain along with the list of my favorite Matchbox cars and the name of the artist who performed 'Pac-Man Fever.' "So I'm like, supposed to get money for signing this?" Gina asks at the end of my lesson, to which Jenna in all of her legal superiority chooses to contribute nothing.

"Tell 'em you want thirty grand to sign it," I suggest.

"*Thirty grand?* I don't want to piss off my boss."

"Think about it: what are the two things that you've been trained to do?"

"Marketing and accounting."

"And what are the two things you're not permitted to do for three years and within 30 miles if you get let go?"

"Marketing and accounting," she repeats. "Thirty grand might be low, even."

"It might be. I don't even think this would hold up in court, by the way. Wouldn't you agree, Jenna?"

"I'm not listening," the lawyer replies with an exaggerated flip of her page. She could get an answer for Gina with one e-mail sent from her Blackberry but won't do it for some reason.

"I'll call your HR director if need be, Gina," I volunteer.

Gina thanks me and returns the document to her bag before moving to a reclining position on her stomach. "Could you undo my top for me?" she asks very casually. I take one of thin strings of black cloth on Gina's bikini between my thumb and first finger and slowly, deliberately pull it until the knot on her smooth, beautiful back becomes undone. She must look *fantastic* in bed from behind. History tells me that I'll never know, but my sex drive unfortunately pushes me to try to make it happen anyway. "Thank you," Gina says to me very pleasantly, like it was such a chore to undo her top. She then starts going through her phone and begins snorting.

"Problem, Gina?" I ask.

"Have you heard, Jenna," says the full-blooded Italian to the half-breed while giggling, "that Woodchuck wants to treat me like a rental property?"

"That's...fucking wonderful," Jenna replies without hiding her disgust. "You're just *so* classy, *Woodchuck*." She pronounces my nickname with an especially derisive sneer. "And I'll have you both know that I'm trying to get this brief marked-up and having to listen to you guys flirting very playfully with each other isn't helping anything."

"Then why are you texting every two minutes, Jenna?" Gina asks in reply. "And we're not playfully flirting with each other or anything. Well, maybe a little. Woodchuck's kinda funny."

"I'm just texting Michael to tell him what time I plan on coming home tomorrow," Jenna explains. "We have dinner reservations at Le Monde."

"I heard that it's only three stars now," Gina replies. "Somebody told me that. I forget who."

"We went there a few months ago and it was wonderful," states Jenna.

"Maybe you can take me there, Woodchuck, after you get a new job," suggests Gina sweetly with a strong smile.

"The menu's not all 'goat balls wrapped in kelp,' or dolphin taint, is it?" I ask.

Jenna exhales and shakes her head in disgust upon my mention of 'dolphin taint.'

"I think there's regular stuff, too," Gina says, ignoring her. "The appetizers are *awesome*. They have really good fried calamari."

"Eh. Not too big on octopi. I'm more of a meat 'n potatoes guy."

"You know what I always wondered?" Gina says with a giggle that tells me something really stupid is coming. "I wonder if you can eat a starfish. Most of them are spiny, aren't they?"

"*I've* never seen one on a menu," Jenna declares like she's some kind of expert and we should be paying attention. Prior to this, her only area of expertise appeared to be some not-yet-named area of litigation practice, having a great body, and being a miserable fucking bitch with an odd pug. I look over at Gina and she immediately starts snorting. "I've had enough with you two," snaps Jenna. "I'm driving over to the beach in Avalon by myself. Maybe I can actually get some work done there." I watch the brunette struggle to retie her bikini top before she exits the roof, leaving me alone with my crush. I can't say that I mind as I take in a generous view of Gina's ever-darkening body.

4:02 p.m.

Harry has arrived at his property for the first time this summer. He drops off his sweet, petite strawberry blond fiancé at 728 and orders me into his F-250 that has a set of brass-colored prosthetic balls hanging from the trailer hitch. My job is to help him put his wakeboarding boat into the water at a nearby public ramp. Harry is about an inch shorter than me and twice as wide. He shaves his head completely cue ball bald. It fits, though. It used to be covered with red hair. He also has very intense, greenish eyes, one of which starts to drift slight to the left after his third shot of Jack. He's the only one at 728 that knows my real story. "You did a nice job with the showers, Food Stamps," Harry says as he sips from a thermos filled with Stoli O and club while he drives. "The ride down today was *brutal*. I take the back roads once I get outta Philly so that I can get a nice buzz on. There might be two other fuckin' cars on these hick roads that nobody knows about. Well, evidently today the secret was out. I sat on this one little county road for 45 minutes without moving. We sat there so long that Marie and I had to stop drinking because we never would have made it here. How stoned are you?"

"Not at all, really."

"Good. Do you want to drive the truck back to the house or the boat?"

"I don't think I could dock the boat."

"That's not always easy for a rookie. How's the job search goin'?"

"It's not."

"Just sit on your ass for as long as you can. Depression's a bitch, man. My dad has it. I think he spent ten years locked in his fuckin' bedroom. Are you really going to score a great job right now, anyway?"

"Not a chance, Harry."

"Exactly. You know how I got my job? I was talking to this random guy in line at a McDonald's one day. This was like, ten years ago, I guess. I had been selling industrial dishwashers to hospitals and schools and shit, and making okay money doing it. Then I got laid off. I was out of work for almost a year and burnt through almost my entire savings just paying my fuckin' mortgage. I'm completely at my wits' end at this point. I was broke as a fucking joke. I shouldn't even have been getting lunch at McDonald's that day. I couldn't afford it. So I'm bullshitting with the guy next to me in line, and he mentions that he was coming back from a sales call to the hospital down the street. So I tell him that I once sold them a dishwasher just to make conversation and he starts telling me that he's trying to sell them a CT scanner and that his outfit is hiring. Gives me his card, I call him a couple of days later, and over nine years later I'm a vice president. And I'm paying *two* mortgages without any problem *and* have a skinny fiancé. I couldn't see *either* of those things happening ten years ago. So you never know what might happen, man. Just stay as fucked up as possible until your time comes and concentrate on getting your dick sucked. Otherwise, you're really going to regret it during your first 60 hour week back at work."

> *5:14 p.m.*

The Board received a message that Mallory has fallen victim to a flat tire while riding her road bike at a location six miles from the house. I was the only one with any ability to drive due to a well-timed nap, so I set out to retrieve the brunette beauty in my Shitmobile. It's embarrassing to me to been seen in this car, but my insecurity is tempered by this exciting opportunity to see Mallory in spandex shorts. I find her and her bike and her legs on the roadside somewhere in neighboring Avalon. Mallory's ass is no larger than the diameter of the steering wheel in my car. I manage to get her bike into my trunk and she takes a seat inside my piece of crap.

"I'm sorry I'm sweating all over your car," she says after fastening her seatbelt.

"This car's seen better days, Mallory. 'Sweaty' is a good look for you, anyway."

The brunette smiles to herself and pulls down the sun visor. "No mirror, Woodchuck?"

"It's a no-frills operation I have going on here. Sorry that someone so attractive has to be seen in such a piece of shit."

"You should be *relived* to drive something like this. It's a good city car. I just paid $40,000 for a new Audi that got hit while I was food shopping last month and I have a $1,000 deductible. That's a lot of money to pay for a trip for low fat yogurt and a box of Wheat Thins."

"Yeah, I'm not about to put $1,000 of body work into this heap."

"Thanks so much for getting me, by the way. I tried calling this guy that I'm kinda sorta seeing but he was too involved in his beer pong to be worried about me."

"Once you sleep with a guy that you're 'kinda sorta' seeing, all motivation to be a nice guy and do favors for you is usually lost."

"I know," Mallory says with a sigh. "I was in a four-year relationship until March and I'm pretty comfortable riding the 'kinda sorta' bus right now."

"What about Blotto?"

"It's cute that you're sticking up for him, but he actually likes me. That's too much to handle right now after four years of dating Satan's pool boy. Maybe after the summer when we don't live together every weekend. There's too much jealousy involved when a couple lives in the same shore house."

"Sounds like you may have made some poor choices in the past."

"I have," she laughs. "Blotto's sweet when he wants to be."

"That makes him totally unattractive, doesn't it?"

"Oh, shut up," is her order. "Let's stop at the Moo Moo and I'll buy you a sandwich."

"You don't have to do that."

"I'm sure something will happen and you can get me back later," she insists. I turn into the parking lot of the deli, almost running over an old lady in the process because of my preoccupation with Mallory's thighs. Fortunately, the old lady was not too shaken up and Mallory found the embarrassing incident to be flattering on some strange level.

9:37 p.m.

A board meeting has been called to order with a large number of participants. Stinky has been a fucking puddle for the past hour because her 'boyfriend' has cancelled both his future East Coast appearance and their relationship. She has pulled herself together somewhat, but only because she is pretty much too stoned to function physically or emotionally. She sits atop the queen between Page and Blotto while staring at an unremarkable portion of the Board Room wall. Gina is also present, along with two other pretty girls that I've met for the first time. One of them is a major FAIL on the feet test. Her pinky toes on both feet jut out sideways in a completely perpendicular fashion. I stare at her feet for a full five minutes, thinking the weed that we're smoking might be laced with some kind of hallucinogen. But it's not. This girl *really* has pinky toes that are completely sideways. She also smokes cigarettes, is a redhead and a serial texter. She may as well have surgery to have her phone permanently attached to her hand. I guess we're all totally uninteresting. This woman does inspire me, though, to take my own phone into my hands and send a text to the woman seated directly next to me on my bunk.

> *Message to: Gina*
> *6/12/10 9:41 p.m.*
> *Lets stay here and make out when*
> *everyone leaves for the trainwreck.*

Gina's phone starts buzzing and making all kinds of noises a few seconds later. I feel slightly nervous as she pulls it out of her purse. She hits a button, takes a look at the screen, and begins issuing snorts that one would expect from a migrating humpback desperately trying to communicate with its wayward pod. This doesn't sound too promising.

> *New Message: Gina*
> *6/12/10 9:42 p.m.*
> *ur a fuking nerd*

I roll my eyes at Gina, who looks at me and continues to snort while shaking her head in the negative. I made my point. She made hers. She exits the Board Room. The redhead with the sideways toes is the next to leave the room, texting the entire time. No one seems to care, including her friend who is currently ripping a hit from a spectacular bowl supplied by Page that is fashioned as the *Millennium Falcon*. Thunderous applause suddenly erupts. I look up to find that a woman with curly, dirty blonde hair and glass green eyes has entered the room. She's dressed comfortably in a short denim skirt, a black Polo with a purple horse and black flip-flops. She greets Blotto, Page and Sharkey with hugs and kisses. She tries the same with Stinky, but receives little response. This girl's legs are fantastic. Looking around the room for a place to sit, she spies me sitting on a bunk, alone. She hops over and takes a seat on my lap instead of the mattress. The girl's body feels so warm and she smells wonderful.

"They always gravitate toward a fucking new guy," notes Blotto.

"Fresh meat," chuckles Page. Stinky mumbles something unintelligible and everyone laughs at her incoherence.

"What's *your* name, cutie?" the blonde asks me sweetly with the fresh scent of alcohol on her breath. I can feel my cheeks flushing red. I'm scared half to death of this beautiful new arrival.

"Woodchuck," I reply.

"Woodchuck, huh? How'd you get that nickname, sweetheart?"

"Umm...my buck teeth in grade school."

Sharkey lets out a powerful laugh. "There's really no way to spin a cool story about *that* nickname, is there, Woodchuck?" he cracks.

"I think it's cute," says the sexy blonde as she runs her left hand through my hair. My cheeks feel so red that I fear that my face may explode. "So what do you do for a living, Woodchuck?"

"I'm unemployed," I admit like I'm under some sort of truth spell. I am, though. The spell is called 'beautiful woman.'

"Oh, dear," replies the blonde, as if I have AIDS.

"Have no fear, Amanda," interjects Blotto. "Woodchuck is an attorney."

"I think that's wonderful," says the warm woman on my lap, suddenly changing her tone. Blotto looks at me and winks. Then I notice the very, very, very large engagement ring on the blonde's left hand. This, I never understand. I appreciate the attention from this beautiful girl, but it's completely hollow unless I know that the relationship vultures are already circling overhead her fiancé. I don't think this girl isn't trying to lead me on, though. She probably just assumes for some reason that I'm not a desperate, pathetic fuck with no options unless they belong in an insane asylum or currently serve as a Weight Watchers 'before' picture. She's just being drunk and friendly toward a new face. I can't crucify her for that. Everyone here in Angel Bay has been very friendly so far save Jenna and Tearsten after too many drinks. "I'm Amanda," the girl on my lap finally says. "And for some reason, you're *really* blushing, cutie."

"Scarlet fever," cracks Blotto. "Sudden onset. Typically caused by hot blondes with big tits."

"By the way, Amanda," says Sharkey, "where's Tony the Douchebag this weekend? Parole revoked?"

"It'd be nice, Peter, if you could just call him 'Tony' when I'm actually sitting in the same room with you," says the blonde, not sounding very happy.

"It's a hard habit for us to break," Blotto says in Sharkey's defense. "Tony himself doesn't exactly help his own cause, either."

"I can't handle you guys sometimes," says the blonde sweetly. "Somebody *please* give me something to smoke. Tony's deep sea fishing in Florida, by the way."

"That's what he told *you*," says Sharkey. "I have a strong feeling that forty kilos are coming up from Columbia and he's there to receive his cut."

"That's not a very nice thing to say, Peter," says the blonde from my lap.

"The truth hurts, sister," he replies. "Sometimes the truth *really* hurts. All you gorgeous bitches are *blind* when it comes to your supposed 'men.' I'm just trying to perform a public service for all of you while I'm drunk enough to get away with it."

It is decided that it's time to head to the Shipwreck. Stinky falls atop the queen now that no one is supporting her body by sitting next to her. Page pauses to cover her useless body with a blanket before we all depart for the bar.

10:32 p.m.

"Can I get you a drink, Jenna?" I ask as I approach her at the Shipwreck while she leans upon the bar awaiting service from 728's regular bartender, Danny. Dressed in a black skirt and heels with a sharp red top, it cannot be denied that Jenna is one absolutely stunning woman. I'm not really intimidated by her, though. Not only do I think she's a bitch, but no one with her looks and salary would ever consider fucking me unless they turned into a homeless smack addict and I was carrying. Since there's nothing to screw up here, there's really no reason to be nervous around her. She ignores my offer for a drink. I repeat it.

"I'm getting a soda," she grumbles back.

"Pregnant?"

"No," she replies with quite a nasty sneer on her gorgeous face as she flicks her hair back dismissively. "I like to be in control. I don't drink alcohol. Ever."

"Me, neither."

"I'm sure."

"Can I get you anything else?"

"Don't waste your time with me, Patrick. My boyfriend is twice the man that you'll ever be."

"Is he going to beat me up?" I ask with a laugh.

"Violence has nothing to do with whether or not someone is a man, as far as I'm concerned."

"You obviously didn't grow up in Philly, then, did you?"

"No, thank god. Huntingdon Valley. Why don't you go find some drunken hussy to give you the cheap blowjob that you so desperately need? It's completely *obvious* that you're on a losing streak..."

I take my Sprite and walk away without comment. Now I'm totally self-conscious because I can't tell if Jenna was being her bitch self or if I really have 'Total Loser' tattooed across my forehead in black. I check my phone. No new messages. I keep checking every six seconds even though my phone is not vibrating and I can't think of any female that would be texting me for any reason. I find Page and we walk into the Disco Room to admire the talent.

1:26 a.m.

I spot Dharma among the dozen or so beauties waiting in line for the ladies room as I endeavor to take care of my own business on that end. Half of them are crying for various reasons. The dirty blonde with the doe eyes spots me and immediately looks down at her phone in hopes of avoiding further contact. "Hi, Dharma," I say as I pass. She doesn't even bother to look up from the screen. "How's it goin'?" I continue in a vain effort to engage her. Dharma gets out of line and butts into the ladies' room in order to escape, causing fierce protest from the other women waiting with broken hearts, broken dreams and near-bursting bladders.

2:37 a.m.

I had thought it might be a good idea to make some smalltalk with Amanda at the Shipwreck, but it was impossible to get anywhere near her. Everywhere she went, she was surrounded by very territorial Hot Dudes who were monitoring the level of liquid in whatever cup she was holding so that they could be the next to jump in and buy her a drink. She did wink across the bar at me on one occasion and flashed me the kind of smile that I have not seen from a woman in quite some time. She's gorgeous. I'm not getting my hopes up, especially when she has a shiny ring on her finger. Not that it really matters in the year 2010. Getting engaged is just something a beautiful woman does for a few months or a few years before suddenly moving on to the next asshole.

Gina ignored me the entire night until the last 40 minutes, and she was piss drunk so we blatantly felt each other up on the dance floor in what amounted to a giant tease. She's now in bed already because of a cursed baby shower for a sorority sister back in the Philly 'burbs tomorrow morning, so I accompany a crew over to Dizzy's place to watch and/or participate in the shenanigans. Dizzy has a long-standing policy that he will provide coke at no charge to any woman that attends late nite topless. Nothing makes women start throwing their clothes around the room like the white power does. As far as I'm concerned, it's cocaine's only redeeming quality.

Despite my one-time desperate foray into the world of smack, I've never done the nose candy. I'm old enough to remember the shock that ripped through both the sports world and society at large when Len Bias, a 22 year-old basketball phenom from the University of Maryland, died of a heart attack brought on by cocaine intoxication. People who weren't alive at that time or who were too young to remember it can't fathom the enormity of the event. At the time of his death in 1986, Bias was the reigning ACC Athlete of the Year and ACC Player of the Year, the second time he had garnered the award in as many seasons. During his senior season, he became Maryland's all-time leading scorer. In 1986, it was the World Champion Boston Celtics that held the number two pick in the NBA draft after making a trade with Seattle two years earlier. Coming off a 67-15 season with a roster boasting four future members of the Hall of Fame, legendary Celtics president and cigar-smoking general manager Red Auerbach felt strongly that Boston's next superstar could be Len Bias. On June 17, 1986, in New York City, the Celtics formally made Bias their man. On June 18, he signed an endorsement deal with Reebok worth a reported $1.6 million, which was a *hell* of a lot of money 24 years ago. The next day, Bias was dead. Perhaps in the internet age, rumors may have surfaced prior to the tragedy that the immensely popular basketball star had fallen in with a bad crowd or had picked up some bad habits on campus. Whether they were true or not wouldn't have been relevant. There would at least have been some predictor of potential trouble on the horizon. But there was no such foreshadowing in 1986. Nobody saw it coming. Larry Bird, who said that he would actually attend rookie camp if the Celtics drafted Bias, told *Sports Illustrated* that the news of his death was the cruelest thing he'd ever heard. Bias had so many reasons to live that most people couldn't even comprehend it. And in a flash, he was gone. The Celtics, who had been crowned World Champions a staggering 16 times since their inception in 1954, didn't win another for 21 years.

I remember asking my dad about the tragedy. His opinion was exactly what I would have expected from an Irish Catholic father. He didn't think it was a tragedy at all. "When you do drugs," he said, "you deserve everything that happens to you." I know that he was just trying to teach me a lesson, but even as an nine year-old I thought that was too simplistic an answer. Still, I promised myself that I'd never do cocaine. I always kept that promise. But I don't pass judgment on those who dabble in the drug, and a lot of people do. Len Bias didn't intend to kill himself that night. Lots of people do things that can be considered dangerous every day. It's dangerous to operate a car in a fierce, driving rain. But it doesn't mean that you automatically deserve to die for it.

I arrive at Dizzy's and follow the old school sound of House of Pain and screaming, giggling, intoxicated women up to the large sleeping area on the third floor. It's like being backstage at a rock concert, except Dizzy and our crew are the stars. There's at least eight topless women present with breasts of varying cup sizes, from Heather's completely flat training bra chest to a surprisingly attractive and freckled redhead who looks to be sporting legitimate Ds. Some of them are allowing a massively obese man do lines off their tits or ass crack in exchange for a slice of pepperoni pizza in a box on the floor. This man, known as Fifty-One, is a walking heart attack. In addition to the pizza, he has a cheese steak, pizza steak, cheese fries, a king size Snickers bar and a Diet Pepsi on a small table next to him. This is what he considers to be an after-bar snack. I assumed he earned his nickname because it was his waist size, but it was given to him in high school because he was so massively fucking fat that people thought that he had a legitimate shot to become the 51st state in the Union. Molly is feverishly running around the room trying to herd the crowd into one corner. But she was bred to herd sheep, not a bunch of drunk women also blasted out of their minds on coke while jumping around topless to early Nineties hip-hop. She eventually realizes that the task is hopeless and climbs onto Dizzy's bed. Molly looks at all of us like we're a bunch of fucking idiots. Dizzy passes me a water pipe. "Welcome to the Big Show," he says with a grin. Heather walks over to greet me with a big, wasted hug and kiss. The skin on her body feels so smooth and soft and warm. After our hug, Heather makes the mistake of mocking Peter Sharkey for his wooly head of hair.

"I think I'd keep my thoughts to myself if I was walking around with a chest as flat as yours, Heather," he says with a laugh. "I've seen mosquito bites bigger than them titties."

Heather tries to ignore the shot, but it's plain on her face that she's pissed at Sharkey. "What the fuck do you tell your hairdresser, Peter?" she asks angrily. "Take a little off the top and make me look homeless?"

"Something like that," Sharkey replies. "Then I bang 'er."

Heather storms out of the room, being one of those women who are very sensitive about their lack of cup size. She may not have breasts, but I note that her golden back is a work of art as she exits. It contains no tramp stamp, either. I've never liked tattoos on women. Female flesh is beautiful enough in itself. When I have an attractive woman on all fours for me, I want to view their body in its purest, unaltered state. It's a crime to defile nature's ultimate masterpiece. It's not like a tattoo is going to get you kicked out of my bed, though, especially these days.

A man named Jake enters the room with Silent John Peters, who rarely speaks because a portion of his tongue was removed due to cancer and a long-standing dip habit. When he does talk, it is with a very pronounced lisp that sounds like a three year-old trying to communicate. It's a shame, because he's a very good-looking guy. The pair carries three acoustic guitars. Dizzy turns off the stereo. The spare is passed to me at my request. Danny, our red-headed bartender at the Shipwreck, appears with a set of congas. Jake is the frontman, since Silent John obviously can't sing. Jake has a powerful, on-key voice that gives him the ability to hold the attention of the entire room as he rolls through a series of covers by The Rolling Stones, Buffett, Springsteen, and original songs about masturbation, being sexy and finding your head trapped between the legs of a woman with large thighs that he refers to as 'cellulite earmuffs.' The raunchy originals get as much attention from the ladies as the covers. Danny's perfectly on-time beats is what keeps the asses moving and the tits bouncing. I manage to follow along and trade lead breaks with Silent John, who is a damn good player. Heather returns to the party just after a nice version of 'Thunder Road.' It is somewhat surreal playing to a roomful of girls blasted on coke who are dancing around with their breasts jiggling up and down. It appears that I've fallen in with the fun crowd here in Angel Bay.

"I didn't know you played guitar!" Heather says to me as I place it aside after our set break. She takes me by the hand and leads me into a nearby bathroom. God, I love that back of hers. Heather walks to the toilet, lifts her denim skirt, drops a pair of black panties that fall to her ankles, and begins to pee. We converse as the sound of her urine stream hitting the toilet water fills the room.

"Have a girlfriend, Woodchuck?"

"Nah."

"Why not?"

"Lots of options," I lie pretty unconvincingly. "I'm waiting until August to make a final decision."

"I didn't realize that you had *soooooooooooo* many women chasing you, Woodchuck," says Heather sarcastically as she prepares to wipe herself with a wad of toilet paper so big that it could shut down an entire landfill. Then I realize that Heather is also taking this bathroom opportunity to change her fucking tampon. I choose not to view this event and instead turn toward the mirror where I pretend to search for zits on my face that don't exist. I hear something fall into a nearby trashcan and the toilet flushes. Heather taps me on the shoulder. I turn to face her. *"Is it okay if I kiss you, Woodchuck?"* she whispers forwardly as she puts her arms around me.

"Do you think you need my permission or something?"

"No," she smiles. Heather's lips taste like hard alcohol. They're fucking delicious. She moves her moist tongue inside my mouth softy and slowly with a smooth rhythm that I wouldn't ever expect from a drunk, coked-out girl past the 3:00 o'clock hour. Having just watched her change her tampon, though, the level of anticipation for this entire episode has been largely muted. I have no urge to pull myself away from her, though. I run the base of my right hand up her spine. Heather's tongue pushes deeper into my mouth and she moans. Our lips separate. We quickly deliver kiss after kiss as we make an attempt to regain our breath. The skin on Heather's face then suddenly turns to a particularly odd shade of green. She spends the next twenty minutes vomiting as I stand behind her, holding her soft blonde hair away from her face.

3:24 a.m.

With Heather safely put to bed on her stomach and with a bucket by her side, I exit her bedroom to find Amanda Liss walking into the hallway after exiting the bathroom. Unfortunately, she is not topless. "Hi, Woodchuck!" she says to me brightly. "What brings you here?"

"Just watching the shitshow upstairs."

"You mean all of the girls running around half-naked?"

"That's what I mean, yes."

"Is it possible that you could get your hormones under control and walk me home?"

"It's possible."

"Let me say goodbye to Dizzy and Peter. Meet me outside, okay?"

I step outside into the cool salt air. Things have mostly fallen quiet, save the sounds coming from Dizzy's place and assorted insects making their varied calls into the night. Amanda exits the house in her black Polo and denim skirt and approaches me on the sidewalk. "It's so nice of you to walk me home, Woodchuck," she says as she locks arms with me. "I'm a *little bit* wasted."

"Too much nose candy?"

"Never!" she exclaims drunkenly and sincerely. "I just like Dizzy and Peter and hearing Jake and John. All of your new friends are really harmless. The first night I met Dizzy and Peter, me and one of my friends had just broken up with our boyfriends so we got so shitfaced that we couldn't even walk. We were sitting on a bench outside the Shipwreck crying our eyes out so they gave us piggy-back rides home. And they just walked us up our steps and didn't even come inside or ask us for our phone numbers. We were both waiting for the ol' *'Can we use your bathroom real quick?'* trick so that they could invite themselves in. We were actually somewhat offended that they didn't. So how was your little make out session with Heather?"

I issue a denial. Amanda looks at me with her green eyes like I just told her that one and one equals 15. "She told me at the Shipwreck, Woodchuck, that if she didn't go home with Kevin Dingle- who is a *major* douchebag, by the way- that she would tell Dizzy to invite you over for late night so that she could get butt wasted and hook up with you."

"So I was Heather's Plan B and she had to be snorting a controlled substance to want to kiss me. That's wonderful. That's really fucking wonderful. Thanks, Amanda."

"She finds you intimidating."

"Intimidating? That's ridiculous. I'm just a regular guy."

"You're an attorney as she's some paper pusher that lasted 18 months at Millersville before permanently getting kicked out. So she has some kind of inferiority complex. And she said she was really fat when you knew her."

"I don't date people based on their SATs or what they looked like in third grade, Amanda. Maybe you can be my dating coach."

"I don't know if I'm quite up to the challenge. You couldn't even look me straight in the eye when I sat on your little lap tonight. Confidence issues?"

"You have to admit that you're kinda stunning, Amanda."

"That was a little better. Maybe there's some hope for you after all..."

"Doubt it. I'm quitting while I'm ahead. So tell me about Tony."

"Umm...I live in the city, he lives in the suburbs? I work during the week, he works managing three beer distributorships all weekend and pretty much ignores me? It's not exactly an engagement made in heaven right now."

"Then what is it?"

"I'd rather not talk about it. It's complicated."

"It's *always* complicated, isn't it?"

"This time it really is, Woodchuck. I'd prefer if we changed the subject, cutie."

"That's fine. So...what was the name of the first boy you kissed?"

"It was Tony. The same one we're trying not to talk about."

"Great. Umm...I got nothin', Amanda."

"I have a question for you, Woodchuck. Why are you smooching Heather if you have such a crush on Gina?"

"Who told you that I-"

"I watched you and Gina molest each other on the dance floor for the last hour or so before last call. Mallory and I were placing bets on what time you guys were going to start counting each other's teeth with your tongues in front of the entire dance floor. You can't get away with anything here."

"I kissed Heather because guys are opportunists," I explain. "You never want to have *zero* options. It's all about having enough horses in the stable to build your cavalry of love."

"So you're comparing women to horses in a sex army? You're reaching a new low every minute. And I'm not really all that crazy about it, sweetie. You seem better than that."

"Do you take your old car to the lot when you're shopping for a new one? Or do you sell your old one first and go without a ride for a week or more?"

"You're obnoxious," the blonde giggles.

"I'm just being obnoxious, I guess, because I'm immature and intimidated by your looks."

"Don't be intimidated. What makes me different from anyone else that you may have dated or been friends with?"

"I guess I'm not allowed to say 'exceptionally large breasts and great legs,' am I?"

"Shut up," Amanda says with one of several versions of her beautiful smile that I've had the good fortune to witness tonight. "So have you ever had your heart broken, Woodchuck?"

"I have."

"Poor baby," the blonde says with mock sympathy. "What was her name?"

"There's a few. Kim, Megan, Brigit, Lori...the list goes on. And on. And on."

"Maybe Gina will heal all of your wounds. Her boyfriend is *the* most boring guy I've ever met. And you're cuter than he is."

"He's that bad, huh."

"I was trying to say that you're handsome, Woodchuck."

"Thank you," I say while feeling my cheeks flush red. "Chas is loaded, though."

"So what? I don't know how you could say that. Money isn't everything. What's most important is what's in a person's heart."

"Money don't hurt."

"No, but it's *still* not everything. Why would you care, anyway? You're a lawyer. I'm sure you do *very* well for yourself."

I ignore that last comment as we cross the Seventh Street Bridge and arrive at the Bunny Ranch, a duplex which is directly across the channel from Harry's place. "If things were different right now, I *might* want to kiss you, Amanda," I somehow manage to say without stumbling.

"Hmmm. What happened to your confidence issues?"

"I dunno," I reply. I have nothing clever to say. I blew my load when I said I wanted to kiss her without screwing it up.

"I'm somewhat tempted," the blonde replies sweetly with a smile. I get an excited feeling inside my chest. A window for further negotiation has clearly been opened.

"Somewhat?"

"If things were different right now, I would," she adds.

"Can we just *pretend* that things are different, Amanda? Let's take a ride on the train to the Land of Make Believe."

"We're already there, Woodchuck. You enter as soon as you get off Exit 15 on the Parkway. But you already disqualified yourself tonight after you kissed Heather and felt-up Gina right in front of me."

"Someone was too busy accepting drinks from a plethora of Hot Dudes to pay attention to me."

"*Plethora.* That's *such* an overused SAT word, Woodchuck. You need to come up with something much more clever than that if you want a shot at *these* lips."

"I'm not that clever, Amanda."

"I'm sure you are when you want to be, Mr. Car Buyer. Just be patient with me, please."

"I can do that."

"Good. I can give you a tiny kiss, I guess, just to say goodnight and for being so nice in walking me home."

"I'm fine with that."

"A-MAN-DAAAA!" suddenly calls a voice from the top deck of the Bunny Ranch. It's Amanda's roommate, and she's in quite a mood. "Amanda!" she repeats harshly. "You get up those steps. Right. Now. Is that a ring I see on your hand, woman? I think you need to learn to respect it a little more."

"I think you need to mind your own business when a friend of mine is a gentleman and walks me home late at night," Amanda shoots back.

"I'm not leaving this deck until you get inside this house."

"That's real mature, Tags."

Amanda looks at me and rolls her green eyes. She gives me a peck on the cheek and walks up the steps to the Bunny Ranch on her wonderful legs. She turns while half-way up to flash me a bright smile and give a wave goodbye.

Sunday, June 13, 2010

5:35 p.m.

With the side yard now devoid of vehicles and people on this late Sunday afternoon, I pull the embarrassing Shitmobile off the street and park it onto the property. I always pull it somewhere onto the street on late Friday afternoon for the benefit of my housemates. There's only four parking spots at the side of the house, one of which is permanently reserved by Harry during the weekends that he is down. I like to make my spot available so that someone frazzled from working 50 hours a week for a bunch of assholes can at least claim a coveted parking sport after their 90+ minute drive instead of endlessly circling the area looking for a place to park. It's the least that I can do as someone who's essentially living at 728 for free. I also don't want to advertise that 'the lawyer' drives such a piece of fucking shit.

Once back inside the house, I survey the situation and take the *Falcon* for a spin. The plan is get high and dream of Heather's soft lips and her thin, topless, golden body in my arms as I tackle the necessary Sunday chores. Then, as a reward for a job well done, I'll permit myself to splurge on a $20 order of bacon-wrapped scallops and asparagus from the seafood joint down the street. My routine is quite uneventful and going as planned until I begin vacuuming the carpet in the Slut Room. Lying on the floor near the closet is a pair of black stripper heels; next to them is a small pile of clothes that I immediately recognize to be Mallory's outfit from the previous evening. Sitting atop this pile is a small, lacy black thong that utilizes so little cloth that it should be a violation of trade to charge over six dollars for it. I turn off the vacuum and stare at this worn black thong as if it is a discovery of great import. I have not smelled the *real* scent of a woman in quite some time. And this little black piece of cotton was fortunate enough to be riding up Mallory's crotch all night. The temptation is just too strong for my stoned mind to overcome. I am therefore compelled to sniff Mallory Jacobson's panties.

I reach down to scoop the tangled strand of cloth into my right hand. I take great care to straighten the undergarment until I am able to properly identify the area which was worn directly against Mallory's sex. I lift the cotton of the crotch under my nostrils and inhale deeply. I am able to identify the scent immediately: *coconut balm*. After hours and hours of drinking and dancing and sweating and chasing men, *Mallory Jacobson's crotch smells like coconut balm*. This great mystery is properly placed into a category with the Pyramids at Giza, the creation of the Universe, and how toothpaste is placed into a toothpaste tube. I must take another sniff to verify my findings. As I deeply inhale Mallory's scent once again, I detect laughter coming from directly behind me. Female laughter. I recognize that laugh. I instantly freeze in place, panties still in hand, as the giggling reaches side-splitting proportions. My face is burning with the intensity of an explosion from a twenty megaton nuclear bomb. I turn to face the Girl with the Coconut Balm Crotch, who is holding a beach bag in her hand. She also happens to be taller than I am.

"Gimme those!" Mallory exclaims as she snatches her panties from my hand and tosses them back onto the floor. "You could have just *asked* if you really wanted to sniff my panties!"

"I'm...so sorry."

"You are *so* red right now! *So* red."

"Umm...is there any chance that dinner on me might discourage you from telling people about this little incident?"

"There's a chance, yes. What were you thinking?"

"Scallops and asparagus from the place down the block. Maybe some corn on the cob, too. Anything you want is on me."

"Hmm. Since you're buying, Panty-Sniffing Lawyer Boy, I'll have a lobster tail- the big one- and a side of coconut shrimp. I love anything with coconut."

"I've noticed."

"You're a perv."

"I'm pretty fucking embarrassed."

"You should be."

"Thank you."

"You're welcome. Now go get me my dinner, bitch."

Mallory continues to laugh at me as I exit the room to order our food. Before I've even returned with our dinner, the entire lower unit learns of the incident via Mallory's texting. Stinky blasts off no less than seven messages calling me a pervert, sex offender, loser, butt gerbil putter-inner, a skullfucker and various permutations thereof, including accusations of homosexual pedophilia and having sexual relations with a head of lettuce and a sea otter. Stinky then had the audacity after hurling all of these varied insults at me to demand to know the reasons why I didn't choose to sniff her own panties instead. The simple answer is because she didn't leave a thong on the floor along with a pair of her stripper shoes, but she doesn't find that satisfactory. When a woman wants to know why you passed on sniffing her dirty panties in favor of her roommate's, insecurity has officially been brought down to a whole new level. I drown my embarrassment with a further ride on the *Falcon* before I sit with Mallory in the living room to eat our dinner. This was not the way that I expected to return the favor of yesterday's Italian hoagie (minus provolone and onions) from the Moo Moo.

* * *

New Message: Heather Ball
6/13/10 9:26 p.m.
did we make out last night?

Message to: Heather Ball
6/13/10 9:28 p.m.
Yes. Right after u changed ur
fucking tampon in front of me.

New Message: Heather Ball
6/13/10 9:31 p.m.
omg

New Message: Blotto
6/13/10 9:47 p.m.
The difference between u and me woodchuck
is that i never got caught.

New Message: Heather Ball
6/13/10 9:48 p.m.
still omg

New Message: Alexander Page
6/13/10 9:51 p.m.
weed is a powerful drug

New Message: Amanda Liss
6/13/10 9:51 p.m.
Bad boy...lol

New Message: Gina
6/13/10 9:52 p.m.
great! its fucking invasion of the panty sniffers at 728.
asshole!

Message to: Gina
6/13/10 9:53 p.m.
LMBB

New Message: Gina
6/13/10 9:54 p.m.
whats that supposed 2 mean???

Message to: Gina
6/13/10 9:54 p.m.
Lick My Balls Bitch

New Message: Gina
6/13/10 9:55 p.m.
fuck off pervert

Message to: Gina
6/13/10 9:55 p.m.
Lose my number. Oh wait- u might have to pay ur own cover.

New Message: Gina
6/13/10 9:56 p.m.
i have my own money. i work and pay taxes to support ur lazy ass.

Message to: Gina
6/13/10 9:57 p.m.
Judge much? Thanks anyway.

New Message: Gina
6/13/10 9:59 p.m.
ur so fucking weird. How ru not a virgin.

Message to: Gina
6/13/10 10:00 p.m.
How'd the non compete work out aft i called ur boss 4 u?

New Message: Gina
6/13/10 9:59 p.m.
why? do u want to sniff it? MYOB.

Wednesday, June 16, 2010

8:17 p.m.

My 3L year was a massive clusterfuck in both the bedroom and the classroom. The final year is supposed to bring relief to even the most battered of law students. For the first time, you can catch a slight glimpse of the light at the end of the long, shit-filled sewer that is law school. Soon, you'll be working full-time and presumably making good money. You've finally become so accustomed to reading all the legal bullshit such that a U.S. Supreme Court opinion excerpt that you would have had to read four times as a 1L is now digested after reading only a half-page. You've already taken all of the courses that are necessary to give you a complete overview of the foundations of the American legal system and its pertinent principles. You're ready to take work assignments involving much more discrete and complex issues of law in the context of real-life disputes where hundreds of thousands, or millions, or even billions of dollars are at stake. Most lawyers, law students and law professors believe that a third year of law school isn't even necessary. (Two-year programs were approved for some schools by the American Bar Association beginning in 2008.) There's really only one reason why schools will continue to cling to that third year going forward: they want that tuition money.

My academic performance during my final year can be summarized as follows: it sucked. I earned 2 A's out of my ten courses; the rest were mostly grades of C+ and B-. Looking back, my ten grades of A or A- over the course of six semesters represented a big kick in the crotch. It's not that they weren't important. Those A's provided a much-needed jolt to a transcript that was struggling on life support after the Spring 2L semester and fading fast toward flatlining. The pain comes from knowing that I still had the ability to perform at a high academic level, but my fucking warped brain wouldn't stay straight long enough to allow me to do so consistently. It is pretty difficult to earn an A in law school given the effects of the curve and the fact that your final (and only) exam is graded against every other exam in the class. In law school, that one super smart nerd who wants to be elected D.A. by age 29 *en route* to becoming Chief Justice of the United States can *really* fuck everybody. She'll take the only A in a class of 105 and leave the rest of us fighting for the remainder. I couldn't be that super intelligent nerd (otherwise, I'd have been an architect or astronomer) but I could work smarter than everyone else. I always performed a Google and Westlaw search on every professor teaching one of my classes. I'd uncover all of the law review articles they'd written and I'd try to read every one. That way, you can often get a sense of the professor's political leanings and are able to see how their outside research topics relate to that semester's coursework. You could make a safe bet that any course-related topics that were of interest in the professor's outside research would appear prominently on the final exam in some way, shape or form.

It's even better when a professor who is teaching a class actually practiced law for a decent length of time. Most law professors have never set foot in a courtroom to make an argument on behalf of a living, breathing client. They go to Stanford, Michigan, Cal, Texas, UNC, Georgetown, Chicago, or an Ivy League program on Daddy's dime, graduate with honors, clerk of a federal judge for a year, write legal memos in BigLaw for a year or so and then run for the hills of academia rather than work 80 hours per week for total assholes. (What do you call a lawyer that's unpersuasive? 'Professor.') Every once in a while, though, a professor's name will come up as an attorney of record on some substantial cases and often it's in the same area of law that the they are currently teaching. If you come across such a case as a law student and fail to read and analyze it, you're an asshole. A professor will usually talk about her work in private practice during lecture if she has any, but often they'll hold one or two cases in their back pocket and use them as a basis for a "hypothetical" final exam question. My Antitrust professor once gave a three-question in-class final based almost entirely on a case he argued before the U.S. Court of Appeals for the Fourth Circuit in 1986. We were permitted to bring "any materials or study aids" to the exam room, and I had a well-worn, yellow highlighted copy of that 1986 opinion with me. Grade: A. I definitely deserved it. Lawyers don't memorize the law, which is impossible; they're simply trained on where to find it, and I found it.

Other A's I earned because I had an interest in the material so I'd prioritize it for study purposes. Between work, school and depression, there's no way that I could do all of my reading every semester. I'd do the reading for the courses I liked. I'd walk into exams for some of the other classes without having read hundreds of pages of course material. It wasn't laziness, even though that's what I told myself when I'd administer my hourly mental beatings. I could have handled school and work by themselves, and I could have handled school and major clinical depression by themselves. But school, work and depression was trying to serve three demanding masters simultaneously, in addition to taking my mom to procedures and appointments on occasion. There was simply no time to read and I was apathetic to the world sometimes for weeks. I had no shot to succeed. The score was already 42-0 when I was taken off the bench and put into the game, and I was no Frank Reich. The best that I could do was to try to make a couple of nice plays so the final would be a more respectable 42-21 for the casual fan reading the paper the next morning. Except it was serious law firms, not casual sports fans, that would be reading my scores and stats in the end. And none of them would be the least bit impressed by my body of work.

My Family Law class that I took during my 3L year provides an excellent example of my futility. It was a fucking joke of course in which I earned a whopping C-, even though I attended every class so that I could sit with my friend Lauren Taylor and fantasize about kissing her red lips for three hours each week. The course documented all of the various ways you can get screwed in a divorce or lose your fucking kids. It's usually presented by examining divorce cases from a community property state like California that involve celebrities or socialites that have big assets and hire big lawyers to shield them from their ex'es, thus generating appellate opinions that become precedential. I know why I bombed the in-class final. I slept for approximately 48 minutes the night before. It was my first exam that semester and my terrified mind went into maximum overdrive. Over a course of hours, things went from *'I think I'm a little nervous about my final tomorrow'* to *'Man, my entire life is pretty fucked up right now'* to *'I fucking hate Regina Pellini but I can't give up that pussy because losers like me are hopeless to get real women'* to performing an online search for handguns that could get the job done for under $200. I could use my last available funds and have it in my hands by the end of finals, I thought. I'd be free of all the worry surrounding my grades and career. Maybe I could just pay someone to kill me if I couldn't get the guts to do it myself. I could drain my bank account when my student loan checks cleared the following semester and throw someone $5,000 to put a bullet in my head, couldn't I? Why not? I got so stressed that I wasn't sleeping that night that I couldn't fall asleep even after hours of this constant dark rumination. And I knew the family law material. I just had the misfortune, after sleeping less than an hour the night before due to ridiculous fantasies involving my own death, to fall back asleep in the law library while conducting a final review of my notes. I showed up for the 3-hour exam almost 90 minutes late. There were 10 essay questions. I had only finished 6 when time was called. That's how you get a C- in a joke of a class like Family Law. That's how you kill your GPA. That's how you wind up practicing ShitLaw.

The funny thing is that most law school exams are open book or take-homes. No professor wants to read blue books filled with the sloppy, frenzied, handwritten ramblings of a stressed-out law student on a major caffeine overload, or trudge through 100 incoherent exams written solely from memory after a fruitless, failed attempt to memorize a 700-page textbook full of horseshit. It doesn't matter, anyway, if you have your book next to you and you haven't done the reading at least once already. It's usually far too late to catch-up during the exam. I know this more than anyone. I spent far too much time sitting in examination rooms while desperately flipping through a 20-page index, engaged in a hopeless search for any random term that might describe the legal concept at work in the fact pattern contained within the essay question that was on the table in front of me. It's a scary thing when you read an entire essay question and *none* of the facts presented jog your memory toward any of the course material. Or, I was just too warped to function properly. I remember that I completely ignored the concept of a 'control person' during my Securities Regulation exam for some reason, even though I attended every class because it was held late afternoons on days I wasn't working. I wound up with a B- in large part due to that. I couldn't win for losing.

My performance in the bedroom during my 3L year was much less impressive than even my meager performance in the classroom. I scored no girls that I would consider A's. No B's, either. College and post-college living brought me some very attractive women. Law school? Eh. The semester had started out with some promise. A half-dozen of us met at a Center City bar on the first Tuesday night after school returned to session and Jessica Jenkins became quite intoxicated. I had always thought that she was cute in some way, even though most of my friends disagreed. Too plain, they said. She was thin but completely flat-chested with little definition or curves on her 5'4" body. Sexy, she was not. She wasn't unattractive, though, either. She was kinda just there. Jessica didn't normally stand out in any way, but she had just returned from ten days in Aruba and had a hint of a tan across her normally pale complexion. For some reason, she became very humored by me at some point past her sixth drink. I could sometimes whip out my old personality in public because I enjoyed the company of my friends. It was the beginning of a new academic year and a new semester and I was filled with hope that I wouldn't have a repeat of the 2.55 GPA I earned during the previous Spring. I also did anything I could to hide the fact that I was depressed. Since I thought it was solely a personal failing of mine, I put on an act whenever I could in order to disguise the fact that I was secretly a fucking freak with a warped brain. It's easy to do, since there's no obvious physical sign of the injury. And that night, for some reason, I disguised it very well.

Even though I dislike PDA, Jessica literally backed me into a corner and began to lean in *so* close while we were talking that it would have looked much more awkward to *not* kiss her. So I did. I drove her back to her apartment 20 minutes later and we had sex for 2 hours. I could have sex for hours when I was in my twenties and not taking antidepressants. Besides, it was the first time I'd sex with anyone since my fateful night with my friend Lori DiDominico seven months earlier. Big slumps were the norm in those days. They still are. Sex with Jessica wasn't half-bad. She may have been plain and relatively unsexy, but she kept it clean and knew how to smoke a pole. I could have licked her for hours. We happened to have Corporate Finance on Mondays from 2:30 to 4:55 together. During the first class meeting following our initial romp, Jessica kept looking over toward me every three minutes or so during a very dry lecture on strategies and methods of choosing a capital structure. This frequent eye contact soon gave rise to a prominent distraction in my pants. A man's penis *always* remembers where it's been. And a woman becomes much, much more attractive when you *know* that she will fuck you. Jessica suddenly wasn't so plain anymore when I could get her naked, throw her legs on my shoulders and get her off. My phone began to vibrate. *'round 2 aft class?'* was the message. *'How bout now?'* was my response, which elicited an electronic smiley face but no firm commitment. She was very smart and was the studious type. Jessica was after it, but not so much that she'd jeopardize her GPA over leaving class to have sex when two hours remained in the lecture. Besides, she was a woman. She could get sex whenever she wanted to. She wasn't a desperate fuck like I was. I still remember that second evening with Jessica. She was one of the few girls I've been with that could cum easily during intercourse. It made me feel like I was the biggest stud on Earth, even if I was far, far from it. Nothing can temper the undeniably massive ego boost that comes with having someone underneath you that is moaning and screaming and sweating through ecstasy because of *you*. We spent two additional Monday evenings and Tuesday mornings fucking before she cut me off for a partner at a major law firm that was forty years her senior. Getting ditched for a dude who was 64 years old destroyed whatever boost to my ego and self-esteem that Jessica had provided. It seemed like one of those things that could only happen to me. And let's face it: it was.

By mid-October, I was up to my old tricks again. Any renewed hope I had for the new academic year was soon dust. I never slept. I was missing classes. I wasn't studying as hard as I promised myself I would. Work was demanding, but I was denied private student loans because I was missing payments on my small amount of credit card debt. Often, I had the money but sending in the credit card bill went to the bottom of the list behind school, work, endless commutes between Northeast Philly and Villanova and Center City, and spending hours and hours thinking about putting gun to my head. Without private loans, I was now forced to work just to cover my tuition bill. I was a vulnerable fucking mess. So when I spied an event planner named Regina Pellini making eyes and smiling at me in a Center City bar during one of the handful of times I was social that semester, I had to approach her. She happened to be out on the town with a female classmate who was a jumbo nerd and ranked #1 in our class. I'll refer to her as Pear Butt. I used this classmate to make the introduction.

I don't think I would have made a move on Regina under normal circumstances despite her exciting dark hair/blue eyes combination, large breasts, and very, very pretty face. She was about 30 pounds overweight, which really put a dent in the attractiveness of my two favorite feminine features, the ass and legs. But I myself was 30 pounds underweight, miserable, and fucking crazy. I took the bait. Things were relatively normal with us for the first few weeks and the sex was fantastic. Regina told me that I was so cute and so good to her in bed that it made her heart flutter if we were in the same room together. In the shape I was in, nobody could have said anything sweeter to me and it instantly endeared me to her. However, it soon became apparent that Regina's only redeeming quality was that she was the only woman within a 900 mile radius who would open her legs for me. Even the most unstable women can usually keep up appearances for the first three months of a budding relationship. Regina could not. By Week Four, her happiness and stability became completely reliant upon the amount of time and effort that I would put into our 'relationship,' and Regina became suspicious or jealous of almost everything I did.

Sunday afternoons became torture. Regina could not handle the fact that I chose to watch the Philadelphia Eagles instead of giving her my time and full, undivided attention. If an Iowa game also happened to be televised that weekend, the complaining would be endless and the tears would flow freely and frequently. It didn't matter that I was watching (or, *trying* to watch) the games at her place. After I got tired of Regina's entire production of stomping and complaining and crying all over her apartment whenever a pigskin appeared on her television set, I stopped watching football at her place and instead met some high school buddies or stayed home to watch it with my dad. You're really supposed to watch the game with your dad, anyway. All of the initial giddiness over each other's company and the hot, new sex became replaced by endless calls, text messages and general paranoia every Sunday. This would soon escalate to every other day of the week as well. She would try to keep me on the phone in-between my classes because she feared that I'd use this time to do something as dangerous as studying or making small talk with some of my female classmates. On game days, Regina would begin flooding my phone approximately ten minutes before kick-off. She'd typically start a conversation by saying something very melodramatic and bitter-sounding like, *'I know that your Eagles game is much more important to you than I am, but there's something you said last Tuesday that I really need to discuss with you and we need to discuss it right now.'* Whatever I allegedly said on Tuesday would turn out to be completely insignificant or completely misinterpreted, if I even said it at all. Regina just had a pick a fight in an attempt to pull my attention away from the game. Negative attention is still attention to a disturbed mind. I'll never comprehend how a woman could have been be so insecure and so needy that she couldn't allow me to relax for a few hours out of my hellish schedule to watch a football game in peace- especially when I was already spending 3-4 nights a week at her apartment. And she was so devious. I noticed that my phone would explode whenever the Eagles were in the red zone or the defense had forced a key turnover. *'Is that game STILL on? Why r u ignoring me? Obviously the eagles r still more important than our relationship. Remember that the next time u want a fucking blowjob u piece of shit.'* This was a far cry from the woman whose heart I supposedly made flutter.

After literally crying several times about my habit of watching the Eagles each Sunday, Regina later confessed that she started watching the games herself at the bar down her street. Though she knew nothing about football, the excitement from the crowd after a certain play or the chatter from the nearby drunk males would give her a clue as to which parts of the game were most important and most critical. Certainly, there was not of lack of guys that were willing to explain to a girl with big tits and a pretty face exactly what was happening on the television screen. So when Regina sensed something significant was happening, that's when she'd start launching more texts or go outside to endlessly call me. The effort on her part to break my stones at the most critical junctures of the contests demonstrated how just fucked up and evil Regina truly was.

I put up with this madness for about two months for one reason only: I knew that I looked like hell and felt like hell and was a piece of fucking shit. I was getting pussy stolen by senior citizens, for fuck's sake. My prospects for finding semi-sane replacement pussy for Regina while in this state were nil. Regina represents the kind of poisonous filth that you're forced to date when you're suffering from depression and feel that you are nothing and have nothing. I *had* to date her. Pussy is a drug, and all men are addicts. There is no cure. The same things that made Regina absolutely fucking crazy outside of the bedroom made her a complete freak *in* the bedroom. I knew that the withdrawal following my latest relapse into the world of the wet hole would prove to be cold, lonely, frustrating and ultimately maddening. I couldn't quit cold turkey. Like any other junkie, I would need to hit rock bottom before I made a bold move. That occurred in early December, when I was in the midst of completing, ironically, my take-home Corporate Finance final in my parents' basement. I had told Regina in no uncertain terms that I was cutting myself off from the world during final exams. I made the big mistake of giving her courtesy call that late afternoon before making myself a sandwich. During the call, one of the partners at the firm where I was working part-time buzzed in order to check on the status of an assignment that I had undertaken right before I took ten days off for exams. Regina was livid that I took that call. *'I thought you were cutting everybody off!'* she shrieked just before I hung up on her. *'And how do I know that it really is a work call?!? Are you just cutting ME off during finals and still finding time for work and everyone else that suits your fancy?'* I couldn't understand what was so offensive about taking a work call, or why she even questioned whether it really was a work call in the first place. Her unfounded, suspicious paranoia showed just how crazy she was. Regina continuously launched ten megaton bombs into my phone for a full thirty minutes. *'Ur a liar! You said u weren't taking ANY calls! To me that includes work! What other lies r u telling me!! Ur such an asshole i cant believe i open my legs and fuck u.'*

I couldn't shut off my phone. The partner I had spoken with directed an associate to complete my assignment in my absence, and he asked that I be available for a phone call so that I could relay the progress and findings of my research to him. Once we finally spoke, I shut it down. Regina was relentless. My parents' landline began ringing immediately. I knew that my mom had just fallen asleep on the couch upstairs after a sleepless night filled with pain. I was livid, but I calmly answered the phone and explained to Regina that my mother was sleeping, that it was very important that I take my part-time job seriously, and that I still had my final to complete. It didn't work. She began yapping back in response, trying to out-lawyer the law student by continuing to maintain that I was a 'lying fucking prick' because I said that I wasn't taking 'any' calls during finals yet willingly spoke with people at work. *'If you have time to talk to work, you have time to talk to me!'* she kept yelling. It was an argument that was far beyond ridiculous. Work calls are just a known exception to anything. Regina just couldn't deal with the fact that my attention had turned away from her and toward my finals for two weeks. I hung up on her again. The landline rang a second time. I heard my mother stir and get up from the couch upstairs. I picked up and screamed that I would drive to Regina's apartment, stab her to death, and set her on fire if she called either of my phones ever again. It was actually my dad on the line. He was startled and confused. He yelled back at me for a bit, then said to tell my mother that he would be home late. The phone started ringing again as soon as I hung up. It was Regina. I issued the same threat. I wouldn't have tried to kill her if she called the landline a third time, of course. I still had my final to attend to.

"Who were you yelling at?" my mom asked from upstairs with much concern.

"Regina," I said. "Dad'll be home late."

"Oh," she replied calmly before opening the refrigerator for a Diet Pepsi. My mother met Regina once and immediately recognized that she was nuts. It was odd that she never was able to recognize that same quality in her own son.

Regina's next call was to Pear Butt, my law school classmate who was indirectly responsible for introducing us. Regina asked Pear Butt to help her file a restraining order against me. After having to take a further time out from my final for a very tense thirty-minute conversation with my classmate, Regina agreed not to file it. Pear Butt then sent me a very sanctimonious e-mail stating:

Dear Mr. McShea:

I am writing to confirm the contents of our conversation today. I will not be filing a restraining order against you as a result of today's incident. However, your explicit threat to kill an innocent woman is nothing short of appalling and is conduct unbecoming of a prospective member of the Bar. It is my position that I am bound by the Rules of Professional Conduct to inform both the Dean and the Board of Bar Examiners of your unwarranted and despicable actions. However, Regina has requested that I not do so at this time. Should you make any further threats against Regina, either explicitly or implicitly, I will not hesitate to report these threats to the Dean and the Board immediately. Be advised that I maintain a strong relationship with the Dean and members of Philadelphia's top firms due to my standing at the law school. Kindly consider this communication formal notice that your behavior will continue to be closely monitored by both myself and other members of our community. Your fate is in your own hands. I would implore you to think carefully before taking any action that will reflect poorly on your character and further demonstrate your lack of fitness to be admitted to the Bar of this Commonwealth. I am sending copies to both your school and personal e-mail accounts to ensure its timely receipt.

Sincerely,

Pear Butt

These are the types of people you have to deal with in law school sometimes. And when you're ranked #166, there's not a fucking thing that you can do about it. I stared at my computer screen for what seemed like an eternity. I was livid, which added yet another distraction during finals aside from my fragile mental health and the knowledge that I was again to be pussy-less for who-knows-how-long this time. And how many people utter the words, 'I'll kill you' every day? Probably millions. How many actually *mean* it? Like, two? My own mother and several grade school teachers threatened to kill me no less than 80 times. Even in my fragile mental state, during which I admit to harboring horribly violent thoughts, I would never have killed someone over waking up my mother with a phone call. I was tempted to go straight to the Dean myself. Pear Butt's e-mail was threatening, inappropriate and probably designed to purposely throw off my game during finals, since the ultra-competitive Pear Butt and I had three classes in common that semester. But I trusted the Dean about as far as I could throw her. A battle between the #1 ranked female student and a male student ranked #166 could only end one way, especially when an alleged threat to 'kill' another 'woman' was involved. I didn't need that kind of attention, especially with the lengthy application to take the bar exam on tap. The Dean herself had to sign-off on it. I kept my mouth shut. For the first three weeks of the following semester, the members of Pear Butt's study group would become noticeably tense if I happened to enter an elevator with them or walk past in the library. That really humored all 146 pounds of me. I didn't like it, though, when people I barely knew would greet me as 'Killer' in the hallways before rushing on and out of sight.

Regina didn't fare very well in the end. Three weeks after my own suicide attempt, I learned that she had been found dead in her apartment after overdosing on a combination of alcohol, sleeping pills, and prescription painkillers. Her fiancé had dumped her the previous day. It was obvious that Regina was having some of the same mental problems that I was, but they were unfortunately left untreated. But I was almost taken aback by the lack of sympathy that I had for this event. I guess that's because I never lashed out at others and tried to make them miserable when I was having my own mental problems. I only lashed out at myself. I didn't attend the viewing or the funeral. I had no desire to see Pear Butt or Regina ever again, dead or alive. I did say a silent prayer for the quick and speedy delivery of Regina's soul to wherever it was destined to be. It was the least that I could do. I secretly hoped that she went straight to Hell.

Thursday, June 17, 2010

   2:46 p.m.

   The rain has been pouring outside for hours. I could smell it coming. There's that unmistakable damp, dusty scent carried by the brisk breezes that start rattling the screens just before it begins falling. My wrists and fingers ache from fighting the high action on my crappy but beloved guitar, so I'm forced to put it down for a bit. I primarily played electric blues until I was forced to sell my Fender '72 Reissue Telecaster and 60 watt all-tube amplifier in law school at a huge discount because my car was repossessed. Given my employment history since graduation, I could never afford to replace them. The only thing that remains from all of my years as a guitar player is this old, battered off-brand acoustic that was given to me by a graduating fraternity brother in 1997. But I cherish it like one would a bottle of authentic Irish whisky or a favorite issue of *Playboy*, especially since the person who gifted it, Brother Marc Goldstein, met an untimely end at the age of 24. One day while bound for Sedona to meet his beautiful girlfriend with an engagement ring in hand, he dropped straight off Arizona State Highway 89A somewhere near Jerome, AZ (elev: 5,080 ft.) while traveling alone in his Jeep after a heavy fog suddenly moved in after a storm. It was so typical of Brother Goldstein. He could have shot up I-17 North instead of winding through the mountains, but that would have been far too offensive to his sense of adventure. It's eerie when people come to a literal crossroads, and in the process of making a completely innocent decision they unwittingly choose their own death. It's such a waste to die so young, especially when you're a medical student at the University of Michigan that's determined to become one of the world's best oncologists. That's just how fragile life really is, and sometimes it really sucks. It makes me sick to my stomach when I imagine his girlfriend Rachel sitting inside her hotel room alone awaiting her boyfriend (and a surprise diamond ring), neither of which would ever arrive. I'm saddled with such guilt putzing around getting high and collecting unemployment while I await the start of my next shitty, unchallenging, low-paying, no-help-to-society legal job when someone who wanted to work tirelessly to cure cancer- and had the brains to do it given the right opportunity and the right people- was wastefully taken from this Earth. If only I could be as lucky as Brother Goldstein sometime.

   With my guitar set aside for now, my stoned and lively mind is forced to turn toward the television for stimulation. I'm not much of a TV guy anymore. The only things I watch that aren't in the realm of sports or nature documentaries are the stoner cartoons on FOX and Comedy Central. I'd almost consider television a sin in Angel Bay, save watching the Phillies. There's too much life here on St. Michael's

Sound to waste time in front of the tube. I find Dizzy's endless ADHD-afflicted chatter during our expeditions to be ten times more fascinating than 90% of what's on TV at any given time. I didn't even know that half of the creatures I see on our trips even existed, let alone in a place like New Jersey. Now I notice all of the long, white necks of the great egrets poking out of the marshlands every time I drive on the causeway leading in and out of town. I note the location of all of the osprey nests with the fierce-looking but doting mothers raising the little osprey chicks inside. I wouldn't have noticed things like this only a few short months ago. My mind was still too wrapped-up in constant rumination over the shitty state of my life. All of the bad things- my grades, my job, my bank account, my sex life- continuously replayed over and over in my brain, especially the things in the past that I couldn't ever go back and change. I'd think about the classes that I fucked up four years ago, seethe about how much I hated a job that I'd already lost and never wanted anyway, and how women long gone in my life had rejected me. I spent a lot of time doing that, mostly while lying on my parents' couch at night or driving my car, and all it succeeded in doing was causing crippling insomnia and making me drive like a madman on the highway.

All things considered, my life is still pretty crappy. But at least my mind is mostly my own now. I can turn off the racing, repeating thoughts a majority of the time. They still take hold sometimes when I'm driving. I can feel my chest tighten as I suddenly begin going through over a half-decade of near-negative bank balances in my head and paralyze myself with a mixture of anger and fear over how much longer this constant instability might continue. It tends to happen a lot when I pass a business or a commercial vehicle that belongs to a company that was represented by the firm where I clerked in law school. (You'd be surprised how often this happens. The firm actually represented Angel Bay's largest realtor.) The worst is when a dude who appears to be my age or even much younger pulls up alongside me while driving a $40,000 car with no massive dents, prominent paint scratches, gaping holes, a duct-taped mirror, a crack in the windshield, and the engine actually roars when the light turns green. And it's not like people are just handed these things. Some undoubtedly are, but the rest of them- people like Blotto- just worked hard and earned them for themselves over the course of years.

I sit on the couch with the remote in my hand punching through the guide screens as the rain continues to beat against the windows, the deck and the sliding glass door which opens to a grand view of the water. I've never relied much on TV for entertainment when I think about it. I spent my days as a kid watching *Speed Racer*, *Bugs Bunny* and *The Smurfs*, then moved on to *Star Blazers*, *Gilligan's Island* and *What's Happening* after walking home from St. Ray's. I watched virtually no television in high school; I was too busy playing my guitar on the afternoons that I wasn't working at the local supermarket to earn money for better instruments and bigger amplifiers. I never saw many movies, either. The first reason is because I was never allowed to see R-rated movies, so I missed out on classics like *Friday the 13th* and *Porky's* and *Caddyshack* and all the other flicks of schoolyard legend that my friends were watching with their older brothers. The other reason is that I never went on any movie dates in high school. My shy demeanor and 130-pound body didn't do much to excite any of the girls in the neighborhood. Not that it matters now, as I sit on the couch at a relatively obese 168.

I find myself at Spike TV, which is showing *Star Wars: The Phantom Menace*. It is almost painful to sit and watch this movie. I want to like it, but I can't. I can emphasize with those who claimed that George Lucas 'raped their childhood' after the first *Star Wars* prequel was released in May 1999. I don't find that statement to be one bit melodramatic nor do I dismiss it as the hyperbole of a maniac, convention-going jumbo geek. To say that *Star Wars* is 'just another movie' trivializes its impact on popular culture in the same way as saying that Babe Ruth was just another baseball player, The Beatles were just another band, or Albert Einstein was just another mad scientist fumbling along in a lab somewhere. *Star Wars* became the standard by which every sci-fi, fantasy or adventure movie will be measured for all time. The impact on youth was enormous. All but the coolest of the cool kids and the poorest of the poor kids had some *Star Wars* action figures or spaceships somewhere in their house. I remember that Eddie Baker had his dad drill a small hole in his Boba Fett figure so that he could run some string through it and wear it around his neck all day. And no one made fun of him for doing so except some dirty kids on Crafton Street whose parents were divorced.

Kids watching *Star Wars* today forget that there was a time when people didn't yet know that Darth Vader was Luke Skywalker's father. These days, it's simply presumed that everybody knows that and always knew it. There's a complete loss of perspective among the people who watched the prequels in movie theaters as their first new *Star Wars* releases. The thing that made the original trilogy so effective was that it was so believable. Sure, there were spaceships traveling at light speed and lasers and the Force and intelligent talking robots, but everything was done on a very human scale. The story and the characters were just as fantastic as the special effects or the look of the movie itself. It wasn't too much of a stretch of the imagination to believe that there really *could* be a world like this in a galaxy far, far away. I think that's one of the many reasons why *Star Wars* became so ingrained into popular culture so quickly. The movies stretched your mind, but without bending the bounds of fiction and reality so far that you would stop relating to the happenings on the screen. I only had a problem suspending my belief when a band of cute, tiny, furry Ewoks began taking out a legion of the Empire's purportedly 'best' troops on the forest moon of Endor.

In retrospect, *Return of the Jedi* provided the first glimpse that Lucas was no longer interested in preserving the believability and integrity of spectacular world he had crafted so carefully in his first two movies. His genius already affirmed, Lucas had nothing left to prove to himself or anyone else. His critics and doubters had been forcefully silenced for all time. He was flush with cash. He had earned the right to full artistic and creative freedom. So Lucas changed his path. He turned into Metallica with Bob Rock at the production helm or Aerosmith after they gave up drugs. Both bands remained wildly successful, but did so at the expense of alienating the core fanbase that got them there. Lucas was no different. He lost the edge that separated him from all of the pretenders in the first place. He shifted his focus toward entertaining children, which is ironic since he had feared after the filming of the original *Star Wars* that he had made "a kid's movie." His vision was that of a space opera geared toward the adult crowd, and it just so happened that kids were fascinated by the movie (and its merchandise) just as much as their older brothers and their parents.

The new trilogy was geared toward children entirely. In fact, it pandered to them. It started with an Anakin Skywalker- the future Darth Vader, no less- that was far too young to have any hair on his chest. The adults of the original *Star Wars* generation couldn't identify with that. The kids could, though, and that was all that mattered. Lucas sold out in order to attract the people of the internet and computer generation toward his franchise. They wouldn't have the attention span for a movie that they couldn't fully identify with, or wasn't replete with special effects, spaceships and characters generated by computers instead of painstakingly crafted models and real actors. The same thing happened with professional wrestling. It would be far too boring these days to have Tully Blanchard vs. Magnum T.A. or Jimmy 'Superfly' Snuka vs. The Iron Sheik. They would be pipsqueaks by today's wrestling standards. Now it's The Detonator vs. Human Death Machine in a steel cage match held twenty feet in the air over a shark tank by two combatants that look like they've been shooting-up steroids daily since they were 2. And people eat it up. Wrestling itself isn't the attraction anymore. Everyone knows it's fake, and no one cares. The true fan-pleasers are the fanfare, the fireworks, and the incredibly built bodies that will lead to a disproportionate number of deaths of current and former wrestlers at an early age.

Lucas dressed-up the prequels the same way. He *had* to know that it would look fake, but that the kids wouldn't care. It was like the grand, noble Jedi Knights of the originals had morphed into the Superfriends, and I found that to be too much to take. Jedi didn't just have lightsabers and do the occasional flip during combat anymore; now they were jumping out of skyspeeders and thumbing their noses at the laws of physics by precisely dropping forty stories to grab onto the rear of an already-moving space vehicle that was piloted by a getaway bounty hunter. Yoda was no longer a wise, 800 year-old sage; he could do backflips and jump to Olympic-level heights while batting humans four times his size. I can't accept that a nine year-old flies through a space battle and blows up a robot command ship, either. I don't care if it's the future Darth Vader. The real-life equivalent would be a fourth grader piloting an F-16 into Afghanistan and precisely firing a missile straight into Osama bin Laden's forehead, or Wayne Gretsky scoring an NHL hat trick while in middle school. That's the stuff Disney movies- kid's movies- are made of. Not *Star Wars*. It wasn't supposed to be like that, at least. The first two installments of prequel trilogy were a giant video game designed to market merchandise, and it was shameless. That's all it is to me. The only thing that's powerful and refreshingly original about the first two movies is the score provided by John Williams. It also didn't help matters for Lucas that Peter Jackson managed to blow people's minds with his work on the *Lord of the Rings* trilogy. If only Lucas could have done the same.

I think the biggest sign of the overall failure of the prequels is the fact that that we didn't see the integration of the new characters, themes and dialog into popular culture the way that we did with the originals. *Everybody* knows who Darth Vader and Princess Leia or Jabba the Hutt are; Darth Maul and Padme Amidala, much less so. The $383 million investment partnership created to keep debt off of Enron's allegedly cooked books was called 'Chewco' after Han Solo's wooly companion Chewbacca. Enron's partnership with the California Public Employees Retirement System was called the Joint Energy Development Investment Limited, or JEDI. Think about that: the business entities that were at the heart of one of the greatest corporate collapses and scandals in history took their names from a Wookie and the heroes introduced to the world via the original *Star Wars* trilogy.

Of all of the prequels, *Revenge of the Sith* was decent at least, which confirmed that Lucas still had the ability to wow us at times. My high school buddies used its release as an excuse for us to get together one Saturday afternoon. We all got high in Mike LaForgia's minivan, which he bought after his third kid. It was a somewhat surreal experience being with a bunch of guys you've known for 15 or 20 years (or longer) and you're all sitting in a minivan together smoking weed in the middle of a

135

parking lot, with much of the group being married with kids. Then we devoured half the menu at the nearby diner before hitting the movie. I was so stoned and the film was so intense that I didn't feel right for two hours afterward. I still get chills when I watch certain scenes play out on my DVD, thinking about the emotions that must have been present in the character's minds as everyone's entire world begins to turn inside out and upside down. Drama and imagination is what *Star Wars* is supposed to be about, not slick CGI characters and pod racers involved in an endless video game with a sprinkle of things from the old trilogy thrown in just to add a purportedly authentic-looking element to the movie. The prequels should have been refreshingly original in and of themselves. They weren't. We're just left to wonder what could have been. Ironically, that's exactly how I feel about my own life after age 28.

I turn the television off and survey the weather situation outside. It's still all dark and gray everywhere for as far as my eye can see. I pick up my guitar once again and struggle through some scale exercises until it's time to make myself a pot of stale pasta for dinner.

* * *

Message to: Heather Ball
6/17/10 9:12 p.m.
We need to do it heather.

New Message: Heather Ball
6/17/10 9:27 p.m.
in the fall cutie

Message to: Heather Ball
6/17/10 9:29 p.m.
aka never

New Message: Heather Ball
6/17/10 9:31 p.m.
ur probably right

Message to: Heather Ball
6/17/10 9:31 p.m.
At least ur honest w me.

New Message: Heather Ball
6/17/10 9:32 p.m.
y do u want 2 fuck me anyway

Message to: Heather Ball
6/17/10 9:34 p.m.
Have u looked in a mirror lately?

New Message: Heather Ball
6/17/10 9:38 p.m.
nevermind. ur not getting it.

136

Message to: Heather Ball
6/17/10 9:40 p.m.
Apparently not. On several levels.

New Message: Heather Ball
6/17/10 9:42 p.m.
theres issues on my end

Message to: Heather Ball
6/17/10 9:45 p.m.
Like what? Besides the obvious.

New Message: Heather Ball
6/17/10 9:48 p.m.
female issues

Message to: Heather Ball
6/17/10 9:48 p.m.
I wont pry then.

New Message: Heather Ball
6/17/10 9:49 p.m.
thank you. goodnight sweetie.

New Message: Mallory
6/17/10 9:52 p.m.
Hows my favorite pervert? Thanks again4 the ride
and lobster! C u soon. xoxo

Saturday, June 19, 2010

3:37 a.m.

A ravenous Stinky is now making love to a slice of pepperoni pizza after spending much of the previous hour bawling her beautiful brown eyes out. Last night, the typically smiling, sexy blonde went home with a Hot Dude with "killer abs and a hot chest" to which she had been attracted to for six summers. She fucked him. Tonight at the Shipwreck, just after midnight, Stinky discovered said Hot Dude in a corner of the Disco Room liplocked with "a trashy girl that was dressed like a total slut and wearing the shortest possible skirt that you can buy without having your filthy vadge hanging out." When Stinky approached him about ten minutes later, the guy acted as if he didn't even know her. Such is the life of an attractive, 30 year-old woman who still gives looks paramount consideration when choosing a man. Stinky has failed to account for the fact that every Hot Dude has a bevy of starstruck girls in their early to mid-twenties that are similarly spellbound by six-pack abs and the layers upon layers of muscles in each arm. This makes any woman who has hit 30 imminently disposable. Stinky may represent the top of the mountain for a regular guy like me, but she'd never settle for my kind. Harry ripped her ruthlessly for no less than 20 minutes about her quest for total assholes, and it was hilarious. It was actually a display of kind genius. Harry has now placed Page into the role of 'good cop' to his bad. Page sits next to Stinky on the couch, simultaneously trying to console her and finally score with his #1 crush. It appears to be working, somewhat. The stoned pair is constantly giggling as Stinky's wet eyes turn dry while finishing her pizza.

I remove myself to the Board Room in order to allow Page to operate without an audience. The room is beset the beautiful scent of the most potent of greens. Notably absent are two very attractive women in short skirts who had joined Blotto and Sharkey for the latest meeting of the Board.

"What happened to the girls?" I ask. "I didn't see them leave."

"They climbed out the window," Blotto says dryly. "Seriously. They smoked our weed, then climbed out the fucking window. They said it made them feel like secret agents. It makes me feel like we were once again used for our marijuana. When is some random woman going to use me simply for my body? I did grab a nice view of the one girl's vagina during her climb over the window sill. No panties."

"Which one?" Sharkey asks.

"The blonde. Dina."

"Shaved?"

"Absolutely. Though I'm probably better off not knowing at this point."

"What's your story, Woodchuck?" Sharkey asks of me.

"I got nothin'," I say as I launch myself into a lower bunk.

"That seems to be the theme around here, and it's fucking pathetic," he replies. "Page still wastin' his time talking to that puddle Stinky?"

"Of course."

"She'll never hook-up with anyone relatively cool or normal. And here's yet another one..."

Mallory enters the room in tight black boyshorts and a red Rutgers t-shirt. It's quite a sight. Her cell phone held tightly in right hand like it's made of gold and worth billions. She climbs into the queen next to Blotto, not seeming like her typically pleasant self.

"What's the problem, bitch?" Sharkey asks.

"This guy," she replies predictably.

"Care to elaborate?" queries Blotto.

"He's just...he's just *such* an asshole. A total fucking asshole is what he is."

"Did you catch him sniffing your panties?" chuckles Blotto at my expense.

"I think the *proper* translation," Sharkey offers, "is that Mallory's dude was hanging out with his ex all night instead of her."

"Pretty much," the leggy brunette admits. "I'm so fucking pissed at him."

"I'm here to fuck- I mean, comfort you," Blotto states.

"Thank you," the brunette replies as she snuggles up to the former football star.

"You know, I might as well just come out and say it," speaks the stoned Sharkey suddenly. "I've sniffed your panties, too, Mallory. Last summer. It was Fourth of July weekend, I think. These purple, lacy-looking things. And let me tell you somethin'- they smelled sa-*wheat*."

Mallory begins snickering from the queen as she cuddles up to Blotto.

"What's so funny?" Sharkey asks.

"I was having my period that week," Mallory laughs. Blotto groans before kissing Mallory's forehead.

"Maybe it was the week after," Sharkey muses. "Otherwise, you must have ambrosia between those killer thighs."

"I'll never understand you guys," Mallory says as she begins to run her fingers through Blotto's mop of blonde hair. "Should I just leave my panties hanging from my doorknob every night when I get home, I guess?"

"We'd probably feel less creepy about things that way," Blotto replies. He receives a punch to the chest which sounds throughout the room as a pronounced thud. "Don't damage the shrine," he says coolly.

Mallory's phone now begins blowing up from its spot on the floor next to the bed. She retrieves it with the kind of speed one would expect from somebody with superpowers. "I gotta go," the brunette quickly declares after reading the screen.

"*That* didn't take long," laughs Sharkey as Mallory leaves the queen. "Now go show that guy how pissed off you *really* are by sucking his cock and swallowing his fucking load. That'll teach 'im not to hang out with his ex all night."

Mallory shakes her head as she heads toward the door via her glorious legs.

"Remember to play with the balls, too," Sharkey adds. "Always play with the balls. I'd lick underneath them, if I were you. Otherwise, that ex is goin' to start lookin' better and better every day."

Blotto sighs from the queen. Sharkey laughs at him. Page enters. He dejectedly climbs into an upper bunk.

"Shot down again, huh?" is Sharkey's comment. "Did you even *try?*"

"Yup," Page replies. "She's 'too upset' to hook-up right now."

"Too upset, my *ass*. If some Hot Dude walked into this crackhouse right now, she'd have her lips cemented to his dick like it was tethered to her oxygen supply. It's officially time to give up, Page. It was time to give up about four years ago, actually. You're a fucking jackass."

"Thanks," Page replies with frustration. "Since we're all lying down right about now, who's going to hit the lights? Not it!"

"I'll get it," I reply as the Board Room door opens yet again. Everyone holds their breath, desperately hoping it is a woman who will enter and that the woman is here to see them specifically. It's Gina, dressed in short gray gym shorts and a tight, plain white t-shirt. "Could you hit the lights?" Blotto asks.

"Sure," she replies. "Move over, Woodchuck."

I'm genuinely surprised that Gina has chosen to enter my bunk after exchanging nasty text messages with "the pervert" all week and completely ignoring me at the Shipwreck. I'm not about to protest, though. She places her wonderfully tan right leg across my body, puts her head on my shoulder and rests her hand on my chest. Her body is warm and comfortable- until her t-shirt starts glowing and vibrating. She is still wearing a bra and has her phone stuffed between her tits. In case Chas decides to call randomly at 4 a.m., I guess. "It's Jenna," Gina reports upon pulling her phone from her shirt. "I better go back upstairs." The sexy Italian-

American leaves as quickly as she had arrived. A muted chuckle from every bunk is heard throughout the room. Yet another cell phone goes off. It's Sharkey's this time.

"Let's see what asshole is texting me at four in the morning," he mutters. "Ah!" he then exclaims. "Mary McDonnell! Let's see what this bitch has to say...*what ru doing?* Ha! She might as well just text, *'Drunk. Legs open. Insert cock.'"* Sharkey climbs out of his bunk and heads toward the door. "I guess I'll see you *losers* later," he says with a laugh as he turns all the lights back on and shuts the door behind him.

Monday, June 21, 2010

   9:02 p.m.

   My introduction to the harshness of the modern practice of law came during my disaster of a 3L year. By way of background (that's a lawyer phrase), I was working part-time for a small team of litigators at Goldman Sharper that primarily represented private, closely held corporations within the region that garnered revenues in the $20,000,000 range. There were only seven attorneys at the firm- five partners and two associates- so I wasn't just assigned scraps. I was intimately involved in discovery and motion practice prior to trial on cases big and small. At any one time, we might have been involved in six different matters for a single corporate client and I may have had a hand in all of them. We'd be prosecuting an arbitration action on behalf the company in a dispute as to whether an executive with an employment contract was dismissed for cause; participating as a potentially responsible party in a defense group arising out of an environmental action brought in federal court pursuant to the Superfund law; seeking a declaratory judgment related to an insurance coverage dispute in which millions were at stake; or, even handling a minor car accident case for the daughter of one of the company's vice presidents. We had clients with business interests funded by Mob money. We had clients who were millionaires twenty times over and put every penny earned on the books as best they could. We represented small, struggling businesses. We advised companies whose products were going national. We had clients who were involved in international disputes over hotel properties in Nigeria. I was entrusted with responding to dispositive motions in cases in which we were up against some of the country's biggest firms and millions upon millions of dollars were in dispute. The most shocking thing to me was that our adversaries at some of these reputable firms, for all of their claims of superiority, were cranking out some fairly shitty work product on some of these cases. I guess they didn't care as much about matters in which less than $100,000,000 was at stake. Bottom line, I was exposed to a wide variety of commercial matters and few, if any, law students get such a golden opportunity. I couldn't believe my good fortune.

   I was first hired by the firm after responding to a post pinned to the corkboard outside of career services one day during the spring of my first year. I remember exactly what it said: 'Small, collegial but sophisticated Center City commercial litigation practice seeks eager first year to handle small projects under direct supervision of a partner. 20hs/wk through August.' Not many firms have any use for first-years, so I contacted them immediately and was called for an interview. I marched into Center City wearing my best $125.00 suit and with a copy of my first semester grades, which were respectable. The partner that interviewed me, John McManus, had a picture of my pee wee baseball coach on the windowsill of his 41st floor office. It turns out that it was his younger brother. If you are Irish Catholic in Philadelphia, there is only one degree of separation between you and every other Irish Catholic in every neighborhood in the entire city. Not only did I have the grades, but I had a ready reference that I did not expect. I was in.

It was intimidating working at a real law firm for the first few weeks. You think you know something after your first year of law school, but you really know dogshit. Experienced secretaries know local court procedure and, in some instances, know the law itself better than you do at that point. They spend all day typing legal opinions, memos and correspondence for big cases. The sharper ones start to pick up on things after a while. I recognized this quickly and was smart enough to use the secretaries as a resource rather than strutting around the office trying to show them what a young know-it-all I was. I was only slated to work 20 hours per week, but it was soon increased to 30 and eventually 50 hours once the partners realized that I was quickly getting a handle on things despite my lack of experience. In August, I was invited to work part-time at the firm throughout my 2L year. I didn't think twice about the offer. I was thrilled.

It wasn't easy taking 5 classes and working 20 hours per week during the fall of my 2L year. It was very stressful. When commuting time was factored in, I had about 30 hours less per week to study than my classmates who had nothing better to do than get drunk and high and go to law school. I'm not going to sit here and tell you that I would have spent the entirety of those 30 hours studying. I wouldn't have. I had my guitar to play, after all, and there was plenty of internet pornography to view and I had a handful of mischievous classmates that I had fallen in with. But I can say confidently that I would have spent an extra 10-12 hours per week with a book open, and I had lost the ability to do that. I wasn't too concerned. I'd just have to work smarter.

It was this stressful work/school schedule that made me think that nothing was awry when I began having difficulty sleeping sometime during October of that year. There were no obvious signs or red flags whatsoever to indicate that I was about to drive straight off a cliff during my 2L campaign. Your mind can betray you completely without putting your un-showered self on a street corner banging a Bible and calling for repentance, or deciding that your next pressing task is to paste the walls of your apartment with your own shit. I would simply stare through the darkness toward the ceiling each night and wonder if working during the school year was really the smart thing to do. I juggled my schedule so that I had no classes on

Wednesdays, so I would spend anywhere from 10-14 hours at the firm instead. Friday afternoons I would leave class at noon and drive right down to Center City and work until past 6. I convinced myself that I had made a smart move. In the end, I was not only gaining incredibly valuable experience working real cases for real clients, but the extra income would save me from incurring tens of thousands of dollars in additional student loan debt over two years. That was worth more to me than gold.

It wasn't just my school/work schedule that I began to contemplate, though. I would lie on that couch at night completely torn up over my recent 4-hour love affair with Lori DiDominico. I'd think about how I experienced love-at-first-sight but ultimately failed with my classmate Megan McLaughlin during my first year of law school. I'd think about my ex-girlfriend Kim. I'd think about Georgie Inammorato throwing me inside a dumpster when I was in fourth grade. I thought about how horrible that made me feel. I thought about how powerless I was to stop the abuse because of my slight build, which is still slight to the current day. I could no longer contemplate the possibility of a successful future. Instead, I thought about how none of my attractive classmates seemed interested in me. No one wants to date someone that weighs 146 pounds, right? Women are supposed to be skinny, men are supposed to be manly, and I wasn't. I wasn't much of anything, really. I knew that my grades would suffer because of my work schedule. I just wasn't able to gauge how badly yet. I was slowly becoming a complete mess, and I was as powerless to stop this meltdown as I was to stop Georgie two decades ago. It never occurred to me that it wasn't really my work schedule that was hurting my school performance. It was my own mind.

For reasons that even modern science cannot explain, my brain chemistry was changing. Things had decided to go haywire. These substances didn't ask for my permission or consult me first. I had no idea it was happening. I never realized that there was this vast middle ground where the substances in your brain become so unbalanced for one reason or another that you are on the verge of a debilitating meltdown and no one- yourself included- fully realizes this. I didn't immediately devolve into a drooling idiot or the *heir apparent* to America's most infamous law student, executed serial killer Ted Bundy. My brain's ego and super-ego was left largely intact, preventing me from doing anything that was seriously criminal, oddly perverted, or blatantly socially inappropriate. Instead, I'd ruminate on things long past and other random thoughts that would shoot through my mind that had nothing to do with anything. Then I'd think about them for hours and hours at a time. I'd spend two hours planning my long-awaited violent revenge on Georgie, and I didn't know where he lived or even if he was still alive. Instead of sleeping 7-8 hours a night, I'd get about four hours or so of staggered sleep. I began showing up late for my early morning classes, if I even made them at all. I beat myself up for being too lazy to get off the couch and go to class. But being 'lazy' had nothing to do with it. When you sleep four hours per night, by the time Thursday rolls around it isn't an issue of not *wanting* to get off the couch; you simply *can't*. I'd fall asleep while studying in the law library on the days I wasn't working. I was unmotivated. I rarely left the couch on Saturdays or Sundays, and I often didn't bother to open a book. I tried, because I felt pressure mounting deep inside my chest because I knew that I wasn't studying enough. So I'd pick up a book. My eyes would start getting droopy before my first flip of the page. I'd put the book down. Now I was wide awake for some reason. I'd pick the book back up. I'd feel sleepy again. Put the book back down. Feel awake again. Pick the book back up. This could go on all fucking day as I fought with my body and my mind to let me read. I always lost. My law school friends said that I constantly looked tired, like someone had poured salt directly into my eyes. Of course I was tired. My friends were going to class 15 hours a week, studying twelve, and getting fucked up the rest of the time inside the condos they rented near campus. I was in class for 15, work for 20 to 25, and spent endless hours sitting in traffic on I-95 or I-76 before I even opened a book. That's why I'm always so tired, I told myself.

I still managed a 3.2 GPA for my Fall 2L semester, my lowest showing at that time. Looking back, it was a fucking miracle and a testament to my natural ability to do things that don't involve numbers. But my first grades in the 'C' range appeared on my all-important transcript. Law school isn't like a graduate program, where you'll automatically be dismissed if you earn grades in two classes below a 'B' over the course of your studies. The reason for this is that classes are often graded according to a mandatory curve in order to prevent grade inflation, and a mandatory curve *requires* that some students in every course be assigned grades less than a B. One professor who had a few drinks in him once told me that the grades of B+, B and B- were 'determined practically by a coin flip.' If law school was run like a graduate program, each year might see half of the class dismissed (along with their valuable tuition money) based in large part upon the results of an arbitrary 'coin flip.' But with the glut of lawyers in America, that wouldn't necessarily be a bad thing.

The whispers in the hallway were that Villanova was on a "2.8 curve," which meant that that the average grade for all of the students taking a particular course must be a B-. This can really screw you if you're one of 12 people in an upper-level seminar taught by an adjunct that is bound to follow the curve. Hypothetically, the mandatory curve would dictate that even if all 12 students handed-in final exams of superior quality, some of them could still walk from the class with a grade of C.

145

Otherwise, the class average could never be a 2.8 for that course. A kind professor will usually assign only one grade of A (or even none) in such a small class in order to mitigate the curve's harsh effects. In a larger class, at least some students will inevitably earn C's on their own and the curve balances out itself without screwing anybody. (The running joke is that C = J.D.) Some tenured professors can't be bothered to strictly follow the curve in a class with 100 students. It's too much of a chore. Still, even in courses with 100 students only 2 or 3 A's will be given out. Potential employers know that an 'A' student from schools that operate on a curve like Villanova or Temple or Law School X really is outstanding and that their transcript isn't simply fluff. With the grade legitimacy that a curve provides, the school's rank in U.S. News & World Report is affected positively, which is the motivation behind almost everything a law school does.

By the end of my 2L year, my transcript had been shat upon several times by C-bombs and even a D+. My GPA dipped below a B+ average for the first time. I was still turning in a high quality work product for the firm, even though I knew deep inside that my efficiency had seriously slipped. My mind was wandering all of the time at work, too. My thoughts turned to suicide. With my GPA in tatters, the firm would be my only chance to escape the practice of ShitLaw after graduation. The unwritten rule is that a firm is supposed to make a hiring decision on a law student during the summer following your 2L year. They were riding me hard during that summer, and I responded. The Great Recession had not yet started, and firm was drowning in work. Still, no offer was made. I was sending out resumes with the little spare time that I had and was getting no responses from anybody. I couldn't list my GPA on my resume and, as you might imagine, the lack of a GPA on your resume immediately raises a red flag.

Fortunately, something unexpected happened that summer. The firm got called for trial in August on two cases in consecutive weeks in which a combined $17,000,000 was potentially at issue. People have the mistaken impression that courts are run efficiently and that trials dates are given well in advance, but that's not the case in the massive clusterfuck known as the Philadelphia Court of Common Pleas. Within a few months after a lawsuit is filed, you'll be called down to City Hall and be given a generic Order with deadlines handed out by some patronage clown saying something like, *'This case should be ready for trial on or after May 6, 2006.'* The chances of that case actually trying on May 6 are slim to none, and Slim has his hand on the doorknob and is ready to leave the room. Every firm prepares as if this is the actual trial date, though. You *have* to. You can file a Motion for a Trial Date Certain, which will be summarily denied 99 out of 100 times. A whole host of things can happen to delay a trial. Some other matter on the judge's calendar that's expected to take five days to try winds up running five weeks for one reason for another, judges take vacations, become ill, or a judge will simply delay calling a case for trial because the issues are far too complex for him to understand so he just hopes it settles and goes the fuck away. (Judges in Philadelphia are elected, so merit or legal acumen has nothing to do with getting on the bench. They're really politicians in robes who were able to raise a lot of money, and to put it bluntly some of them are really fucking stupid. At one time, the going rate to get on the official ballot endorsed by the Democratic City Committee for distribution at polling places was $40,000 and a whole lot of *pro bono* work for the party and members of the city's labor unions.) What really winds up happening with cases that are going to be tried is that the judge's tipstaff or clerk will call you Tuesday at 3:30 p.m. on August 9 for the case that was supposed to try May 6 and say, *'You're picking a jury tomorrow. Be in Courtroom 285 at 9:00 a.m. sharp.'* Needless to say, this instantly turns even the most diligent and prepared lawyers into a bunch of human-sized chickens running around with feathers a-flapping but without their heads. The exhibits have to be taken out of storage and dusted off. Clients and witnesses have to be flown in from Houston and Austin and Sacramento on a second's notice and prepped again. At a small firm like the one where I was clerking, it can be a disaster waiting to happen. And in the August following my 2L year, judges pulled this shit in back-to-back weeks. It provided me an outstanding opportunity, however: by default, I was given sole responsibility for the *RedLine Environmental* appeal brief to be filed with the Supreme Court of Pennsylvania. Law clerks simply don't get those kinds of assignments. But I did, and I ran with it. The question to be answered on appeal was as follows:

"Under Pennsylvania law, is the introduction of parol evidence admissible when a purportedly 'fully integrated' Asset Purchase Agreement makes no representations or warranties concerning the basis for Plaintiff's claim of fraud?"

Our case had been thrown out by the trial judge upon a defense motion and we lost the appeal of that decision at the Superior Court level. The Supreme Court was our last chance, and I learned as I read the various trial and appellate court opinions on the subject that it was a complicated issue that had confused the courts themselves for decades. In fact, two different judges of the Philadelphia Court of Common Pleas had answered the same question in opinions handed down during the same week in 1992 and each came to a completely different conclusion based on the same appellate precedents from the 1950s. I worked night and day on that fucking brief when I wasn't running to a courtroom in City Hall to deliver something left at the office or doing quick research on an evidentiary issue on which the trial judge had reserved a ruling from the bench. The attorneys reviewed the brief after trial some days when they could, but they didn't really do much reviewing. They were fucking burnt from a full day of trial when you have to be on your toes every single second and everything you do or say is scrutinized by the judge, a live jury and your own clients. This brief was filed with so little oversight that it actually concerned me. You can't fuck up a Supreme Court brief filed on behalf of one of the firm's biggest clients when over $11,000,000 is potentially at issue. The entire matter sat like a rock in my stomach as we awaited the decision of the Court.

Once school was back in session, I continued working hard. I'd slip into the office sometimes on Saturdays even if I knew I was too distracted to get much done. Just the fact that I was seen on the premises and answered a few e-mails was impressive enough in some of the partners' eyes for someone who was still a student. Some days, I'd somehow make it to the office by 6:30 a.m. and put in some time before heading to my 9 a.m. classes, then I'd come straight back to work at noon until 6. I was running a big risk of burnout, and there was no guarantee I'd even be hired after graduation. The firm hadn't hired a new associate in four years. But during the third week of March, we discovered that the Supreme Court ruled in our favor in the *RedLine Environmental* matter. The firm treated me like I had just been named MVP of the Super Bowl. Mr. McManus called me into his office the following day in order to finally gauge my interest in sticking with the firm permanently. He told me that everyone was impressed with my largely unsupervised work and my dedication to the job. He felt that I had an incredibly bright future in the law and said, quite frankly, that my work product was the most impressive he'd seen from the dozen or so students employed by the firm over the years. We discussed salary during another meeting the following week. It was a small firm, so I didn't expect to be blown away by their offer. It appeared that I would start in the range of $75,000 plus a year-end bonus of $10K-$15K. Since all of the partners except the already-divorced Marcia Goldman were family types, a typical work week would never be more than 55 hours unless the firm was again placed in Trial Hell or you had the misfortune to be jammed up on your own deadlines.

I was fine with my proposed salary. After not working full-time for three years and taking on massive amounts of student loan debt, it would keep me in the basement for a bit longer and I'd probably have to push the Honda past 150,000 miles. But I didn't care. I never had that kind of money in my life. Before I knew it, I would be renting my own house or apartment again. I would have a beloved Corvette, albeit a very used one, before my hair was all gray. I'd keep my Honda as a beater to drive in the snow and become the lone person in America who has a 'My Other Car is a Corvette' bumper sticker on a hunk of shit and it would actually be true. It was a damn good start for me, especially with the way my grades had shaped up. I never had any desire to work 80 hours a week for $135,000 at some legal behemoth that didn't see it fit to confer partnerships upon Irish Catholics until the late 1970s. A formal offer letter would be prepared during the week, I was told. No one at the firm ever asked about my grades. My work product for real-life legal disputes was all the proof the partners needed that I was more than capable.

Mr. McManus again called me into his large corner office overlooking Center City the following week. I marched down the hallway with a big smile on my face, carrying a silver pen engraved with my initials in case I had to sign any necessary papers. My deceased maternal grandfather had given me the pen for my high school graduation. I didn't think too much of the gift at the time (not that I even expected anything from him) but I took it to Iowa with me and always kept it in the top drawer of whatever dresser I was using. When he died during my sophomore year, I realized why he gave it to me- no one ever throws or gives away a pen with their initials on it, so it would always be a simple reminder of him. I walked into Mr. McManus' office with gusto. The expression on his face was grave. "Shut the door and sit down," he said firmly. Marcia Goldman, the firm's primary rainmaker, had received a call from her niece who was attending Berkeley's prestigious Boalt Hall School of Law. She was set to start working for one of San Francisco's top firms, along with her fiancé, in September at a starting salary of $160,000. Her fiancé suddenly dumped her. She certainly couldn't work with him any longer. She didn't even want to be on the West Coast anymore. All of the other big firms from coast to coast had already filled their classes and it was too late to apply for a clerkship with a federal judge. Ms. Goldman offered my job to her niece.

Mr. McManus and one of the other partners took serious issue with this, so it was agreed that the final hiring decision would be made the only fair and objective way possible: by an evaluation of our respective law school transcripts. The look on my face when I heard this must have told the entire story already, so I was straight with Mr. McManus and gave him the truth. There was no ammunition with which he could go up against the partner that provided the bulk of the firm's gravy train. Despite this enormous slap in the face delivered by the firm, I still had to stick around for another month because I needed the money. I had a list of ten assignments on my plate. I finished eight before I broke down and couldn't handle being in the office any longer now that the dream was over and I needed to search for a job. The firm hadn't exactly done anything to inspire my loyalty, either. I handed things over to Mr.

McManus and quietly walked away from my office during the second week of April. I didn't even say goodbye to anybody. I had already lodged the first massive failure of my legal career, and it was under particularly rotten circumstances. The only positive was that I'd have some extra time to study for finals. Of course, Ms. Goldman later sent me an e-mail bitching that I left without completing those two assignments, even though neither of them was under any deadline imposed by rule or court order. Lawyers, especially the female ones, are relentless. I had put my own interests before the firm and its clients, she wrote, and called my work ethic into question. Ms. Goldman let it be known that I would never be welcomed back to the firm should a position ever become available- all because of those two lousy legal memos. Lawyers always like to forget facts that they find inconvenient to their positions. Marcia Goldman always liked to forget that I was actually a law student who needed to find a job and not a full-time lawyer with the firm. In fact, she used to bitch about me taking time off for finals. *'You can't take time off for finals in the real world,'* she'd say very snottily. *'There's 24 hours in a day, and 7 days in a week. There is NEVER an excuse for not getting something done. The first deadline you blow as an attorney will be your first stop in the unemployment line, and I'll be proud to be the one to put you there.'* It certainly made sense that she was divorced. I didn't bother to respond to her e-mail because I just would have called her a cunt.

Mr. McManus and one of the other partners did make some calls on my behalf. Three firms contacted me, all of which were respectable mid-tier firms that had some interesting and complex practice areas. Two of them insisted on having copies of my transcript and verification of my class rank prior to scheduling any interview, despite my strong writing sample and Mr. McManus' unequivocal support. This automatically took me out of the running. Legit firms don't want to see a 2.62 GPA and a class rank of 166 out of 222, no matter how great the *RedLine Environmental* brief was. Academic white trash isn't going to get an invitation to the legal country club, no matter how great of a golfer you might be. The third firm interviewed me twice but instead hired a classmate whose father owned several businesses that could serve as potential source of revenue for the firm. It was already far too late in the hiring game at many places. My lone job offer wound up being from a ShitLaw firm in cahoots with some shady chiropractors and doctors that carried an endless inventory of bullshit neck and back cases. My starting salary was $42,500. After two years honing my skills on legit cases for the firm and three years of law school, I was slated to become an ambulance chaser. I was devastated, even though I knew deep down inside that I had gotten exactly what I deserved.

It didn't seem possible, but I began sleeping even *less*. I literally wanted to die and often fantasized about hurling myself off a bridge. I even conducted research to see which of the several bridges in the area had the span that was set furthest above the water. I learned that two people had jumped from the bridge that was walking distance from my parents' house, the Tacony-Palmyra, and survived. I made a mental note to avoid it if I suddenly became overcome and got the guts to make the final move. The Ben Franklin Bridge that connected Philadelphia with Camden, NJ would be my springboard of choice, since the pedestrian walkway on the Walt Whitman was closed due to sandblasting and other construction. There was still one month to go before my last set of finals. I barely cracked a book and missed a lot of classes. I felt numb to the world. Except for a B+ in Taxation of Partnerships and Corporations, which was earned on the back of my friend Maria, I bombed my final semester. I didn't care. My fate had been sealed long before.

Despite the protest from my sickly mother, I didn't even bother to attend my law school graduation. There was nothing to celebrate. I ordered Jenna's cousin her bouquet of roses before walking down the corner to smoke a few bowls behind the post office. Next on the Graduation Night agenda was a handful sleeping pills. I knew that I had fucked up so badly that the end of my three years would bring only financial, mental and physical pain. I couldn't tolerate seeing the sense of accomplishment and relief on the smiling faces of the much more successful graduates when I had a job offer for only $42,500 in hand. Some of my close friends had starting salaries $90,000 *higher* than mine. But my pain had little to do with greed. I didn't need to make $135K. But I needed a hell of a lot more money than $42,500 with my student loan burden, and I knew I needed a job in which I would actually use my brain or I would drive myself even further out of my mind. I had a law degree but would still be living in my parents' basement well into my thirties. How the hell do you explain *that* to a woman you meet at a bar? I gambled on law school and rolled craps. I'd have no quality of life and would be working solely for the benefit of my creditors for years with nothing tangible like a home or a reliable car to show for it. They only thing I had to my name was a worthless piece of paper from Villanova Law.

I constantly replayed the past two years in my head at all hours of the day, even though I could do nothing to change any of it. I blamed myself for everything. *Wouldn't it have been smarter to take out an extra $20,000 in student loans to keep my grades up instead of working during my 2L year? Couldn't I have at least held my credit intact so I could have taken my 3L year off from work? Couldn't I have tried to hit the books a bit harder despite my grueling schedule?* Studying for the bar became much more of a project than it already was. When a man has no goals and no dreams that are realistic and obtainable, all hope becomes lost. I saw no point in living. I couldn't sit still for more than a few minutes at a time. I would drive and drive and drive the I-95/676/I-76 loop around the city blasting music at deafening volumes for hours every week just to avoid studying. I had nowhere to go. I had no money. I had no pussy. I thought about taking my Honda up to 110 m.p.h. (if it could still go that fast) and driving it straight into a concrete wall along the highway. But I was gutless. I never did the deed.

Even though I spent most of my time driving pointlessly around the city and ruminating about my fucked up life and my own death, I still managed to pass the Pennsylvania and New Jersey bar exams in July. The names of those who pass are published online and appear in all of the local legal periodicals, so everyone knows exactly who failed when the results are released in October. I knew one guy carrying a 3.4 GPA who walked into an $105,000 job litigating copyright and trademark cases and failed the bar exam the first time. He kept his job and passed in February. I knew a girl who graduated with honors and had a $135,000 job who fucking failed it *twice*. Law school grades are not always an accurate indicator of how a person will perform when all of the answers can't be found in one textbook sitting on your coffee table. Students with a C average have gone on to become legal legends in Philadelphia. But firms have nothing else to go on. The person who graduated with honors and fails the bar twice is still deemed far superior and far more intelligent than the guy with a 2.6 who passed the bar exam while fucked out of his mind. And they should be. No one cared about my work product for the firm during law school because I wasn't a lawyer and couldn't sign off on anything I wrote. Your GPA and class rank are the only two metrics that will ever matter. That didn't make much sense to me, but that's the way it is. I'm still pretty bitter, though. I think I have a right to be, even though the rules were set long before I ever attended law school orientation.

I'm fairly certain that God was looking over my shoulder while I was taking the bar exam. Now that I'm an adult, I know that He is no longer out to make my life miserable at every turn. Had I failed, I'm sure that I finally would have crossed the line that separated the internalization of all my self-hatred, jealousy, fear and hopeless despair into overt acts of insanity and unconscionable violence. I searched for Marcia Goldman's niece online after the firm extended my job offer to her. Sure enough, I found several articles about Marna Goldman on the Cal Law websites. She was a member of the moot court and helped organize a Women in the Law forum at school that was attended the three federal judges. I found a few pictures of Marna, too. She was *great* looking. I always admired Jewish girls. The last one to admire me back was during my sophomore year at Iowa. Marna was pretty special with her dark hair, dark eyes, olive skin, great build, and a very fake, very suspicious-looking white smile that screamed 'bitch.' I'd fantasize about raping her for hours. Not only fantasizing about it, but *plotting* it. I'd know exactly where to find her. The security guards in the building all knew me. I'd have no problem getting upstairs to the firm's suite. I'd head straight to my (now her) office. The door did lock, didn't it? Yes, it did. I locked myself out once when I went to take a shit and the office manager had to let me in. Marna would certainly be there, since she wouldn't have enough experience to be sent to court or conduct depositions yet. And I'd strut into that office like the madman I was and slam that big, heavy wooden office door behind me, locking it tight before barricading it with a file cabinet. I'd say something ominous to the bitch like, *Today is not your day, Ms. Goldman.* I'd see the confusion and fear in her big, brown eyes. Confusion turns to terror when she realizes that I mean fucking business. A hard hand right across her fucking face will tend to do that. And another slap. And another. It feels *so* good to finally beat a woman! All they've done is beaten me around for *years. Don't grab that big stapler on your desk, Marna.* That could be a mistake. The piece of metal in my own pocket is much more deadly. She doesn't like the sight of the blade, so she does the only thing she can. She cries. That's all women seem to do these days is cry. Every girl for some reason thinks that her slit is a license to turn on the faucets. I'll pause to enjoy her tears for a bit before I pull her toward me by her hair. *You have such long, beautiful hair, Marna.* And I'll keep pulling and ripping that dark hair of yours violently before I try to tear your skirt off. And I *will* tear that skirt off you, you skinny little Jew bitch. You have such a sexy little body, and since I'm not good enough anymore for girls with skinny, sexy bodies I'm just going to have to fucking take it. You won't like it very much, either. Just like I don't enjoy you taking everything away from me because Seth is apparently a very smart man and decided that you were too much of a fucking bitch to spend the rest of his life with. *You have such a nice little ass, Marna.* A nice little Jewish ass. You cry out in pain as I decide to fuck it. I feel your body rebelling and trying to push back, but I'm coming in whether you like it or not. There's nothing like the tightness of pushing past your asshole, especially when you don't want it. *I'm so sorry that I have to do this to you, Marna.* Just like I was so sorry to hear about your fiancé and your $80,000 pay cut, too. You're only going to make about $85,000 with your bonus this year. How will you survive? How will you be able to admit to your friends in the honors club that you make so little money after the rigors of attending classes 15 hours per week in sunny California for three years? Your classmates with federal clerkships will make almost as much as you will! For a *government* job! But you didn't pay for school, did you? All of that money, all of that fucking money you'll earn after Uncle Sam takes his piece will go right in your own fucking pocket. No government loans. No private loans. I've seen the files, Marna. I know that one of Daddy's companies- The Goldman Group, LLC, I think it was- turned a $6.2 million profit last year. Daddy paid for everything, didn't he? That's why you have to pay right now, Marna. I'm violating you, and I like it. You'll feel the mental pain that I feel every day for the rest of your life. And I'm sure you will, you fucking bitch. One good cut deserves another. *How does it feel, Marna! How does it feel to be bent over and have a stiff cock forced up your fucking asshole! That's what you did to me! Aunt Marsha bent me right over her desk and fucked my life. You whore!* The door to the MY office is shaking and trembling from everyone out in the hallway trying desperately to force it open. People are yelling and screaming and footsteps are rushing all across the gray patterned carpet. I have no worry. I'm ripping Marna apart and I can feel it. I can smell the stench of her blood and her sweat and her shit coming from her body. Each one of her frenzied, tearful screams is more exciting than the last. I release my seed and am dizzy from the rush. I remove my bloody spear from Marna's anus before punching the bitch in the back of the head as hard as I can. She falls unto the floor, her skirt missing and her black stockings ripped to shreds like her little bleeding bare ass now is. With Marna filled with my cum and disposed of, I grab my swivel chair and lock the legs. I'm not going to jail for felony ass rape. No fucking way. I smash the chair repeatedly against the office window until it finally cracks and shatters. The air is cool. I'm so high up that I can see all of the little green treetops stretching and curving down the Delaware River across three different states. It's beautiful. Marna is screaming and crying. My office door is about to burst open. I *have* to jump now. I've finally run out of excuses to live. I don't look down first. It's no use. Changing my mind means prison and 10-20 years of my own ass being raped. I'll never get off on an insanity rap because I'm not insane, right? I'm just a guy who fucked up really badly and committed these crimes in order to finally force myself to kill myself. I jump. I'm in free fall from 41 fucking stories up. There's definitely nothing stopping me. This is for real. It's over. Omigod it's fucking over. Mom's not going to believe this! Something's stuck deep in my throat. It's my heart. I'm dead before I even hit the ground.

* * *

When I sit here on the sound under a sky aflame and listen to the pop of the fish jumping in its calm, orange-tinted waters, I can't even begin to comprehend how badly I was out of my fucking mind for the past five years. The demarcation of reality and insanity is a fragile line at the mercy of cells and chemicals with their own intuitive ways and means of doing things that no one will ever truly understand. And even the most stable man still has a crease of darkness deep inside his mind near the part where his naturally irrational and insatiable sex drive is stored. But few people lie awake at night fantasizing about anally raping a girl that you know exists because you purposely sought her out on the internet, but never met. I couldn't even begin to entertain such thoughts in my brain right now. I couldn't have prior to my second year of law school, either.

Everyone has thought about committing crimes in a hypothetical sense. You wouldn't ever have enough jail space if people could be held criminally liable for mere thoughts. Six of us were once sitting around my fraternity house on a random Tuesday night in the dead of winter while stoned out of our minds. We carefully concocted a plan to rob the First Iowa Bank & Trust of all its available funds, which we estimated to be at least $6,000. We discussed the timing of the police patrols, when the particular block where the bank was located was lit by the sun or when it was cast in shadow, what artificial light sources were in the area, etc. No turn of our plan went un-stoned. Mark Richmann was a bank teller during the previous two summers and provided his keen if indecipherable insight. It was decided that Rob Bird would drive the getaway car, which would be stolen from the driveway of a rival fraternity and replete with Kappa Sigma stickers. Brother Bird once set the land speed record for an '86 Oldsmobile in making it to the liquor store just before closing when practically an entire sorority showed up on our doorstep one evening because their fire alarms and sprinkler system had gone off unexpectedly. There was no other person in which we'd rather trust our fate with federal time on the line. We talked about using the robbery proceeds to buy weed, porn, and expensive lingerie for our girlfriends. Maybe we'd send the pledges over to the Delta Gamma house under the guise of reinstalling their cable lines and have their entire house wired for closed circuit television beamed straight into our rooms in a real-life application of *Revenge of the Nerds*. We had a great laugh about it, and then everybody went to bed or downstairs to the basement to drink cheap beer and play Zoo Keeper in our mini-arcade. The peace and dignity of the State and the Nation would remain safely intact, at least with respect to the instance of the Great Iowa City Bank Robbery of 1999.

In contrast, the hair on my arm stands on end when I think about how close I came to effectuating one of my awful fantasies during the last few years. My super-ego, my own conscience, had melted away to the point where shooting myself in the head became just another life choice. I lost all ability to think into the future. I gave no thought as to how putting a bullet though my head might affect my mother. She always told me that she would jump into my grave with me if I somehow predeceased her. My dad, tough as he is, probably would have dropped dead when he heard the news. Who would have had to identify my body? I'd like to think that I smoked heroin that day because I subconsciously held out some small hope that life really *was* worth living and I knew I'd probably get too blasted to ever finish the job. I never got to the point where my conscience slipped so far away that I'd consider bringing harm to others the way I would bring harm to myself. But I had to be close. Very close. Too fucking close.

If I had failed the bar exam when the results were posted in October, I might have marched right down to my old office and executed my deranged plan against Marna Goldman. It's not the kind of legacy one wants to leave behind, even though there would be people who could view the crime scene, view my body, and speak to the rape victim and still not believe that Patrick McShea could have committed those horrible acts. That's one of the reasons why depression and criminal mental illness perpetuate themselves. I always hid the fact that I was depressed. I'd be sitting on a chair outside a classroom waiting for lecture to begin, thinking about all the endless ways that I could end my own life. A familiar face (or even and unfamiliar one) would walk by and say 'Hello,' which would make me snap out of my thoughts for a spell. I'd force a smile and say 'hi' back, or maybe even start a small conversation. I had to. Otherwise, I was convinced, these regular humans would know how crazy I was. They would *know* that I was weak. They would *know* that I was worthless. They would *know* that I wanted to kill myself. And the women would realize that they shouldn't ever fuck a piece of garbage like me who was going nowhere fast despite the fancy classes he was taking every day and fancy work assignments he was completing every week.

I felt like a freak. My friends were the best therapy, but I didn't always make myself available, worked a lot, was exhausted all of the time, and found that serious study was best a solitary task. I was confident that I was the only person who ever felt the way I did, and I only felt this way in the first place because of my own unique set of circumstances- just like I had convinced myself that I was the 'only kid' at my high school who had ever done something as vile and disgusting as masturbating. Everything that happened with my life was my own fault and wholly of my own doing. I took a job during school because I was too cheap to take on more debt, I thought. And because of my hectic job/work schedule, I stressed myself too much to even sleep at night. And since I didn't sleep at night, I became too lazy to study, too lazy to do anything, and now I'm a piece of fucking shit who's going to drown in student loan debt and still be living with Mom at 40 because I'm a total fucking idiot who deserves ShitLaw and deserves to die and be rid from the face of the Earth. I was convinced that I should left to deal with these many failings myself. I couldn't admit them to anyone else. I couldn't even admit them to myself sometimes. I denied that I had a problem for five fucking years. It's not an easy thing to admit that your own mind is a much more powerful force than you yourself and that you have little control over whatever's really going on in there.

I still don't have 100% control over my mind, but only a robot ever could. Everyone plays the 'what if' game sometimes, but it's always a losing proposition as I try to heal and move onward. My grades and employment history cannot be changed. I can't travel back in time to the Fall of my 2L year and call Dr. Karlis for help immediately. I can't wonder about all of the girls I might have slept with if I wasn't a depressed mess. I can't wonder about the interesting, high-salaried job I might have, or the house I might own, or the car I might be driving if I had performed up to my academic potential. There's no need to contemplate what awful things I might have done to others if I failed the bar exam, or my mom died, or some other untoward event added to the collection of stresses and unbalanced chemicals in my corroding brain. Sometimes I do, though.

I still keep in touch with Mr. McManus. I saw him a week before the summer started at his brother's viewing. He retired from the practice of law to open a restaurant in the Chestnut Hill neighborhood, and business is good. He told me that Marna Goldman left the firm after only eight months because "the pay was insulting." Had I heard that while I was still depressed, I probably would have literally killed her. Fortunately, I never did any awful things to others. I'd like to think that I never would have under any set of circumstances. I certainly wouldn't now. The only things I'd like to kill are the mosquitoes commencing their vigorous post-sunset attack on my skin.

Tuesday, June 22, 2010

> *"Lord, let me be chaste- but not yet."*
>
>   *-St. Augustine*

1:44 p.m.

I like to talk a lot, but the truth is that I've never been comfortable with my own sexuality until I was at the University of Iowa and far away from any strong Irish Catholic influence. It's not that I've ever struggled with my sexual identity or suffered any criminal abuse other than my brief assault at the hands of Franny the Retard, which has been both forgotten and forgiven. It's because it took me *years* to shake the Catholic notion that sex in all its forms is the greatest evil ever bestowed upon mankind, to the point where it's considered truly unfortunate that sex is a biological necessity in order to create life. The first time I ever had sex was traumatic, and I mean that sincerely. I was alone, of course. Before my mother got sick, my parents had a small vacation house three blocks from the water near the tip of the Delaware Bay side of South Jersey. It's not that we were rich; society was just different then. In 1981, my dad was offered an opportunity the buy the "bay house," as he called it, and he seized it. A new development was being constructed in Cape May County on land that was considered undesirable for some reason. I couldn't understand why at the time, but it wasn't because of any environmental issue or anything dangerous. With the gas crisis of the Seventies still fresh in everyone's mind, developers were uncertain if Philadelphians and their suburban neighbors would travel almost 100 miles to a relatively remote and undeveloped area of South Jersey that was mostly filled with retirees and white trash that was so poor that people would use the old backyard outhouse when the water got shut off. Even though the Delaware Bay was only blocks away, the houses were priced as high as the real estate market and regional demographics could possibly allow: the exorbitant sum of $31,000. My dad knew he could bartend during the entire summer at one of the nearby vacation towns and make enough money for the family to swing it. He decided to live the dream.

One hot and humid August night when I was 13, I was lying upstairs in the queen-sized bed in the bay house fruitlessly trying to sleep. My 10 year-old brother was on the other side of the mattress. There was not a breeze to speak of that night. The Hunter fan was spinning in the nearby window but provided no relief. We had those fans forever. To this day, I can still hear the unmistakable, dull, rhythmic hum of the blades when they first start turning at medium speed and the air begins to push through them. I was wearing only a pair of old tightie whities that night and was sweating into the sheets. Air conditioning was not an option. Central air was only for the truly rich. Portable units would wreak too much havoc on the electric bill, I was always told. It was also pointed out repeatedly that Our Lord suffered on the Cross for three hours without the benefit of air conditioning. Even if we had the money, my parents' Irish Catholic consciences would not have permitted the use of such a sinful luxury. I was always told to offer up my discomfort for the souls in purgatory. No one will ever gain Heaven without a healthy measure of willful discomfort, anyway. The hallmark of being Irish Catholic is doing things that you absolutely don't want to do, and experiencing things you definitely don't want to experience, for the benefit of your own and others' souls. In some odd way, I think my Dad took on the second mortgage for the bay house to keep his Irish Catholic conscience in check because it would force him to work harder and leave him with little comfort financially. Comfort always leads to eternal damnation for the McSheas, even if it doesn't for anyone else. That's why virginity and celibacy are revered by the Church. It's the ultimate denial of pleasure and relief to oneself, and will surely put one on a higher cloud in Heaven.

My discomfort on this eventful night wasn't just because of the heat and dreading the return of school in less than two weeks. My penis was in a particularly turgid state for no known reason. I was far too uncomfortable in the heat to be having sexual thoughts, especially with my little brother in such close proximity. My erection was unrelenting nonetheless. There was so much blood flowing through it that it was throbbing and twitching of its own volition. It was poking clear out of the top of my underwear, with the elastic band cutting across a very sensitive area. I tried to ignore it. It was impossible. I'd try to sleep on my left side. My right side. On my back again. Lying on my stomach was certainly not an option. This went on for almost two hours. It was shortly after one a.m. when I finally got out of bed and went into the downstairs bathroom to see if this condition could somehow be remedied. And I fucking remedied it. And once I started my self-made remedy that night, I refused to stop until it was all over. I couldn't have stopped if I tried. It was my first high of any kind and represented the ultimate 'fuck you' to my Irish Catholic repression. In the moment itself, I loved it. My entire body was shaking before it was all over. And it had nothing to do with sex. I wasn't even fantasizing about anybody. I just wanted to get rid of this problem penis and go the fuck to sleep. When it was over, the gravity of what I had just done was immediately apparent. The evidence was everywhere, in fact. I got rid of it the best I could while I dealt with the psychological frenzy starting to run through my brain now that my condition had turned from that of a hormonal beast intent upon releasing its seed at all costs and now back to a normal human male again. I instinctively knew that there was no way that something this intensely pleasurable couldn't be inherently and gravely evil. Surely, I had stained my soul with its first mortal sin. And not only that, I was entirely convinced that the other kids at school couldn't be as evil and perverted as I was in touching my own penis. Not only was I a sinner, but I was the worst kind of sinner: a masturbator. Deep inside, I knew that I was very weak and would probably wind up sinning again.

My knees were still shaking as I exited the bathroom and headed back up the stairs to the sauna disguised as a bedroom. I heard something stir in my parents' room. My father was still out tending bar, so it was my mother that entered the hallway immediately to investigate my activities.

"Why are you awake?" she asked, like sleeping in 88 degree heat in the same bed as my brother with no air conditioning and an ineffective fan was ideal. But it was still cooler than Hell will eventually be, I guess.

"My stomach was bothering me."

"Why didn't you use the upstairs bathroom?"

"I don't know."

"Did you eat or drink anything just now? If you left any crumbs or spilled anything down there, with the Lord as my witness..."

I ignored her and climbed into bed. I was really tired of her whole 'I know that everything you do must be sneaky and evil because of what you did in third grade' act. And the fact that I couldn't be left the fuck alone after such a profound, confusing moment in a young man's life really bugged me. My mom was up my ass 24/7 and there was never any way to escape her in our small Philadelphia rowhome and small bungalow by the bay. She marched down the stairs to inspect the premises. I was terrified that some 'evidence' of my crimes may have remained. I heard lots of lights being turned on and mom stomping through each room to make sure that nothing was out of place or I hadn't left a crumb anywhere. She was convinced that if one single, microscopic speck of food remained anywhere that roaches secretly hidden within the walls would immediately invade by the millions. We even had to clean our trash. I once threw a can of lemonade away without first fully rinsing out the aluminum with warm water and was nearly shot for it. As the only teenager in the household, I was already labeled as the worst offender in the crumbs and spills department. Mom would leave no stone unturned in investigating my activities. My heart was pounding as my mom came back up the stairs. *If she knew what I had just done!* It was bad enough that God Himself and all of my dead relatives already knew. Mom walked back into her own room without comment. I breathed a huge sigh of relief and immediately fell asleep.

I didn't always attach the highest of evils to women and sex. I've been a raging heterosexual from an early age, and it's definitely been for the worse. In kindergarten, we'd line up at dismissal in one row each of boys and girls to walk out of the classroom and down a long flight of concrete steps to the exit and our parents waiting in the schoolyard. While Mrs. Blumenthal had her back turned in order to lead us out the door, I would sometimes hold hands with Melanie Morrisey during our walk down those steps. I don't know how all that business started; what I knew is that I was able to recognize at age 5 that Melanie was blonde and pretty with little pink barrettes in her hair and that I was very attracted to her. She used to look at me with this wide smile with every step until we reached the door and hastily let go of each other so that our activities would remain safely hidden from our mothers. I never ran into her after school because she lived on the 'other' side of Frankford Avenue, and the other side of Frankford Avenue was over eight blocks from our rowhome on Revere Street so it may as well have been in Timbuktu. I used to think about her a lot, though, and I can attest that on several occasions I wound up with a semi-erection while lost in thought about her. I didn't know what sex was or even what a girl looked like naked. I just knew that Melanie had a very pretty smile and I liked it.

When I look back now, it was completely fucked up that I was horny at age 5 and able to trigger blood flow to my little stump of a wee wee. You're supposed to be free of that burden at that young age. And it is a great burden. I'm tired of sanctimonious and self-righteous statements from females about males and their sex drive. If a woman was forced for a single day to switch her ovaries (which produce a *single* sex cell once per month for a finite number of years) with testes (which produce *tens of millions* of sex cells *per day* until death), I think a woman would go absolutely insane by the end of the first conference call of the work day. It's tough to concentrate on business when you're constantly obsessed with thinking about your secretary walking into your office, shutting the door, and giving you the most incredible blowjob along with her best friend. And Heaven forbid if the day of the Big Switch was a Friday or Saturday. It would be quite a sobering experience for a woman to suddenly be saddled with 30,000,000 more reasons to pay attention to an opposite sex that has 29,999,999 less reasons not to give a shit about her existence. Not to mention the increased expense of having to pay for all of those drinks herself.

I remember looking for Melanie on the first day of first grade when I was enrolled in the Catholic school across the street, St. Raymond's. I was disappointed that I didn't see her and assumed that she was continuing her education as a filthy public school heathen. But Sr. Mary Margaret clearly called out the name 'Melanie Morrisey' during roll. I perked up and looked excitedly around the classroom to see if I had somehow missed her and she was indeed in Room 103. Her name was called again. There was no response. I was so disappointed. Circumstances were already intervening to frustrate my progress with girls in the first fucking grade. It was surely a sign. I should have given up on women right then and there.

The end of seventh grade is when I became aware of girls again, even if I didn't touch myself until that August. Once a male starts getting some hair on his balls, pussy becomes obsessive and his mind is burdened by completely unrealistic sexual fantasies every six seconds from puberty to the grave. Threesome, foursomes, fivesome, sixsomes...nothing is beyond a man's perverted imagination. If having sex with one girl is great, sex with three of her friends, too, is even better. Frankly, it's sometimes torture. Like every other young male, I wanted to hook up with many of the cute girls that I knew at school and in the neighborhood. This was a problem for me, because I was painfully shy with women unless they made a real effort to engage me for some reason. I was also subconsciously terrified that my interactions with girls might lead to situations where I'd go past second base and be struck with lightning bolts sent from on high. Plus, all of my beatings had made me feel worthless and lower than fucking dirt. It didn't make any sense to me that someone might find me attractive. I didn't even like looking in the mirror at myself when getting ready for school. I remember having to sit next to Donna DeAngelo for homeroom in eighth grade and it drove me fucking crazy. In Catholic school, you were grouped into 'tracks' based on standardized test performance and your perceived abilities. I was a Track 1 nerd. Donna was in the lowest track, Track 5, so we would only be mixed together during our homeroom period. Like many girls that are considered dumb, Donna was fucking hot and a member of the 'in' crowd. The 'dumb' girls were really much smarter than anyone ever gave them credit for. They knew that grade school and high school would be their only time to shine. That's why they started doing things in sixth grade that other people put off until college. Donna found my existence alone to be completely offensive and never said a word to me. On the first day of eighth grade, she was lean, mean and 14 while fiercely strutting into homeroom on summer legs that were as dark and mysterious to me as the Amazon at midnight would be. I swear that Mr. Olsen used to send her on errands just so he could step out into the hallway and watch her walk to the other end of the building.

Donna took her assigned seat next to me and the following three half-days of homeroom-only instruction were thirteen hours of pure fucking hell. She refused to pull her blue uniform socks up to her knees, which was a status symbol of rebellion among all of the cool girls along with smoking and getting fingered in the local movie theater on Saturday nights. She would have them pulled down just underneath her shapely brown calves, which only served to completely accent them and wreak havoc on my suddenly exploding hormones. For every minute of the next three days, I was obsessed trying to get a good look at her legs out of the corner of my eye without getting caught. I thought I was being discreet until Day Three when Mr. Olsen left the classroom, presumably to take a piss. Donna immediately stood up and sneered, "Stop staring at my legs, Woodchuck, you fuckin' pervert!" and kicked me as hard as she could with her saddle shoes in the shin. Her boyfriend, my nemesis Georgie Inammorato, was also in the classroom. He was not pleased. Georgie walked to my desk and flipped it over with me still in it. That was pretty fucking humiliating. That's the kind of shit you have to put up with when you're in eighth grade and weigh 122 pounds. Most of the girls snickered at me. Most of the guys were deadly quiet and thankful that they hadn't gotten busted staring at Donna themselves. The worst part is that I still had to deal with sitting next to her legs during homeroom for the entire school year. She is solely responsible for unearthing my horrendous obsession with Italian girls and their olive legs, and it appears that it will remain unfulfilled for all time. Still, that lust burns hopelessly strong and I am powerless to stop it. It wouldn't matter if I got to choose the women I'm with, but I don't and never will unless I somehow come into some serious coin or confidence. One usually correlates to the other. As for Donna, she died of a drug overdose at 19. My mother sent a Mass card to the DeAngelos on behalf of our family.

I'm still not completely comfortable with girls almost twenty years later. Most of them are far too intimidating to me in the shape I'm in right now. But I have to laugh every time I hear these self-esteem challenged women in Angel Bay tell me that they 'look like shit.' Women don't realize how attractive they *really* are. And they never will. Women don't see women, and themselves especially, the way that men see women. I'd venture that 99% of men do not care that their girlfriend wore the same outfit two weeks ago, or that she's not wearing make-up on Sunday afternoon, or that her eyes are slightly puffy and red in the morning. It's her features themselves that he's enamored by, and a shower and a little make-up aren't going to change a woman's eye color, the shape of her calves, the shape of her ass, the position of her cheekbones, or the way that her lips part so perfectly when she smiles at her man. A man's attraction to a woman is from head to toe and encompasses *everything*. And few of these things are affected by whether or not a woman is wearing any eye liner or is having a bad hair day. If a man is strongly attracted to a woman, she becomes every bit as hot and sexy to us as any woman on a movie screen or the pages of a swimsuit catalog. Our women are *real*, not some far away, Photoshop fiction in a calendar or on some slick centerfold. I'll never meet Miss July and I really don't care to. But if I do, I'll probably be very disappointed to find out that she isn't *really* turned-on by 'regular guys who are a bit nerdy and shy' like myself. *Playboy* has been selling magazines by giving men false hope for 50 years.

The reason why I reflect on all of this is because I haven't had an erection in five days. No longer having a sex drive is somewhat of a relief right now, but it may possibly be the oddest thing that I have ever experienced- even moreso than my semi at age 5. Morning wood has always been a universal constant, like the tides or the force of gravity and the speed of light. Thoughts of sex now pop into my mind and leave just as quickly, dispersing into the nothingness via the synapses and neurons and neurotransmitters and stray electrical charges present inside of my bruised brain. Instead of thinking about sex every six seconds, it's more like every six minutes or sometimes even every six *hours*. If I had a job, I'd certainly be a billable hour machine right now. I don't even look twice if a young woman passes by me in a tight jogging outfit or a bikini while I'm walking the streets of Angel Bay. The biological processes that stir a man's mind and body whenever an attractive woman is within ten yards are completely absent. My testicles seem vacant. Seeing a woman as just another human is indeed strange. My eyes don't dart around their bodies, sizing up every feature and its proportions while trying to lock in on something that I may find especially enticing or worth fantasizing about later. I hold a conversation with a stunning woman and I don't find myself glancing down at their lips, filled with the desire to kiss them. *Why would I ever want to be anywhere near a girl's dirty mouth?* It's almost like women aren't even there. Now that I have no sexual urges whatsoever, I realize how powerful they truly can be. They're the only reason why I've ever been driven to ever talk to a woman in the first place. Otherwise, why would any man bother? Biology knows we wouldn't. That's why we have functioning balls.

This new and significant change in my body is at the forefront of my mind as I enter the musty old brownstone at 882 Pine Street and walk toward the office in the back. I'm actually early for once, so I sit on the bench outside the closed door of Dr. Karlis' suite as Vivaldi's *The Rite of Spring* plays on the ancient radio nearby. I'm always nervous before a doctor's appointment, even though I know that nothing physically invasive is going to occur and that my lack of sex drive is probably just a side effect of my meds. I release my nervous energy by thumbing through a random issue of *National Geographic* from the pile lying on the table next to the radio. I pause at a photo feature on the numerous natural wonders along the U.S. Rt. 163 Scenic Byway that cuts through the remote landscapes of Southeast Utah. The strikingly unique features of places like Monument Valley State Park, Natural Bridges National Monument, and Valley of the Gods Road are documented in all of their natural splendor. As someone raised in the Rust Belt, I've never seen anything like this before. The landscape looks more like Mars than these same United States. The central photograph shows the silhouette of the stately, ancient Mittens of red and orange rock jutting from Navajo land as the golden light of a cold, cloudy, wintery Utah sunrise softly illuminates the snow-kissed landscape. This odd, striking beauty instantly makes me forget that I am a nervous, unemployed law school failure who can no longer even function as a man. This single photo immediately fills me with the sublime in the form of a personal acknowledgment of the existence of the Deity, a channeling of this country's bygone Manifest Destiny, and a sense of the insignificance of man throughout time.

Then I wonder: how many times has a *lawsuit* elicited such strong feelings? It has happened, to be sure; there have certainly been cases during the history of the United States that filled its lawyers with a sense of noble purpose while they vindicated an oppressed underdog in a triumph of individual rights over the awesome power of the State. But lawyers often relentlessly tear people down all day, sometimes with no reason and no purpose. Is that really the way that I want to live my life going forward? I did a fine job of tearing myself down. Is that what I want to inflict upon others? Unfortunately, my loan burden requires that I work in a high-paying profession, and I will get there eventually as an attorney. I can't wait tables and pay off $90,000. But I'd rather be at Monument Valley taking pictures of the Mittens any day of the week. And I don't even know how to operate a real camera or how the fuck I'd get to Monument Valley in the first place. Maybe Dizzy knows, even though he doesn't seem to be very interested in photographing things that don't have tits or wings.

The nearby door swings open and the balding, gray-haired Dr. Karlis greets me before extending an invitation into his suite. It's odd seeing the couch inside the office. You see the proverbial psychiatrist's couch on television shows and in movies your entire life. You just never think you'll actually be lying on one yourself. "So how are you feeling?" asks the bespeckled 63 year-old after I recline. It's the first question that he always asks before taking a sip from a 16oz bottle of Diet Coke with lime and seating himself in the nearby chair that is so large it might swallow his five-foot, six-inch body whole.

"I'm pretty crappy, Doctor."

"Why."

"Financial stress."

"What's the bank account look like?"

"A little more than two grand."

"That's not 'zero,' is it?"

"Might as well be. My loan payments alone are supposed to be $995 a month. At the last hellhole, I was clearing $568 per week after my contribution to my own health insurance. You try starting from zero, then paying $995 a month right off the top on a salary of $45,000 with car insurance, maintenance, dental work, credit card payments, lunch...the list goes on."

"Aren't your student loans deferred?"

"Most of 'em, yeah."

"Why not all?"

"The private lenders require good faith payments every month."

"How much?"

"About $200."

"Two hundred dollars isn't $995, is it?"

"No."

"We can't worry about things like loan payments that don't exist right now, Mr. McShea. Have you found yourself diving into dumpsters for food yet?"

"No."

"Some of the attorneys I've treated have."

"That's a low standard, isn't it, Doctor?"

"Low. But very real. Some of my patients have drank and gambled and snorted away millions of dollars. You lawyers are an especially destructive bunch. High stress and a high income is often a recipe for disaster. Consider yourself fortunate that your experience will lead to a greater level of perspective and maturity when you begin making the big bucks yourself. Any further suicidal ideation?"

"I think those days are over. I might actually sleep for seven hours straight for two, sometimes three nights per week."

"That's an improvement from zero. Medication seems to be working?"

"It does. Probably too well at this point."

"We'll address that. What about the nightmares?"

"Still have 'em a couple nights per week. During the day, even, if I take a nap for some reason. I don't think they're going anywhere for a while."

"Probably post-traumatic stress. Your father on board yet, McShea?"

"No, Doctor. He's convinced that this is all stress-related. And because of 'the drugs.'"

"It's a convenient scapegoat, isn't it? And one your skeptical father is able to easily understand."

"I guess that's it, yeah."

"So he wants you working again."

"Yes."

"Right away."

"Of course."

"Tomorrow isn't soon enough to have a new job."

"Exactly."

"You'd agree with me that most working Americans experience some form of stress, don't they, Mr. McShea?"

"Certainly."

"Overworked, underpaid, a real dickknocker for a boss, office politics, asshole co-workers, that type of stuff..."

"Everyone does, Doctor."

"Do they all drive down to Kensington Avenue to grab a bag of smack and a gun?"

"Of course not."

"Have you tried to explain this to your father?"

"I'd rather not deal with that. I had a hard enough time convincing *myself* that I had a real problem. I thought it was all stress-related, too. My dad thinks it all boils down to my false sense of entitlement. Since I didn't walk into a $100,000 job with a reputable firm after graduation, now he thinks I'm rebelling in the office and somehow trying to flush my own career down the toilet. I've gotten lecture after lecture about how he taught Catholic school for $13,000 a year in the Seventies. He thinks $42,500 out of law school might as well be a million."

"Do you happen to know how much your parents paid for their home?" asks Dr. Karlis.

"I think, $22,500. And it's paid off now."

"Your father never heard of the housing bubble, I take it. Do you think that you could find yourself a house or a condo in a decent neighborhood for about twice your salary these days?"

"Twice my salary is zero, Doctor."

"I meant, twice your past or prospective salary."

"Not in a million years. Not to mention my credit hurdles. The Philadelphia real estate market is completely screwed up right now. There are townhouses selling for $425,000 that are one block from the ghetto and you come out for work in the morning to an open-air drug market right on your corner and chalk lines in the street. But I don't need to convince my dad or anyone else that I was legitimately fucked up. If trying to blow myself away and getting fired from three jobs in a row wasn't enough to make him believe that I have a serious mental health problem, nothing ever will."

"Fair enough. Think you're ready to start poking around for a job?"

"I have been. It sucks."

"Of course it sucks. Looking for a job is boring, tedious, and can be quite stressful. And the goal we have set here is to limit your stress to acceptable levels before you throw your suit back on and jump into the lawyer game again. Just don't expect to hit the first pitch out of the ballpark, especially in this economy. You need to stay strong and prepare yourself for the possibility that it may take as long for you to crawl out of the this hole as it took you to get trapped inside it."

I've come to recognize this fact, and I'm not happy about it. I can't imagine waiting until 2015 to achieve some measure of stability. But it's a possibility. It's very possible. Too possible.

"There is a light at the end of the tunnel," Dr. Karlis tries to assure me, "and right now it may seem like a pinhole. With each passing day, that pinhole becomes larger and larger and larger and eventually you will find yourself basking in the sunshine again. But there is no timetable. Setting timetables in this instance will just give you another reason to believe that you are failing when you are really progressing. And progress is not always linear. Things could change for the better with one phone call, or there may be peaks and valleys. But there will always be a light in front of you. And do you know what that light is called?"

"It's not Jesus, is it?"

"No. It's much simpler than that. The light is the future. We need to put the past behind you and get it out of the rear view mirror. Living in the past will never help you move forward."

"I think the only thing that's going to help me move forward is some success."

"Aren't you successful now? You're a young, handsome man with a law degree."

"I don't consider myself much of a success, Doctor."

"If you measure success by what kind of car you drive, or how big your house is, or which country club you belong to, then, of course, you are not successful. But that's not what 'success' is. Success is falling down ten times and getting up eleven. You fell down hard. And you dusted yourself off and got right back up. How is that a lack of success?"

"I'm not trying to be greedy, Doctor. I just want to survive."

"Aren't you surviving now? You're living, breathing, you have family, you have friends..."

"I mean, survival with money."

"There's nothing wrong with the security money can provide. That's completely understandable. But security takes time. And patience. And common sense. So who are you fucking these days?"

"Umm...nothing has changed on that front, Doctor."

"Why not?"

"No finance, no romance."

"Did you ever stop to think that some woman might just appreciate you for who you are, and not what you have? Or don't have?"

"This is Philadelphia in the year 2010, Doctor. We just spoke about housing prices. This isn't *Leave It to Beaver* where a house with a white picket fence in the suburbs costs $4,000. I won't be able to be a provider for years. And in a city and region of millions, there's plenty of providers out there for these women."

"Who says you need to be a provider?"

"Women in their thirties are brutal, Doctor. *'Do you want kids?'* comes up within 24 hours of meeting someone sometimes. They start jumping the gun from Minute One. I can't afford a fucking kid. I don't want one. If I'm able to put this past me, I want peace and quiet and money to spend on myself- not on baby formula and diapers and a mortgage. I can't fuck right now, anyway."

"Why not?"

"I don't think it works any longer."

"By 'it,' do you mean your hammer?"

"Yes, Doctor."

"You know the difference between 'anxiety' and 'panic,' don't you?" he asks.

"I don't."

"'Anxiety' is the first time you can't get it up a second time. 'Panic' is the second time you can't get it up the first time. So which are you?"

"I'm anxious, I think. Or panicked. I don't really know."

"You don't know?"

"No. I just woke up this week and I was-"

"Flat as a pancake."

"Yes. It's dead. It's fucking dead. It urinates. That's it."

"Not an uncommon side effect with your medication," the doctor explains. "I can prescribe another pill to counteract the diminution in your sex drive, if you'd like."

"I'd like that. Is it expensive?"

"There's a generic. But think about this for a second, first. Some people feel much more focused without a preoccupation with sex. They become more driven in other ways. Your mind becomes free to explore other areas and avenues of interest, unburdened by the inevitable fantasy that enters the brain several times per minute."

"I think I'd rather have a functioning dick, Doctor. I thought I'd like taking a vacation from my sex drive, but it's way too weird and unnatural. I mean, there aren't many things in my life that are actually pleasurable right now. That's my only chance."

"If you're living in Angel Bay for the summer, I'd recommend the supplemental medication," says the doctor. "I have a hunch that you don't want word getting around St. Michael's Sound that Patrick McShea is a gelding instead of a stud."

Wednesday, June 23, 2010

7:27 p.m.

I returned to Angel Bay immediately following my appointment with Dr. Karlis yesterday. I didn't even stop home to see my parents. I feel like such a failure. I see no need to face them. I'll be back in their basement soon enough. Upon arriving at an empty 728, I hopped on a kayak before making myself a pretty shitty dinner. While out on the water, I encountered a very strange bird with bluish-purple feathers that was clearly drunk. It ran and stumbled and tripped through a large area of the sound at low tide while searching for fish to eat. Prior to striking the water with its pinkish, spear-like beak, the bird would get its apparent intoxication under control and raise its beautifully-feathered wings for one second before quickly striking for prey. I think it nailed a fish 3 out of 4 times. I had never seen anything like it. I reported the sighting to Dizzy, who was back in Philly on donut business, via text upon returning to the house. Consequently, the two of us have now been anchored near the Old Wharf for over six hours while Dizzy has a camera with a massive lens set up on a tripod. He is convinced that if this unknown drunken bird were to re-appear in Angel Bay that it would be here at the Old Wharf among the other wading birds where the fishing is plentiful. Dizzy suspects that I saw a tricolored heron while on my solo run, but after viewing several images on Google I was convinced that I had indeed seen something similar but something else. To pass the time, we have been smoking weed and drinking Gatorade over Dizzy's constant chatter about anything and everything. He has also been photographing a number of diving common terns for over an hour. A dozen of these birds have been tweeting like hell and hunting for fish next to the boat for most of the day, and it's become entertaining watching Dizzy trying to capture the action as the birds move at breakneck speed. He gets excited whenever a particularly clear or cool-looking exposure of the birds as they emerge from the water with dinner is captured. Dizzy uses the common tern to make his own point about women.

"Everything you need to know about the interaction of the opposite sex, you can learn right here in this marsh," he declares. Dizzy points to a small bird with a white breast, gray-feathered wings, and a black head with black eyes that sits alone on a piece of driftwood near where the line of green grass begins. "That's a female tern," Dizzy begins to explain. "The female-"

"How do you know it's a female?" I ask. "Do you use that big lens to see into its vagina?"

"No, smartass," he replies sharply. Dizzy can get quite testy if you mock his bird photographing activities, like earlier this afternoon when he repeated called me a cockgobbler and threatened to throw me overboard after I asked him if he tracks certain birds by tracing their shit patterns floating in the water. "You can tell it's a female, Woodchuck, because like its human counterpart she's a fucking whore," he continues. "All she does is sit there on her *ass* and wait for a male to bring her over a fish as a bribe to mate with her. The message here is clear: if you want my pussy, then I want my fish, bitch. It's amazing how animals and humans are similar in so many fundamental respects. Women just have to sit there and have all of us assholes fight over them simply because they have a pussy. Think about it: some animals fight to the *death* to be inside a pussy. To the death! Do you ever read *National Geographic?*"

"I was reading it at my doctor's office yesterday," I reply as Molly exits the cabin, where the hairy bitch was hiding from the harsh sun. She approaches and sits next to me, placing her right front paw on my lap. It's her signal to commence petting at once. I comply.

"A year or so ago, *National Geographic* ran this story about these pink dolphins that were found swimming around in the Amazon," Dizzy begins as I run my hands through Molly's soft fur. "Weird-looking things, man. After doing some more research, they discovered that the dolphins really weren't pink. They were gray like most other dolphin species. Their pink skin was scar tissue from the males constantly beating the fuck out of each other to attract the attention of the females. It's no different than some of these younger dickheads we see at the Shipwreck every weekend. Females have *such* an unfair advantage because of their pussy. The good part about it is that most of 'em are too stupid to realize it."

"You don't seem to be hurting for women."

"I'm not. But women that I actually *like?* That's something beyond the simple *lust* stage? I'm no different than anyone else, brother. I get all tongue-tied and twisted-up and have to compete with every other asshole out there. It's frustrating sometimes. Getting ass is *easy*. Getting ass you actually *want?* That's a topic for a different day. I don't have an answer for that right now. Speaking of ass I don't want, I think I created a problem last Saturday night."

"Explain."

"I'm lying on my living room couch piss drunk with a serious coke hangover at about 4:00 a.m. You left my place at a good time, man."

"Being only stoned and not being drunk, I can sense when things are about to spiral completely out of control. It's like a sixth sense."

"Well, things did spiral out of control," Dizzy laughs. "The chicks all start crying over these total assholes that won't fuck them, Heather's nose won't stop bleeding- surprise, surprise- and all this other bullshit starts happening. People are screaming about calling for help for Heather, which is going to bring the cops to a house filled with weed and coke and E, so I send her out of the house and leave my own room to sleep downstairs on the couch. My phone starts blowing up. For some reason, I actually bothered to check it. I have no idea why. So it's Stinky. She's like, *'I need company.'* So I text back, *'Isnt page or anyone at ur house?'* So then she's like, *'I need UR company.'* So I'm all fucked up and I'm like, *'Just come over.'* I really just wanted her to stop texting me. So in the ten minutes it takes her to pull herself together and walk over to my place, I pass the fuck out. She wakes me up, and then asks if the couch pulls out. It does. So I get up- somehow- and pull the couch out. I lie down. Molly jumps up with me. I can't even speak at this point. Stinky doesn't say a word and starts pulling off my shorts. Next thing I know, she's giving me head. She didn't say a fucking word, man. I pull out the couch, she starts sucking my cock. Can you imagine doing that to a woman? You'd go to jail for ten years, man! I can't cum, naturally, so she eventually gives up asks if I have any protection. I don't. She hops on top anyway and rides me like a bull for almost a half-hour. Right in front of Molly, too. I never have sex in front of her. She's almost human to me."

"Were you scarred for life, Molly?" I ask the panting, smiling dog. She looks at me with her brown eyes before looking back toward her master.

"It makes me feel dirty, man," Dizzy explains. "It's like having sex in front of your daughter. I don't know how I even stayed awake through the whole thing, quite honestly. The sun's coming up by this point. So Stinky gets off, literally, and passes out next to me. So when we wake up, she's like, *'Take me to breakfast.'* Now first, I was miserably tired, depressed and hungover so I wasn't going *anywhere.* Second, I didn't want to be seen out on the town with her in case we ran into Page. And third, I don't want her getting any ideas that we now have a budding romance just because she practically raped me. So I just roll over and snuggle with Molly, and she storms out pissed off and crying. Is she hot? Yeah. Is she a fucking mess? Definitely. So do I bother to tell Page, or what?"

"I'd file this one under, 'What you don't know won't hurt you.' She actually turned him down on Saturday night about a half-hour before she texted you. Said she was 'too upset.'"

"See? Now I feel like an asshole. Thanks."

"You're welcome."

"Women are such whores, aren't they?"

"Yup. Except Molly. Right, pretty girl?"

The dog looks up to me and smiles as if she knows she's been paid a compliment.   She probably does know.   I'm convinced that she completely understands spoken English.

"I hate to hide shit from Page," says Dizzy, "but you're right, Woodchuck. What he don't know can't hurt 'im. He'd do the same fucking thing if the roles were reversed, anyway.   When you're drunk and some hot chick starts pulling off your shorts, no one ever really says no. Not that I was even able to." Dizzy then begins to look through his viewfinder at the tern sitting on the driftwood. "You know what the entire secret to getting women is, Woodchuck?" he suddenly asks.

"Sure. Enlighten me."

"It isn't really always about looks, or at least it shouldn't be at this point in life. For women, at least. Guys will never change. It's not always the guy who's able to provide the fish, either, although that doesn't hurt. There's a reason why all of these asshole birds are continuing to dive all around the boat for fish, and it's because it works. But to me, it's all about finding religion. I don't necessarily mean God, but it could be if you're so inclined. But you need to find something in your life that you're so passionate about that it gives you a similar kind of excited feeling in your chest like when you're excited about a new woman in your life. Now don't get me wrong: there is *nothing* like being excited about a new, attractive woman in your life. *Nothing* duplicates that high, at least nothing that we'll ever experience in our lifetimes because we'll never sell out the Spectrum, or play in the World Series, or throw the winning touchdown pass in the Super Bowl. Now for me, my religion is my photography. When I check the tide charts and see that the low tide coincides with the soft light of the rising or setting sun, I get excited for *days* thinking about the opportunity for photography under those perfect conditions.   Women don't understand that. Or *won't* understand that. Women can't understand how anything can excite you other than a relationship or a job promotion. See, most women don't have hobbies. Their passions are usually jogging, drinking, crying and shopping for shoes. Maggie used to jog a lot. If she got up at 6 or 7 on a Saturday morning to go for a run, I didn't give a fuck. That was her thing, man, and I wasn't going to get in the way even though I would have rather had her lying in bed next to me naked. But if you can find something that gets you almost as excited as a new woman in your life, whether it's your guitar or even if you score a job in some really interesting law practice, women lose the total grip that they've had on you since you were 13 just as they themselves are peaking sexually. If you can't get pussy in your thirties, you'll *never* get it. It's the one point in a man's life where the woman no longer holds all of the cards. A man can start to sometimes think about things other than pussy. Very briefly, but you can. And that brings confidence. You don't need to place all your happiness in a woman any longer. You have some coin. You have your religion. And as soon as women sense that you may have things in your life that may be more important to you than *they* are, it completely puzzles them. It's like bees flocking into a hive at that point. Except the hive is in your pants, and there's always room for more bees."

Dizzy stops speaking and starts rapidly firing off his camera, which is still aimed steadily at the female tern on the driftwood. For the first time today, a male tern is hovering just over her left. Not only is the sun illuminating the fluttering bird perfectly, but it is also not obscuring the female in Dizzy's lens. She opens her orange beak as if she is smiling. The male continues to hover, then offers the fish into the beak of the waiting female. Dizzy dials through his results of this exchange and seems pretty excited. *"All* day I waited to get this shot, Woodchuck!" he exclaims. "All fucking day. But it was totally worth it. I just captured nature. It's the entire cycle of life and death, man. Fish is swimming around, fish is captured, fish dies, terns mate, new chicks are eventually born. Now that's what I'm talkin' about. That's my religion."

Dizzy surveys the position of the sun in the sky and checks the time on his cell phone. "Looks like capturing this alleged drunk bird will have to wait for another day," he says. "I want to get back to my place before dusk and give Molly a b-a-t-h. I can't say the word. She'll hide in the cabin and not leave it. And's she a bitch to carry up the dock, especially at low tide." Dizzy orders the anchors raised and we cruise back through the sound under a low-lying sun hanging in a cloudless sky.

New Message: Amanda Liss
6/28/10 9:02 p.m.
I am SO sorry for last Sat. Seriously.
I couldn't stop crying over it.

Message to: Amanda Liss
6/28/10 9:14 p.m.
Don't worry abt it.

New Message: Amanda Liss
6/28/10 9:16 p.m.
I will make it up 2 u. I promise!

Message to: Amanda Liss
6/28/10 9:17 p.m.
Looking fwd 2 it.

New Message: Amanda Liss
6/28/10 9:17 p.m.
U should be! I will see u thurs.

Thursday, July 1, 2010

When a man sits with a pretty girl for an hour, it seems like a minute. But let him sit on a hot stove for a minute and it's longer than any hour. That's relativity.

- Albert Einstein

7:15 p.m.

A new month has brought new trials. The 'highlight' of last weekend was the first Angel Bay appearance of Amanda's fiancé, Tony the Douchebag, after he took a rare weekend off from work. He was massive, and he looked exactly what you would expect a douchebag named Tony to look like except his dark, slick-backed hair is clearly unable to respond to Rogaine in any appreciable way. At approximately 2:25 a.m. on Saturday night, Amanda greeted me much too enthusiastically for Tony's tastes when I saw her at the Moo Moo at while I was in search of a soft pretzel, a 7UP, and any drunk woman that might want to take me home. Once outside, Tony unexpectedly grabbed me from behind and repeatedly slammed me into the nearest parked car. My entire body hurt like hell afterward, but I was uninjured. I didn't even mention it to the Board or Dizzy because I knew it would lead to Bloodbath at the Bunny Ranch and Amanda was already pretty upset about it. She has agreed to cook me dinner as an apology and has placed Tony the D-Bag on 'probation' as a result of this incident, whatever the fuck that means. She probably won't blow him for a week and then everything will return to normal.

I'm not concerned about the status of Amanda and Tony's relationship, though. My only focus tonight is the meal itself. I am absolutely starving as I leave for the Bunny Ranch in a white Iowa golf shirt and the same pair of khaki shorts that I wash about every seven days or so. I feel like such a beaten man. I have spent my entire day vomiting due to stress. Dr. Karlis' light at the end of the tunnel has been reduced to a size so small that I'd need an electron scanning microscope and a pair of mighty magnifying goggles to see it. My last receipt from the ATM at the Moo Moo has revealed that my lone bank account has an available balance of $0.67. That's not a typo. After seven years of schooling, running back and forth between class and work like a lunatic, bar preparations, aggravation, frustration and $90,000 in combined student loan debt, I have sixty-seven fucking cents to my name. I stared at the receipt for about ten minutes. The numbers didn't change. It quite literally made me sick. It was only within the last hour that I stopped vomiting and my stomach finally settled down. I'd still be puking if my mother hadn't volunteered to FedEx $100 to me that will arrive tomorrow.

Amanda had called and asked me to bring a bottle of wine to dinner. I initially agreed out of habit, then had to call her back and tell her that I had no coin "because I lost my ATM card." It's pathetic that I couldn't even bring this girl a bottle of wine to compliment the free meal. I can't even afford a fresh pack of gum to constantly chew the rotten taste out of my mouth. I'm stoned, though. Really fucking stoned.

My bankrupt bank balance is because of last night. I awoke with pain in my mouth at approximately 3:30 a.m. I immediately knew what it was. My dentist had warned me six months ago that I had two very deep cavities in two molars that would eventually require root canal. I had no coin and my low-rent law firm offered no dental insurance, so I put the treatment off as long as possible. Consequently, both of these teeth decided to become infected. The pain from an infected tooth is unbearable. It starts rather calmly, feeling like a piece of chicken or meat stuck between two teeth. Except, of course, you can't remove it because it's actually inside of the tooth itself. This becomes annoying. Then this piece of food that you can't remove starts to throb and itch, and you certainly can't scratch your tooth to gain any relief. The pain continues to throb and sometimes turns sharp, feeling like bolts of electricity coursing through your mouth. Pus and other agents pour into your tooth below the gum line. Since these substances can't go anywhere because of the crown of your tooth above, they expand outward forcing a large, painful bubble to form in your gum below the infected teeth. The pain becomes so unbearable that you can't even sit still. And if left untreated, of course, the infection can kill you.

Come morning, I found an endodontist in Cape May County that agreed to see me on an emergency basis. Treatment for my two infected abscessed teeth (including scraping the bacteria from the infection from my jawbone), the antibiotics, and the hydrocodone script that I couldn't help but fill have unexpectedly set me back $2,140. This does not include $1,400 worth of crowns that these teeth will also need; nor does it include the cost of a crown for another tooth that received root canal almost a year ago. When I finally am working again, I feel like half of my income will be going straight into my mouth. The other half will be going toward my loans, of course. None of the money will make it into my own pocket for years.

I walk across the Seventh Street Bridge to the top floor of a small bi-level directly on the sound and ring the bell. I am greeted by a curly-haired brunette with dark eyes and olive skin that stands about 5'5". She is presumably Italian and is very good-looking, but not very pleasant. Then I realize that it's Amanda's roommate Tags. Fortunately, she doesn't remember me.

"Is Amanda here?"

"Who are you?" she snaps.

"Patrick."

"I don't know who you are."

"I'm Patrick."

"You just said that."

"Well, that's who I am."

"Who do you live with?"

"Harry Trimble."

The brunette rolls her brown eyes and sighs rather melodramatically. "I don't allow marijuana to be smoked in this house," the woman spits. "Is that understood?"

"Yes."

"Is that understood?" she repeats.

"I'm not getting my milk and cookies today, am I, Teacher?"

The woman stares me down for a few seconds before walking past and down the steps. I walk into the house and follow the delicious scent of food cooking to the kitchen, where I find Amanda standing over the stove wearing a plain white shirt and a pair of very short plaid shorts. Her feminine presence alone is a soothing balm to my tortured soul. "Hi, Woodchuck!" she says very pleasantly. Women rarely greet me with such enthusiasm these days, except for my grandmother and Dizzy's dog. And Heather when she's blasted on coke. "Did you ring the doorbell, cutie?"

"I did, Amanda."

"Going forward, just walk in. Nobody ever locks their doors. The only people around here who knock or ring the bell are delivery people and the cops. So you formally met Tags?"

"Unfortunately. She's a little too pretty to be so fucking miserable."

"Yeah, she's a little uptight sometimes. I'm sure you've already noticed. She was much worse last summer, which was right after her fiancé dumped her. She gets a bit needy for attention, I'd say. You can watch tv in the living room while I finish up, Woodchuck. Or you can sit at the table and watch me make a salad, which doesn't sound too exciting."

"I'm not much for tv," I reply and take a seat at the kitchen table, which is already adorned with two settings. "Sorry about the wine fiasco."

"That's okay. It's so inconvenient to lose your ATM card! Did you bring any weed?"

"I have some, but Tags..."

"Screw Tags!" Amanda says emphatically. "She's not my mother, although she tries to be. So you went to Iowa, Woodchuck? Or do you just wear that shirt because you look really cute in it?"

"Iowa, then Nova Law. You? I never asked."

"Yes, we got too caught up in talking about the size of my breasts, sex armies of horses, car shopping, and Mr. Rogers and the Land of Make Believe."

"You make me sound like such a freak, Amanda."

"I wasn't in much better shape than you were, sweetie. That's why you had to hold me for the entire walk home."

"I thought you just wanted to touch me."

"You're really stoned, aren't you?" I nod my head, even though Amanda's back is turned toward me and she can't possibly see my affirmation. I'm *that* fucked-up. "You've gone from having no confidence to obnoxious to cocky and who knows what might be coming next," says the blonde. "But I'm not putting my money on 'charming.' That's my goal for tonight. To get one comment out of you that is actually charming."

"I still don't know where you went to college, Amanda."

"Oh! I went to Wisconsin."

"Madison is a great college town. I road tripped for a football game there once. One of my fraternity brothers was like the walk-on fifth string punter or something."

"I dated our punter while I was in school for two years. He was *such* a sweet guy but he wanted to move back to his parents' farm way out in the boonies, and I just couldn't picture living my life as a farm girl. But I probably should have. Sometimes I think I'll regret it for the rest of my life."

"You'd be hot as a farm girl, Amanda."

"I'd be hot as anything, Woodchuck. And don't you forget it, you little fucker."

I am immediately silenced. The blonde is quiet for a few seconds before she begins laughing at me. "That line from you was *waaaay* too weak and predictable, Woodchuck. And it's *so* easy to push your little buttons. And so fun."

"Thanks. I'm glad I can provide you such entertainment."

"You know, I played field hockey at Iowa a few times. It's beautiful. It's one of those places that you think would totally fucking suck, but it was a pleasant surprise."

"Is that where your legs come from? My guess was tennis."

"Do you like my legs better or my breasts?"

"I know I'm supposed to say 'both,' but I'm really more of a legs guy. It's always the first thing I look for."

"I'm jealous of Mallory's legs. They're about four miles long and she has great skin."

"I'm sure your own legs have gotten you everywhere you've ever wanted to go, Amanda."

"So is that your favorite feature of mine?"

"No," I lie. "It's your eyes."

"I'm impressed," Amanda says as she turns away from cutting up a cucumber for a second. "That was *actually* pretty charming."

"I lost my virginity to a girl with blonde hair and green eyes. Is that TMI? I talk too much when I'm wasted sometimes. We can make a sex tape if you want."

Amanda turns back toward me and gives a cold stare. She resumes cutting-up vegetables, then immediately turns toward me again and giggles. "So how old were you when you lost your virginity, sweetie?" she asks.

"I was 31."

"I don't know if I'd believe that, Mr. McShea. I don't think you could have kept all the girls away from that handsome face of yours for 31 years."

"Thank you."

"You're blushing. Don't get many compliments?"

"Probably not as many as you do, Amanda."

"Is that your stomach growling, you poor thing?"

"It is," I say, taking a deep breath and hoping that nothing decides to spontaneously eject from it. "How many people live here?"

"Nine people, all girls," Amanda replies. "That's why we call it the Bunny Ranch. How many are in your house with Harry this year?"

"Eight."

"So why'd you go all the way out to Iowa City for college? Chess scholarship?"

"The farm girls."

"That figures. So what did you study aside from your amateur gynecology?"

"Architectural history."

"That's really interesting."

"It was the most academically taxing material that I've ever studied."

"Really?"

"No. How 'bout you, Amanda? I never asked you any questions about what you do."

"That's okay. Nobody really talks shop on weekends. But I majored in astrophysics."

"Is that a joke, or..."

"Charm school's on the line! There's an emergency in the kitchen at the Bunny Ranch!"

"I'm sorry," I say softly as Amanda giggles at me. I notice that my confidence in the conversation wanes every time Amanda bends her ass at a certain angle and I realize how incredible it looks. Guys like me don't get their hands on asses like Amanda's very often. For lack of a better term, it's depressing. "I'm giving up on charming you, Amanda," I say. "So whadda ya do with your degree?"

"I teach high school physics and college remedial math during the summers. I'm here almost every other Thursday night through Sunday, which is nice, depending on whatever mood Tony is in."

"Tony's a pretty charming guy himself," I say quite sarcastically.

"I gave up on him a long time ago."

"Well, obviously not. You're engaged to him."

"You knew what I meant. Don't be an asshole, Woodchuck. Is that really too much to ask while I'm cooking for you?" Amanda walks toward the stove in order to point out tonight's menu. "So," she begins, "I made you pork chops that I'm covering with baked apples and...fresh broccoli and...stuffing and...baked potatoes. Is that okay?"

"That's wonderful. Seriously. Thank you."

"I hope you're hungry!"

"I'm starving."

"Good. I made the potatoes because you're Irish. Irish people like potatoes, don't they?"

"Of course."

"Sorry about my cooking clothes, by the way. I know I look like crap tonight."

"I think you wore those tiny shorts on purpose, Amanda."

"I think I haven't done laundry and this was all I had left."

"Do you like my legs better or my breasts?" I repeat in a mocking tone.

"Oh, shut up," laughs the blonde. "This should all be done in a minute," is her promise as she walks back to the counter to continue cutting up some vegetables with her back turned to me. Women have become such alien creatures to me since The Episode and The Slump began. But my new meds must already be working to return my sex drive to my brain, because my male mind quickly devolves to its most primitive state as I stare at Amanda's legs while she begins to slice into a tomato: [where the fuck did u *ever* get those legs amanda? ur achilles goes long and strong into ur golden muscular calves. ur legs are a gift running so shapely and smooth from the cloth at the bottom of your shorts down to the thin line of whitish skin tracing ur arches where the tops of ur tanned feet meet the plantar skin of ur un-sunned soles. i want 2 walk right up 2 u amanda u bright gorgeous little pixie u. id take ur slim waist and warm body into my desperate arms while softly kissing the gold-toned skin of ur neck. ur breathing becomes more labored and more excited for me. u lift ur head and offer ur entire neck to me. my tongue licks u from underneath ur ear lobe and down to ur shoulder. u moan. thats right u pretty little bitch. u moan because u want me and my cock and my cum inside u, dont u amanda. i unsnap and unzip those little plaid shorts that are riding straight up ur ass and have been torturing me since i sat in this fucking chair. i want 2 taste u ms. liss. i want to hear how ur sweet voice sounds when its excited and calling my name and asking me to do the dirtiest things to ur toned sexy feminine body. ur ass looks so tight amanda. so tight! i need to taste it. i drop to my knees and i pull ur shorts and those most unnecessary panties from ur hips and sex and down ur lengthy legs. u step out of them and widen ur stance on ur pretty bare feet so that i can see ur cunt and its small pink lips swelling and glistening with excitement 4 me. i take ur tight tiny ass into my hands and open it so that i can see and smell everything that u have to offer amanda. i grab ur ankles and hold u still as i prepare to feast on u. i somehow show patience slowly running my tongue back and forth between ur moist lips savoring every bit of ur wetness and ur sweet taste running into my watering mouth. then i reach the skin over ur clit amanda. i know how sensitive it is so my tongue tickles it slowly and softly in circles to start even though i want u to be my whore NOW. u begin 2 moan my name. i love hearing my name in ur sex voice u little slut u. now its time 2 use long, slow strokes from ur clit to ur asshole and back again and again and again and again. my cock is throbbing for u amanda. everything about u from ur legs to ur smile to ur mind makes my cock get hard and throb and pulse with wonder and excitement and longing for ur mouth and ur skin and ur touch and ur cunt. ur taste and ur voice and the scent of ur sweat and wetness between ur golden thighs makes my head dizzy amanda more than any drug ever could. i stand 2 bend u right over that fucking counter u sexy little bitch u. that ass looks so good amanda. but its ur cunt that i want u gorgeous fucking thing. u reach behind to grab me and place my stiffened flesh at ur hole. i push. ur damp skin resists but i can feel the wetness and warmth in the waiting stratosphere beyond. ur getting wetter 4 me amanda. *i want it* u moan. *be rough with me. just push it. push it inside me patrick.* ur body gives way 2 me and i sink so softly so slowly into ur warm wet tight hole with a masculine groan. i thrust and thrust, my body smacking against ur tight ass as i give it 2 ur pussy. *pull my hair* u moan. oh i will pull ur long dirty blonde hair u bitch. i take it into my fingers and rip it straight down ur arched back as my eyes move from ur ass 2 my cock thats fucking u 2 ur smooth, golden thighs topped with tiny blonde hairs down 2 ur muscular tanned calves 2 the red-painted toenails on ur feet. *u like getting fucked from behind, don't you, u little slut u?* i ask as my balls begin to stir from my constant thrusting into ur cunt. *i love when u fuck me from behind patrick* u moan excitedly. *now cum inside my dirty little pussy 4 me* u squeal as i thrust harder deeper faster until u open ur mouth and say]

"Did you hear what I just asked you, Patrick?"

"Umm...I was distracted, Amanda."

"*Distracted.* That's cute. You were a little more than distracted, I think. In fact, you were staring straight through me. You certainly are a little lawyer, aren't you, Woodchuck? I asked if you wanted to smoke on the deck before we eat."

"Sure."

"You're blushing again. Do I want to know what is running through your mind right now?"

"It's all rainbows and unicorns, Amanda."

"I'm sure," the blonde replies quietly with a smile before leading me out to the nearby deck.

9:01 p.m.

The night is so still that it is slightly uncomfortable. Eerie. The water on the sound is like glass, reflecting the last blues and purples and reds of a cloudless civil twilight that was painted across the sky by the hand of The Maker himself. The intoxicants have highlighted the serenity of the sunset, allowing me to gain some release from the forty tons of stress pushing firmly against my chest wall and down into my gut. Dinner was delicious. I was so stoned that I fed some of it to Amanda airplane style, which she found to be incredibly entertaining. I doubt Tony the Douchebag does fun, silly stuff with her like that. He fucks her instead. Amanda and I wound up talking until my high wore off and I ran out of things to say. I excused myself for some bullshit reason that I can't even recall now that I'm stoned again. I feel very comfortable with Amanda because she's clearly very intelligent and is humored by my obvious lack of confidence. That's really the trick to clicking with any woman- you have to find someone that thinks your unattractive and awkward qualities are cute.

My long, horrible day vomiting has been somewhat redeemed by the company of a flirtatious and very sexy girl, a good meal, and a great sunset. I don't want to retreat into depressing thoughts, but I do. Having sixty-seven fucking cents to your name will make you tend to emphasize the negative. Like a lot of people, Amanda asked me over dinner why I decided to go to law school. There's a lot of little reasons, none of which provide any sound basis for why a person would want to go. One of them is that, unlike Amanda, I can't do math. I was never able to conquer pre-calculus in either high school or college. In high school, I cheated my way through. Despite making an effort to learn the material, I ultimately realized that it was

184

hopeless. Plus, I was fifteen. I didn't give a fuck about pre-calculus. I wanted to spend my time playing my guitar and fantasizing about what the girls in my group of friends might look like and smell like underneath their uniforms. Cheating enabled me to do both. My pre-calculus teacher, Mr. Andrew McDonough, was a high school legend. 'Stinky Drew' weighed well over 400 pounds and could be smelled within a radius of several hundred miles on his best day. The problem was that he was so massively obese that he couldn't even reach around to wipe his own ass after a dump. He'd sometimes have shit stains visible on the back of his pants as he walked down the hallway. Anyone who dared to mock him would be 'escorted' to his next destination under one of Stinky Drew's armpits. His act would not have flown if there were girls at school. Fortunately, there weren't any. My mother went to grade school with him and said he came from a good family. He only weighed a svelte 275 then, she said. She asked me to pray for him, which I did. He was well-liked as a teacher, provided you were lucky enough to be assigned a seat at the back of the classroom like I was. His life couldn't have been much fun. I give him a lot of credit for trying to be as normal as possible in his condition.

Stinky Drew taught two pre-calculus classes to juniors. One was held during fourth period; the other was during sixth. As luck would have it, two of my best friends had the class fourth period. We all had fifth period lunch. The answers to the multiple choice Scantron tests were provided to me at my lunch table on a small slip of paper torn-out from a page of a notebook. I'd mark one or two answers as purposely wrong on the green Scantron sheet, along with whatever my friends may have gotten wrong on their own just to make it all seem legit. I managed an 87 average for the entire year. It was bad for someone who had all of the answers, but it was pretty damn good for someone who should have failed the class every quarter.

Stinky Drew may have been fat, but he was no idiot. He had a suspicion that this kind of thing may have been happening, so on a snowy day in March of 1993 he gave my sixth period class a test with the questions in reverse order from the earlier exam. "Answers" already in hand, I had time to waste. I worked my way through the 10 problems or so out of 30 that I could actually perform just to humor myself. One of these problems was a pre-calculus equivalent to $x + 2 = 4$ that I can't recall specifically now. My answer was C. I panicked when I saw that the answer on my cheat sheet was A. I was 99.999999% confident that, in this one instance, I was right. From my position in the back row, my eyes darted around the room looking at my known fellow cheaters and those that I suspected were cheaters. All of them had their heads pinned down toward their desks, robustly filling out their Scantron sheets with a flurry of #2 graphite. None of them gave any sign that something was awry. But I was confident that I had uncovered Stinky Drew's nefarious plot. I couldn't be 100% sure from my brief analysis of a handful of problems that a true reverse had been called, but I went with my gut and assumed that he would take great pride in tricking us in the easiest way possible. My gut was correct. I scored a 93. I was a dirty fucking cheater, but I was certainly no fool. Nine of my classmates carrying averages above 90 were busted when they clocked-in with test scores between 0 and 16%. Two members of the National Honor Society were also busted stone cold and bounced after they tried to tried to claim very unsuccessfully that they mistakenly used a No. 2¾ pencil for the exam. That was a pretty stupid thing to do. It's fucking high school, and an all-male Catholic high school despite some ridiculous policies and paranoia usually operates as some sort of loose brotherhood. No one was trying to ruin anyone's life over a Scantron test until people had to make up lies about the grade of graphite in their pencil.

This all did catch up with me. While studying architectural history at Iowa, I got the bright idea that I might want to be an actual architect. Calculus and physics were required, and I registered for college-level pre-calculus in order to learn what I was supposed to learn in the first place in high school. My first attempt resulted in a big fat F. The second attempt resulted in a D+. My GPA bruised and battered, I tucked the dream of being an architect away to a place where it would never resurface. Cheaters never do win in the end, and I think I have paid more than a heavy price for never taking Mr. McDonough's class seriously.

There were other reasons why I went to law school. I wanted an intellectual challenge. I felt that my complete lack of knowledge concerning the business world was a detriment. I also thought that I might have the good fortune to meet a pretty, intelligent girl ("PIG") and get married. But the real reason why I went to law school was *Saturday Night Fever*. It had nothing to do with John Travolta prancing around Brooklyn in a white leisure suit when not mixing paint for Mr. Fusco. My dad was a Catholic high school teacher and didn't make a dime, of course. My mother always called it a 'vocation.' That's because she felt it would be sacrilegious to admit that the Church, flush with hidden reserves of cash, might be shortchanging its own teachers. Mom saw no contradiction between the Church preaching social justice while paying its own employees nothing. But my dad, like many Catholic school teachers, had little choice. The old school Irishman didn't have the temperament to last even thirty seconds in front of a Philadelphia public school classroom. The first dirty white kid who said 'fuck you' to him would have been thrown out into the hallway and beaten to a bloody pulp. But I digress, as I often do when my mind is filled with intoxicants.

My dad nearly killed himself tending bar all summer and every single Friday and Saturday night during the school year for fifteen straight years, and worked other odd jobs on the side, to provide for his family and pay the mortgages on both the Philadelphia and Cape May County houses. My mom was only 21 when I was born, so she was left home alone with me every weekend night at an age far, far younger than I am right now. I was her sole source of entertainment while my dad was out working. She would put Lawrence Welk on the old Philco television in the living room or spin the *Saturday Night Fever* soundtrack on the record player so that we could dance across the horrendously green carpet in the living room together. And when I say that green Seventies carpet in the living room was horrendous, I mean it was *horrendous*. It looked like a giant cat had swallowed balls of green, yellow and white yarn and just vomited it out over an entire 10' x 20' area. My two favorite tracks on the record were 'Stayin' Alive' and 'A Fifth of Beethoven' because I recognized the signature riff from watching cartoons. My mom used to pick me up from the floor so that we could slow dance to 'How Deep Is Your Love' together, which always embarrassed me because she would keep laughing and I thought I was doing something wrong. She wasn't laughing at me. Mom just thought that I was adorable. So that's the real reason why I became a lawyer. I had seen my father work two and sometimes three jobs until he was well past 50. I'm a lazy fuck, myself. I thought that I could go to school for another three years and go to *one* job in *one* office, and be put on the salary fast track, even if I was working 60 or more hours a week. It just seemed a lot easier. Dad's down to only two jobs now, but he'll have to work forever just for the benefits in case my mom's remission doesn't last and she gets sick again. He's trapped. That's a place that I never wanted to be. Ironically, I am.

My parents sold the site of my first mortal sin for $65,000 when my mom got sick. One year later the house next door, which was on an even smaller lot, went for $153K. My dad laughed about it, but I think he really wanted to jump off the Walt Whitman. He didn't, though. He knew the life insurance policy he had through the Archdiocese was shit, too. As for Stinky Drew, he's still teaching at my high school. Although I'm no longer religious, I remain spiritual. I do pray for him sometimes. I think about the rejection I've faced because of my slight build at times. It couldn't ever compare to what the massive Mr. McDonough has had to face during his lifetime. So even though I have only $0.67 to my name, I guess I don't realize how fucking lucky I really am.

Sunday, July 4, 2010

12:43 a.m.

The birth of our great Nation was celebrated via Dizzy's annual Pimps 'n Ho's Party, which was quite a sight to behold. Girls will spare no expense in trying to out-whore each other for these events. Gina and Jenna didn't even come to Angel Bay, filled with fear that they would be seen in facebook photographs near the women dressed in lingerie walking down St. Michael's Drive in broad daylight and standing in line at the Moo Moo for cigarettes. Stinky and Mallory were among the most conservative, dressed in bikinis with matching heels. Amanda and her entire house dressed as slutty schoolgirls. Amanda herself looked amazingly blonde and sexy while greeting me with a soft, wet kiss to the lips. She's never done that before. I was granted the honor of sitting-in with Jake and the Pantydroppers. We were set up in the rear of Dizzy's boat so the sound would go toward the party and not down the channel where some senior citizen is always itching to call the police to break-up a good time. We played two sets with a DJ in between. Silent John continues to impress me as a guitar player. It's inspiring to watch someone who really knows how to play a musical instrument so well.

The party itself was madness. By 10:00 p.m., many of the fishnet-clad and heel-wearing girls were making out with each other or hanging all over us as we played the last songs of our final set. Naturally, I hit it off with the one girl who was *not* dressed like the sexiest slut on the planet. She was in from St. Paul, Minnesota to visit her now passed-out cousin and was not adequately prepared for the event. Still, she was a pretty blonde-haired girl with brown eyes, a nice tan, a nicer body and a short skirt. We're currently in the back of Dizzy's boat together while he is inside the cabin having sex with a stunning brunette. My blonde is topless and wearing only her beige, plaid-themed skirt as we sit across from each other. She has legitimate D-cups that I played with like I was 16 again. Combined with my solid performance with Jake and the Pantydroppers and the free lingerie lesbian show offered by the party itself, this has all of the makings of the best night of my post-depression life. What a turn-around from only a few short days ago, although my gums at the rear left are still slightly swollen from the surgery and it makes kissing this blonde just slightly less enjoyable than it should be.

"You do this every weekend, I'm sure," says the Midwestern visitor as we take a brief pause to giggle and listen to Dizzy's current conquest moaning in ecstasy behind the cabin doors.

"I'm with at *least* three girls per weekend," I reply, my voice dripping with sarcasm. That may not have been a smart response, since Midwesterners rarely pick-up on East Coast sarcasm. My roommate at Iowa seriously thought that me and 'my boys' from Philly were gang-banging drug dealers for at least six weeks.

"It wouldn't surprise me if you hooked up a lot," the girl says with a sly smile as the moonlight illuminates her soft, brown eyes.

"Why."

"You play the guitar, you're funny, you're handsome...and you're a great kisser."

"I'm not always surrounded by a hundred women in lingerie and short skirts that are loaded by 10 o'clock." I'm not always very funny, either, but it's hard to be intimidated by a native Minnesotan. The Midwestern girls always liked me, even though I was never able to measure-up on my home turf.

"I'm sure you find your way around," says the nice-looking girl. I fail to issue a denial and kiss her soft lips once again before this stupid conversation goes any further. Perhaps inspired by the goings-on only a few feet away in the cabin, she grabs the back of my head and begins to kiss me much more aggressively. Not sloppily, but aggressively. My right hand, which along with my left has been massaging her dark thighs for a time, moves toward the front of her panties. They're soaked straight through the cloth, which only whets my appetite to taste her more. I push them aside and slowly slide my middle finger between her moist and swollen lips from bottom to top. I've been here hundreds and hundreds of times and it never gets old or boring or plain. I'm in my thirties. Things are rarely going to stop here. I've always had a soft touch with everything- my guitar strings, my penmanship, my pet hedgehog (you kinda have to) and my women. I lightly massage underneath her hood until her moans almost reach that coming from the cabin. Then I grab the sides of her panties and prepare to pull them from her slim waist. She stops me immediately.

"Can I ask you a question?" the blonde says as the sound of the current can be heard gently brushing against the vessel.

"Sure."

"What's my name?"

I draw a complete blank. My only two options right now are to guess 'Jennifer' or be annoying and answer her question with a question of my own. I chose the latter. "What's mine?"

"Patrick Aloysius McShea," she replies without hesitation.

"How the *fuck* did you remember that?"

"You showed me your driver's license when I said you had more of an accent than anyone from Philadelphia ever could. Then I showed you mine because you said you'd never seen a Minnesota license."

189

"I just wanted to see how old you were without asking you directly."

"So how old am I?"

"December 1984. Twenty-six."

"Twenty-five, genius. What day?"

"The eighteenth?"

"The fourteenth."

"I was only off by two..."

"Answer my question, Mr. McShea."

"Tina."

"Wrong! It's Tara."

"That's pretty damn close for knowing you less than three hours."

"'Close' isn't going to get my panties off."

"I'm really good at oral."

"I'm sure you are. But that has nothing to do with anything."

"Sure it does. Is anything more frustrating than bad oral sex?"

The blonde pauses to think for a second. "Probably not," she admits. "I just want you to remember my name, that's all. Is that *really* too much to ask?"

"In the shape I'm in?"

"It's four letters, Patrick. I think you can manage. I heard a rumor that you're a lawyer."

"It's only a rumor. Trust me."

"Then what is it that you do for a living?"

"Sales."

"And what do you sell?"

"Urinal cakes."

The girl bursts out laughing and pinches my cheek. "You are such a fucking...*idiot*," she says with a bright smile before planting another soft kiss on my lips. Excited, feminine cries of *'I'm cumming! I'm cumming!'* are now heard behind the cabin doors. *"What* are they doing in there?" Tara asks with slight disgust in her tone.

"I would imagine that they're having sex, Tina."

"Tara!"

"Tara. Sorry."

"Ugh! I'm going to ask you my name again in five minutes. If you get it wrong, the panties are staying on and you're walking me straight back to my cousin's house."

"Deal."

I sink back into the blonde's soft lips. *"You're so cute,"* I'm suddenly told in a whisper. Our kissing continues as our tongues dance inside each other's mouths. My finger slides between the heavens previously guarded by her tanned things. *"You are so good at that,"* the woman moans as I again massage the area around her clitoris. Passing shorebirds squeak. The water continues to roll against the boat. A gentle breeze blows off the sound. The woman pulls her lips from mine.

"What's my name, Mr. McShea?" she asks again.

"Tina," I reply confidently without a second's pause. The woman immediately grabs the rest of her clothes and storms off the boat to get dressed.

Wednesday, July 7, 2010

> *I do not believe in the God of theology who rewards good and punishes evil.*
>
>   -Albert Einstein

8:58 p.m.

Gina has developed a habit of asking me to attend church with her on Sunday mornings before she leaves for Philly. Even though she usually wears a sundress and looks fantastic, I can't do it. Going to church was ruined for me for all time because of my upbringing. I hated God and Jesus by the fifth grade. Those fuckers were always out to get me and there was no way to hide from an omnipresent deity. After the Choir Loft Incident, every single word and deed of Patrick A. McShea was under intense scrutiny from four eyes at all times. I was under a microscope and the viewer was God Himself, both from above and manifested on Earth through the existence of my parents. It was drilled into me that the Almighty was not pleased and I knew not the day or hour of His wrath. And I got his wrath through Georgie and Franny the Retard. Even if I never took a seat behind the organ that fateful day, though, I'm not sure things would have been all that much different. Even before all that shit started, my mother painted always me as a spoiled rotten little boy that had no right to complain about anything at any time because I did not have cancer and none of my limbs had yet been amputated. If I said I was bored as a child, like all children do at one time or another, my mom would angrily snap, *'How would you feel if you had no legs and were confined to a wheelchair the rest of your life? Then you'd REALLY be bored, wouldn't you? A lot of bored people wind up in Hell when their days on Earth are over, you know!'* Then my dad would march into the room and immediately demand to know what his spoiled rotten son who was blessed with two arms and two legs had dared to complain about this time. *I was eight years old, you fucking assholes!* Spoiled? You were making $23,000 per year in 1986, Dad. I don't think we had too much to feel guilty about, even though we all had our limbs intact.

  To add to this madness, my mother's best friend gave birth to a boy named Kevin that had the misfortune of being cursed with one of the most dreadful diseases that mutated DNA has ever wrought, cystic fibrosis. He suffered constant, horrific lung infections and was dead by 12. This served as a valuable lesson for me. If I complained of any pain whatsoever and mom wasn't buying it, I'd immediately be hit with an angry, *"Your stomach hurts? How would you like to be Kevin Boyle? He can't even breathe! You need to get down on your knees and pray to God that you were born with two arms and two legs and a functioning body."* The goal was to make me feel guilt with every breath I took because I was among the 99% of Americans not born with this affliction.

Of course, no Irish Catholic household would ever have been able to function properly if the world was a better place and people were not starving in Africa. The constant reminders of the Potato Famine were bad enough. But I heard about the people in Africa so much that I actually began to resent them. One Wednesday night while I was in seventh grade, my mother had made ham for the third time in two weeks. It must have been on sale somewhere. I rarely complained about my mother's Irish cooking, but I hated ham. I don't think my dad liked it, either, but he just kept his mouth shut. Ham was always plain and boring and there was nothing short of a half keg of ketchup that could make it palatable to me. On the night in question, I was picking at my food and clearly disinterested in my supper. My mom started her 1,000th speech about the people starving in Africa and I decided to put this to an end once and for all. I stormed out of the kitchen, grabbed a big manila envelope from my dad's teaching supplies and wrote 'TO AFRICA' across the front in big, bold, block letters. I went back to the table and dumped my entire plate of ham and green beans and canned creamed corn (barf!) and applesauce into it, sealed it, and dropped the envelope onto the counter where my mom had placed several bills that needed to be mailed. My athletic, pre-cancer mother sprung up from her seat in a flash and punched me so hard in the chest three times that I almost fell over. I was shocked. There's nothing more emasculating than being punched by your own mother. You're defenseless. There's nothing that you can do because you can't hit her back. Even my dad was floored by the violence. He never went against my mom, so Dad must have wanted to slide all of the shit off his plate and into the envelope, too.

I retreated to my room. I grabbed a Butterfinger that I had stored in my bookbag and strummed my guitar for a while. My dad came upstairs some time later, opened my bedroom door, and looked around. *'Don't let your mother find that candy wrapper in your bedroom,'* he said before leaving. That was the Irish Catholic Dad checking up on me. There was no need to speak about the incident itself as long as I was in one piece and playing the guitar. He went back downstairs and started watching the Sixers from his chair. My mother apologized two days later, but she still had completely freaked me the fuck out. Having your mom wind-up and deliver close-fisted blows when you're almost a teenager was weird, even if you were being a huge smartass. Georgie hit me when I was younger, now that I was older it was my own fucking mother. The message was clear: this house will be ruled with an iron fist, even though you are carrying a lifetime 'A' average, skipped a grade, and go to church every Sunday- which were all things I was supposed to be doing anyway, I guess. I

193

never showed her the bruises or told her how it would hurt whenever I would breathe deeply over the next few days. It would have been useless given the unfortunate Kevin Boyle. He struggled with almost every breath, Mom would surely point out. Further, it would only have been viewed as evidence of how my diabolical ways could drive even a good Christian mother to the fiercest anger.

My mother reached new lows in the game of guilt on a regular basis. Once a week all of the kids in the neighborhood would gather at the nearby playground to play football or baseball or street hockey, depending on which season it was. Everybody played. Even though some of the kids that tended to pick on me would be there, that stuff was all put aside when it was time to play sports. Street hockey was scheduled for Wednesday, which was the same day my mom had set aside for our weekly visit to my paternal grandmother's. I told my mom that I wanted to go to the playground and play hockey instead. She reacted as if I had asked to stay home alone so that I could worship Satan and kill goats. Mom concluded her angry, impassioned lecture with, '*You can go play hockey if you want, Patrick. But just remember that if your grandmother dies tomorrow, your last words about her were, 'I don't want to go visit grandmom today.' And you'll have to live with those words FOR THE REST OF YOUR LIFE!*'

Only an Irish Catholic mother could correlate the desire of a nine year-old to play sports with harboring a death wish for his grandmother. (Grandmom, by the way, is 96 and still quite alive.) I think most kids would have realized how fucking warped this was and just walked out the door with their hockey stick. But I didn't. I was such a pussy in grade school because I knew God was out to get me, and He would get me for every deliberate and inadvertent act of disobedience no matter how big or how small. I never thought to question why God didn't seem to be getting revenge on the neighborhood kids who were breaking car windows, writing graffiti all over the local businesses, and getting piss drunk in grade school. Maybe it was because they weren't Irish, so they were already cursed enough. I remember one morning during my sophomore year of high school, I came downstairs into the kitchen and wasn't wearing a belt. It wasn't a fashion statement or for any particular reason. I had forgotten while in the midst my early morning haze to put one on. My mother exploded. I could not understand this. It was a fucking belt. It's not like I tumbled down the stairs in the morning and a bag of coke fell out of my pocket. Just yesterday, Mom informed me, my own father had given a student detention for not wearing a belt to school. Now I was flaunting the authority of my father, of all the teachers at my own high school (many of whom knew my father, who was big in the union) and of the Pope himself. I was a malcontent, a heretic, and a disgrace- because I forgot to put on a fucking belt. In fact, the Romans that nailed Jesus to the Cross probably weren't wearing belts, either. *That's why they needed to gamble for Our Lord's clothes as he hung!* How was I any different than those that drove the nails into Our Lord? I lived in fear. What if I came home drunk one Friday night? If putting dinner in an envelope was worth three punches in the chest, and not wearing a belt lead to a verbal bitch explosion, I'd surely be stabbed to death for drinking. It was a good thing that my IBS prevented me from ever having to suffer such a fate.

Needless to say, I never even considered skipping Church during my seventeen years under that roof. I wasn't even allowed to wear jeans, since hippies and public school kids wore them. Missing Mass and being caught would have made my life Hell. I badly wanted to skip church, because I saw no need to fall upon my knees in worship for some asshole that was intent on making me miserable all of the time. There was no question that God would command that I be pasted all over the highway by an 18-wheeler if I ever committed such a sin as missing Mass, though. And my blackened soul would shoot straight to Hell via the express lane. Go to Straight Hell, Do Not Pass Go, Do Not Collect $200. I almost felt the same way about the greatest evil of all, premarital sex. Although my expanding and developing mind was starting to feel that some of this Catholic Church stuff was total bullshit by my senior year of high school, I couldn't bring myself to aggressively pursue having sex with anyone other than my best friend, Brigit O'Brien. She was fucking adorable. Brigit had curly brown hair and big tits, and was every man's fantasy while dressed in the blue uniform of St. Bernadette's Catholic High School for Girls. Every time the phone rang, I prayed that it was Brigit on the line. I'd have butterflies each time my mother would scream, 'Patrick! Phone!' from downstairs. When Brigit's friendly voice responded to my typically disinterested 'Hello' with an excited 'Hi!' the butterflies increased tenfold.

The two of us spent countless hours on the phone and at the mall together. I spent an equal amount of time fantasizing about Brigit sitting in her favorite ugly gold chair in her parents' living room with her legs wide, wide open so I could go down on her while she was wearing only her dark blue school socks. That fantasy was always out of reach. She was far too busy hooking up with the rest of the neighborhood instead, although her virginity remained intact. I had already 'frenched' Brigit once in eighth grade but she was never willing to step it up to anything else with me. My mom always liked to call Brigit 'my girlfriend' but that was not the case. I couldn't ever have been that lucky. Mom only called her that to reassure herself that I wasn't gay. She had realized through conversations with other parents that I didn't receive half the calls from girls that my friends did. Truth be told, only Brigit ever really called me. I wasn't surprised by it. High school relationships are based solely on looks. Guys tend

195

not to look too good when they're over 5'9" and weigh only 135 pounds. My mother was blind to that fact because of the deep but sometimes obscured love for her son.

By the spring of our senior year of high school, the girls from the 'nerdy' contingent of our circle of friends began sending out feelers to the guys to see which of us may be interested in destroying their virginity before everyone left for college and separated, possibly for good. The guys called a high-level meeting in Matt McCrory's basement one Friday night in April after he had been relayed a message that the girls would be making decisions that very week. If you were picked, a girl would call and ask you to have sex by using the code phrase, 'I was calling to see if you wanted to get together one day after school this week.' We reached a consensus that the girls were most likely to gravitate to their closest guy friend to do the deed. The crew unanimously believed that I would finally achieve my dream of Brigit and offered me congratulations. I accepted, even though I knew full well that they were premature. But I couldn't sleep for days as I pondered the possibility that I wasn't quite out of the running yet to finally see her naked. I launched myself so quickly toward the telephone every time it rang that week that I wound up breaking a toe on that Monday. I thought about making a mix tape for the grand event, probably with some Def Leppard on it like 'Hysteria' or 'Animal.' I was a little apprehensive about the whole deal, of course. A decision as to whether or not to engaging in such a mortal, deadly sin was not to be taken lightly. In the end, though, I felt that instant eternal damnation would be a small price to pay if it meant losing my virginity to the incredible Brigit and all of her feminine wonders. There would be no reason to live after fucking her, anyway. Life would already have gotten as good as it could ever possibly get.

I was never faced with making such a choice, though. Women are best friends with certain guys for a reason, and that reason is because they find them to be totally, completely, utterly unattractive. After a couple of days of procrastinating, Brigit was the first to act. She went right to my good friend John, who was the stud of our high school wrestling team. John, who was loyal to a fault and secretly screwing three different girls from three different high schools, asked her point blank why I wasn't getting the call instead. Brigit's response was that she wouldn't have sex with me if I paid her and took her to Hershey Park the next day. I felt completely betrayed by that statement. It's one thing to prefer John. It's another to completely denigrate your 'best friend' in the process. I never told John not to do her, though. How could I? We were 17 years old. There is *nothing* more important than pussy when you're 17. Nothing! It wasn't going to help my cause, anyway. That decision had been made. I just told John that I didn't want to hear about it afterward. I stopped returning

Brigit's calls, which made her livid. She fired off a six-page letter to my parents' house and had her sister address the envelope so I wouldn't recognize her own handwriting and trash it. Women do not appreciate it when someone that they have placed firmly into their 'friend' zone gets too big for their britches and stops fully embracing their role. I was supposed to humbly accept that I was Brigit's permanent shoulder to cry on and nothing more. Developing feelings of like, love, or lust for her was clearly not part of my job description. *'I can't believe how selfish you are being after all we've been through together over the past six years,'* the whore wrote. *'I always thought that you would be here for me for good times and bad. True friends don't walk away from each other over this kind of shit. If you refuse to be friends with women just because they won't have sex with you, then you are in for a rough, lonely life.'*

Thanks, Brigit. I was leaving for the cornfields of Iowa in four months, anyway, and she was set to attend Seton Hall. I did miss the times during the late spring when she would invite me over to keep her company while she was laying out in her back yard in a bikini. I could have looked at her for weeks in a bathing suit, even though my raging curiosity about what lie underneath its cloth was torture at times. Looking back, I think in some twisted way she knew this. Her boyfriends always tortured and cheated on her (which is why she never wound up sleeping with them), so I think Brigit made herself feel better by asserting her dominance over me. My mom asked me why she stopped calling. I lied and said she had a serious boyfriend, which really confused Mom because she was convinced that I was Brigit's boyfriend. It's not like I could tell her that we stopped talking because she decided to lose her virginity to Big John Stud instead of me.

Since my buddy John was considered the top prize in our crew and there was nowhere to go but down, the rest of the girls held what could best be described as a sex draft. I was picked second to last by Kelly Schmidt aka Kelly Shit. She was overweight, appeared to have a moustache, and sometimes smelled funny. It was an awkward conversation when I received the call:

"Hello?"

"Woodchuck, this is Kelly Schmidt."

"I know."

"Umm...do you wanna...gettogetheronedayafterschoolthisweek?"

"Excuse me?"

"I asked if you want to get together after school this week."

"Why?"

"Umm...you know, to like, to *get together*, you know..."

"Us?"

"M'mm."

"I have to do my math homework. I'll call you back."

There was no fucking way that I was going to risk the pains of Hell to have sex with Kelly Shit, but I couldn't say 'no' to her directly. I'd been denied far too many times myself to be comfortable in the role of the rejecter. I never called her back and graduated from high school a virgin. Even worse than being drafted by Kelly Shit in the first place, though, was the realization that the girls in my circle of friends probably viewed me in the same light as the guys all viewed Kelly Shit. My buddies tried to assure me that this was ridiculous, or I never would have been picked to escort the semi-legendary Diana Maciejewski to her prom and touch her breasts afterward. She was openly searching for a date because her 25 year-old boyfriend happened to be in jail at the time. She picked me because I seemed 'harmless' and she was one of the few girls in the entire neighborhood who thought that it was cool that I played guitar. I was thrilled to experience the unforgettable first touch of the soft flesh of a female breast, but I still felt the sting of my Brigit dream crumbling to pieces.

It took me over two months at Iowa to finally forget about Brigit's betrayal and God trying to kill me all of the time. But I did manage to normalize myself. On one cold Sunday night in November 1995, I finally crossed two equally dangerous thresholds: I missed Mass for the first time *and* had premarital sex. I never went to church on Sunday mornings in college, instead opting for an 8:00 p.m. Mass at a chapel about 150 yards from my dorm. By November, it's pretty fucking cold in Iowa City. It's the kind of cold where you step outside, take one breath, and the snot inside your nose freezes *instantly*. As I listened to a fierce, stiff wind shaking the windows of my dorm room on that Sunday night, the prospects of venturing out to perform my duty to God were dwindling by the second. My agnostic roommate from Chicago Heights, who may have been tripping on acid, informed me that I had the look of a man who was going to Hell. He left to stay in his girlfriend's room for the night. I was in a quandary. There was only a five minute window for me to leave for Mass before I would arrive very late. There was a knock at my door, and it was an angel. Not a messenger from God, but a girl named Angel Brooks who hailed from somewhere way outside of Peoria, IL. She was a blonde farm girl living on the floor upstairs that had straight hair, green eyes, very fair translucent-like skin, and she was dressed simply in jeans and a dark flannel over her thin body. Angel also had a right superior canine that was dead fucking sideways, so she sometimes looked semi-retarded when she laughed or smiled particularly wide. But there was no question that she was cute in a 'starter girlfriend' kind of way, which is exactly what the doctor had ordered.

Ironically, I had masturbated to her that very morning after my roommate left for the dining hall without me.

Angel and I were assigned three of the same first semester classes, so we always ran into each other on the elevators and walked to class together. Sometimes, we would eat lunch or dinner and she would chew my ear off about what a bastard her high school dropout boyfriend back home was. On this cold November night, she asked me if I happened to have any pot and if I wanted to smoke it with her. I invited her into my room and tore off down the hallway to see Ed Marker, a junior from Ewing, NJ that always had weed. Fortunately, he was there. He usually was. I really don't know what he did with himself besides going to class and getting high. I threw whatever bills were rolled up deep inside the bottom of the pocket of my jeans onto the small wooden coffee table where Ed always burned his incense and candles. I demanded that he roll two joints immediately. I returned to my room with the goods in less than three minutes. Angel wasn't there any longer. She had wandered down the hall to pee before becoming trapped in a conversation with Blake Ditchwicker, who was arguably the weirdest dude ever. He always introduced himself as 'Blake Ditchwicker, Time Lord' and had two hamsters in his room that he referred to as his 'assistants.' No one knew exactly what these hamsters were supposed to be assisting him with, although one resident of the floor declared on one Saturday night at 4 a.m. that he believed that they helped Blake watch TV. Exactly how a fucking hamster was supposed to help someone watch TV was never adequately explained by this drunk. The only things that we were able to figure out with certainty were their names, Iscandar and Bella, and that Blake read to them for at least 30 minutes each night. It was mostly comic books and science fiction that no human would listen to voluntarily.

Angel managed to extricate herself from the conversation just after Blake asked her if she knew anything of the search for the theoretical Higgs boson. She returned to my room, where we made ourselves comfortable on a small, obscenely red couch that my roommate had since he was five. You could not walk more than four sequential steps in any one direction in our cramped dorm room, but we did have a flaming red couch. It did not take long for Angel and me to get completely toasted. We wound up listening to *Paul's Boutique* and trying to do impressions of what our middle-aged, female writing professor might sound like in bed with her lesbian lovers. Angel was convinced that she would be very proper and mature, saying things like, *'I would much prefer if you would increase the velocity of your licking implement while stimulating my clitoris orally. And I would request that you maintain such a speed until I have managed to achieve climax or suddenly become flatulent, whichever comes first. No pun being intended.'* After much more stoned silliness,

Angel turned to me and said very calmly and very casually, "Umm...you're kinda cool. Do you wanna have sex with me?" I thought she was kidding until she flashed me a wide, sideways-tooth smile and reached over to kiss me. I was so curious to give her oral sex and pulled her jeans off as soon as it seemed appropriate. I was hooked on it for life at her first moan. I should have had her return the favor. The first of the three times we had sex that night lasted about nine seconds. I felt so lightheaded afterward that I rolled off the couch and onto the floor with a thud. Technically, I was raped. Having skipped second grade, I was still 17 for another three days. Angel had repeated first grade due to some scary-sounding illness and was 19. I accepted responsibility for my role in this horrible crime and declined to go to the campus police.

The next morning provided the real moment of truth. After Angel returned to her room, I hopped into the shower and got myself ready to leave for my 10:00 a.m. class. There was an extra spring in my step, having finally experienced the unique thrill of a wet pussy for the first time. I was steppin' tall until I exited my dorm and reached Davenport Street. This was perhaps the most critical moment of my young life. I looked left. I looked right. I looked left again. I looked right again. I stepped off the curb. I started walking very briskly toward the other side of the street. In fact, I fucking ran. I couldn't believe it when I reached the far curb and stepped back onto a sidewalk. I had skipped church and had sex only 12 hours before, *yet made it across the street without being hit by an 18-wheeler the next morning.* Surely a greater punishment awaited! I went to my writing class. Angel skipped it. She met me at the dining hall for lunch. I figured that my food would become a vicious poison in my system. It didn't. There was no vomiting afterward and I shit only twice, which was standard for dining hall food. Angel and I had sex *again* that night. Three times! The next morning, I saw a great light in my eyes. I was convinced that the Lord had taken me in my sleep, and now I had to answer for my great sins before my soul was cast into Hell to rot until it was finally destroyed on the Day of Judgment. I was still alive. The light was coming from a giant flashlight in the hands of my roommate, who was breaking my balls because he had an early class and I didn't. I remained alive and retained all of my limbs throughout the ensuing 24 hours. My colon didn't fall out. I didn't get cancer. My grandmom didn't die, either. I had never felt so fucking free before.

Ironically, the last person that I had sex with over 400 days ago was Brigit O'Brien. She has two kids and divorced her husband, a cop, after he was sentenced to jail time for planting evidence and stealing from drug dealers and the innocent alike. I knew the guy from high school, and he was a fucking nutjob. The fact that the City had given him a license to carry a gun is mind numbing. I remember when someone had first made an off-hand remark at a local gathering of the neighborhood crew at a smoky bar on Frankford Avenue that Brigit had started dating him. My heart sank like I was in high school all over again. Now many years later, Brigit and I agreed to meet up one night while her kids were with her parents. I hadn't seen Brigit in over 10 years, and I already knew from her facebook photos that she didn't look exactly like the woman I had so loved and so lusted for in high school. I kept my hopes up, though. I needed to. I had not one positive thing in my life. Brigit had the same smile that she always had when she answered the door to her apartment, which instantly gave me Goosebumps. But her face looked far too full and the crows feet around her eyes were very pronounced. When I entered, I was disappointed to discover that Brigit had gained at least 40 pounds. Her breasts looked saggy and her tight-as-a-button ass had expanded far beyond my wildest imagination. Women either peak at 16 or 30. She was the former. But it was Brigit O'Brien, so I had to sleep with her if given the opportunity so I could literally put that failed chapter of my life to bed. We talked and laughed on the couch for about an hour before Brigit pointed out that we kept moving ourselves closer and closer toward each other as the conversation continued. *'It might be time for you to kiss me again,'* she said with the same smile and slightly mischievous brown eyes she always had, even if the body had completely changed. It still gave me the chills. She was a *fantastic* kisser, just like she was 18 years ago when we paused at the corner of Knorr & Battersby Streets so I could collect on my promised goodnight kiss for leaving the Friday night dance early to walk her home.

We wound up in her bedroom fairly quickly. Hearing her moan my name in her sex voice was jarring the first time. I had fantasized about hearing her talk to me that way more times than I could ever count. In real life, her voice sounded so much sweeter and so much more excited. But physically, it was no longer there for me. As a single, never-married, never-engaged man with no kids, the small scars from Brigit's C-sections completely freaked me the fuck out. I never in a thousand years thought the tables would turn like they did. We had sex on only three occasions before I cut it off. I was at the height of my depression at that time, and sleeping with Brigit actually made it worse despite my need for sex. Her attention gave me neither solace nor any reason to celebrate. Now filled with carnal knowledge of my high school love, I tortured myself with my failure to secure her body when it was every bit as lovely and exciting as her kisses and her personality and everything else that made her Brigit. I was only good enough for her now that she was divorced from some total asshole and her body was twice put through the ravages of pregnancy and childbirth, I told myself.

And how incredible would life have been if she had picked me and we had spent the last month of our senior year of high school exploring each other's bodies? I couldn't comprehend it. I just couldn't fucking comprehend it, and it bothered me that other guys got to experience the old Brigit when it was I who would have appreciated it most. That's the kind of useless crap you think about, though, when your mind is not working properly. You lose a lot of sleep over things that can never be changed and have no real effect on the present.

I may have cut off sex with Brigit, but I didn't cut off the friendship. We still message and call each other. She's dating a divorced fireman now and is pretty happy. As for my first, Angel, we became almost disgustingly inseparable for the six weeks that remained in the semester following our first night on the red couch. We both lied to our parents about when our finals were over so that we could lock ourselves in a dorm room for two extra days and do nothing but eat, breathe and have sex. I *loved* fucking that girl. She would look at me with the most excited green eyes the entire time I was inside her, which made me feel like a world champion. A man needs to feel that way sometimes. We did it 13 times in two days. During that winter break, Angel got knocked up by her bastard boyfriend and never returned to campus.

Though my sexual hang-ups have been largely expelled and I again have a functioning penis, I have no doubt that living on the couch in my parents' basement to help my mother and to save money during law school contributed to my demise. Having returned to the scene of the crime, so to speak, I think the "spoiled rotten" little Irish Catholic boy still living inside of me was very uncomfortable on some subconscious level that the good grades that I initially earned would entitle me to walk into an $80,000 to $105,000 job following graduation. That was just *so* much money to me and our humble family. *Too* much money. I hate to think that this was one of the factors contributing to my failure to get professional help promptly, but it certainly was. In some way, I've sabotaged my own self because I felt I didn't deserve the success and the comfort that comes with financial stability. That's something I simply can't deal with unless I'm way high as I sit here broke as a fucking joke right now.

New Message: Amanda Liss
7/08/10 8:46 p.m.
I had a dream abt u last night.

Message to: Amanda Liss
7/08/10 8:52 p.m.
Good or bad?

New Message: Amanda Liss
7/08/10 8:54 p.m.
Both

Message to: Amanda Liss
7/08/10 8:55 p.m.
Do explain.

New Message: Amanda Liss
7/08/10 8:59 p.m.
I dreamt I gave u head.

Message to: Amanda Liss
7/08/10 9:00 p.m.
Did u swallow? lol

New Message: Amanda Liss
7/08/10 9:03 p.m.
Ur disgusting.

Message to: Amanda Liss
7/08/10 9:04 p.m.
I said lol.

New Message: Amanda Liss
7/08/10 9:05 p.m.
It wasnt necessary. I cant help what i dream.
U can help what u text.

Message to: Amanda Liss
7/08/10 9:06 p.m.
Back atcha Ms. 'I Dreamt I Gave U Head.'

New Message: Amanda Liss
7/08/10 9:06 p.m.
Oh fuck u woodchuck.

Message to: Amanda Liss
7/08/10 9:07 p.m.
Did u dream abt that 2?

New Message: Amanda Liss
7/08/10 9:07 p.m.
Don't flatter urself.

Message to: Amanda Liss
7/08/10 9:07 p.m.
Thanks 4 playing. Stay in touch with urself.

Saturday, July 10, 2010

5:28 p.m.

Harry summons me upstairs to hand me a retainer agreement with an architect and several construction contracts from companies for work on a new bulkhead and construction of the new dream house for him and Marie. I can tell immediately that most of them were pulled right off some internet site instead of being drafted by a real lawyer. There's shit that's even badly misspelled. It's such a fucking disgrace. "You don't need to look at everything right now, obviously," says Harry as he digs into a sandwich at the dining room table with five empty bottles of Corona in front of him.

"I'll take a quick look," I reply as I take a seat, only because I want to eye-up Jenna for a spell. She is perched on the couch in denim shorts and a red bikini top over her C-cups. She is presumably watching the Phillies, but instead just stares blankly at the television screen while she's sucking on a lollipop or taffy of some kind. She twirls the white stick in her fingers while gliding the candy around and over her tongue. Then she dips and moves the stick so that the purple-colored lollipop is slowly sliding in and out from between her pink lips. I find myself very jealous of the confection in Jenna's hand. Much too jealous. It's been far too long since I've received the kind of attention from a woman that this purple taffy is now getting.

"*Somebody's* not getting enough action from her boyfriend," cracks Harry with a mouthful of his turkey sandwich.

"I get *plenty* of attention from Michael," Jenna snaps back after pulling the lollipop out of her mouth with a pucker.

"Really?" Harry replies. "Your brother told me you're so fucking miserable that he's tempted to return the minivan and take back the $90,000 Mercedes that he sold you for thirty grand. He said you don't deserve it any longer. I think Miss Love needs *you* in her mouth, Woodchuck."

"It's a possibility," replies the brunette to my surprise before adding, "if I happen to die and go straight to fucking *Hell*." Her Blackberry starts vibrating on the coffee table. "It's my cousin Maria," she announces for no reason before grabbing her device and leaving the couch.

"Tell Maria I said 'hi,'" I say to the brunette as she heads toward her room. She responds by giving me the finger.

"If there's a woman on Earth who needs to be fucked in the ass more than she does, I haven't met her," is Harry's final say on the matter.

1:16 a.m.

Tearsten has jumped on the Rock Room stage at the Shipwreck to assault the drummer, whom she has been seeing for nearly two weeks. The crime? His sister walked over to give him a hug and a kiss at his drum kit before the third and final set started. This is completely unacceptable in the drunken Tearsten's mind. Storming onto the stage like she is charging across a Civil War battlefield, cymbal stands are now falling all over the place, drums are being violently rearranged, and the drummer is receiving several blows about the head and body by the drunken, red-faced danger to male society. The bouncers quickly move in and dispose of this madness. She tries to cry to me for sympathy on the way out but I'm hearing none of it.

Aside from Tearsten's antics, the Shipwreck is a raging clusterfuck of loud music, alcohol, short skirts, and girls stumbling around and crying for any one of the following reasons: they saw an ex from six years ago; they saw an ex from last week; their boyfriend is talking to a woman that is prettier; their boyfriend is talking to a woman that is fatter; their boyfriend is talking to any woman whatsoever; they don't have a boyfriend even though they really want one but only if he's fucking hot; or, they are just crying because that's what they do when they're drunk. In other words, it's a typical Saturday night here.

Gina is drunk but not crying. Instead, she has unexpectedly lead the panty-sniffing asshole to the Disco Room where she has her arms wrapped around me as we groove to some trance tune with a hypnotizing bass riff that I couldn't ever name. Gina and I are pretty locked in at this point, and I'm starting to think that I might finally have the green light. I grab her hips. She twists them up and down and back and forth like she means it. I pull her up against my body. She's so near now that I can feel her breathing on me. The anticipation is fucking killing me, and it's amplified by an entire host of reasons including my current slump with both Italian and regular women alike. She turns her body and plunges her tiny ass into me. The trance track gives way to the soft piano riff from Ne-Yo's 'Because of You.' DJ Buttfuck couldn't have played a better song for the moment if I had slipped him $20. I lock my arms around Gina's waist and begin to softly kiss the brown skin on her neck. I can taste the salt from her sweat on my lips. She reaches up with her left hand as she continues to slowly dance in rhythm with me, putting it on the back of my head so that I can't stop kissing her. She lifts her head and I can feel her exhale. My lips work up her neck to her cheeks to her ears. She turns her head toward me and we lock eyes for the briefest instant. She slowly closes her eyes and moves her red, wet lips toward me. I close my own eyes and await the receipt of Gina's first kiss. This is such a profound moment in my twisted, awkward life. Gina's lips never arrive. She is ripped from my arms by Jenna Love, who screams at her about having a boyfriend. She immediately leads Gina away from the dance floor and toward the nearest exit.

Message to: Maria Napoli
7/11/10 8:22 p.m.
Is jenna love REALLY ur cousin?

Message from: Maria Napoli
7/11/10 8:56 p.m.
Yes! Where did u meet her?

Message to: Maria Napoli
7/11/10 9:01 p.m.
Im texting u from the ninth level of hell.

Message from: Maria Napoli
7/11/10 9:03 p.m.
Oh stop it! Im pregnant again!

Message to: Maria Napoli
7/11/10 9:06 p.m.
Congrats! Jenna lives upstairs from me in angel bay.

Message from: Maria Napoli
7/11/10 9:07 p.m.
Lol lol lol...u must be the stupid little stoner she told me about!

Message to: Maria Napoli
7/11/10 9:06 p.m.
*I dont want her 2 know the truth about career and my head
issues. I don't really deal w her.*

Message from: Maria Napoli
7/11/10 9:07 p.m.
*Understood. Shes been a terror lately. Job and bf stuff.
Every big firm is facing huge layoffs.*

Message to: Maria Napoli
7/11/10 9:09 p.m.
Its a brutal market. Congrats again! Tell bob i said hello.

Thursday, July 15, 2010

7:07 p.m.

It's pouring rain outside again, as it has for far too many days this summer. When Dizzy's not around, I've gotten into a routine of taking a kayak out for a solo spin around the sound each night as the sun begins its descent toward the blue and watery horizon. When I'm out on the sound, I don't think about anything untoward. I'm only concerned with pushing the paddle forward, each smooth stroke through the water bringing me one bit closer to yet another place I've never been and never seen. Not just physical places; my mind often turns completely quiet while I'm out on the water. I suppose the realization that a small oar, a small kayak, and my own meager strength are the only three things coming between me and 20 feet of water and muck has a way of clearing my mind of some extraneous concerns. I like looking at all of the different houses along the water as the soft golden light hits their exteriors. Some are very big and new, some not so big and older, and some have boats docked outside that are about as large the houses themselves. The lifeboat or dingy attached is usually three times the size of the kayak that I'm paddling. I might fantasize about living in such a place with a beautiful wife, but I feel no jealousy or envy toward whoever the current owners might be. Some of them probably worked hard for 30 or 40 years to get these things. I don't need a mansion and a yacht handed to me to be happy; I just want to be put in a position as an associate at a place like Goldman Sharper where with some hard work I could be secure somewhat at some time. That hasn't happened yet.

I sit on the couch and think about this stuff while waiting for the latest potential disaster to finish cooking in the oven. Eating well, though not cheap, helps keep my IBS in check. You can't put a price on that. So I bought some large pork chops at Angel Bay Market and asked the butcher to slice them down the middle. I somehow had gotten the idea to place stuffing of some sort inside. My goal is to be spared trichinosis and have a dinner that will taste at least average. I've prepared by smoking a good bit of Grapefruit so that I'll devour the entire thing regardless of how it might turn out.

The Phillies are on a West Coast trip, the rain is continuing to pour and I'm much too lazy to retrieve my guitar that I left at Dizzy's house after a late night jam, so my stoned and unoccupied mind next turns to fish stories, namely Megan McLaughlin. I was floored by her. I used to think that love at first sight was a great farce designed and perpetuated by Hollywood to keep women buying movie tickets. It fits so well within the female concept of victimhood in that they are forced live on this Earth with a bunch of intolerable men who never understand them, never listen to them, don't know how to spoil them, and have hairy backs. But then, that one person will walk out of the men's room at the local bar that is absolutely 100% physically, intellectually and financially perfect. He will rescue this woman from her endless misery. She deserves it, of course. No woman should ever have to compromise or settle for anybody since all women are 100% perfect and logical themselves. All of the men in their lives over the past two decades were just too dumb to see that.

My staunch skepticism surrounding love at first sight was shattered the second I saw Megan walk into the moot courtroom during law school orientation. What a brutal kick in the balls, that was. She wasn't exactly dressed to the nines in her Providence College t-shirt and gray gym shorts with flip flops, either. Still, I think every cell in my body imploded. She's the only girl that I've met in my life that literally made me speechless. Megan made me forget about *everybody* for a spell, including my previous obsessions named Kim and Lori DiDominico. Oddly, she wasn't hot. It wasn't one of those scenes where I suddenly became enamored by a girl with mile-long legs and movie star looks along with every other asshole in the room. But Megan was so fucking adorable that my mind's eye couldn't have ever imagined that a woman could look anything like she did. And she seemed to carry herself so well. I couldn't stop staring at her. My cheeks and ears burned a bright red because I felt so self-conscious about it. She had this curly, shoulder-length brown hair, big brown eyes, an incredibly kind face with dotted with little freckles, and a nice tan that you wouldn't normally see on a woman of Irish decent. She wasn't built like a stick figure, either. She had some meat on her bones, but it was good meat that was spread evenly along her 5'6" frame. It turns out that she was a rower in undergrad, so she had a legitimate "athletic" build that was not a euphemism for "fat and overweight." I had to have her for myself.

As luck would have it, Megan and I were placed in the same first-year writing section and she was assigned a seat right next to me. That's when I first noticed the large engagement ring on her hand. I also realized that I was powerless to say anything to her beyond 'Hi.' I don't know if it was because I was so freaked out by my genuine 'love at first sight' experience or if this was simply a defense mechanism left over from high school when girls thought I was a total fucking joke. This would lead to a lot of uncomfortable moments for me, because Megan was very reserved. She wasn't chatty, which is normally a very positive quality in a woman. In this instance, it was a detriment because it didn't add up to much conversation during the course of the semester. It wasn't because she was snotty or couldn't be bothered with me. She always greeted me with a nice "Hello" and asked me how I was doing every time I saw her. She had such a great voice. It is impossible to accurately describe sound in words, but it was sweet and soft yet maintained its confidence. It made me think that Megan could play both the motherly role and sexy role of a woman equally well. I remained terrified of her. It wasn't necessary because she was low maintenance and carried no attitude or airs, which was probably because she was from a small town in Vermont and not the Philadelphia region. I didn't care that she was already engaged. Boyfriends and fiancés come and go like the tides. You just have to be there and be ready when the boyfriend finally fucks up that one last, unforgivable time.

It's time to check on the pork chops. I walk over to the oven, and find myself bathed in the stifling heat that exits when I pull the door down. The chops and stuffing actually smell like real food, but I'm a bit skeptical of their appearance. My mom always overcooks everything until it is near bone dry, ever-paranoid that some lurking germ is otherwise going to kill the entire family. I've acquired some of that paranoia, so I close the oven door and head back to the couch for another toke from the *Falcon*. It's not like I have anything else to do on a rainy day. Not that it would matter if I did, anyway.

Back to Megan. Her boyfriend did fuck up, apparently. Halfway through our second semester, she showed up at our Constitutional Law class with the ring no longer on her hand. I almost fell out of my chair. I knew that the only solution to normalizing my relationship with Megan was a serious hook-up. Once I tasted some success, I was pretty sure that I could be a normal person around her. Until then, my raging infatuation with her turned me into a socially awkward megadweeb- and this was *before* my depression struck. I'd have trouble making eye contact. I'd jumble all of my words. I'd be so nervous about having to speak with her that I'd just blurt out something way too intensely because I was about to explode. This was not the University of Iowa frat guy that didn't even need to openly flirt with women because I could bullshit with anybody about anything. But somehow, I arranged a couple of study sessions with her in the law library after classes. I let it be known to a mutual friend that I had an interest in Megan, and word was passed on. She obviously wasn't freaked out by it, because we continued to study together. I swore she gave me several extra smiles when I saw her around school, but I was probably just imagining it.

Megan actually made the first move by inviting me over to her apartment one Friday night for an 8 p.m. book date. I felt like that I had just hit the lottery. After class ended at 1:30 p.m., it seemed like every hour took three to pass. I was so nervous and excited that my IBS started to flare. After shitting my brains out and showering, I finally made my way to Megan's apartment for some long-awaited alone time on non-law school property. I arrived and experienced one of those moments where you're so frazzled that you can't even decide whether you should knock or ring the doorbell when you arrive. I chose to ring the bell because that's what people always do in movies. It's much smoother than banging on a door. Megan answered wearing jeans and a black sweater, which was all she needed to look completely stunning in my eyes. "Hi!" she said sweetly. I think my knees melted away. I was somehow able to follow her lead into the kitchen. Our classmate John O'Halloran was already seated at the table with a book open. "You know John, don't you?" Megan said as I took a seat. We shook hands since it was our first formal introduction. It seemed pretty obvious that Megan and John were either together or headed down that road. I looked up to ask a question while reading *Moore v. City of East Cleveland* and clearly caught the two of them making eyes at each other. It felt like a punch to the gut. I sat there for a very tense and awkward 80 minutes before I excused myself, claiming Friday fatigue. I had no idea why Megan would have invited me over to watch her study with her new boyfriend that she had never mentioned. I was very bitter on that ride home. My sources later informed me that John and Megan had attended Providence together and that he'd been chasing her for years unsuccessfully before finally giving up. When Megan had mentioned to him that I was coming over for a study date, he showed up unannounced with two dozen roses a half-hour before I arrived in order to cut me off at the knees. Maybe that was her intent in telling him. I don't doubt that she may have had some interest in me, but the reality probably was that John was Plan A and Megan simply used me to prompt him to make a strong move after beating him back so many times before.

I kept tabs on the situation throughout the remainder of law school, even though I wouldn't have had a prayer of developing anything with Megan while I was depressed if she suddenly became available again. She couldn't have been the magic wand that cured me, anyway. No woman would have been able to reach into my skull and make an adjustment to the screwed-up recipe of chemicals in my brain. She wouldn't have hurt, of course. But it may have been worse to date her, only to drive her away later with my illness. I'm sure I would have done that. I disliked myself so much when I was depressed that I would have resented her for liking me. I wouldn't be able to grasp how someone so sweet and so smart and so adorable could want to spend time with an ugly, lazy, worthless madman and do something as intimate as sleeping with him. That's as low as you can go as a human, when you dislike people for their belief that you have positive and likeable qualities that you refuse to see or acknowledge yourself.

Megan did marry John after graduation. I would not have wanted to stand in the way of true destiny. My only hope is that I will be better prepared if another Megan McLaughlin unexpectedly walks into my life like she did during law school orientation six years ago. I'm a hopeless romantic. I'd like to think that people still get married because they are wildly in love. That's not reality, though. All I see is people settling because they're too insecure to be alone, or the biological clock is down to its last few ticks, or they're just tired of sifting through all the shit that is floating around in the dating pool. People don't marry the person they feel is the best for them; they marry the best they think they can get. That doesn't make me feel like I have much to look forward to should I get myself out of this fine mess that I've gotten myself into. In the meantime, it smells as if my pork chops have finally burned off all of their deadly parasites. I hope so, because I'm starving and tired of throwing up these days.

* * *

> *New Message: Dizzy*
> *7/15/10 8:48 p.m.*
> *Just checked the tide charts. We will be busy next week.*

> *New Message: Amanda Liss*
> *7/15/10 9:16 p.m.*
> *Hey*

> *Message to: Amanda Liss*
> *7/15/10 9:49 p.m.*
> *Whats up, miss pleasant.*

> *New Message: Peter Sharkey*
> *7/15/10 9:53 p.m.*
> *Keep scratchin ur balls bitch. Thats abt all ive seen*
> *from u this summer.*

> *New Message: Amanda Liss*
> *7/15/10 9:59 p.m.*
> *Come over cutie. Im here and have weed.*

> *Message to: Amanda Liss*
> *7/15/10 10:00 p.m.*
> *Im sold.*

> *New Message: Amanda Liss*
> *7/15/10 10:00 p.m.*
> *Shocker! Lol see u in a minute.*

Tuesday, July 20, 2010

5:06 p.m.

I had a good time with Amanda last Thursday and we spooned for the night at the end of our pot smoking session. Simply having her feminine body in my arms and the sweet smell of a woman next to me was soothing. We laughed a lot and I was permitted to massage her wonderful thighs. She explained that she was quite drunk during our text exchange the previous week. I raised the possibility of making her dream come true, but I was rebuffed with a playful slap and a giggle. I think the door to Liss bliss is ajar. I just have to be enormously patient and wait for Tony to totally fuck-up again. We spent some time together at the Shipwreck during the weekend. We have a unique ability to hang out with each other in silence in a loud bar and it's not awkward. A small crush on her is certainly brewing inside me. Well, it's more than a 'small' crush. I just tell myself it's 'small' in order to protect my fragile ego.

Blotto and Baxter have arrived for some vacation days this week, and I'm enjoying the company of both. We pass the time on this rainy late afternoon by sitting in the living room smoking marijuana while playing bubble hockey and Stratego. Stratego is our current thing. I've just made my first attack, and a bomb placed randomly in Blotto's first line of defense takes out one of my four Captains early. It's my own damn fault for failing to send out my Scouts.

"Sharkey told me to ask you about Trisha," I say as I take the piece from the board.

"That's because Sharkey's a dick," my opponent replies with a chuckle. "But I will tell you about her, anyway. Trisha was my one-time fiancé, but I now I just regard her as a nasty whore with maggots living in her cunt. Big maggots, too. Like they were put through some kind of thermonuclear radiation or something. What the fuck are we talking about? Yeah. If I had only been smart enough to see Trisha for the low self-esteem, daughter of a no-good alcoholic father and whore of a mother that she was from the very beginning. I mean, from Day One. High school orientation, as it was. But, just like a woman always does, I ignored every giant red flag that she was waiving and dove-in head first. Actually, to say 'red flag' sells it short. The Goodyear Blimp was painted red and flying over my fucking house with a spotlight. And I still ignored it. I was particularly vulnerable at the time, though. I had just gotten permanently sent home on a plane from training camp in Mankato, had no job, no money, a major concussion, was living with my parents, and was pretty much miserable. I'm sure you can identify right now, except for the brain injury. Four."

"Six." Fuck. Yet another Captain down early. Blotto is employing a particularly aggressive strategy, rushing out with two Majors and a Colonel early to rip apart my forward positions. I usually lead with a line of 5, 6 and 7. My theory is that I gain an early psychological edge by taking out a nice chunk of my adversary's army early, even if they're a bunch of cheap pieces. It also allows me to get a feel for the enemy and their strengths without revealing or sacrificing any of my higher ranked soldiers. It's not working so far today, especially with Blotto's randomly placed ordinance in the front row taking out my first Captain right from the gun. I anxiously await Blotto's runaway Colonel walking straight into a well-placed bomb in the middle of my defenses. "Three," he declares.

"Boom!" I exclaim as Baxter issues a cough worthy of a coal miner with black lung disease. He decides to lie on the floor at my feet.

"He okay?" I ask.

"The vet thinks so," Blotto replies. "The problem is that no one knows how old he really is. And he can't tell me. I wish he could talk sometimes. I'd like to think that he has more wisdom and intelligence than most humans. That ain't sayin' much, though. I have no idea what I'd do without him. Coming home from work or yet another bad date or yet another drinking binge and not having him there to greet me...fuck it, whatever happened to that bowl?" I pass Blotto the *Falcon* just before he dusts my bomb with a trailing Miner. It's just one of two decoys, though. My flag is on the right side of the board. Fortunately, Blotto begins to cut left after taking a toke. I take one of Blotto's useless Scouts before he diffuses the second bomb. His eyes reveal that he feels that he is on the road to an early capture of my flag. Then I take out the advancing Miner with a seven. "What the fuck were we talking about?" he asks as he puts the defeated piece back into the sleeve holding his casualties.

"Trisha."

"Yeah. In any event, I run into her at a convenience store one night when I stopped to get a can of dip. That was a bad habit I picked-up in college. I didn't finally quit until they removed half of Silent John's tongue. He was a trial lawyer, too. Kinda affected his ability to do his job. So we make smalltalk and I ask for Trisha's number. Again. I think the last time was my sophomore year of high school. We wind up going out one night for drinks. It was probably a bad idea to start that way because her father was a raging alcoholic. Trisha was a cheerleader, so her dad used to come to all of my football games to watch her cheer. He was usually so fucking bombed that they used to have to ask him to leave for being so drunk and belligerent- at a fucking high school game. One night, they had to bounce him because he was screaming at the opposing cheerleaders that they were "a bunch of cocksucking sluts that will get drunk after the game and suck on each other's tampons." He had to be semi-retarded. Needless to say, Trisha would get pretty embarrassed and I'm sure it sowed the seeds of some serious self-esteem issues. So instead of being with me in high school, she dated my total asshole teammate who got kicked off the team and kicked out of school for punching an assistant coach in the jaw. That was the first red flag right there. It was obvious that she was inclined to date total assholes and fuck-ups like her father. Three."

"Two." Blotto's aggressive attack on my left flank is defeated.

"Shit. So it turns out she got knocked up right after I went away to college to become a football star. By the time I got back home for good, the father of the kid is in jail for his third DUI, then he attacked one of the other inmates and a guard with a weightlifting bar and got handed an extended stay in his cell. This should have been another indication to me that Trisha was not capable of making the best choices. But I ignored it, and we start dating."

"Five."

"Six. So I get her wasted that first night. I don't even know who was watching her son. That was never really explained. We had *fantastic* sex that first night, so I was hooked right away. That was almost ten years of pent-up testicular frustration that finally got blown-out full force. Long story short, we wind up dating for three years and we start looking for a place together. Her son Todd is 8 at this point, and I'm really tight with him, too. Very cool little kid. He called me 'Dad,' even. I gave him the helmet that I stole from the Vikings when I got cut. They even billed me for it, those bastards. I still have that bill somewhere. I never fucking paid it. So one Saturday I score great seats for the Phillies and I'm supposed to take him. He was so excited to go, but we're driving down I-95 to The Vet in my Dad's old '87 pick-up he gave me and Todd's not saying a word. Totally doesn't seem like himself. So I'm like, *'Everything okay, big guy?'* and he's like, *'Mommy told me not to tell you.'* I figured something must have happened at school, or with a girl, or he flunked a test or something. So I prod him a bit and bribe him with an offer of a hot dog and a soda, which I was going to get him anyway. And he just blurts out, *'There was a bad man at the apartment last night and he was showing mommy his pee pee.'* I nearly drove right off the fucking road. I knew a little kid wasn't going to make something like that up out of nowhere, especially Todd. Boom!"

My all-important Spy has now been wasted by a bomb.

"So this is like, fifteen years ago now. There was no cell phones or text messaging. So I had to go sit through that entire fucking game with my stomach completely twisted up in knots with absolutely no explanation. I couldn't eat, I couldn't drink, I couldn't sit still. But I wasn't about to ask Todd exactly what mommy was doing with said pee pee. The game went extra fucking innings, of course, and they *lost*. I tried calling Trisha on a pay phone at one point, but she didn't answer. She went to the bar to get trashed by herself, it turns out."

Blotto starts coming down the center again, this time toward my right flank. He's already taken out most of my left, even though the attack was ultimately thwarted. He knows where my flag is. I have no idea where his might be hiding.

"Long story short, we get back to the apartment and Trisha is nowhere to be found. Todd goes into his bedroom and falls asleep. I wait. And I wait. And I wait. I have to. Like I'm going to let Todd be left alone in the apartment? Holy irresponsible mother, Batman. Trisha finally shows up piss drunk, in tears, and tries to walk straight to her room. That wasn't happening. So I'm like, *'Company last night?'* and her entire face dropped even further than it already was. So she runs into Todd's room and starts *screaming* at him for being honest with me. What a great lesson to teach your son, huh? So eventually the truth comes out. She fucked this guy I used to play football against in high school. Kevin Dingle. Total fucking douchebag. I still see him at the Shipwreck sometimes. But that was Trisha's speed. She only felt comfortable with total fucking assholes. She did me a favor, really, because it took that incident to finally admit it to myself. I'm sure there were others. It was so much easier to get away with cheating back then without cell phones and the internet. Now, everyone knows from the pictures on facebook where you got fucked up last night, and with who, and even what you ate for breakfast the next morning- whether you want them to or not. Why do people always post pictures of food on facebook? I never understood that. But the hardest thing I ever had to do in my entire life, aside from walking into my mother's viewing, was to sit down with Todd to tell him that I wasn't going to be his father anymore. He kept crying and crying and asking if it was all his fault. It's wasn't, of course, but I couldn't tell him the truth which was that his mother was a fucking whore."

"Ever see 'im again?"

"In court this past May. Trisha married some other dickhead a few years later. This is where things really get complicated but I'm fucking wasted and you're a lawyer so I'm sure you hear a bunch of fucked up stories all of the time. Can we consider this attorney-client privileged?"

"Sure. You can consider it friendship privileged, as well."

"I appreciate that, brother," Blotto says as we bump fists. "So I'm really drunk a year or two ago at about 4 a.m. and I try to look Todd up on facebook," he continues. "And I find him. And not only do I find him, but his profile picture is the Vikings helmet that I stole when they cut me from camp. Just a plain purple helmet with the adhesive tape still attached to the front that said 'Bristow.' You have to *earn* the right to wear one with actual Viking horn, you know."

"I understand."

"So I had no idea what to do at that point. I cracked emotionally. So I just pretended that I never saw it. Todd never contacted *me*, either. So this past winter, I find out from my dad of all people that Todd- who is 23 now, by the way- is being sentenced for vehicular homicide. He drove home drunk from a party and killed a three year-old. So he's pretty much going away for at *least* five years. I struggled with what I should do, but I decided to show up for sentencing. Trisha's entire family is there, so I sat in the back away from those assholes. Her dad was drunk in the courtroom, of course. Todd is lead into the room in cuffs and an orange prison suit just like it's a TV show. We make eye contact a split fucking second later. I could have died. I hadn't seen him in fifteen years, but there was no question that this was the same eight year-old that went to the Phillies with me that day. Same eyes, same features, except he's going away to jail for a long, long time instead of a ballgame. I just felt- well, I couldn't even describe it to you. It felt like my soul was melting out of my body when he stood behind the defense table to hear his sentence. I sat through the victim impact statements, which were heartbreaking. I was impressed with the way Todd handled himself and apologized to the family, though. I know it's just words, but it seemed sincere- especially since his fate was already sealed. Seven to ten years, he gets. So he's being lead away after sentencing, Trisha's screaming and crying, and Todd looks right at me and yells, *'This never would have happened if you had been my father instead, David!'*"

"I'm...*so* sorry, man. I don't know what else to say."

"It's okay, Woodchuck. I didn't know what to say, either. The entire courtroom turned around and looked *right* at me. So I just ran out of there. I never ran away from anything in my life, but I could have set an Olympic record running out of that fucking courthouse. I would like to think that Todd wasn't being malicious. He was just telling the truth, I guess. He's probably had that bottled up inside himself for a while, just like I did. I haven't slept since that day, unless I'm completely wasted. You may have noticed that I drink and smoke a lot."

"I've noticed," I say and we share a stoned laugh.

"When I can, I'm going to sit down and write Todd a letter. I can't right now. I just can't. It may take me another year. Or two. He's not going anywhere, though. So the moral of the story, Woodchuck, I guess, is this: the only thing that can completely destroy a man's life is a woman. You'll always know deep down inside if you've fallen for the wrong person. Don't do what I did and squash the voice of reason living inside your head because of something as shallow as a mega-attraction to someone. There's plenty of attractive women around, and believe it or not some of them are very good people with an actual conscience. So the next time you sense in any way that a woman is bad news, run like hell, man. And don't stop running until you're on your very last breath. It will save you a whole lot of pain later. One."

"Flag."

"Thought so, bitch. Your turn to grab dinner. Actually, I'll pay for your unemployed ass tonight. I'll buy, you fly."

I grab a large umbrella from the nearby closet and set out alone for the four-block walk to the Moo Moo, since the Shitmobile has had problems starting in the rain lately.

Wednesday, July 21, 2010

1:27 a.m.

I think the Gina D'Amico dream- however baseless it was- died at the Phillies game tonight courtesy of a change-up fouled off by Chase Utley. It sailed straight into my hands. It's strange that a stray foul ball can provide insight into a person's character. Things all started at approximately 4:00 p.m., when Peter Sharkey called Blotto to offer him one of four tickets directly behind the dugout to the 7:05 Phillies game. He didn't want to interrupt his vacation or cancel his bar date with a sexy blonde named Dina that was last seen escaping panty-less from the Board Room window, so I drove the 86 miles back to Philly to meet Sharkey at a bar on the corner of 24th & Fairmount called The Bishop's Collar. Sharkey also gave one ticket to Gina and the other to his hairdresser, a cute girl named Olivia, that he has been sleeping with for six years with no firm commitment. Everyone was already bombed when I arrived at the bar at 6:30. We grabbed a cab and headed straight for the stadium.

The seats were fucking spectacular. We were so close that one of the opposing players actually cracked a smile while the drunken Sharkey was heckling him. I was seated in between Gina and a 7 year-old boy who was at the game with his dad, who was a Philadelphia police officer and got the tickets from his "much more successful brother, who's a lawyer." The kid looked like he had died and gone to Heaven. He was sitting there awestruck in a little Phillies cap and Phillies t-shirt with his baseball glove anchored onto his left hand as he awaited his opportunity to strike gold by scoring an authentic Major League baseball from the field of play. I long for the days when nothing was more important than baseball. Then you discover pussy and your life goes completely down the shitter because it's something you can't control and watching isn't as fun as actually playing.

Gina was being her usual drunken self, which means she was laughing at everything I said, touching me a lot, sending me goofy, flirtatious and sexual text messages even though I was sitting right next to her, and doing all of those other subtle things that a woman does when she wants to fuck you on some yet-to-be-determined level. Occasionally, she'd throw a barb my way and then apologize for it just as quickly. Then, in the sixth inning, Chase Utley hit that that foul ball directly into my hands. I didn't think twice about it. I handed the ball to the kid next to me. I *was* that kid once. He didn't know whether to shit or cry. I think he did both. The father was *thrilled* by my off-hand gesture. He couldn't stop thanking me. Gina herself was *livid*. She did not say one word to me for the rest of the game. That's when I realized that nothing was ever going to happen between us. She just doesn't get what I'm about. Kim wouldn't have cared if I gave that ball to a little kid instead of her. She would have *expected* it. Even Vanessa the Annoyer, who used to secretly watch me playing Wiffle ball with the neighborhood kids in Manayunk from her window, would have been positively wet in her panties from this unselfish display of 'good father' genes. Not that I want Gina to think of me in those terms, but I knew right then in Row 1 of Citizens Bank Park that any dream of love or lust with her was dust. If she couldn't appreciate what I had just done, there was no way that she'd never be able to appreciate me for who I really am. It finally made me realize that Gina is nothing more than a selfish bitch. Sharkey didn't help matters. He teased her unmercifully for being so bitter about it. He would have done the same thing I did. We're older than 75% the players on the field now. I actually have a license to represent them. We don't need their baseballs. We just want to enjoy a game on a summer night and see them win.

I know I did the right thing tonight, but doing the right thing is usually the last thing that helps you to get laid. It's a shame it has to be that way. I'm actually surprised that I managed to catch the ball given the amount of time I spent staring at Gina's thighs tonight. Even if I'm questioning her as a person, I'm still held hostage by an ever-expanding, festering lust every time she's near me. There's nothing that I can do about that, and it's a very troubling conflict. It's been 20 years since the late Donna DeAngelo awakened me to the wonders of Italian girls before calling me a pervert and kicking me in the shin for my wandering eyes. The only quality Italian pussy I have to show for it is one fucking night with Lori DiDominico.

The kid's dad did give me an FOP card, though. I'll certainly need it because I can't afford to pay a speeding ticket any time soon.

Monday, July 26, 2010

In the real dark night of the soul it is always three o'clock in the morning, day after day.

-F. Scott Fitzgerald

[broke. unemployed. loveless. sexless. ugly. dependent. stupid. pathetic. tortured. hopeless. powerless. aside from a child molester and a man with a darkened and malignant heart who has committed murder, is there any human lower than i am right now? NO! so just take that fucking lighter into your hands, asshole! take it! fucking pain is what you deserve. horrible pain! how dare you sit here on the rolling waters of angel bay, you unemployable son of a bitch, spending your government check on drugs and guitar strings and who knows whatever else you waste it on! you don't even deserve to see the light of day or the fading sun sinking beneath the sound in all of its splendid colors ever again! you should be working you lazy fuck! and your delusions are absolutely laughable. laughable! you know it, too. you can deny deny deny all you want but you know that you will NEVER be good enough for a tight tanned toned blue-eyed blonde or a woman with big brown eyes and brown legs and a killer smile that makes you giddy with all kinds of excitement! NEVER! who the fuck do you think you are?!? your own best friend in high school couldn't *wait* to get fucked before she left for seton hall and she said *she wouldn't fuck you if you paid her and took her to hershey park the next day.* until she was divorced and gained 40 pounds, of course! when will you learn that this isn't iowa, dickweed! this isn't a bunch of hick sorority girls who don't have the capacity to realize what a worthless fuck you are! those girls would date ANYBODY, even you! but this is philadelphia! this is angel bay! this is the REAL WORLD! you have to EARN your pussy now! and in the real world you are broke and muscle-less and rotten and disturbed and you'll be lucky to find yourself with a fat piece of fucking trash like regina pellini ever again! do you think that you are above certain women? you are shit! you thought you were above dating maria napoli didn't you? she wasn't good-looking enough for you, was she? again: who the FUCK are you! you broke that poor little girl's heart, and you will pay! NO woman with pretty eyes and a pleasant face and pleasant body will EVER lower herself to pleasuring a piece of human garbage that is so fucking bankrupt in so many fucking ways. not to mention that you wasted $90,000 to litigate bullshit slip & fall cases for no pay you stupid fuck!! you must cleanse your heart, your soul, your shit of an existence! *now do it.* do it! *flick*...the flame it dances orange and blue and inviting...it moves closer, warm but soft in the blackened darkness of this room. closer. closer! hot. hot! just push it! push it! PUSH IT! now! now! just get it over

222

with! hothothothothothot...it burns! it fucking burns! just another second...the pain! THE FUCKING PAIN! the pain of this burning flesh is unbearable! inhuman! evil! stop. enough! now do it again. AGAIN! you deserve more pain, you fuck! smell that burning human flesh! that's right! scream, you fuck! scream until you are satisfied that you have inflicted the horrible pain you truly deserve!]

* * *

> But kiss me out of desire, babe, and not consolation.
>
>   - Jeff Buckley

9:11 p.m.

I can't believe I fucking did this to myself. This weekend was a confluence of clusterfuck that has destroyed what little remaining ability that I had to think rationally. The end result leaves me standing over the kitchen sink as the cool water runs over the blistering, reddened mess of burnt flesh that I just created on my own forearm using my yellow lighter with purple polka dots. It fucking hurts and burns like hell while the rest of my body shivers with an especially cold chill.

If someone had told me on Friday night that I would get Heather Ball naked and unexpectedly make out with Gina D'Amico while she was wearing her hottest outfit of the summer, I would have thought that an outstanding weekend was on the horizon. And I would have been wrong. Things seemed to be trending upward on Friday night but it only got progressively worse. After continuously lamenting to myself about my perceived failure with Gina, Heather went home with me after shoving her drunken tongue down my throat so many times at the Shipwreck that it was starting to become embarrassing. I finally pulled her out of the bar just after midnight and took her back to the Board Room for some entertainment before the rest of the boys returned for a meeting. Heather and I were holding hands, giggling, bumping ourselves into each other and doing all of the other things that wasted people do when they're walking home from a bar with someone that they want to fuck. It's always a good feeling to be one of those guys. She looked spectacular. She was wearing a way-short red skirt with a slutty, glistening black top and black stripper shoes. The sound of Heather's heels clapping against the sidewalk alone was turning me on enough, let alone her tan legs, her face, her eyes, her blonde hair and her constant wet kisses over the course of the night.

We entered 728 to find the entire downstairs vacant. I was attacked. I hadn't felt wanted like that in forever. Only three minutes later, Heather's golden legs were spread eagle in my bunk. She was wearing only her heels and staring me down with her baby blue eyes as my eager tongue tickled her bald, pink slit. I licked it like it was the best pussy I had in years, because it was. Heather was moaning with delight and revealed a very, very dirty mouth. Her phone began blowing up to the point where the constant buzzing and Lady GaGa ringtone became very annoying and distracting. Heather retrieved it from her nearby purse while I continued to imbibe on the sweet nectar flowing from between her golden thighs. I assumed that she was grabbing her phone to shut it down. With my tongue slowing moving toward her anus, I looked up to find Heather vigorously tapping away at the keys on her phone. And she kept tapping. And tapping. And tapping. Finally, I had to ask:

"Umm...Heather?"

"What," she replied with great impatience.

"What the fuck are you doing, exactly?"

"Hold on. I really need to send this text."

"Is somebody dying right now?"

She suddenly slammed both her phone and her legs shut, left my bunk, and began fishing around for her clothes. There was no emergency. Heather readily confessed that she was ditching me mid-cunnilingus in favor of someone else six blocks away. I was incredulous. She had the right to do that, of course, just like I have the right to dangle a fresh steak two inches from the face of a homeless mother with a starving child. Just because you have the right to do something doesn't change the fact that you're a total *asshole* for doing it. To add even further insult to injury, the person's name was her former third grade nemesis that constantly made fun of her for having three chins, Dino Morelli. He had recently resurfaced at the Shipwreck as a Hot Dude after a lengthy stint in the Marine Corps. Showing neither any conscience nor remorse, *she asked me to walk her over to his house.* Even I'm not *that* much of a sucker. The drunken Heather never made it there. Without my escort, she tripped over a curb and cracked her head open. A bike cop found her lying on the ground bleeding and called an ambulance. She refused to go to the hospital, was taken anyway, and then arrested on an outstanding jaywalking citation from 2006. I can't say that I have any sympathy for her. She's almost a bigger trainwreck than I am. Almost.

I spent a great deal of a beautiful Saturday afternoon pacing around 728 while everyone else was wakeboarding on Harry's boat. It was very non-productive. All I did was curse and mumble prayers for the death of Heather and Dino and my tortured balls. My dad interrupted with another long lecture via cell while he informed me that the Philadelphia Sheriff paid the house a visit on Friday afternoon to serve a lawsuit that my credit card company brought against me for $8,426. (The actual balance was $2,422 and my purchases themselves were paid for. The rest was interest, late fees, and fees for the interest and late fees putting me over my $5,000 limit.) They must have bad lawyers. A simple investigation would have revealed that I'm already $90,000 in the hole with no assets. Even if they obtain a judgment against me, there's no way of collecting it.

I went through the package of mail Mom had sent to Angel Bay and uncovered rejection letters from eight additional law firms. At least they bothered to respond. Twelve other firms still haven't. I've also been rejected for several pseudo-legal positions at various universities in the Philadelphia area. They feel that I'm overqualified for a job paying a miniscule amount like $65,000 because I have a law degree, whereas the law firms think I'm under-qualified because of my beyond shitty credentials. That brought the grand total to 18 outright rejections and 33 non-responses for the summer. One of my rejections was from a firm that practices lemon law exclusively. Think about that: a firm has already adjudged, my twenty years of schooling notwithstanding, that I'm not competent enough to represent people who own a car that has had an excessive number of trips to the mechanic for repairs. And it's not like I'd even want such a horrendously shitty job, anyway. *"You say it's a '06 Chrysler, ma'am? And after the first time the Check Engine light came on, what exactly did you do? No, ma'am, I am taking your claim very seriously. This is exactly why I went to school for seven years, ma'am, and spent over $80,000 so that you could tell me about all the problems you're having with your Chrysler fucking minivan."* I was staggering and stumbling from taking blows to the head and heart from all sides. The bleeding had started in earnest. And there was no cut man in my corner or any referee to stop the carnage. Not wanting to admit these things to anyone not named 'Dr. Karlis,' I felt all alone and just had to deal.

But fortunes change in Angel Bay like the direction of the breeze across the sound. On late Saturday night, I waved the white flag and bailed on the Shipwreck early. At approximately 1:36 a.m., Gina unexpectedly stumbled through the screen door ahead of the pack returning from the bars. And when I say she 'stumbled' through the door, I mean she *stumbled* through the door. She tripped right through the screen, leaving only the white metal frame standing. With my help, she was able to again stand on the slinky heels that put the exclamation point on her uncharacteristically un-conservative purple mini-dress. What a hot fucking mess she was. She began a serious snorting fit. It didn't make her appear any less delicious. We then had a very brief exchange when the snorting stopped that went like this:

"Hi, Woodchuck!"

"Hi."

"Umm...I broke up with Chas."

"You did?"

"M'mm. And I'm *really* fucking wasted."

It sounded like she was over the fact that I sniffed Mallory's panties or gave the baseball hit by Chase Utley to the kid instead of her. It was time to act and to act boldly. I pushed the giggling Gina into the Board Room, shut the door, threw her on the queen, and launched myself atop her. She didn't resist. She tasted like alcohol, which is an incredible turn-on because you know that means you are dealing with someone with much-lowered inhibitions. The skin on her thighs felt so smooth and warm in my hands. We kissed only for a few minutes before the rest of the Board began to shuffle in from the bars. Gina used this as an excuse to run upstairs without me and go to bed, locking her bedroom door behind her so that I could not pay her a surprise visit. I knocked on the door continuously until a positively annoyed Jenna cracked it open and launched a glass of water into my face.

Gina made herself scarce on Sunday and didn't return the text message I sent her. I assumed that she had already driven back to Philly for work on Monday, but I was delighted that I finally experienced her sweet, soft lips for a few minutes' time. I thought about her brown legs the entire day. My mind was incapable of being interrupted by anything else for any great length of time, whether it was my lack of a job, my poverty, or the fact that I was named as a defendant in a lawsuit that I would have to report to the Supreme Court of Pennsylvania. I wandered around the Moo Moo for twenty minutes while grabbing lunch because I was so stoned and excited for Gina that I couldn't even focus or think straight enough to decide what I wanted to eat, grab it, pay for it, and go the fuck home. When I finally got in line with my chips and a sandwich, I realized that I had left the house with no wallet and no coin.

In the end, this few minutes of bliss with Gina revealed itself to be only a drunken pity kiss from an attention whore. She was the final nail in my coffin of sanity that was slammed into place late Sunday night. I returned from a quick supply run to Angel Bay Market to find Molly in the living room. Dizzy himself was nowhere to be found. I didn't think it was unusual. I gave him blanket permission to drop Molly off at 728 any time that he might be heading out to A.C. on an all-night cocaine binge with a stripper or a quick overnight run back to Philly to check on his donut operations. I always enjoyed her company. After sitting outside for a spell with the friendly dog and smoking copious amounts of marijuana by myself (Molly declined), I retreated to the Board Room to hit the sack. While being snuggled on the queen by the affectionate dog, I heard Gina laughing her ridiculous laugh in her bedroom above. This was odd, because she never stayed in Angel Bay on Sunday nights. She avoided the Drive at Five (A.M.) back to Philly on Monday mornings for work like the plague. About five minutes later, I could hear her climb into bed. Then the bed started squeaking in a very distinct rhythm. And it kept squeaking. It became more intense. I could hear Gina moaning loudly and clearly. Apparently, somebody was 'so deep' inside of her and it was driving her out of her mind as I lay with a hairy dog only ten feet below on the same bed where we made out the night before. I looked out the window and checked the side yard. Chas' Porsche was nowhere to be found, so this wasn't a round of make-up sex. I had no idea what the fuck was going on with this latest turn of events. All I knew was that the same gorgeous legs that I'd been dreaming about all day were wide, wide open for someone else and it was going down right under my own nose. My stomach twisted inside out. I couldn't sleep. I couldn't sit still. My whole world was crumbling and there wasn't a fucking thing that I could do about it. I felt stupid more than anything. *How could I have thought for even a single second that a girl who looks like Gina would be interested in me?* I sent out a text to Dizzy to see where he was. His phone began going off on the coffee table in my living room. I felt so many simultaneous emotions that I had a complete brain freeze. I took some sleeping pills passed out on the living couch with Molly on the floor next to me. When I awoke in a haze the next day at about noon, 728 was vacant.

Further, Tony the Douchebag was placed off probation and is firmly back in Amanda's good graces. He appeared with her at the Shipwreck this weekend, and she completely ignored me like Dharma the Ghost Kisser-er always does.

Finding myself alone tonight with my thoughts and unable to sit still, the only way to release the demon created by the cruel, crippling confluence of poverty, unemployment, stress, tension, the lack of real intimacy, self-hatred, and pure hell boiling inside my body was to cause myself a destructive orgasm of indescribable pain. I'm so helpless. I'm not afraid to admit to myself that I'm weak and I simply can't deal. I'll have to call Dr. Karlis tomorrow. I need very strong tranquilizers. But most of all, I need to find religion. And just like Blotto did with Trisha, I'm so pissed that I refused to listen to the voice of reason in my head. I should have run like hell from Gina the very second I met her. It had EPIC FAIL written all over it.

I'm such a fucking asshole.

Tuesday, July 27, 2010

1:28 p.m.

My emergency appointment with Dr. Karlis today is the most humbling experience of my life. I rolled off his couch and straight onto the floor, where I placed myself into the fetal position and cried like a baby pining for a pacifier. I'm so fucking ashamed. When a grown 'man' with a ton of friends and a law degree has cried his eyes out on the carpet of his psychiatrist's office- with burns of his own making up and down his arm, to boot- he's *really* hit rock fucking bottom. I'm only a small, single step above a person sucking dick for crack at this point. I'm a broken person who can't handle himself, can't handle everyday life, can't handle his career, and can't handle his women. Dr. Karlis was silent and allowed me to release my pent-up frustration with reaching my early thirties as a completely powerless person financially, socially and mentally. I feel no different than being 17 again, except I have less money and much more debt. I finally composed myself and climbed back onto the couch as the good doctor polished off another Diet Coke with lime.

"Do you feel any better, Mr. McShea?"

"A little."

"Irishmen aren't supposed to cry, are they?"

"No. But I did."

"That's better than destroying yourself, isn't it?"

"I started destroying myself five years ago."

"How so?"

"I should have called you then. I should have called you during my 2L year. Not three years following graduation, after I already destroyed my career and tried to kill myself."

"Depressed people don't usually make those calls for help, Mr. McShea. Why? Because they're depressed. You know that. You lived it. You *must* move forward."

"How?"

"What if you had gotten cancer during law school, Patrick, and you finished with the same grades? Would you be beating yourself up like this right now?"

"Of course not."

"Why."

"Because you can't help getting cancer."

"How is that different from depression? Some people get cancer, some people get MS, some people get depressed. And as far as depression, there's no obvious sign that your body is breaking down like you might find preceding a diagnosis of cancer or multiple sclerosis. You didn't even know you were sick."

228

"A managing partner *might* understand bad grades because of cancer treatments. Mental illness? You might as well walk into the partner's office and piss all over his desk. No one's going to take that risk unless you have a close connection somewhere in the firm. It's not normal to lie awake at night for three or four hours a night and want to kill yourself."

"You're right. It's not. Just because help comes later than you would have liked is not necessarily a bad thing. You might be dead right now if we hadn't met at all."

"And I would be far better off."

"Can you honestly say that, Mr. McShea?"

"Yes, I can."

"You have a journey of 1,000 miles ahead of you. You're throwing in the towel ten minutes in. You can will yourself to failure, you know. So I have to ask you this sincerely: are you a quitter?"

"At this stage? Yes. Absolutely. And I'm not ashamed. I can't take another ounce of failure with anything. Next time, I'll grab a gun again instead of a lighter. The way I live...it's not natural."

"I believe that you're a stronger man than that, or you wouldn't have even made it this far."

"I don't want anything to do with a fucking 1,000 mile journey, Doctor. I've been broke since I left the womb. I went to Iowa to better myself. I went to law school to better myself. I still have nothing. Fuck it."

"For the first time, I'm hearing a sense of entitlement from you."

"I know. I'm sorry. Now that I've entered my thirties, I have a lot of *very* successful friends and fraternity brothers, Doctor. It's hard."

"No apology is necessary, Mr. McShea. We're simply examining here. Are you jealous of your very successful friends?"

"Not at all. They've earned it themselves. They didn't get tripped up like I did."

"Now who says that you have nothing?"

"I do. And that's the only opinion that counts."

"Do you have a caring family?"

"Yes."

"Before law school, when you worked as a juvenile probation officer in North Philly, did those children all have caring families?"

"Some, yes. Others, the mom would disappear for days smoking crack and leave the 12 year-old in charge of the four kids."

"I don't doubt that. Do you have friends?"

"Yes. Good ones."

"You need all the friends you can get, including yourself."

"Very true, Doctor. I think that's my problem these days. I'm not at all content with myself."

"Someone of your intelligence will eventually find contentment with himself in some way."

"Who says I'm intelligent? I can't do math to save my life."

"So what? I'm a medical doctor and I can't spell. Now, you can't honestly say that you have nothing, can you?"

"No, Doctor. I can't."

"Good. After your episode this week, that's important for you to recognize right now. I'm not trying to sound like your Irish Catholic parents, but some people *really* do have nothing. On the other hand- and this might sound callous or cold- that is *none* of your concern, Mr. McShea. Comparisons can be deadly. If you compare yourself to someone who has less, then you're placing yourself in a position to apologize for your own existence. You should *never* apologize for who you are, or for what you have earned with your own money, blood, sweat, tears and brain. But if you compare yourself to someone who has "more" than you might, you will never measure up in your *own* eyes. There will *always* be someone with a better job, more money, a nicer car, a bigger mansion, and more girls than you have. Always, always, always. Guess how much my last patient yesterday made last year?"

"I dunno. Five-hundred thousand."

"Two million. And he sat there and bitched to me for an hour because he's no longer getting invited to the cocktail parties by the lawyers who made five, ten or twenty million last year. The more you compare yourselves to others, especially the ones that you perceive to have more than you do, the greater harm you will do to your own self. And you may see someone your own age step out of a $90,000 Mercedes, but you don't see the bill for the car payment every month, do you? He's probably *drowning* in debt. It's the American way. Have you ever been to India?"

"No."

"Some of the people there literally have nothing except the clothes that they're wearing, if that. People sleep in the streets as a way of life. And they have smiles on their faces. There is no crime. They feel blessed. Admittedly, American capitalism and our society make it much more difficult for you to feel blessed, especially when you grew up in a major city and see all of the money in Angel Bay. But don't *ever* say you have 'nothing.' You do. Otherwise, what's to stop you from leaving my office right now and jumping off the Walt Whitman Bridge?"

"They're still sandblasting it, I think."

"They are. But answer the question: what is stopping you from leaving this office and making a jump off a bridge?"

"Hope, I guess. I'm hoping that things will turn around. Somehow. But they won't."

"How can you say that with a straight face? Even Yoda can't predict the future."

"Yoda didn't have $90,000 in student loans to pay, didn't graduate from a Tier Two law school with a 2.62, and I doubt he lived in his parents' basement at 300 years old."

"Never saw him with a woman, though, did you?"

"Me, neither, Doctor. Not in years."

"I get the sense, Mr. McShea, that you're chasing a bunch of women with something between their legs but nothing between their ears. A big present all wrapped-up with a bow but nothing inside the box, so to speak."

"Isn't that *all* women, Doctor?"

My psychiatrist pauses to chuckle. "It certainly may seem that way at times, Mr. McShea," he says. "But deep inside, you know that simply isn't true. There's no need to go around chasing the Flavor of the Month at your age. There may be someone closer than you think. But in the meantime, you need to see my dermatologist friend down the hall. I'll buzz ahead to let him know you're walking down to see him now. I'm concerned that your burns are deep and starting to show some early signs of infection."

At the end of the appointment, I'm prescribed a powerful but non-habit forming sustained release tranquilizer that has a generic version which I'm able to afford. My next appointment is scheduled for one week. I shake hands with my doctor, then head toward the office door with a destroyed ego and moist eyes.

"Listen," says the doctor as I head out the door. "Remember one thing."

"What's that?"

"All bleeding stops, Patrick."

I walk to the receptionist to hand her a $200 check. Sitting on the bench across from the reception window among the piles of *National Geographic* and *Golf Digest* is a beautiful brunette in glasses wearing a sharp blue suit and pink blouse while thumbing through a court opinion of some sort. Her legs are a work of art, and

I'd recognize them anywhere. I silently try to sneak out of the suite without making eye contact with Jenna Love but fail.

Wednesday, July 28, 2010

> *6:51 p.m.*

To: *PMcShea77@junkmail.com*
From: *karen.lardo@smithstaffing.com*
Subject: DMI Communications, Inc. Litigation

Mr. Mcshea:

This is to confirm that you will be a member of the document review team in the above-referenced matter. The hourly rate is $26.00 and your work week is 40 hours. There are no benefits and no overtime will be offered. Your estimated start date has been moved from August 16 to September 13, 2010, due to ongoing motion practice regarding the documents to be produced. The assignment is expected to last 6 to 12 months and may possibly continue longer. Please be advised that you will have little or no warning when this assignment ends, as a potential settlement of this case is beyond our control.

There is no opportunity for permanent placement with the firm for which you will be reviewing the documents.

Since we always receive questions regarding this subject, please note that you will NOT have access to the cafeteria at the firm. The firm has also requested that you do not eat lunch anywhere in or within 20 feet of the building in order to ensure that there is no contact between the members of your team and any of the firm's attorneys or its clients. Contact between you and the attorneys of the firm and/or its clients will result in immediate termination. Additional information will be provided when your assignment begins.

Thank you again for using Smith Attorney Staffing.

Karen Lardo, Esq.

* * *

To: *PMcShea77@junkmail.com*
From: *jenna.r.love@wwwmslaw.com*
Subject: (no subject)

Mr. McShea:

I write to address our encounter in the offices of Andreas N. Karlis, M.D. on or about July 27, 2010. For your information, I am not under psychiatric care as a patient of Dr. Karlis or any other mental health service provider. As a member of the Philadelphia Bar Association's Women in the Law committee, I was assigned the task of interviewing Dr. Karlis concerning any particular trends or unique mental health problems affecting women in the profession. As you may or may not know, the State of Connecticut at one time forever disbarred any lawyer who had received psychological or psychiatric care at any time while practicing law or otherwise. Since our firm has a national practice, I have been admitted pro hace vice in both federal and state courts in Connecticut. As an associate at Philadelphia's top firm, I will not allow my employment to be jeopardized by any baseless speculation or rumors that you may spread amongst your friends or former colleagues concerning my presence in the office of Dr. Karlis on that day. Any such statements will be considered defamatory and I will proceed as warranted with the full power and resources of this firm behind me.

Thank you in advance for your understanding and cooperation in this matter.

Jenna R. Love, Esquire
Associate, Litigation
Wheat Winkelspect White Morgan & Straw LLP
1901 Market Street, Floor 61
Philadelphia, PA 19103

CONFIDENTIALITY NOTICE: This communication is attorney-client privileged and confidential and solely for the identified recipient. Any disclosure, copying, distribution, or use of the contents of this communication is strictly prohibited. If you have received this e-mail in error, immediately notify the sender by reply e-mail and permanently delete this transmission.

TAX ADVICE DISCLAIMER: Any federal tax advice contained in this communication (including attachments) was not intended or written to be used, and it cannot be used, by you for the purpose of (1) avoiding any penalty that may be imposed by the Internal Revenue Service or (2) promoting, marketing, or recommending to another party any transaction or matter addressed herein.

To: PMcShea77@junkmail.com
From: angelbaygina@junkmail.com
Subject: (no subject)

hey asshole

first, dizzy hasnt returned my calls or texts all week so im sure u told him to stop hooking up with me. it is none of your fucking business who i hook up with. none! second, what would EVER make u think that i would date you. i had no interest in u at all and ur NOT very attractive. ever hear of the gym? maybe u should stop lifting the bong and start lifting the weights instead. the two of us were FRIENDS and thats it. u obviously couldnt take the hint. thats not my problem. ur not very smart for a lawyer. i guess thats why u dont have a job and live with ur parents u fukin jerk off.

* * *

PHILADELPHIA- The venerable Wheat, Winkelspeckt, White, Morgan & Straw announced changes to their method of calculating associate bonuses today, citing the current economic conditions as a factor. "We have been looking to alter our methods of distributing associate bonus compensation for some time, but with the economic climate as it stands we decided that the moment to act is now," said firm chairman C.G. Thaddeus Boldecker IV. Associates previously garnered a bonus of $10,000 for each year of service to the firm at the close of each fiscal year, which ends in July. Instead, first and second years will receive no year-end bonus but find that their yearly raise will be bumped slightly higher. Those in the third through eighth class years will receive a flat bonus of $30,000 going forward, plus the standard $20,000 retention bonus at the end of year three and $45,000 at the end of year eight.

"To those analysts who cast doubt on the ability of the Wheat firm to recruit and retain the best and the brightest from our nation's law schools given this change, I shout a hearty 'pish, posh' to you," said Boldecker. "Wheat will remain competitive in the legal marketplace, just as we have for the past one-hundred and sixteen years."

There were some grumblings on several legal blogs concerning the scaled-back bonuses. A recent internal survey found that almost 40% of Wheat associates carried a median of $40,000 in student loan debt. "I'm here at Wheat to work hard and serve my clients," said one senior associate who declined to be named given the nature of his comments. "The bonus structure at Wheat always gave me peace of mind that I could get my loans paid down and still maintain a high standard of living. I recently purchased an investment property, and I've been distracted at work ever since it was leaked that slashing bonuses could be a possibility. I think the partners were short-sighted in making such drastic cuts to our compensation so suddenly in this economy."

The base salary of Wheat's first-years currently stands at $145,000 in Philadelphia and $160,000 in San Francisco and New York. Boldecker stated that this is not expected to change for the 2011 and 2012 fiscal years, but will be reevaluated against the prevailing economic conditions. In fact, Wheat had planned to raise first-year associate salaries in New York to $200,000 before the current economic downturn began in earnest in 2008. Boldecker did make clear, however, that there would be neither raises nor cuts to associate base salaries under any circumstances even though the October 2010 class of associates has had their start date deferred until October 2011. Under a deal reached between the 21 incoming Philadelphia associates and the firm, they will each be paid $70,000 in bi-monthly installments for one year in lieu of reporting to work this October. Firmwide, Wheat's deferral packages are expected to save over $7.6 million in salaries, bonuses, taxes and overhead associated with each new hire in the form of tax and retirement contributions, malpractice insurance, support staff and supplies. The dismissal of 37 members of Wheat's secretarial and support staff is also expected to save the firm an additional $3 million this year.

Boldecker declined to address whether Wheat was also slated for a massive round of layoffs of associates, dismissing such talk as "rumors without basis."

Thursday, July 29, 2010

7:58 p.m.

Today was not a good day and I'm glad the sun is finally setting upon it. On the heels of my self-mutilation incident and some disturbing dreams, I spent most of the morning and early afternoon vomiting. Even though I've scored a job as a member of a team of misfit attorneys like myself reviewing 11,000,000 documents in connection with a securities fraud lawsuit, I know that $26 an hour isn't going to get me out of the basement on Revere Street when almost $1,000 comes straight off the top for student loans. Document review projects are also notoriously fruitless exercises because any true smoking gun is surely at the bottom of the Atlantic right now in between hundreds of barrels marked 'Caution: Biohazard' and a couple of dead bodies. It's also one step above red light/green light on the 'boring' scale and hurts your resume just the same. All of this constant stress and my unmet goals and expectations have now caused my stomach to become an acid factory that never shuts down, pumping forth much more product than I could ever possibly handle.

I ate a harmless breakfast this morning that starting burning so badly inside my body that my brain decided to give the launch command. And I kept launching long afterward with the kind of prolonged, intolerable vomiting that causes you to gag and be completely unable to breathe. Stress and self-hatred do not make for very good neighbors inside of your body. It's easy for anyone to understand why I'm stressed or hate myself. It manifests itself physically as a rock inside my stomach and chest that never leaves except when I'm really fucking high, out on the water, watching some of the antics of the Board, or, presumably, if I was getting a blowjob. I think a man needs to have much greater problems than I do to be distracted when a woman has her lips wrapped around your pole. But I had no prospects to deliver me a BJ after I was done puking and had no money to drive up to A.C. to pay for one, so I passed out on the living room couch while listening to a mix of mostly singer/songwriter stuff like David Gray and Ray LaMontagne, since that's the only good music being made these days aside from dance music that I was in no mood to listen to. I was starving when I awoke from my nap, but I saw no need to again anger the Gods of Acid living inside my body. Instead, I ate a handful of pretzels (I scrapped off the salt) before setting out on the sound with Dizzy to search for wading birds foraging at low tide.

Our time on the water turned into a dramatic three-hour expedition deep into the marshlands on Gatorade and some badly bruised bananas. We first got sidetracked by an osprey nest, where two fledglings were getting their flight lessons from mom and dad. There were several hard landings under the watchful yellow eyes of the parents, but no apparent injuries to the young birds. Dizzy, who has been watching this nature show unfold over several summers, pointed out that one of the juveniles was landing with its talons improperly extended. Dad was not very pleased when one of his own offspring landed directly atop his back, claws out. It made for some spectacular photos, though.   After Dizzy documented the flight lessons extensively, we paddled out to the Old Wharf in search of his precious snowy egrets. He photographed several of them strutting and chasing each other around while foraging for worms and small fish during the low tide. Unfortunately, Dizzy became so involved with his photos and I got so involved with watching everything myself that we got stuck between two channels as the tide continued to recede. This forced us to disembark so that we could push the kayak toward water by sinking knee-deep into the snail and crab-filled black muck at the bottom of the emptied marsh. The stench, caused stirring up wet mud that had not been disturbed in centuries, was epic. Now my fucking arm hurts and itches as I search through my belongings for clean clothes to wear after my much-needed upcoming shower.

I'm very pissed at myself for causing this painful inconvenience on my own body. I can't say that I'm shocked, though. I've never been happy with my body or my looks. Why should I be? In grade school, my small size got me pummeled by the Crafton Street Crew. In high school, my slight build and total lack of confidence in it spurred rejection after rejection from girls. In college, I was too far away from home and too busy with women and fun to ever give my body a second thought. My body type was irrelevant out there with tens of thousands of girls at my disposal, which killed any motivation I had to improve it. Then I returned to blue collar Philadelphia and the rejections began to pile up again and again save Vanessa the Annoyer and a couple random one and two-night flings with personal friends, and friends of friends who were visiting from somewhere far away that I wouldn't ever see again. Then there was the meltdown, and depressed people aren't motivated to do *anything* to improve themselves. Three lost jobs stole all of my coin and confidence. Then there was the suicide attempt. There's been little or no interest from women again. Dr. Karlis said I looked half-dead when we first met. (I asked him to beat me half to death and finish the job.) I don't look half dead at all now. I've gained a lot of weight. I can't see my own ribs anymore. My stomach is flat rather than looking like it's always sucked in and vacant. I'm 168 pounds instead of 146. I'm a 32 waist instead of a 30. There is actually some muscle tone present from my hours upon hours of kayaking through the sound.   My eyes still look sad but are much brighter.   I have an unemployment tan. I can't enjoy this improvement, though. Every time I look in the mirror, I still see that defenseless, helpless kid that got pounded by Georgie

Inammorato. It makes me feel like human garbage. And until I achieve some tangible success with something, I probably always will.

I know that I'm not the only person that feels this way when they see themselves. We rarely see ourselves the way that others do. Except for Heather and a few run-ins with Harry over the years, none of the people here in Angel Bay knew me before Memorial Day. They've only seen the same thing I see in the mirror now. But I carry all of that other stuff with me like an invisible albatross around my neck. I know that Heather Ball is a nutjob because she still sees a pudgy little girl with three chins looking back at her in the mirror instead of her gorgeous, golden body and blue eyes. I used to think psychology was total bullshit, but people really do carry around things in their past whether they realize it or not. Before I get too wrapped-up in further self-hatred and baseless over-analysis, a woman in the form of Jenna Love scares the living shit out of me by suddenly walking into the Board Room on a Thursday with a smiling, panting Princess in her arms. The sight of this bitch causes my already malfunctioning stomach to twist with hatred on several levels. My rage is only contained by my new tranquilizers and the presence of this pathetic pug that I've grown very fond of.

"What's that...*smell*?" Jenna asks with a sneer as she stands on her dark summer legs while dressed casually in tight gym shorts and her favorite Penn Law t-shirt. The sight of Jenna Love in spandex is pure torture for a man who hasn't had sex in forever. The fabric grips the tops of her tanned thighs so fucking perfectly. My chest immediately burns with yet another mix of anger, despair, sexual frustration, and deep, deep self-hatred. "Are you going to answer my question?" Jenna asks as I try to ignore her.

"It's the foul stench of mental illness," I reply. "I'd advise that you leave before it sticks to your clothes and you get disbarred."

"Seriously, Patrick."

"Did you *really* threaten me with a defamation suit? Get the *fuck* out of my room."

"Watch your mouth. And it wasn't a threat. It was a promise. I take my career *very* seriously."

"Leave me the hell alone, Jenna. Please."

"I need a small favor first."

"Showerhead getting moldy again? You've got some guts asking me for any favors."

"I'm just asking for you to watch Princess for me. I took a vacation day because Michael is coming down tonight and we're staying in Atlantic City for a couple of days. It's kind of a spur-of-the-moment thing."

"You took a vacation day from Wheat? You're fired. And give back your $50,000 bonus immediately, please."

"How the hell do you know how much my bonus is?" Jenna asks with shock as if I possess some very sensitive information, like her dress size.

"Evidently, Mr. Boldecker the Third thought it was worthy of a press release to the entire free world."

"He's the Fourth," Jenna quickly corrects. "And I don't make those decisions. I earned every penny of it. What was *your* bonus this year, Patrick?"

"Is Michael a big dude?"

"About your size. What does *that* have to do with anything?"

"Because I just wanted to tell you that you're a fucking *cunt* without getting my face smashed in later."

Jenna gasps in horror and quickly exits the downstairs with Princess still in her tanned arms, finally leaving me alone but not at peace because of the image of her thighs being permanently burned into my mind. She may be the biggest bitch in Angel Bay, but she'll always be the winner because every man in town would fuck her in a heartbeat. Even Peter Sharkey, despite his statements to the contrary.

7:28 p.m.

The dank smell of the sound in the Board Room seems to have abated. This has been aided by my showering and the scent of freshly burnt Blueberry being exhaled throughout the premises. It was the least I could do to further the return of the Board Room air to an acceptable quality. The next task is to apply ointment to my badly blistered forearm before taking at least three times my prescribed dose of tranquilizers. My phone begins to vibrate on the nightstand:

New Message: Maria Napoli
7/29/10 7:46 p.m.
Ru ok? Please tell me that ur not the same
patrick who just called my cousin that vile word!

Message to: Maria Napoli
7/29/10 7:48 p.m.
Guilty as charged. Check ur email. She is insane.

New Message: Maria Napoli
7/29/10 7:53 p.m.
Omg. Defamation? She is out of control.

Message to: Maria Napoli
7/29/10 7:53 p.m.
Ya think?

New Message: Maria Napoli
7/29/10 7:54 p.m.
Im supposed to meet her sat night in a.c. w bob.
Can u please watch the dog? For me? Shes crying
like a baby.

Message to: Maria Napoli
7/29/10 7:55 p.m.
Jenna or the dog?

New Message: Maria Napoli
7/29/10 7:59 p.m.
I told her 2 leave the dog upstairs and u will come
get princess later. Deal?

Message to: Maria Napoli
7/29/10 8:01 p.m.
Only 4 you. I hate that bitch.

New Message: Maria Napoli
7/29/10 8:03 p.m.
Stop! She is having a rough time w everything right now.

Message to: Maria Napoli
7/29/10 8:04 p.m.
She can join the fucking club. And I dont have an
extra $50K to fall back on.

New Message: Maria Napoli
7/29/10 8:05 p.m.
What has happened 2 u patrick? Im really concerned abt u!

Message to: Maria Napoli
7/29/10 8:06 p.m.
I can handle myself. Enjoy ur weekend and say hello 2 bob 4 me.

I shut my phone down and walk to the kitchen to grab a 7UP with which to down my pills. I notice some dude who is noticeably thinner than me and about two inches shorter walking through the back yard dressed in a very un-summery outfit of a plain white t-shirt and death black jeans with a black Jeff Cap. This guy looks like he was just got off the bus after a lengthy stint in the state pen following a conviction for ritualistic animal sacrifice. His arms are covered by a series of disturbing, dark tattoos, each anchored by a large skull with worm-like insects and other things of general grossness crawling out of the empty orbits. The man's face is dotted with an array of silver piercings about the nose and eyebrow. He also has one of those stupid fucking black rings in his left ear that leaves a giant, gaping hole. Jenna, wearing her version of the little black dress and insanely hot black heels that would put to shame at least two-thirds of the footwear donned by America's best strippers, tries to greet him with a kiss to the lips but he turns his cheek toward her. I might be clinically nuts, but I can't believe she's fucking this dude. They drive off to A.C. together in a shiny, black C6 Corvette. That's just far, far too cruel for me to take. It almost seems like a conspiracy. I spend a few minutes in the bathroom vomiting again before I walk upstairs to take possession of Princess. She is sitting in the living room by herself, taking advantage of her alone time to whirl away on the carpet and scratch her butthole. I grab her from the floor and take her downstairs. This living thing is a calming presence in my arms. I place her in the lower unit living room and return to the Penthouse to grab her water bowl and food dish. When I return downstairs, Princess is again spinning. I entertain myself by watching for a few minutes while downing three tranquilizers to replace the ones I just vomited and augmenting them with several flights on the *Falcon,* along with a painkiller left over from my infected teeth. I lay on Couch #1 exhausted. Princess the Spinning, Butthole-Scratching Pug stops whirling and jumps up onto the couch. Evidentially, she's already getting very comfortable with me. She walks onto my reclining body and plops herself onto my chest with a sigh. I place my right hand atop her body and massage her crusty fur as I watch her eyes slowly droop lower and lower. The pug, who I have decided is so ugly that it actually succeeds in making her completely adorable, is soon snoring away. As I drift off myself, I no longer have the urge to silently pray that only one of us wakes up.

Friday, July 30, 2010

11:52 a.m.

I'm awoken by a pasty tongue licking my face repeatedly. The good news is that it's a female, but of course it's the dog. I'm groggy as hell with a serious case of brain fog. I slept for approximately 14 hours, and I feel like shit. I also smell it. I discover that Princess has already had an episode of explosive diarrhea all over the kitchen floor. In addition, I've slept so long that I pissed myself like a 2 year-old. I can't in good conscience discipline the dog when I'm having accidents of my own at age 32. And it's not this little pug's fault that her weekend caretaker decided to load-up on pills in a half-hearted attempt at an overdose and slept way past the time for her morning walk. I simply point to the mess on the kitchen floor to ensure that Princess doesn't get any ideas about a repeat episode. She waddles into the corner of the living room, lying down with a sad look upon her face that makes me feel quite guilty. It's not your fault, Princess. You're spending the weekend with the biggest failure from the Villanova Law Class of 2006. In fact, I pity you, you poor thing. Surely you deserve better and more capable company. I begin the rather unpleasant task of cleaning up both the dog and human accidents at 728.

7:48 p.m.

Potentially, there will be no arrivals at 728 this weekend. Harry's bachelor party is taking place in Las Vegas, and every male from 728 and Dizzy's house will be in attendance. I pity whatever poor soul wound up getting stuck sitting next to Fifty-One on the plane. I was invited to the party, but obviously couldn't afford the trip even though both Harry and Dizzy offered to spot me. I couldn't accept. I hate owing friends money, and who knows when the hell I'd be able to pay either of them back. Marie is having her bachelorette back in Philly, and Stinky and Mallory are both at the same wedding in New York City. Jenna is obviously in A.C. That leaves only one potential housemate for the weekend: Gina. I'm hoping that the lack of a weekend crew will discourage her from coming to Angel Bay. Like every other hope I have, it is dashed as I am relaxing in the backyard stoned with my new friend Princess on my lap while awaiting the sunset. An $112,000 Porsche 911 GT3 painted in a beautiful aqua blue metallic enters the side yard and parks next to my embarrassing blue heap. It's quite a study in contrasts. It's a shame Dizzy's not around to photograph it. Gina has apparently waived the white flag on being single after only one distressing incident of disrespect from Dizzy. This shows how mentally weak some women really are. An attractive woman could never live the life of a regular guy and receive only 20% of the sex, attention and affection to which they're accustomed.

Though my back is basically turned toward the house, I move my head slightly so that I can get a view of the legendary Chas in my peripheral vision. Guys are always curious to see the men that women fuck after they receive a hard rejection from the woman in question. He clocks in about 6'2", so he definitely wins the height advantage. Chas' most attractive quality, however, appears to be his wallet. His complexion is three shades paler than my own (*before* the summer started), he has at least 20 extra pounds of gut sticking out from underneath his white Polo, his blonde hair is beyond thinning, and he is committing the high crime of wearing socks at a shore resort. The ultimate test is the handshake, but I won't interact with Gina so I doubt I'll have the opportunity to judge. One of two things is at work here: I'm either much, much less attractive than I already think I am, or Gina is purely a golddigger. In this one instance only, I believe it to be the latter. Then again, it's no crime to be successful in your late twenties or early thirties- even if most of the success comes courtesy of Daddy. Women want men who can provide. Houses cost an exorbitant amount of money. Kids are expensive. I simply can't be a provider. Gina knows that. She's still a complete bitch in my eyes, though. There's ways of letting people down easy and not completely leading them on. She obviously missed those lectures. Or just doesn't care.

New Message: Harry Trimble
7/31/10 2:23 a.m.
Do u have a nevada law license.
U might make a killing this wknd.

New Message: Peter Sharkey
7/31/10 2:36 a.m.
These may possibly be the fattest hookers in las vegas.
And they were def not cheap. Not spending less than
2500 on 2morrows. Thin 2 win baby!

New Message: Dizzy
7/31/10 3:13 a.m.
What is the penalty 4 getting caught w coke on a plane.
This shit rules out here.

Message to: Dizzy
7/31/10 3:14 a.m.
Gina already back w chas

New Message: Dizzy
7/31/10 3:13 a.m.
Hahahahahaha that fat rich fuck

New Message: Page
7/31/10 3:23 a.m.
U should be here bro. Just sayin'

New Message: Blotto
7/31/10 4:16 a.m.
Fat hookers + alcohol = green chip on 26 black and a cool $875.
Twice. Id advise that u drive 2 AC and hop a redeye.

New Message: Peter Sharkey
7/31/10 4:34 a.m.
Getting laid right now? My guess is no.

New Message: Harry Trimble
7/31/10 4:46 a.m.
I can now cross freebasing cocaine off my bucket list
hahahahahahaha

New Message: Jenna Love
7/31/10 5:02 a.m.
Hows my princess?

Message to: Jenna Love
7/31/10 5:05 a.m.
I was about 2 text u the same thing. Not.

New Message: Jenna Love
7/31/10 5:06 a.m.
Seriously. Grow up.

Message to: Jenna Love
7/31/10 5:07 a.m.
Its 5 in the fucking morning jenna

New Message: Jenna Love
7/31/10 5:07 a.m.
Just answer my fucking question.

Message to: Jenna Love
7/31/10 5:08 a.m.
Shes snoring away on my chest.

New Message: Jenna Love
7/31/10 5:08 a.m.
Aww...really? Why are u up so early?

Message to: Jenna Love
7/31/10 5:09 a.m.
Going 2 kayak at sunrise. Very peaceful.

New Message: Jenna Love
7/31/10 5:10 a.m.
We do need 2 talk. Ur not who i thought u were.

Message to: Jenna Love
7/31/10 5:11 a.m.
U need 2 get over urself first.

New Message: Jenna Love
7/31/10 5:12 a.m.
Ur an asshole

Message to: Jenna Love
7/31/10 5:13 a.m.
That was a quick 180. Put ur phone down ur throat
and choke on it. Please.

Sunday, August 1, 2010

1:45 p.m.

I did spend a lot more time with Princess this weekend rather than being at the Shipwreck. I circled the place several times each night trolling for someone to hook up with, but was ultimately unsuccessful. Princess and I went on several walks during which I was forced to deal with additional explosive diarrhea. We bonded while playing with a stuffed mouse that has a small bell on it. I put her in a child's life vest and we went for a spin around the sound in a kayak last evening about an hour before sunset. She barked at every bird she saw, especially the seagulls. Ultimately, I found Princess to be more entertaining and better company than 99% of the women I've met in my Philadelphia days. I can now completely understand why Dizzy has such a close bond with Molly.

I'm currently in a stoned, half-awake/half-asleep state with Princess again snoring atop my chest. I've been awake since 6 a.m. and was on the kayak by 6:30, so I feel no guilt about this early Sunday afternoon nap. The Board Room door creaks open. I'm hoping it's due to a slight breeze from a window that I didn't completely close after airing the smell of both dog and human diarrhea out of the place. But it's Jenna. Michael stands behind her and tries to look menacing, but his 145 pound build mirrors my own during my depression years and doesn't exactly strike fear into my heart. I'd love the opportunity to beat someone senseless and relive my lingering frustrations with my life, but I'm too stoned and tranquilized to care about this d-bag. Jenna snatches Princess from my chest without comment. The pug looks at me with a confused, sleepy look in her brown, bulging, snotty eyes and extends her front paws out toward me. I smile at her and close my eyes afterward. Michael slams the Board Room door behind him with such force that I'm shocked it doesn't become unhinged. What a punk. He's lucky Harry's not around, who would provide a sound verbal or physical undressing for abusing his property.

"You're welcome, Jenna," I say fruitlessly before falling off to sleep. If only some other, more useful object aside from a woman had been gifted a pussy.

Wednesday, August 4, 2010

3:24 p.m.

I've been wandering down the middle of St. Michael's Drive since 7th Street. I'm on 13th now. So far, no one has run me over while I stumble along the double yellow line on my way to Angel Bay Pharmacy. I haven't taken my medication in four days. The events that occurred late Monday evening are the reason for this, and they are mostly my dumb fault. Things started going downhill on late Monday afternoon. I tried to take my car for a spin to the Angel Bay Market, but it refused to start and it wasn't the battery. It was towed to a nearby service station, and there was found to be an electronics problem. It also needed new spark plugs and maintenance to the distributors. That's why my car wasn't starting in the rain any longer. It all cost me $648 to repair. This brought my bank account down to $37.48 as of Tuesday. After returning to 728 from the station and smoking my stress away, I realized that I hadn't taken any of my medication the day before. I pocketed the precious bottles containing my little peach capsules and white 'bump' pills, then walked into the bathroom so that I could down the pills, take a piss, and brush my teeth. I first brushed my teeth. Next I pissed. Then I washed my hands. This is where my actions begin to make less sense. Without drying my hands, I reached into my pocket for my meds and one of my prescription bottles slipped away as I turned the cap, launching every remaining capsule for the month down the drain. I called Dr. Karlis, who I knew was on vacation on some island somewhere. Within an hour, and with the island breezes whistling through his cell, he called and said that Angel Bay Pharmacy would have the prescription ready the following day. I had no money to pay the $202 cost, though.

My unemployment funds finally cleared today, Wednesday. My body is a mess. The withdrawal from my antidepressants is brutal. The interior of my skull is a cloud of thick fog inhabited by electric insects that give me pins 'n needles and random tingling sensations all over my face that become annoying. And I'm not even high. My entire digestive system is off-track. I'm nauseous just to the level below where I'll actually vomit, and have been for days. It only fades if I'm really concentrating on something, like reading a book, or playing a difficult scale exercise, or I'm deep, deep in thought about my life. I've had constant diarrhea and beyond painful stomach cramps. My sense of reality and equilibrium fades in and out like the signal on an old television with a coat hanger antenna. I know that I'm not supposed to walk straight down the fucking middle of a two-lane roadway. But my brain fails to make the connection that I should move to the sidewalk instead. So I stumble along in the middle of the street as drivers honk their horns and scream that I'm an idiot and a junkie and a thousand other things. This aggressive jaywalking is the criminal equivalent to murder in Angel Bay, so it's not long before a police cruiser with flashing lights pulls up alongside me. Two bike cops cut off my progress, with one of the assholes almost running me over in the process. The window to the cruiser rolls down. It's an older officer with a balding head of gray hair and a gray moustache. He doesn't look very threatening, even though he's a much larger man than I am.

"Whatcha doin', son?"

"Walkin'."

"Isn't that what the sidewalks are for?"

"I dunno."

"Lemme see some ID."

I fumble through my pocket and manage to produce my license. One of the officers has flipped open his trusty ticket book and is writing up violations as fast as his hand will allow. The other officer is staring me down with his right hand on his holster and his eyes are filled with hope that I do something violent. He can't be more than 20 years old, either. It's fucking terrifying that someone this young has a license to carry. I realize for the first time that I'm not even wearing a fucking shirt. I must look like one of those dudes who wanders the city preaching repentance, except that I showered within the last 24 hours and my shorts are somewhat clean.

"Step inside the car," says the officer in charge. I enter the back of a police car for the first time in my life and take a seat as a small crowd of senior citizens gathers on the nearby sidewalk to see the outcome of the police encounter with the terrorist from Philadelphia.

"Am I being arrested, Officer?" I ask. That would be something else that I'd need to report to the Supreme Court of Pennsylvania, along with the lawsuit from my credit card company.

"Not unless you're going to try to kill me," says the cop. "How's your mother?"

I guess I'm in the company of my father's high school baseball teammate. An Irish Catholic connection through Philadelphia's neighborhoods is at work once again. "Umm...she's doing well, Chief."

"I saw your father a few weeks ago at the Communion Breakfast."

"He never misses a Communion Breakfast."

"Your parents don't sleep at night, son."

"I know."

"What's the problem today?"

"I haven't taken my meds in days. I was walking to the pharmacy. I need my pills. I don't even feel human."

One of the bike cops hands a fistful of violations through the window. "Looks like you've also managed to rack-up $497 in fines today," Chief reports. That's another $497 that I simply don't have. My stomach turns and I vomit into my own lap. "Just relax for a minute, son," he continues as he flips though the paperwork. "Now what can I do right now to help you, Mr. McShea?"

"Just shoot me, Chief. Please. Please just fucking shoot me."

9:57 p.m.

Chief Fitzpatrick declined my request to shoot me, and this afternoon did end on a positive note. The Chief, after driving me back to 728 to get a shirt and shower, took me to the pharmacy and assured me that my citations would all be dismissed administratively. Only two hours after taking my meds, my brain and body felt completely normal again. The transformation was so subtle that it didn't even dawn on me that I was okay until long after it had already happened. But when I finally did realize that my head and stomach was working semi-normally again, it was such a great relief.

A storm rolled through at approximately 7:30 p.m., but began to break-up as the sun began its decent toward the horizon. The remnant black storm clouds reflected strongly off the water, while the others turned a bright pink atop a strangely purple sky as the sun lowered. Dizzy has stopped by with Molly after photographing the sunset from the Seventh Street Bridge. We share a jay of Sour Diesel that he has on hand. The photos he has taken are so impressive that they look completely fake, even though I personally saw him take them and I am viewing the results in-camera before any kind of downloading or post-processing is performed. As I scroll through the pictures, we talk about Gina. Dizzy had no idea I had a serious crush on her until after the fact, for a simple reason: because I anticipated failure, I never told him so I wouldn't be embarrassed when she finally kicked me in the teeth. He picked up on the barbs and commentary from the Board about my thing for her, but there's so many pretty girls in Angel Bay that all of us have a 'thing' for at least a half-dozen women each. No one had any idea of the true depth of my feelings, or the lifelong cycle of failure that it represented for me.

Dizzy apologizes profusely before delivering an extensive lecture on my poor self-confidence. He sees no reason for it. If only he knew what was going on inside my brain for the past five years and how fucked-up my career and sex life really is. He's one of those regular people that subscribes to the false convention that all lawyers make $100,000 no matter what and assumes I am flush with cash reserves and the sense of calm and relief that will come with the ever-elusive financial security. Dizzy makes a shitload of money, and once you have money yourself you completely lose the ability to understand why somebody else might not. He looks down at the floor and exhales a potent stream of smoke before he again speaks. "Gina, my friend, is *crazy*," he states as fact.

"Let's hear the evidence. I'm curious now."

"Evidence? I got plenty for ya, brother. First, she steals my number from *your* own phone while we were out on the sound together. Then, behind your back, she blows me up left and right until I finally give into temptation and fuck her even though I already have six other chicks on my plate. So on Monday afternoon she stops by my place before driving back to Philly. I'm cleaning the cabin of the boat, so I don't know she's even at the house because I left my phone in the living room. And Molly ain't much of a barker. I mean, look at 'er. She's 80 pounds, but someone could try to rob the place blind and she'd try to lick their face while they were carrying the television set out the door. So after I'm done in the cabin, I head back into the house and upstairs to take a shower. And Gina is sitting on the living room couch going through my phone. I mean, what the *fuck* gives a woman the right to do that? And it's not just texts from other chicks I don't want girls to see, but I have financial information from my businesses and shit in there. And even worse, I just happened to clear my phone before she stopped over. So then Gina starts giving me shit about deleting my *own* texts from my *own* phone! *'Like you don't get any text messages? What are you trying to hide from me?'* and all this shit. And I'm like, *'Excuse me! Are you my fiancé? Have we been dating three years?'* And she's like, *'We're having sex. It doesn't matter.'* Oh, really? That's news to me. I didn't realize that my penis now suddenly provides a woman access to my text messages and e-mails. I did you a favor, Woodchuck. She's an insecure stalker, and now on my lazy list."

"Lazy list?"

"Yeah. When I want to get laid but don't want to make any effort. That's my lazy list. They're on the B-team and C-team. There is no D-team."

I decline to admit to, or discuss, *l'affaire Heather*. She may not even remember it, anyway, and I doubt she would make herself look like such a whore by telling anyone even if she did. Dizzy and I make plans to kayak the following day before he departs for Atlantic City to meet a stripper. He leaves the affectionate and obedient dog in my care, along with some treats, a large brush and a copy of Molly's favorite CD, Lionel Richie's *Greatest Hits*. The company is very welcome.

* * *

New Message: Amanda Liss
8/04/10 9:59 p.m.
No more tony :)

Message to: Amanda Liss
8/04/10 10:02 p.m.
Dinner 2morrow night?

New Message: Amanda Liss
8/04/10 10:04 p.m.
Sure! U can explain 2 me what money laundering is :(

Message to: Amanda Liss
8/04/10 10:07 p.m.
Ouch! Call me 2morrow when u get down.

New Message: Amanda Liss
8/04/10 10:08 p.m.
*I will wave to you from my deck. Wait until u see
the red dress and hooker shoes im bringing. Ur
stoned little eyes will pop out of ur head woodchuck.*

Message to: Amanda Liss
8/04/10 10:09 p.m.
My eyes pop out of my head every time I see u amanda.

New Message: Amanda Liss
8/04/10 10:11 p.m.
Aww...i will see u 2morrow when i get there.

Message to: Amanda Liss
8/04/10 10:12 p.m.
Sounds good. Goodnight.

New Message: Amanda Liss
8/04/10 10:12 p.m.
Goodnight woodchuck xoxo

* * *

From: happyharry666@junkmail.com
To: marie1973, jennajenna82, angelbaygina, vikingsreject61, mascotman1,
          psharkey420, PMcShea77, stinkybeavergirl, mallory76
Subject: Flotilla

As you know, Flotilla, aka Party of the Century, is scheduled for this Saturday. Here is all you need to know:

1.   All of the doors to the house will be locked. I have made keys for each of you so that you may enter the house at any time. To the Board Room: KEEP THE FUCKING WINDOWS CLOSED AT ALL TIMES.

2.   We will have 5 port-a-potties outside. NO guests are permitted to use the bathroom inside the house unless they are an attractive female that offers you a blowjob. I do not expect to see ANY strange dudes in my property during the party. This is directed at Stinky, Mallory, Gina and whoever else likes to suck the most degenerate, pus-dripping cocks that Angel Bay has to offer. If anything belonging to

anybody gets stolen from my house by some Hot Dude nobody knows, I am holding you three accountable.

3.   If you are thinking about coming out of the closet, this is definitely not the day to do it.

4.   Woodchuck negotiated for a manned patrol car to be parked outside to discourage teenyboppers from coming onto the property to drink. The fine to me as the homeowner for each underage offense is $5,000. We have also hired some of our favorite bouncers from the Shipwreck for the day from our pool of $6,000. If you see someone who looks underage, politely ask them to leave. If they don't, start being a dick and find our main man Tyrone or the police.

5.   I spent $700 of our funds for a $2,000,000 insurance rider for the party and hired a lifeguard.

6.   The schedule is as follows:
          12:00 Shotgirls from the Bunny Ranch Arrive; DJ Buttfuck
          1:00 Jake & the Pantydroppers w/ Special Guest Woodchuck
          1:45 DJ Buttfuck
          2:30 Jake & the Pantydroppers w/ Special Guest Woodchuck
          3:15 DJ Buttfuck
          4:00 Jake & the Pantydroppers w/ Special Guest Woodchuck
          4:45 DJ Buttfuck to end of party

7.   DJ Buttfuck used his connections to get us 15 kegs of good beer for dirt cheap. Thank him but not too much because he gets a big head sometimes and turns into a douche. If that happens, I suggest that one of our girls give him a blowjob.

8.   Blotto has the t-shirts for the house, the band, and the DJ. They are awesome. Great job. I'd be remiss if I did not also mention that he flew back from summer training camp against his coach's orders during his first year of college so that he could fuck Sharkey's sister behind his back. He told his coach she was pregnant and he had to accompany her to the abortion.

9.   Have a great time and don't die. If you do, please die on public property or in a state waterway and not on my premises. Thank you.

- Harry

Thursday, August 5, 2009

"[My] dick is like the Titanic. Large but full of failure."

-Texts from Last Night (513)

* * *

New Message: Amanda Liss
8/05/10 2:54 p.m.
Wont be in AB 2night. Not feeling well at all :(
Sorry woodchuck.

Message to: Amanda Liss
8/05/10 3:42 p.m.
No red dress? Sorry 2 hear. Hope u feel better asap.

* * *

7:01 p.m.

I'm stoned and now walking past the Crow's Nest with a much-needed spring in my step. It's always fun to check out the talent sitting on the bar's outside decks. On a Thursday it's is a mixed young/older crowd of people, typically those on vacation for the week. There's a very noteworthy brunette in a short, shimmering aqua-colored dress sitting at the tables with a regular-looking guy like myself. You can tell by the way she's looking at him lovingly with her soft brown eyes that it's not his sister. Guys always size-up other men that are seen out with beautiful women and wonder what separates the single, downtrodden 'you' with the guy sitting across from the stunner that you can't get yourself. I always wonder if I'll be lucky enough to be one of those guys again. I'm ever-filled with hope that I will be, but I know exactly what the things are that separate me from the guy sitting at that table right now. And except for my exceptional ability to eat pussy, none of them are good. After taking only a few more steps, I freeze in place right on the Seventh Street sidewalk. Sitting at a table on the outside deck, plain as day, is the supposedly sick Amanda wearing her spectacular red dress and matching platform stripper heels while having dinner with my summer band buddy Silent John. After the initial shock wears off, I walk a slow pace so that I can observe for a few seconds. They're definitely communicating, laughing, touching...and then Amanda reaches across the table to give him several slow kisses on the lips. Silent John is giving Amanda her fish, bitch. Then he's getting her pussy. I'm not. It's a sickening fucking feeling. I've been duped yet again.

* * *

Message to: Amanda Liss
8/05/10 7:21 p.m.
U seem to have made a quick recovery from ur illness.
Not lol.

New Message: Amanda Liss
8/05/10 7:46 p.m.
There was never going 2 b anything btwn us woodchuck.
May i suggest u mind ur own business.

Message to: Amanda Liss
8/05/10 7:49 p.m.
May i suggest u stop being a lying fucking bitch.

New Message: Amanda Liss
8/05/10 7:56 p.m.
Asshole!

Message to: Amanda Liss
8/05/10 7:57 p.m.
Look in the mirror whore

New Message: Dizzy
8/05/10 8:08 p.m.
Yo bro. Stop drinking the haterade and blowing up
amandas phone. SJP needs her more than u do.
He cant even talk for fucks sake. And u guys have
the gig of the century together on sat. So shut it
down man. xoxo

* * *

To tell the truth, it's hard enough without a lover/ who you want to hide your darkness from so they don't let you down.

- Ryan Adams

9:14 p.m.

I complied with Dizzy's admonishment via text and shut my phone down. I admit that it was a low-rent move to blow-up Amanda's phone while she was out on a date, even if she completely fucking lied to me. Though always feeling greatly disrespected by Jenna and now suddenly by my 'friend' Amanda, I've never been such a bitter asshole before. And no one will remember the fact that Amanda dissed me after already making plans for a date. The last thing that people will remember is that I responded to it by being a jerk off. There were probably over a dozen dudes who have been waiting for *years* to pounce on Amanda once Tony was finally tossed aside. Men are no different than a band of wild monkeys chasing after a banana when it

254

comes to grabbing a chance for some superior pussy. I had the good fortune to be in the right place at the right time. I just wasn't picked. And it never stings any less.

I'm not naïve; The Slump is surely the primary cause of my behavior. Intimacy is a real human need. I know what people who knew the truth about my involuntary celibacy would be thinking: why not just grab one of the dozens of overweight, wounded gazelles stumbling out of the Shipwreck each weekend and take her for a ride before never acknowledging her existence ever again. I'd like to be able to take my conscience out of my pocket and put it in a drawer for a few weeks so I could ride a few hogs. There's three reasons aside from my lingering Irish Catholic guilt why I don't do this. First, I don't drink so I'm not susceptible to beer goggles. Second, I did just that with Regina Pellini with extremely poor results. The third thing is that I think it would just depress me more. The entire time in bed, as I watched the fat on the woman's ass, back, and gut jiggle around on their bodies like a bowl of hospital Jell-o being invaded by a plastic spoon, I'd probably be thinking, *'This is the best I can get? I'm such a fucking loser anymore.'* I have no desire to confirm that. It's not what I want to see in bed, and I never had to go that route before law school and my depression. To the feminists out there everywhere: sex *really* is a mostly visual experience for a man, and it's somewhat fortunate. Strong mutual emotional bonds with women are *so* hard to come by that men would go sexless potentially for years in this modern, fast-paced, way-too-busy global society if they waited for a true connection to occur before jumping into bed with someone. And no man is going to take a strong stand and go sexless for years in the name of preserving the sanctity and sanity of women at the expense of his own needs. So stop telling people that the visual aspect of sex is bullshit in order to make the less attractive women in the world feel better about themselves, or chastising men that fear commitment when our DNA simply isn't wired that way. Even men that don't fear commitment get second thoughts via the constant intrusions into our privacy through our text messages, cell phone call logs and various other means before we've even had a chance to decide whether we truly want to go forward with someone. Heaven forbid that you forget to logout of your facebook or e-mail account on your laptop. A woman suddenly morphs into an FBI agent gathering intelligence against Al-Qaeda as she pours through every available message in your inbox and outbox. It doesn't matter if she finds no incriminating evidence. Her paranoid mind just assumes you hid it well.

The media is a convenient scapegoat to explain a man's fear of commitment and attraction to the 'skinny bitch' type, isn't it? The media glorifies skinny women to the exclusion of the world's 'real' women, and we dumb men buy right into it, correct? To paraphrase Chris Rock, when I have an attractive woman in bed, it's not the media that's getting me off. Some feminists love to point to Manet's *Luncheon on the Grass* (1863), where a plump, naked woman with 'curves' and rolls is seen at a picnic with two men in a contemporary French setting. This painting is not evidence of a cultural shift into a conspiracy that occurred between 1863 and the present that was spearheaded by the mainstream media to fool us all into believing that thinner women were more attractive. The painting was considered scandalous and painted for shock value; nudes were formerly reserved only for classical, not contemporary, settings. Napoleon III criticized the painting for being 'immodest' and the body of the non-idealized woman was lambasted by some. Art historians believe that the body of the naked woman depicted is that of Manet's own wife. It does not represent the feminine ideal in any way. And neither does a rib-showing runway model that looks like she's addicted to smack. The anorexic and heroin chic look isn't embraced by most men, either. But a great body is priceless.

I should know more than anyone. I've been physically pulverized because my body doesn't fit the masculine ideal. I've been rejected by women solely because of my body well over two dozen times. In fact, I've just been rejected in favor of a man with half a tongue but a much nicer body. But it wasn't the media that rejected me. It was Amanda Liss. I'm not blaming *Muscle & Fitness* and *Men's Health* and its pages and pages of dudes with rock hard biceps and perfect 6- or 8-packs for it. No one stops me from heading to the gym except myself and my own apathy. It's my own fault. I'd rather play my guitar or read and get high. It takes a big effort to learn to play an instrument, but I enjoy the journey as much as the destination. I thought a high-paying job and a career would enable women to get over the fact that my body itself isn't very attractive physically. Hell, it works for a lot of men. In a place such as the Northeast United States where the cost of living can be so high, money, average looks and a barely tolerable personality can lead to great success with women.

I don't want to leave people with the mistaken impression that I look deformed or something. I don't. At 168 pounds, I look like an average guy when I'm walking around the Shipwreck in my khaki shorts and collared shirt. The problem, for reasons unknown, is that I was born with an extremely low level of baseline strength and muscle mass. (A drug that my mom was prescribed during pregnancy was eventually banned for use in pregnant women due to the possibility of birth defects, but no one could ever state with any certainty whether that was the culprit- or whether it made me susceptible to depression.) I'm well aware women will always like bigger guys, but I find lifting weights to be boring as hell. It doesn't help that, given my physical limitations, my level of commitment would have to be twice that of a man with average baseline strength in order to achieve half of the results. I guess the weights will take the place of the kayak over the winter months. Otherwise, I'll simply need to deal with the muscle lust that's etched into the DNA of most women. It's not only women that are programmed that way, though- *all* mammals are. That's why bucks clash during the rut. It's why bighorn sheep crash their massive horns against each other with such force that it is almost painful to watch. It's why giraffes swing their long necks and use their heads as weapons to bash their male rivals. Elephant seals are known to fight to the *death* for the chance to mate. Nature dictates that only the strong are to survive and procreate in order to propagate the species. Whether it's in Yellowstone Park, the African savannah, or on a remote beach somewhere in South America, pussy is earned only through the most dramatic and gruesome displays of violence imaginable.

Since ancient times, the idealized man has been portrayed as athletic and muscular. Anyone who has taken a survey course in art history knows that. Witness the Discobolus or even the passed-out drunk Barberini Faun. Nobody *really* knows what King David looked like, but every major sculptor save Donatello has depicted him as a mighty, muscular hero. No society wants their heroes and legends depicted as pussies. And a complete lack of sex is so devastating for a man. Women could never realize how essential pussy is, which is fortunate because then even average-looking girls would hold out for real estate moguls and surgeons. Man, have I become jaded and cynical. Fortunately, I am not also beset with the Irish Curse- but that is not always easy to advertise legally, or to speak about without sounding like an insecure braggart. Guys who are legitimately hung or really know how to please a woman sexually rarely need to speak about it. Word will travel fast enough on its own.

The sliding glass door suddenly slides open as I sit alone smoking in my classic black Iron Maiden t-shirt that depicts *Aces High* on the front and *2 Minutes to Midnight* on the back. It's Jenna fucking Love, and she admittedly looks *spectacular* as I sit on the couch having taken-on a real life appearance of the infamous cartoon Butthead. She's wearing a pair of short, short, short dark gray shorts that barely pass the tops of her wonderthighs on her long, dark legs. Her top is black, tightly hugging her C-cups. Her beautiful hair is down and she smells like a garden of earthly feminine delights. I immediately look down toward the stained, beige carpet on the floor. I feel so inadequate in her presence. It's like being in high school and seeing the super hot cheerleader in the hallway that will never date you and rather get cancer than to be caught saying 'hi' to you. You'll never get her, and it sucks. Tonight, I'm worthy of a greeting. "Hi," the brunette says softly with a complete absence of the usual confidence and bitchiness in her voice.

"Hi," I echo quietly while my eyes focus on an orangeish-stain in the carpet that in my stoned state resembles an upside-down elephant trailed by a green comet of some sort.

"I tried texting you earlier."

"My phone's off, Jenna."

"Umm...I just..." begins the brunette rather uncomfortably, "I believe that some apologies are in order. For both of us."

"Who goes first?"

"You do, of course, Patrick."

"Why me?"

"Because was you said to me was *so* disgusting and..."

"Rock, paper, scissors."

"Fine," says Jenna with an exasperated sigh. I manage to rise from the couch for the match, but stumble awkwardly in my stoned and tranquilized state. "Are you okay?" asks the beauty.

"Why wouldn't I be?"

"You seem a bit unsteady."

"Just a little head rush. I've been on the couch a while."

Taking lots of drugs, I fail to add.

I approach and go through my strategy in my mind, which at this time seems much, much more important and serious than it really is. My final determination is that Jenna is definitely throwing scissors. I can feel it. There's nothing she likes more than to cut and stab at people. Consequently, I throw out a firm, confident rock after a count of three. Jenna throws...*paper*. She's totally out-smarted me. "Look me in the eye, Patrick," she commands. It's a fierce struggle for me to look into those wonderful ice blues, but I somehow manage because there's something 'off' about them. Like myself at times recently, Jenna's clearly been crying. At least I can always deflect the blame for my own puffy eyes toward the potent marijuana that I'm smoking in order to forget about what an incredibly spectacular loser I am. This sign of weakness in Jenna's eyes allows me to get out a stoned apology.

"I'm sorry for the way I acted toward you on Thursday," I manage to mutter. "It wasn't appropriate." Jenna's not satisfied, of course.

"And I'm very sorry, Jenna, for calling you the most vile, disgusting word that the English language has to offer with respect to a beautiful, intelligent woman like yourself."

"Can I just say that I'm sorry for throwing out the c-word?"

"No, you may not," she insists very impatiently. "Be a fucking man and apologize." Surprisingly, I'm able to offer Jenna the apology she wants verbatim despite my mess of a mind right now, which is thinking about everything from my build, to Amanda, to fighting pink dolphins, to mating elephant seals and everything else in between.

"Thank you," Jenna replies with a surprising, quiet sincerity. "And I'm very, very sorry about that *nasty* e-mail that I sent to you."

"It *was* nasty. Do you know how I felt walking out of Dr. Karlis' office on literally one of the worst days of my life and finding *that* in my inbox when I got back here? I'm not your adversary in a $100,000,000 antitrust suit, Jenna."

"And that's why I just apologized."

"Congrats," I say like the smartass I am.

Jenna's phone starts buzzing. She takes it from one of her much-too-tight pockets, looks at the screen, and puts it away. "That was the Eighties texting me," she says. "They're wondering when they get their t-shirt back."

I wasn't expecting that one. I think it was the first time in about five years that a woman actually made me laugh out loud. "Since when do you have a sense of humor, Jenna?"

"I'm not the total bitch that you think I am."

"I'm *dying* to be proved wrong about that."

"I'll prove it right now. Step closer and give me a hug, please. I think we both need one." I take one step forward into Jenna's slender, brown arms. She grips me much more tightly than I ever would have ever anticipated. My hands wrap around her back. Feeling her slender, feminine body in my arms causes a further pinch of inadequacy in my chest. I haven't had a body like Jenna's in bed in forever. It reminds me of exactly what I've been missing all these years. "You smell good, Patrick," she says before unexpectedly placing her head on my shoulder.

"Thursday is my shower day, Jenna."

"Why didn't you tell me you knew my cousin, you fucking idiot?" she breathes onto my neck.

"I didn't want to mix worlds. It doesn't really matter now, though."

"Maria said the most wonderful things about you at dinner. I can't *believe* that you're the same Patrick that sent her roses to her graduation. I was there. She *cried* when she got them. She was 25 and never had a boyfriend in her entire life. So there was no one that had ever done anything for her like that. She *loved* you."

"Don't remind me."

"Why?"

"I kinda felt badly about the whole thing."

"There's no requirement that love be reciprocated."

"That's exactly why it fucking blows, Jenna."

"She's worried about you, Patrick."

"I see Dr. Karlis for a reason. We're not golfing buddies. I'm really twisted up right now."

"We both are," the brunette replies before she suddenly begins to cry on my shoulder. My hardened heart toward her slowly begins to melt away.

"What's wrong?" I whisper into her ear as I start to run the fingers of my right hand through her brown hair. It's as soft as a cloud.

"I lost my job," Jenna says through her tears. "I worked *so* fucking hard, Patrick. All through undergrad and law school and from my first day at the office, and..."

"Shhhhhhhhhh. Did you get your bonus, at least?"

"I did. Then I was out on the street with 75 other lawyers."

"Seventy-five? Holy shit..."

"M'mm. They let go of 75 of us just in Philly."

"Wanna do it?"

"You're an asshole," the brunette quietly sniffles.

"Now listen to me, Jenna. I saw a classified for an IP litigator that's been running for three weeks, even in this economy. They handle lots of high-end nerd disputes. I've already been rejected. You'd be perfectly qualified."

"I've never *not* had a job before, Patrick."

"You're 28 years-old. You'll adjust. I've been fired three times."

"Three times? Maria told me you were brilliant."

"Never mind what Maria said. I graduated from 'Nova with low honors."

"I'm sorry. I am. Really."

"I believe you. Otherwise, you wouldn't have bothered to come downstairs to visit me in this crackhouse."

Jenna lifts her head from my shoulder and wipes her blue eyes clear. I remove my arms from around her body, as much as I don't want to. It would just be awkward not to at this point. "I always thought that you were just this...stupid stoner with nothing going for you," she says.

"You were right, Jenna."

"That's not true," she says as she grabs the front of my t-shirt in both of her hands. "Iron Maiden?"

"I've liked them since eighth grade. I'm in my thirties. I have a law degree. I can wear whatever I want and I really don't care."

"You shouldn't care," Jenna replies. "But I have a proposition. I'd like to smoke some pot with you."

"I'll be forced to notify the state bar."

"Oh, fuck you," she says with a slap to my chest and a hint of a smile. Any bodily contact from a woman to a man usually indicates some sort of interest or attraction, but nothing is ever as it seems here on St. Michael's Sound. I propose that we sit on Harry's boat with a recently-obtained jay of authentic Reclining Buddha, of which we have four saved in the Board Room- one for each of us. They are reserved solely for smoking solo with a beautiful woman, even though it's a high crime to waste such righteous buds on a rank amateur like Jenna. It doesn't matter. There's no one else.

10:07 p.m.

Over two hours past sunset, the night is still so warm that steam is rising off the waters of the sound. Even with the fog and light pollution coming from the homes surrounding the channel, there are still 20 times more stars visible in the Angel Bay sky than anywhere in Philadelphia. Jenna and I are sitting on a blanket next to each other in the aft. Being a weeknight, it's very tranquil. The only sounds to be heard are the occasional passing car and the current hitting against the sides of the boat. I've made sure to hide my left arm at my side so that I don't have to answer any questions about it.

"It's such a beautiful night," observes the brunette.

"That's because you're stoned, Jenna."

"That has *nothing* to do with it. I haven't smoked pot in years, though."

"I didn't figure you to have too many vices."

"I do."

"Like what? Ending sentences in prepositions?"

"*With* prepositions."

"Whatever, Jenna."

"I like to play blackjack," she replies.

"Are you gambling away the mortgage money?"

"Of course not."

"Then it's not really a vice. It's just entertainment. That's totally acceptable."

"Thanks for your approval. What's your biggest vice? Besides endlessly smoking pot all of the time and walking around like a stoned idiot..."

261

"Italian women with great legs. Which is probably why I endlessly smoke pot all the time and walk around like a stoned idiot..."

"Well, I'm only half Italian. My father is an Israeli Jew. Only my mother is Italian. Sorry to disappoint you."

"You're not disappointing me. The combination works very well, obviously."

"It was a crime that my parents had to elope in order to spare the families the drama of an actual wedding. Nobody really cares about that stupid shit now anymore."

"In our parents' day, a 'mixed marriage' was an Italian girl marrying an Irish guy. In South Philly, it still is."

"What's your feeling about that?"

"I like exotic-looking girls. It'd be nice to marry an Irish girl and keep the McShea line 100% pure, but I don't see it happening."

"Why not?"

"They're cold. And I'd never marry a girl with my own skin tone. I like 'em a few shades darker."

"Like me?"

"Like you, Jenna. But not you specifically."

"Why not?"

"I just have no desire to feed your already-massive ego. I have a really good idea, though."

"What's that, genius?"

"I think we should play Seven Minutes in Heaven." The brunette glares at me like I've just said something *terribly* inappropriate. "Sorry, Jenna."

"That comment was *so* juvenile."

"Guilty as charged."

"And it's Seven Minutes in the Closet, by the way."

"That must be the suburban version. So tell me about the first time you ever played..."

"I never did. I was never into any of those ridiculous boy-kissing games."

"I guess boy cooties ran rampant in your neighborhood."

"What about you, Patrick?"

"Oh, I definitely have cooties. Double cooties, even."

"You knew what I meant," Jenna says with a stoned giggle.

"I played a couple of times. I always one of the last guys to get picked, if I was picked at all."

"Really? Why?"

"I went through a really awkward phase. It ended about two weeks ago."

"I happen to think you're handsome."

"I was very shy in grade school and high school. But thank you, Jenna."

"I was a big, shy nerd, too."

"A hot nerd, I'm sure."

"Is that all that matters to you? That I'm 'hot?'"

"It don't hurt."

"Oh, shut up. You're blushing, by the way. Don't you take compliments very well, Patrick? That a sign of a person with low self-esteem or a poor self-image."

"Is that what your Psych 101 professor taught you at Dartmouth?"

"How'd you know I went to Dartmouth?"

"I stalked you on the internet. Every big firm lawyer has a bio out there. It said that you earned three varsity letters."

"I played tennis. They called me 'No Love Jenna' for my first two years on the team."

"Why's that? Did you suck?"

"*No,*" Jenna replies emphatically. "I don't 'suck' at anything. I just kept to myself when I first got to college. I went to practice and went to the library. That's about it. No boys."

"I'm sure most of them had cooties, anyway."

"They did. Double cooties, even. Just like you do, Patrick."

"What does your middle initial stand for?"

"Rose."

"Jenna Rose Love. That has a nice ring to it..."

"What happened to your arm?"

"Uh...close encounter with the grill upstairs," I lie.

"I thought it was out of propane."

"It definitely is *now*..."

"So, as far as all of the pot smoking goes, what is it that's missing in your life that you're trying to compensate for?"

"The word 'for' would be a preposition, correct, Jenna?"

"Do you ever answer a question directly?"

"Does any lawyer?"

"We're not lawyers right now. We're two friends discussing things on a beautiful summer night together."

"We're friends?"

"Yes, we're friends now that I know the truth about you. Does that bother you for some reason?"

"What's the truth?"

"That you're this caring, sensitive, intelligent guy who hit some bumps in the road, apparently."

"I did," I say quietly as I stare up into the sky. "But let's hide that 'sensitive' and 'intelligence' stuff from the rest of the girls. There's no bigger turn-off to a woman than intelligence."

"That's so ridiculous."

"It's ridiculous because it's true. Remember, I grew up in Philly."

"So talk to me, Patrick."

"I can't. I hide things from people I find attractive."

"You find me attractive?"

"I do. Who wouldn't?"

"I've only had four boyfriends in my entire life."

"By choice, I take it."

"Kinda. It's somewhat complicated."

"If I had a nickel for every woman that used the word 'complicated' to describe their love life or their relationships, I'd be a billionaire. Bye-bye student loans."

"This really *was* complicated."

"Tell me about it, then."

"No. You first."

"Rock, paper, scissors again?"

"Actually, no. I really don't feel like talking about it."

"You know what?"

"What, Patrick."

"You're *gorgeous*, Jenna."

The blue-eyed brunette cracks a Mona Lisa smile and looks down toward the bottom of the boat while running the fingers of her right hand through her hair. Then she looks up at me. "Umm...wow," she says, which doesn't tell me all that much. She's either completely flattered by my diversion from telling my story, or now thinks I'm totally creepy. "Where did that come from?" she asks curiously.

"My lips."

"Obviously. I meant, what was your motivation?"

"The truth, I guess. I just happened to look over at you, and..."

"Sure," Jenna says skeptically.

"Why so cynical? You suck to smoke with, Jenna."

"We've been over this already, Patrick," the brunette says firmly. "I don't suck at anything."

"I gave you an opportunity to prove yourself by casually suggesting Seven Minutes in Heaven and you didn't seem too receptive."

"Because that's, like, completely imm-mah-tour."

"That's one of my biggest pet peeves, Jenna. The word is 'immature.' Now say it: immature."

"No. I'll say it my way."

"Now who's being 'imm-mah-tour?'"

"You're not going to get anywhere with me by making references to grade school bullshit that was just a poor excuse for guys to get up a girl's shirt."

"We're stoned, Jenna. Some people enjoy silly conversation when they're stoned. You don't, obviously."

"Maybe I resent the fact that you're suggesting these things while I have a boyfriend."

"Your boyfriend is not my problem or concern."

"You're such a...*guy*."

"I hope so."

"You are, but most of it is an act to hide your sweet side."

Jenna's spot-on analysis gives me a chuckle.

"What's so funny?"

"You're a very smart girl. That's what's so funny."

"Why is being smart 'funny?'"

"It just is. So what's Michael's deal? Is he complying with his stipulations for parole?"

"Oh, fuck you. Soooooooo...who have *you* been hooking up with this summer in secret? There has to be someone..."

"Why does there have to be someone?"

"*Everybody* hooks up down here. You have to be like, the troll living under the bridge to not hook up when everybody's wasted."

"I guess I'm just the troll that happens to be living *next* to the bridge, then."

"What about Amanda?"

"Just ditched me for dinner in favor of Silent John."

"Seriously?"

"Seriously."

"I don't think he's that cute."

"Evidently Amanda does. And it's only her opinion that counts."

"Okay...Heather."

"I hate her."

"'Hate' is a very strong word, Patrick. I never use it with respect to people."

"You're a better person than I am, then. I certainly have no love for her."

"The opposite of love isn't hate. It's indifference. Hate shows that you care about her on some level, which is senseless. Why would you *ever* waste your time with her?"

"Did I have a better option? She's a *very* attractive, Jenna."

"So what's so attractive about her? I don't see anything special. The way she carries herself isn't very attractive at all. She has a really nice body, but-"

"That's really all that matters sometimes. Not every woman needs to be the future Mrs. McShea."

"My opinion of you is dropping by the second."

"Then tell me about Michael and I'll shut the fuck up. You smell good."

"Thank you," Jenna laughs. "That was kinda slipped in randomly..."

"We're stoned. That's how these conversations typically go."

"Why don't you drink, Patrick?"

"That wasn't the question on the table, Counselor."

"Just curious."

"My body simply can't tolerate it. I'd love to be able to tell you stories about bar fights involving broken chairs and unruly midgets with 60 days residential and a prison sentence, but that's all it is. What about you? Terms of your probation?"

"I had a bad experience with it at 17 and...I never really drank ever again."

"Is it something you want to talk about?"

"No. But here's all you need to know about Michael right now: we haven't had sex in almost three months."

There's a few seconds of silence before Jenna asks for another hit. I pass her the necessary implements. She certainly needs them. Jenna manages to exhale a pretty impressive hit for a woman and immediately begins a coughing fit. I offer her my 7UP and begin to massage her warm back through her top. I didn't think about it first. I just did it reflexively. I might be enjoying the company of this beautiful pest more than I'd care to admit.

"Thank you," Jenna says after a lengthy sip from my drink. "Think about it, Patrick. You'd probably want to kill yourself if you had to go three months without sex."

"I probably would. I definitely would."

"Oh, don't be so dramatic. I love what you're doing with your hand. It's so relaxing."

"That's the point, Jenna. You can thank my old, crappy guitar for my strong fingers."

"Michael would rather commit fucking suicide than touch me sometimes."

"Now *that's* something that's ridiculous. Why do you tolerate that?"

"Well, I know that he has intimacy issues, and-"

"*Obviously* he has intimacy issues..."

"May I finish please?"

"Sure. Why not."

"Thank you. His mother was such an alcoholic that he had to be taken out of the home at one point and separated from his sister. His dad provided the only income and was always on the road for work. So, he's not very affectionate or trusting sometimes. Most of the time. Can you imagine having to grow up like that, though?"

"I can't," I say as I stare up into the thousands of stars in the Angel Bay sky.

"Are you hot?" Jenna asks.

"Apparently not. Silent John is, though."

"I mean, the temperature, jackass. I'm all sticky. And don't be so down on yourself. I've already said you were handsome. A lack of confidence is *not* attractive."

"People can 'say' anything, Jenna."

"Like when you said I was "gorgeous?""

"Touché."

"Let's go inside into the air conditioning."

"Your place or mine?"

"Mine. We can keep Princess company."

"That'd be nice."

"She *loves* you, Patrick. She ran up onto the bottom deck and was pawing at the downstairs door when we got here tonight."

"I'm flattered."

"You should be. Dogs can tell when someone has a gentle soul."

"Can you?"

"I can," she assures me softly before we rise to exit the boat.

10:57 p.m.

Jenna has decided to give me a stoned, impromptu dance lesson while in the confines of her bedroom. This weed must be even better than I had thought. "Your entire technique on the dance floor is to simply molest someone," the sexy brunette lectures as some upbeat dance track plays from her iPod dock. "That's not going to get you anywhere with anyone special." She attempts to instruct me on how to properly move my body while Princess pants and watches the entire stoned affair with her bulging eyes. "Now put your hands on my hips," Jenna orders while the dog continues to watch curiously from her bed.

"I feel like I'm in an Eighties movie and the hot girl is trying to teach the dorky guy a new trick."

"So what happens next in your movie?" Jenna asks with a very flirtatious smile.

"You take your shirt off."

My dance partner puts her own hands on her hips and stares through me. "Can you say something clever or complimentary or...*romantic* for once instead of being obnoxious?" she says with a sneer. It seems to be a common complaint around here.

"I act obnoxious whenever I feel awkward," I explain.

"Don't feel awkward. We totally stoned and just having a good time together with no witnesses or interruptions."

"Princess is a witness."

"Princess can't talk and won't make fun of you, Patrick."

"I'm not so sure. Have you seen the look she's giving us?"

"She's just being protective of me."

"I'm quaking in my shoes."

"Over Princess? Or over me?"

"Clever, Jenna."

"Answer the question, my dear."

"I'm here for the dance lesson. I'm not so sure about this other stuff. You snotbag."

"Excuse me?"

"Nothing. I'm ready to continue my lesson."

"Fine. Start by you putting your hands on my hips again. And you're going to move with a rhythm that's not like a humping dog."

"That's a tall order," I say as my hands settle into the wonderful curves of Jenna's body.

"What color are your eyes, Patrick?"

"Hazel. They're more green or more brown depending on the light and what color shirt I'm wearing."

"What if you aren't wearing any shirt?"

"Then my eyes are usually closed."

"Your rhythm is becoming much better."

"I do play guitar, you know."

"Say something nice to me, Patrick," is Jenna's request as the music from the iPod dock suddenly shifts to Sade's 'By Your Side.' I get a lump in my throat the size of a grapefruit. "Is this music okay with you?" asks my dance partner.

"Anything but this song," I say softly. "Slow is definitely cool, though."

"Bad memories?"

"Kinda. Sorry to be such a bitch."

"It's not a problem," Jenna says as she walks over to her iPod. The beautiful mellow of 'La Cienega Just Smiled' starts pouring from the speakers. "How's this?"

"It's fucking prefect."

"Good," Jenna says as she unexpectedly places her slender arms onto my shoulders and locks her hands around the back of my neck. My heart rate increases by a factor of twelve. "Is there anything you'd like to talk about, Patrick?"

"No. I'm very comfortable right now."

"Good. Say something nice to me, then."

"What do you want to hear, Jenna?"

"That's your call. There are some things that I just can't do for you."

"I can't believe how beautiful you looked in your dress last weekend," I say as we instinctively start to sway slowly with the music.

"Thank you," Jenna says with some pep in her voice. "I didn't even realize that you saw me in it."

"It's kinda burned into my mind at this point."

"I would have walked in the house to say 'hi' to you but you had to be such a fucking *asshole* to me."

"You're not always such a treat yourself, Jenna. That's why we started the night with apologies, remember?"

"I know. I've kinda been having a rough time with things."

"Me, too."

"All bleeding stops, Patrick."

"Excuse me?"

"I said, 'All bleeding stops.'"

"You're a patient of Dr. Karlis, aren't you?"

"*I am,*" Jenna confesses quietly. My anger must be written all over my face. I rip my hands from her hips. "Hey!" she says in protest.

"I'm pissed at you. Seriously. Lie much?"

"*Listen to me,*" the stunner whispers, placing her hands on my chest. "You know that e-mail was a total CYA. There were rumors that layoffs were coming and...c'mon, you know the deal."

I do know the deal. I feign being pissed for a bit longer, than offer my forgiveness as if I wasn't going to offer it regardless.

"Thank you," Jenna replies sweetly. "Now put your hands back where they belong, please."

"Twist my arm."

Jenna smiles a million dollar smile at me. It's definitely time. Yet, I hesitate.

"Is something wrong, Patrick?"

"Not at all."

"Then why won't you kiss me?"

"Because I'll never stop once I do. What if it leads to heavy petting? I don't want to make a sinner out of someone who's so 'mah-tour' and respectable."

"I think I can handle it. Jackass."

"You can?"

"I can," she again assures me.

I slowly move my lips toward Jenna's. I can feel her warm breath on my face as I inch closer and closer. She breaks into a beautiful smile just before our lips touch. Hers are as soft as anything I could ever have imagined.

11:37 p.m.

[ur wonderful feminine curves make u look so incredibly sexy when ur naked jenna. ur skin is so smooth and unblemished and dark as the night itself. and no tanlines from secretly sunbathing on the roof naked u naughty thing u! but as excited as i am 2 have u naked in ur bed i am also greatly humbled. urs is a body i have dreamt about every fucking day since seventh grade yet rarely had for my own. but for now i do. ur olive-toned legs are a work of art in and of themselves but the rest of u is equally stunning. u have been kissed by god just a bit longer than most other girls have ever been. i could run my tongue all over ur smooth stomach forever if i wasn't so overcome by my desperate desire 2 take ur cunt. i want 2 taste and please u and make u cum so badly jenna love. my mouth is watering as i move my lips further down ur body to ur right inner thigh. u moan because u know where i'm headed jenna. i reach the notch where ur wide open leg joins ur body and kiss it. i'm so close to ur sex but still can't detect ur scent. i bite down on ur hip adductor. hard. *omigod please don't tease me, baby* u moan. *its been so fucking long for me, patrick.* and whose fault is that, jenna? such a stupid bitch for someone so smart. women will put up with absolutely anything if they think they are in love. but no matter. i have a gorgeous girl spread out in front of me who needs her clit pleased. badly. my face is now directly over her cunt. my heart is about to shake out from my chest. its shaved save the slimmest possible strip of hair just above her hood. her pink lips are clearly swollen but still slight. its a beautiful sight. how any 'man' could not want 2 lick this top-shelf pussy is beyond any human comprehension. ive secretly been dying for it jenna since the second i laid eyes on u. ur so clean that i'm forced 2 inhale *so* deeply just 2 take in ur scent.   its the most wonderful smell 2 be had anywhere on the face of the fucking earth. i push my tongue directly into ur wet fuckhole. u squeal like i never could have imagined in my endless secret perverted fantasies about every inch of ur beautiful body jenna. i lap ur taste into my mouth. its like water smoothly flowing tasteless and thin. i knew it would be. i leave ur hole and slowly glide my tongue back and forth between ur lips until i reach ur hood then dive straight back down 2 take in more of ur taste. ur soaking fucking wet at this point miss jenna rose love so its finally time 2 lick u where u want it. i slowly circle ur clit 4 a spell before i start 2 attack it. *omigod! omigod! omigod!* u moan more strongly than i ever would have thought. u poor girl. u have been so sexually neglected by every reject and misfit and nerd in ur life. and i haven't even started my act yet. i allow u the pleasure of my fastly flicking tongue for a minute or so before i slowly suck every inch of ur hood and clit and lips into my mouth to massage them. *my god what the* fuck *are u doing to me patrick!* u exclaim with delight as i suckle on ur entire vulva. i release it with a pucker only because i need to taste that asshole of urs. my tongue slides through and past ur wetness as u push ur right foot against the stiff cock throbbing inside my boxers. this drives me fucking crazy. *ur so fucking bad* u whisper as my tongue tickles u from below. i sink my nose inside u. my right knuckle massages ur clit. u cry out loudly. and more loudly. and louder still. u have never had ur pussy eaten like this. and if u have then its been forever and a day since. i couldnt ever taste ur body enough 2night from those soft red moist lips to ur tongue to the wonderful scent on the nape of ur brown neck. and those breasts! so round and supple with perfect quarter-sized nipples that were impossible 2 ignore on my way down 2 tracing ur hips with my tongue while moving toward ur greatest prize. my tongue moves back 2 ur hood jenna. i dig underneath the wet folds of ur skin in my mouth in search of ur bare clit. and i fucking find it. ur entire body flinches like u just put a gold key into a live socket. *too intense, baby!* u say with a pronounced shudder. i squeeze ur clit out of my mouth and push my tongue against ur hood, moving it in slow, strong circles. *lick it, patrick! fucking lick it! now!* u command excitedly. i dont dare disobey. *omigod* u breathe. *that's the perfect spot. right there! right there!* ur deep hurried breathing sounds angelic to my ears. ur hips move up and down in rhythm with my tongue.

then ur dark precious august thighs start to quake jenna. ur so fucking close. and this bankrupt endlessly rejected misfit attorney is the cause. *ru ready for me, baby? ru ready?* u ask in a pitch approaching sexual frenzy. of course im ready jenna. i was ready the second i laid eyes on your gorgeous legs and unforgettable blue eyes. *dont u dare stop u fucking bastard!* is ur latest order. why would i ever stop jenna? making ur gorgeous self cum is a bigger accomplishment than anything i ever did as an attorney.   i lick so intensely 4 u that i practically forget 2 breathe. i am so rock fucking hard from tasting u and seeing u naked and taking ur commands and listening to the sound of ur sex voice as u hit the edge of ur ecstasy. u put forth ur loudest sexiest moan yet. i have u at my mercy jenna and i love it. but i could never pull away from u. u have no idea how excited i am 2 make u cum sweetheart. i will be so relieved when my mission is accomplished. *omigod im gonna cum* u cry out just as i feel a sprinkle of ur taste shoot into my mouth and ur lips swell slightly larger for the briefest instant. and ur quite the narrator u little slut u: *omigod! patrick, im cumming! im cumming right now all over your handsome face! taste it, baby! taste it! omigod, ur making me cum so fucking hard.* i slow my tongue to half-speed until u push ur head away from me and lie on ur side so that i cant take any more tastes from ur magic. i bite into ur trim beautiful tan ass that's lying right in front of me. u kick me and giggle before I can stick my tongue right back into it like the horny beast that i am 4 u right now. ur blue eyes look at me and u say]

"Water, please," which is the first thing almost every woman says after an orgasm. I walk to the refrigerator rock hard and find two bottles inside. One is marked with a tell-tale pink cap indicating that it contains 4-Hydroxybutanoic acid- otherwise known as GHB- which is the preferred drug of choice among those who get tested regularly at work or have government clearances. I take a sip from the other unopened bottle and don't immediately pass out or see pink elephants walking around the room, so I assume it's safe. I deliver it to Jenna. "Thank you, sweetie," she says as I climb back into her bed without disturbing the ancient pug on the floor. "My *entire* body is still shaking. No one's done that for me in *forever.*"

"I could lick you all day as long as someone dropped food and water outside the door every few hours."

"You're such a silly boy," Jenna says before kissing me. "Now lie down. I need to talk to you, even though you won't want to hear it."

"Which disease is it?"

"Shut up, Patrick. It's got nothing to do with anything like that and you know it. Four boyfriends, remember?"

"It only takes one."

I lie down and Jenna begins rubbing my chest while soft her brown hair falls all over me. *"You're so handsome,"* she says soothingly before planting a long kiss on my lips. "You smell like me."

"I'm going to be licking around my lips all night."

"Now listen...I can't return any favors for you, okay?"

"And why not?"

"I've already told you that we're not having sex."

"That was *before* you pushed my head down between your thighs."

"Did I really do that?"

"Yes. You did."

"I just...I haven't gotten any attention like this in so long."

"Cry me a river, Jenna."

"Oh, fuck you," she laughs. "Look, technically I'm still seeing Michael. I haven't sat down and spoken to him yet. I can't be involved sexually with two guys at the same time. I just can't. It's not me."

"Umm...isn't having a guy going down on you being 'involved sexually?'"

"That's different. And you know it."

"How is it different?"

"I'm not doing anything involving penetration or sucking on anything, okay?"

"That's real fair, Jenna."

"If you're patient, Patrick, you'll wind up getting anything you want from me."

"Anal?"

"That's so imm-ma-tour. We've hooked-up now, okay? Stop with the obnoxious, insecure bullshit every time you feel nervous or awkward. There's no need for it at this point. You licked my *ass* forgod'ssake."

"I didn't hear any complaints..."

"You happen to be *very* talented, as much as I hesitate to admit it. I've never let *anyone* do that before."

"I'm a full-service kind of guy, Jenna."

"Just be patient with me, okay?"

"I'm just running out of patience."

The brunette gives me another prolonged kiss before settling underneath the covers with her head on my chest and her shapely right leg across my body. Princess jumps up onto the bed and settles herself in next to my head. She immediately starts snoring directly into my ear. "I'm feeling really relaxed," Jenna says quietly. I take her hand and place it firmly on the front of my boxers. "Omigod," is Jenna's lone comment.

"It's not easy to sleep with this," I reply, sounding admittedly high school-ish.

"Blue balls, Patrick? How many pathetic eighth grade flashbacks are we going to have tonight?"

"Sorry, Jenna. I have a silly sense of humor when I'm stoned."

"It's somewhat endearing, actually."

Jenna, apparently subconsciously, continues to run one of her fingers up and down the prominent bulge in my boxers.

"You're not exactly helping matters, Jenna."

"Oh! I'm sorry. I like it."

"No need to apologize. It's been a good night. I'm just asking you to make a decision one way or another."

"Fine," Jenna says with a hint of annoyance in her tone. "I'll jerk you off, okay? That's it, though."

"You can't."

"Why not?"

"Handjobs are illegal after you graduate from college. Does it say *magna cum laude* on your diploma?"

"It does..."

"It translates from the Latin as, *'From this day forward, use your mouth only to please a man in the absence of intercourse.'*"

"You have *such* an adorable face," Jenna replies. "I just can't believe some of the things that come out of it." She suddenly escapes from her bed and leaves the room momentarily. The shapely brunette returns and a fruity smell enters the air. "Pull down the covers and take off your clothes," she commands, then straddles me with her naked body after I comply. "Do you mind your penis smelling like Fresh Melonberry?" she asks jokingly as her soft hands rub cool lotion onto my stiff shaft. "It's my body lotion."

"That's some very lucky lotion."

Jenna giggles and smiles a wide smile, her pearly white teeth glowing in the darkness of the room. "If you're lucky enough, maybe you can rub it all over my body after my shower someday."

"I'd like that. You look amazing naked."

"Do I?"

"Of course you do. That feels *so* good, Jenna."

"I knew it would, you obnoxious little boy. I'm *very* good with my hands."

"I bet you're very good with your mouth, too."

"And why's that?"

"You're a great kisser."

"Thank you. I could drive you *insane* with my mouth, Patrick."

"I don't doubt it," I say as I place my hands on Jenna's thighs and let out an involuntary groan the second I touch the ultra-smooth, sun-kissed skin of her body.

"*Somebody's* getting excited, Patrick."

"Somebody has gorgeous thighs and a beautiful set of tits."

"Thank you. I don't hear that enough."

"You're fucking sexy."

"How'my doing, sweetie?"

"Pull it straight up. It's more intense that way."

"Like this?"

"*Omigod, just like that, Jenna.*"

The stunning brunette quietly laughs to herself.

"Proud of yourself, Miss Love?"

"Kinda," she smiles. "Should I go faster or slower?"

"It's all in your hands. I trust you."

"I just want to make sure I'm pleasing you, dear."

"I'm pleased just to see you naked."

"Maybe it should become a habit..."

"I hope so. I can't wait to *fuck* you, Jenna."

"You wanna *fuck* me, Patrick?"

"You need it, Jenna."

"I *do* need it. *How would you give it to me?*"

"I want those gorgeous legs of yours on my shoulders."

"So you can watch me getting fucked by you?"

"M'mm."

"That's *really* sexy...you'd get so deep inside me with this hard dick of yours, Patrick. *So* deep."

"You have such a tiny little waist, Jenna. I'd destroy you."

"*Is that what you think?*"

"That's what I *know*, Jenna."

"You're *so* much more confident when you're turned on, Patrick."

"I'm so much more confident once I already have you naked."

"So is that your plan? To get me as naked as often as possible?"

"Absolutely."

"You're *so* fucking hard for me right now."

"Not as hard as I was when you were cumming in my mouth..."

"I *never* should have let you do that. Now I'll get wet every time I lay my eyes on you. *Ridiculously* wet."

"Are you wet for me now, Jenna?"

"Of course I am. I'm *so* wet with your cock in my hands. You love hearing that, don't you?"

"Who wouldn't?"

"Are you planning to cum for me any time soon?"

"Be patient, Jenna."

"I'm sorry. You were so good to me. I'll shut up."

"Don't shut up."

"You like hearing me talk dirty, Patrick?"

"I *love* it. I'm so excited for you, Jenna."

"You don't know what 'excited' is until I actually let you inside my pussy, Patrick. You want to be inside my pussy, horny boy?"

"You don't know how badly I want your pussy, you sexy bitch."

"Yes, I do. Your dick got harder as soon as I said the word. You like that word, 'pussy,' don't you? You're a *dirty* little boy..."

"I'm *so* dirty, Jenna. You have no idea."

"I can't wait to find out. I'm going to be so fucking tight for you, Patrick. My pussy is going to be *so* tight for you. Think about your hard cock sliding deep inside of it. And it's *so* soft, and *so* wet..."

"Omigod, I wanna fuck you."

"I know you do, Patrick. Are you gonna pull my hair when I let you fuck me from behind?"

"Yes, Jenna."

"Promise?"

"I *promise* I'm gonna pull your hair when I fuck your pretty pussy from behind."

"You've *never* had an ass as good as mine, Patrick. It's going to drive you *crazy* to see me spread out on all fours. And you better fucking spank me."

"You're a bad girl."

"*Am I?*"

"You know you are."

"You're getting harder..."

"You're gonna make me cum, Jenna."

"You *better* cum for me. I'm not doing all of this work for nothing, Patrick. I'm doing it because I want your cum."

"You want my cum, Jenna?"

"Of course I want your cum, sweetheart. Are you ready to let me have it?"

"Omigod, I'm so ready, Jenna."

"What's my name, Patrick?"

"Jenna."

"Say it again, you bastard."

"Jenna!"

"Louder."

"Omigod, Jenna!"

"Who's pussy do you want, Patrick?"

"Your pussy, Jenna. I want *your* pussy."

"You want my pussy? Is that what you want, huh?"

"I'm *so* fucking close, Jenna. So fucking close."

"Give Jenna all of your cum, baby."

"Is that what Jenna wants?"

"Yes, sweetie. That's what Jenna wants. And Jenna *always* gets what she wants."

"Omigod, here it fucking cums, Jenna!"

"Say my name, bitch."

"Jenna! Jenna! Jenna! Omigod!"

"That's it, you bastard. Omigod, you're cumming so *fucking* hard for me."

"Jenna! Jenna!"

"That's it, sweetie! Say my name and let it all out. Just let *all* of your warm cum out for me."

"Omigod, you're amazing, Jenna," I say between heavy breaths.

"I try," she says with a devilish little smile once she's satisfied that all of my seed has been expelled onto my chest. Jenna surveys the scene and is more than impressed by her handiwork. "Omigod! Where did all of that come from?"

"It's all your fault."

"My god, let me get you a towel..."

Jenna leaves the bed and digs around her belongings, returning with both kisses and a cleaning implement. She does all of the work herself with great care before casting the towel aside and climbing back into bed with me.

"Feel better?" she asks as she cuddles up to me.

"One-hundred percent better."

"We're both naked together, Patrick."

"I know. I like it."

"Me, too. I just...I have another side to me and I wasn't exactly sure that I was ready to let you experience it. Michael can't stand it. He gets all bent out of shape if I act 'un-ladylike' and don't just lay there and moan in bed."

"When he even bothers to have sex with you..."

"Exactly."

"Why are you even dating him?"

Jenna provides the stock answer. "I don't know," she says quietly.

"You know exactly why you're dating him, otherwise you would have cut it off months ago." Jenna has no response. "Do you really think I'd hold it against you that you let your guard down in bed?"

"You never know. Some people are very judgmental."

"I'm not judgmental."

"Obviously. I wonder why you're not. I assume that you went to twelve years of Catholic school..."

"You already know that I see a psychiatrist. Who am I to judge? It's changed my entire perspective on things."

"I wanted to talk to you about that."

"Ugh."

"I just...there's so many contradictions with you. Maria said you were brilliant, yet you've been fired from three firms that no one's ever heard of..."

"I worked for Goldman Sharper in law school. It's a boutique, but..."

"I've heard of them. They didn't make you an offer?"

"It came down to me or Goldman's niece. Guess who won?"

"I'm sorry."

"Not your fault."

"It's your personality though, too. You were such an *asshole* to me, yet so sweet with Maria. And you were so attentive to me tonight. So I'm not really getting you."

"My story is too personal. Too soon."

"And you sticking your tongue into my *ass* isn't 'personal?' Or me saying p-words while I'm jerking you off?"

"You can't say the word 'pussy' if you're not turned on, can you?"

"Shut up."

"Just say it."

"No. I'm a good girl when I'm not acting like a tramp."

"You're not a tramp, Jenna. Humans are sexual beings."

"I'm just never with two guys at once. It's a rule. I never break it."

"Is dating a guy that ignores your needs and refuses to have sex with you a rule, too?"

Jenna sighs and begins to rub my chest. "We'd have *amazing* sexual chemistry," she opines in avoiding the topic.

"Amazing sexual chemistry occurs under only one of two scenarios: incredible mutual attraction with mutual respect, and incredible mutual attraction with absolutely no respect between the parties."

"So which are we, Patrick?"

"Do you really need to ask? If I didn't respect you, I just would have annoyed you into having sex with me, and left if you didn't."

"I can't see you doing that to anybody."

"I can be a bastard. You know that. The fact that you're intelligent helps, too. I'm not going to be able to pull the wool over your eyes like you can with 99% of the women out there, if you have the desire or confidence to."

"So why aren't you out there pulling the wool over the eyes of all these sluts running drunk around the Shipwreck?"

"Lack of confidence. I'm not in a good place right now. I'm not sure if I would, anyway. I like good girls with a dirty side."

"Like me."

"Yup. That's the way my favorite college girlfriend was. All class in public, all whore in private."

"I'm sure she appreciates *that* description," Jenna says sarcastically.

"She knew it. Only I saw the private side, anyway."

"What happened to her?"

"She's a professor of economics at Cal-Irvine and is married with kids. At least that's what I gleaned from the public portion of her facebook profile."

"My college boyfriend was such a dork."

"So am I, Jenna."

"No, I mean he was an annoying dork. And *so* boring in bed. I can't believe I even slept with him in the first place. Same with my law school boyfriend."

"Hopefully, you'll have the same regrets about me some day."

"I doubt it."

"So we're never sleeping together?"

"I didn't say that. I just don't think I'd regret it. Are you going to answer my original question, Patrick?"

"What was it, again?"

"About Dr. Karlis."

"You don't think that's too personal at this point?"

"I'm not exactly having an easy time, either. That's why I see him myself."

"You just seemed to be overwhelmed and disillusioned with the profession. I'm clinical. There's a difference, Jenna."

"I'm not here to judge you. Otherwise, you never would have gotten my shirt off. And my shorts. I'm just trying to reconcile the two Patricks that I know. And maybe we can help each other."

I look up at the ceiling and sigh as Jenna continues to rub my chest and breathe her warm breath onto me. She knows something of my condition already. I don't want to seem like I'm in avoidance mode. It's probably better that I just fill-in the gaps in her knowledge so she's not left speculating or wondering if I'm hiding something evil. She's already caught me red-handed in my shrink's office on my second-worst day. She's already admitted that she's a patient herself. So I spill almost everything. The sleepless nights. The racing thoughts. The bad grades. The full story of getting screwed by Goldman Sharper. Working for bad firms. Working for boring firms. Working for shady firms. Being completely broke. Feeling hopeless. Buying a gun. Blasting heroin. I don't admit to my current 15-month sexual strikeout. I don't admit to my violent fantasies or self-mutilation, either. That's too creepy. I'll never feel comfortable talking about those things to anyone aside from Dr. Karlis. I won't even tell my future wife, if there ever is one. I pause as I finish my story and wait. Jenna speaks.

"I'm so sorry, Patrick," she says sincerely, to my relief, at the conclusion of the toned-down version of my tale. She takes my face into her hands, looks at me with moist blue eyes, and begins softly kissing my lips again until we drift off to sleep in each other's arms.

Friday, August 6, 2010

9:01 a.m.

The naked Jenna opens her eyes and rises from the bed, immediately walking her heavenly ass over to the nearest mirror. It's so small. So fucking small. Her ass, not the mirror. "I look like shit," she declares, even though Jenna is one of those girls who looks *exactly* the same in the morning as she did when she went to bed the night before. She grabs her bathrobe and some clothes from the nearby dresser, then plants several kisses on my lips and orders me from her bed. "You're coming to the beach with me in Avalon," are my instructions before Jenna heads into the shower. "Sober," she adds before closing the bathroom door.

3:37 a.m.

Jenna and I sat on the beach for a few hours together this morning while she wore this stunning red bikini and movie star-sized D&G sunglasses. I kept staring at her perfect legs out of the corner of my eye, still incredulous that I was between them last night. I was very relaxed, even though I obeyed orders and didn't go to the beach with her stoned. She told me that I was handsome or cute every forty minutes or so and pinched my cheek. It was quite a change from her usual attitude toward me, but that tends to happen when a woman actually finds you attractive, her boyfriend won't have sex with her, and she knows that you can make her cum. I was forced to take a stupid quiz from *Cosmopolitan* or some other slut magazine on relationship potential. Jenna refused to tell me whether I passed or not, although she snickered at some of my answers. I suspect that I did pass because I lied whenever plausible or convenient. She hung onto her grade school buddy Gina at the Shipwreck so I didn't see much of her at night. While on opposite sides of Danny's bar, we made eyes and smiled at each other with that silly grin that only comes after you get someone you like naked for the first time. Mallory was the only one smart or sober enough to catch us, but I trust her to keep things on the down low. I hope she does, because the image-conscious Jenna would rather die than be labeled as a cheater.

Jenna is now sleeping in her room with Princess and Gina. I am reclining in my seat on a large circular raft for Naked Late Nite. Stinky is seated directly to my right and is not crying. I have been caught staring down at her thighs and/or tits three times already. She does not care. "We're all friends here," she says. Mallory is directly across next to Blotto, which gives me a great view of her crossed thighs and nicer-than-expected B-cups. Page, Sharkey, Dizzy, Fifty-One, Amanda and Silent John round out the participants. Seeing Amanda and her giant balloons of breast tissue holding hands with Silent John stings a bit, but Jenna the Lifesaver has taken 95% of my frustration with this situation away. Still, it represents a *lot* of flirting and a ton of unlikely-to-be-met sexual fantasies being flushed down the fucking drain. I have no problem with SJP himself. We're all chasing the same thing. Amanda picked him. It's something I just have to accept.

"Do you think there's any chance that we'll have sex over the next 30 days?" Blotto asks aloud to Mallory. "I'm just trying to figure out where I should be concentrating all my firepower at our party tomorrow."

"What about Dina?" asks Sharkey. "She'll be lookin' to smoke your pole now."

"Dina is conveniently at an out-of-town wedding to which I was not invited," reports Blotto with a devilish grin.

"Sounds like one of her exes will be balls deep inside her by midnight," is Sharkey's take.

"Probably," Blotto admits. "Is there any among us who has not pointlessly banged an ex?"

"It's not pointless," says Dizzy, "as long as you get your shit off."

"'Pointless' may have been a poor choice of words," Blotto replies. "I should have used the phrase 'randomly banged an ex.'"

"I don't randomly bang my ex'es and I'm not a cheater," says Mallory. "Which is why you should concentrate elsewhere tomorrow, old friend." Every male groans at the Mallory directing the f-word toward Blotto, except Fifty-One who giggles at his expense. "I'm still kinda sorta seeing this guy from the beginning of the summer."

"Is that the guy that, whenever he fucks up, you punish him by setting a new world distance record for the space between each of your ankles?" Sharkey asks. Mallory looks down toward the water and says nothing.

"And when does 'kinda sorta' evolve into an actual dating relationship?" asks Amanda.

"It won't," Mallory replies to the blonde with a straight face. "I'm not all that crazy about him, but I don't want to see him hooking up with other girls at the Shipwreck, either. So I just kinda sorta keep him around until Labor Day. Then he's out."

"Whatever," mumbles Sharkey. "I wish I could 'kinda sorta' have you smoking my fucking pole. How's that sound?"

"Not very appealing," replies the naked brunette with a smile.

"Ditch that zero now and start workin' them legs around town for the last few weeks," Sharkey says to her. "Home stretch, people! Time to see who qualifies for the Fall."

"I wonder if there's any fish in the channel here," Stinky suddenly asks for no reason.

"There's not," Blotto replies. "There's a giant sign underneath the Seventh Street Bridge that says, 'Notice: No Fish Beyond This Point' and they all turn back around toward the sound. Are you really that fucking stupid?"

"Remember," says Sharkey, "that we're talking about a girl who was once asked to name the star closest to Earth, drew a blank, and then was shocked to find out that it was the sun."

"It was a trick question!" Stinky insists. "That's why I hate rainy days down here. We all wind up playing these retarded board games and people find out how stupid you are when you're not even really drunk yet. It hurts my self-esteem."

"What doesn't, Stinky?" Sharkey asks in response.

"Our toilet," she replies. "I've never had my self-esteem harmed by a toilet."

"A toilet is an inanimate object," says Blotto over raucous giggling from the girls aboard. "Your self-esteem can't be harmed by an inanimate object."

"Sure it can," Stinky replies. "My jeans hurt my self-esteem all the time. The ones that I can't fit into any longer."

"They shrink in the wash," says Mallory.

"Is that the latest excuse?" says Sharkey. "I could be wrong, but I thought it was due to a combination of old age and cellulite."

Stinky punches me because she's left-handed and I happen to be closest male. Then she hits me again for no stated reason.

"I saw you making eyes with someone tonight, Woodchuck," says Mallory drunkenly.

"I plead the Fifth," is my reply.

"She's beautiful."

"I know."

"Spill it, 'Chuck," says Page. "We are here in the Circle of Trust. No lies are told, all sins are forgiven, and no judgments are made. And to top it all off, we're all naked." He laughs to himself before downing another beer.

"Loose lips sink ships," cautions Blotto. I nod in agreement.

"Somebody needs to get that bitch Jenna down here," Sharkey says coincidentally. "She could probably float all the way down to South America on them titties." He then starts obnoxiously bellowing for Jenna from the raft as I try not to cringe. He stops when Mallory uncrosses her long legs, takes them out of the water, and decides to sit with her legs up on the raft with only the front of the soles of her feet blocking the view of her vagina. The raft falls silent as the brains of all of the men drift into stray fantasies. Before anyone can think to engage me with further questioning, Stinky lets out a ferocious scream and rips her legs out from water. She excitedly claims to have just been attacked by a shark. The girls all shriek while Amanda also pulls her golden legs out of the water. The guys look around at each other and do nothing. We note that none of us is attacked in the several ensuing minutes. Blotto implicates seaweed drifting with the current as the suspected 'shark.' Peace and calm again returns to the raft.

"It's a rough life we lead here," says Page with a smile as he cracks another can of suds. "Rafts, beer, weed, water, titties...it's so tough to cope." He again laughs before taking a long gulp of his beer.

"Does anything ever bother you, Page?" asks Amanda.

"Stinky not fucking him," says Sharkey.

"Sure," Page replies after swallowing while ignoring Sharkey's barb. "Sometimes I wonder what may have happened if I hadn't failed out of Miami after my first two semesters and spent four or five years in the same baseball program instead of jumping around to community college and then the 'other' Miami on North Broad Street in North Philly. The one *without* the women walking around in bikini tops in January..."

"Seriously, though," says Fifty-One. "How are you supposed to study at a place like that?"

"Typically with a book open inside a building called a 'library,'" says the snarky Sharkey. "I know that the concept of 'reading' is foreign to some of you people, especially the women, but it does happen on many college campuses across the country, including the University of Miami."

"I would just sit in my dorm room with a pair of high-powered binoculars all day and masturbate," chuckles Fifty-One. Stinky is quite humored by this statement. She turns to me and giggles, which allows me a great view of her perky B-cups and hard, dotted nipples. It's a shame the pretty thing is such a mess inside.

"I'm not going to bitch about things," continues Page. "I still got my shot in the minors, but..."

"Page won't ever tell you this," Dizzy interrupts, "but he was even on a baseball card. Can you imagine being on a fucking baseball card? I can't. Take note of that, Stinky."

"Take note of this, asshole," Stinky says before burping loudly. Then she looks over at me and laughs, giving me another great view of her tits. If the water wasn't so cool, I'd be embarrassingly hard as a rock.

"I was on one of those Topps 'Future Prospects' cards in like '03 or something," explains Page. "I still have one somewhere. Every once in a while I dig it out and cry a little bit over a few shots of Jack."

Sharkey offers his commentary: "And in some basement somewhere, some little kid is going through his baseball cards right now and asking his dad, '*Hey Dad? Did Alexander Page ever do anything in the majors?*' And he'll be like, '*No, son. He's probably pumping gas somewhere to support his illegitimate children like most failures in sports do.*'"

Page has a chuckle at his own expense and takes another sip before speaking. "There were three guys on that baseball card. One guy threw a no-hitter for the White Sox last week. The other guy wrapped his car around a tree while drunk and killed himself. I had surgeries on both shoulders and lost my cannon for a right arm. I couldn't hit a slider to save my life, either, but that's beside the point. Would I love to be crouched behind a plate catching for some guy throwing a 97 m.p.h. fastball in front of 40,000 people and making beaucoup bucks? Sure. But all things considered, I guess I really have no regrets. I'm still alive. And if things had been different, I wouldn't be out drifting on this raft naked with all you motherfuckers at 4:00 a.m. And, quite honestly, there's really no place I'd rather be right now."

"Except inside my butt," Stinky offers casually.

Saturday, August 7, 2010
Flotilla

10:02 a.m.

"Rock 'n roll, pussyhole!" Stinky exclaims as she enters the Board Room in her favorite blue bikini with fingers raised Dio-style in mock heavy metal tribute. "Who's ready to par-*tay*?" she then asks while performing a little dance on the carpet.

"Who's ready to shut the *fuck* up?" Sharkey replies. "I am *so* tired and hungover."

"If you don't get off that bunk soon, Blotto might wake up and start dropping The People's Elbow around here," laughs Page.

"Drop this," Sharkey replies with a blatant blast of death gas.

"I'm just going to pretend for the rest of this day, Peter," says Page, "that you're really not here. If I focus hard enough, and drink hard enough, and smoke hard enough, and do some 'shrooms, maybe, I'm fairly certain that I can ignore your existence entirely."

"Good luck," says Sharkey. He follows this by raising his leg and issuing another powerful, room-clearing blast from his decrepit anus. Stinky screams and seeks shelter in the bathroom, returning to the Board Room with some far-too-potent air freshener. She sprays it generously into the ceiling fan before realizing that it's actually a can of Raid. Sharkey pukes from the top bunk onto the carpet. Baxter is the next to vomit. The groggy, sleepy Blotto rises from the queen, thoroughly fucking confused. He begins a horrible coughing fit and struggles to make his way off the bed and out of the room behind a hacking Page and I. He runs into the bathroom and becomes the third to barf. He was also pretty hungover, though, anyway.

"You are such a fucking *whore*, Stinky!" exclaims Sharkey as he stumbles out of the room. "I have pukefoot now! And I don't know if I stepped in my own puke or Baxter's."

"I grabbed the wrong can by accident!" the blonde claims. "Sue me, okay?"

"Didn't the giant fucking black roach on the front of the can tip you the fuck off?" Sharkey screams at her. "Or was the box that says, 'Warning: Causes Death to Living Things' not big and red enough for you?"

"Yeah, Stinky," says Page. "I thought you were supposed to be a *good* reader."

"Oh, fuck off," she says. "It's all fucking Peter's fault for making the room smell like a giant sack of assholes when we were trying to smoke weed and gossip before our little party."

"If anybody really cares," Page says, "I hooked up with Mindy Miller last night."

"No one cares!" yells Sharkey from the shower while Blotto continues to hurl.

"She's really pretty," Stinky says. "I give it a week before you screw it up."

"Whatever, bitch," chuckles Page. "You almost just killed the entire Board. And your tag's sticking out of your bikini bottom."

"Omigod! Fix it for me! I don't want anyone to know what size I wear."

"No," says Page as he takes a seat on the living room couch to again light the *Falcon*. "If I get too close to your ass, I might try to eat it."

Harry enters. "Can't you assholes stop smoking weed for ten goddamn minutes?" he asks, annoyed. "We have 15 kegs coming in about fifteen minutes. Who the fuck is going to help carry them all?"

"Your mom," calls out Sharkey from the bathroom. 'Mom' jokes have even more impact in your thirties because no one expects them.

"Fuck it, I'll smoke," says Harry and takes a seat. "I got pulled over and got a ticket for having those balls on my truck yesterday," he says to me with a laugh. "I need you to go to court for me next Tuesday. I don't even know what the fuck I got cited for."

"Being a bitch," says Sharkey as he enters the room. "Stinky, you need to grab some sawdust, a wet vac, and say three Hail Marys. Pronto."

"I am not cleaning up anyone's puke!" she insists. "If it wasn't in my stomach than it's not my responsibility!"

"I think you're in the clear, Stinky," the shirtless Blotto reports as he walks gingerly into the room, looking like hell. "I didn't see any regurgitated sperm on the carpet. But we need to get everything cleaned up before Baxter tries to eat it."

"Clean this," Sharkey says while delivering yet another blast. Since none of the vomit belongs to me, I seek refuge in a shower outside and dream of Jenna's lips while I scrub. Her 'other' lips.

11:16 a.m.

The all-important Port-a-Johns arrive in the side yard.

11:45 a.m.

Amanda Liss and the ladies of the Bunny Ranch (the uptight Tags excepted) have agreed to serve as shotgirls for our event. They are running around upstairs in a giggling swarm of tan legs and hair spray as Jake, Silent John, Danny the Bartender and DJ Buttfuck set up the PA and other equipment on the upper deck. My current job is to tune-up all of the guitars. Amanda struts onto the deck dressed in a black one-piece with a black bowtie and white bunny ears in her blonde hair. She approaches. "I think you owe me an apology," she says. *For what?* is the first thing that comes to my mind, but I'm not about to disrespect Amanda with SJP lingering nearby. That just wouldn't be cool.

"I'm sorry for the text messages I sent you on Thursday," I say as I look down toward the tuner built into Jake's guitar. The hot sun is going to wreak havoc on our instruments today.

"Can you look me in the eye and say that?" the blonde requests. I do as she asks, painful as it is. "And I'm sorry for the way things turned out for us. I just..."

"You don't need to explain anything, Amanda." I'm not taking the high road. I just don't want to hear the latest fucking excuse a woman has for not picking me, happy as I am to have had my night with Jenna. Rejection always sucks despite whatever success you may have otherwise. Amanda plants a most hollow kiss onto my cheek. The blonde departs for the back yard with a tray of Jell-o shots and whipped cream for the early arrivals.

Jenna is the next to exit the house. Her hair is down and she's wearing her spectacular, sparkling pink bikini from the first time I saw her sunbathing on the roof. I have to pause to catch my breath, of course, although she looks totally freaked the fuck out. "Hi," she says to me awkwardly before going right back inside. It's not an encouraging sign.

12:15 p.m.

DJ Buttfuck has his equipment up first and is spinning a series of mellow instrumental dance beats and some reggae through the large speakers. All fifteen kegs have been placed into the back yard, where up to a hundred guests have already assembled to get a head start on becoming falling down, piss-your-pants fucking drunk courtesy of 728. Half of these High Noon arrivals are women wearing bikinis. Ninety percent of them are *really* attractive. The first line of floats, rafts and boats begins traveling under the Seventh Street Bridge toward the party, led by with a gorgeous blonde riding a giant smiling yellow octopus that has been marked 'My Other Pussy' by a large black Sharpie. She is followed by a large raft filled with Hot Dudes designated the U.S.S. Shit Show. The second vessel to follow is a dinghy filled with skinny stoners like myself christened as the A.S.S. Balloon Knot. In the meantime, Blotto, Page, Baxter and I are creating the house punch in a 30-gallon trashcan. We've already filled the can ¼ of the way with several large bags from Sea Isle Ice. Next, a dozen 2-liters of green Hawaiian Punch is dumped in, followed by a dozen 2-liters of red. Page begins to stir the concoction with a broomstick as eight bottles of Malibu and 12 liters of vodka are added. Another four bottles of something that smells like liquid shit is put into the mix.

Tearsten approaches. Baxter growls. "Where did you go last night? What have you been up to? What are you doing?" she asks of Blotto as the resident mutt stares her down. Her questions always seem to come in threes for some reason, which is convenient because you can usually get away with answering only the least dangerous of her queries.

"I wasn't in Angel Bay last night," Blotto lies in order to keep the peace. Reporting that he participated in Naked Late Nite would certainly cause an epic eruption.

"Why? Where were you? So what are you doing?"

"What does it look like I'm doing, Kirsten."

"I mean, besides making the punch."

"I'm not doing anything besides making the punch right now."

"Did you try some? What's it taste like? Is it good?"

"You can have the first sip, Kirsten," offers Page.

"*Before* we put the roofies in it," Blotto chuckles.

"Are you really putting roofies in it? Who has roofies? Why are you guys doing that?"

"That is such a stupid question, Kirsten, I'm not even going to dignify it with a response," says Blotto. "Why would we put roofies into the punch, which are highly illegal, by the way, and put half of our good friends in the hospital? Not that many of them would really mind..."

"Ummm...I have a really big float that fits two more people aside from my roommates," Kirsten announces.

"We'll be in the water when we're done our duties here," Blotto assures her.

"I still need to try the punch," says Tearsten, grabbing a cup. She makes a funny face after downing it, then quickly drinks two more cups before deciding that she doesn't really like it. She heads to the water with her float and incredibly sexy body. There is a few seconds of silence as Page continues to stir whatever is brewing in our trashcan.

"I accidentally fucked her on Tuesday night," Blotto confesses. "There was an offer of meatloaf involved."

"You...*moron*," is Page's take.

"Have you ever had her meatloaf?"

"No. Why would I ever have had her meatloaf?"

"She makes it with the brown sugar and ketchup sauce. It's out of this world, man."

"There goes *your* Saturday afternoon..."

"Not all of us can be lucky enough to hook-up with Mindy Miller, Page. How'd that all go down?"

"I saw her coming out of the Moo Moo about 2:15, just before I came back here for Naked Late Nite. So I just walked her home on a friendly basis. She invited me in, and no one else is around the house for some reason so were just standing in the kitchen drinkin' and talkin' and whatnot, and all of the sudden we both weren't saying anything. And she starts lookin' at me and I'm like, *'I think this is on.'* So I start kissin' 'er, and she didn't stop me. I was kinda surprised, really."

"Did she touch your pee-pee?"

"Nah," Page confesses. "I started playing with her titties a bit- big massive *bombs* she has- and was about to reach under her skirt when a whole bunch of people poured in from the bars. So I excused myself and came back here."

"Good job. So anyway, I'd feel better if we put this trashcan full of punch behind a makeshift bar and have the girls take shifts bartending. It only takes *one* asshole around here to spoil a really good time."

1:01 p.m.

Jake approaches the lead microphone stationed on the top deck. "Testes, one two," he says. "Testes, one two." Though it would sound cheesy with a lesser voice, I'm pretty humored by his variance from the stock, 'Check one. Check one.' *"How's everybody doing on this gorgeous day far away from working in the city?"* he bellows before we start our first set. The crowd, which now numbers at least 150 on land and several dozen floating in the water, lets forth a nice cheer. I play a G chord on the spare acoustic-electric guitar that Silent John has provided me today in order to see if it's still in tune. It sounds so clear through the $2,500 PA that I can't believe it's actually me playing it.

We first break into 'Why Don't We Get Drunk (and Screw)' by Marvin Gardens aka Jimmy Buffett. We've agreed to keep the first set pretty mellow so we don't blow our wad too early. The rest of it consists of some more Buffett, Bob Marley, 'Welfare Music' by the Bottle Rockets, 'Hangin' Around,' by Counting Crows, 'Friends in Low Places,' two of Jake's original songs about being sexy and selling Texas back to Mexico, and a set closer of Ramble On>Not Fade Away during which Silent John and I exchange some lengthy leads in front of the ever-growing crowd. We take our guitars inside the upstairs to let them cool off while things are turned over to DJ Buttfuck for the next hour or so. Heat wreaks havoc on the wood in the instruments which seriously affects their ability to stay in tune, so we let them sit in the air conditioning for a spell as Silent John produces a jay of Catpiss. Harry enters the living room giggling like a schoolgirl and plugs his police scanner into a nearby outlet as we smoke:

Dispatcher: *We have multiple reports from the party at 728 St. Michael's that women are exposing their breasts. Can anyone confirm.*

Police: *I'm on the Seventh Street Bridge with Chief Fitz. I haven't seen any exposed breasts yet. I'm trying. I'll certainly keep a look out, and a camera handy. For evidence, I mean. That all sounded pretty bad, I guess. Hope nobody's listening...*

Dispatcher: *I've gotten 36 calls already today. What do I tell all of these people?*

Police: *Tell them to get out of their chair and have a beer. The 70 year-old neighbors are here, for god'ssakes. And the wife is dancing with her cane to 'Whoot! There It Is!' And Fr. Murphy is here, too. 'Hey, Padre!'*

Dispatcher: *Could I have a real answer, please?*

Police: *It's an owner-occupied property so there's not all that much we can do unless there's violence or underage drinking. The owner asked us to put a cop outside the house to discourage underage patrons from trying to sneak in. I say we let it go 'till 6 and call it a day.*

Police: *Check to see if there's any outstanding violations on the owner. It's Harry Trimble. T-R-I-M-B-L-E.*

Dispatcher: *We have them dating back to...let's see here...it looks like 1986, but they've all been paid except for one last week. Something about prosthetic testicles hanging from his trailer hitch?*

Police: *Excuse me?*

Dispatcher: *Apparently P/O Dirk cited him for Disorderly Conduct because he has fake balls on the back of his truck.*

Police: *When's the hearing? This I gotta see...*

Dispatcher: *Could you just tell the DJ to keep it down a little? That might stop some of the calls and make my day a little easier.*

Dispatcher: *Somebody just called to say the band sucks, too.*

Police: *Wait a minute...I see some exposed breasts on a boat docked in the channel. Wait. Nevermind. It's an extremely obese white male with his shirt off. Somebody issue him a citation please. He looks like a beached whale. That's really offensive.*

2:07 p.m.

Screams of bloody murder are coming from within the Board Room walls while I piss in the downstairs bathroom. I place my penis away and immediately rush to the scene to see what woman hath brought such rage into our sacred confines. A browbeaten Page is standing alone with a beautiful dark-haired woman in a flowery bikini. She is possessed of both large breasts and by Lucifer himself. I make a time out signal while Sharkey enters behind me issuing a shrill whistle. Both Page and this wench are silenced.

"Who are you, and what the *fuck* is going on in here," Sharkey inquires of the attractive beast.

"This is Mindy," replies Page. "Mindy Miller."

"The broad you hooked up with last night?"

"Excuse me!" the woman shrieks. "I am not a broad, okay? And why are you spilling our business everywhere, Page?"

"I'm not spillin' it *everywhere*," he replies sheepishly. "Just this room, pretty much."

"Whatever," the girl replies quite dismissively.

"I don't give a shit about any of this nonsense," Sharky declares. "I just want to know what the *fuck* all this hootin' 'n hollarin' is about during our party of the century."

Mindy begins rattling off the high crimes of Page without so much taking a breath. First, he hooked up with a friend of Mindy's three summers ago and failed to disclose this information, even though Page was unaware that they even knew each other. Secondly, Page is facebook friends with Mindy's "bastard ex-fiancé," who was a classmate of his at Temple. Page didn't realize this, either. Third, Page seemed a little too flirty while sharing a raft and talking to a girl who happened to be his high school prom date *and is at the party with her husband.*

"I'll give you five seconds to run out of here," says Sharkey to Mindy after hearing the trumped-up and baseless charges. "If you don't leave immediately, I'm going to set you on fucking fire. Deal?"

The flowered bikini-wearing brunette with a killer tan, large breasts and serious security issues promptly exits in a huff, her tits bouncing up and down inside her bikini top. The positively perplexed Page grabs the *Falcon* and packs it for a good, long trip into hyperspace.

2:45 p.m.

There's a mass of people and bikinis and floats down the channel as far as the eye can see as we take the upper deck for the second set. There's probably 400 people in the back yard, and at least as many in the water. A small U.S. Coast Guard vessel has arrived to keep an eye on the proceedings and maintain a clearing in the channel. You know that your party is fucking big time when the Coast Guard is on hand. Additional kegs are being carried into the yard with the assistance of several Hot Dudes and various bouncers from the Shipwreck. We break into 'Ice Cream Man' followed by 'Pride and Joy,' 'Sweet Home Chicago,' 'Rock 'n Roll,' and a mean version of 'Surrender' that eclipsed any performance by Cheap Trick themselves. You would think that these would be tough to pull off with three acoustic-electric guitars, but Jake's booming voice and the microphones hung above Danny's congas make things groove well enough for our guests. The sound coming from the PA is clearer than the late summer sky today. Any musician will tell you that when your tone is good, you'll play a hell of a lot better. This is the most fun I've had since Iowa.

  With the women getting much more drunker-er, a half-dozen groupies in bikinis join our band on the top deck. The first thing that they do is head straight to Danny and his congas to add several very off-beat booms to the music. Dharma the Ghost Kisser-er appears in a black bikini and leans herself against the deck facing me, her sunglasses resting atop her pretty little head. Her bikini bottom is hanging low, revealing a most sexy of a tanline far below her belly button ring. With the painfully adorable blonde's brown eyes firmly planted on me, I trade lead breaks with Silent John over an odd but workable segue of The Beatles' 'It's All Over Now' into Guns 'n Roses 'Used to Love Her.' Just as I completely settle into the groove, my B string suddenly snaps while I'm bending notes like a madman. What a buzzkill. I'm forced to unplug and retreat into the house to change it.

  2:55 p.m.

  I'm desperately searching through every guitar case and gear bag for a spare B string. It's the string that always seems to break most often, so sometimes there's not a ready spare available. Whether or not physics is the culprit for the breakage because the B is the only one of the six strings tuned to a fourth, I have no idea. I finally manage to find one stuffed into a wrinkled pack of strings at the very, very bottom of Jake's gear bag. My relief is temporary, because drama bombs of thermonuclear proportions are only minutes from exploding inside the Penthouse.

  I take a seat on the nearby couch and use a Guitool to remove the peg on the bridge that holds the B string in place. Dharma, of all people, enters through the sliding glass doors that lead out onto the deck. "I had no idea that you played guitar!" she exclaims with a mixture of genuine excitement and intoxication. She sits herself on the couch so close to me that her smooth, golden left thigh is touching my own hairy leg. I glance at the tanlines surrounding her crotch out of the corner of my eye.

She's such a sexy bitch. "You're hairy," she giggles while pulling on my leg. "Is your back really hairy, too?"

"I use Nair."

"Seriously?"

"No," I reply with a subdued chuckle.

"C'mere," now says the blonde, placing her hand behind my head and pulling me toward her moist-looking lips. It would simply be rude to resist, even though Jenna is now my true hopeless crush. Changing my string and my night with Jenna quickly becomes secondary to the taste of alcohol I'm stealing from Dharma's soft lips. There's 1,000 drunk and high idiots outside- many of whom I now count as my friends- but the sounds of their afternoon revelry all fade away as my fingers trace the smooth curves of Dharma's body while we kiss. Then a pronounced groan of some sort emanates from somewhere in the area of the kitchen. My lips separate from Dharma's as we look around to investigate. I'm the first to spot a piss drunk, completely naked Blotto sitting atop the gas range with a Cheshire cat grin on his face. He looks over at me and tries not to laugh. He is receiving a blowjob from a thin woman with long, blonde hair in a sea green bikini. It's not Blotto's on-again/off-again hook-up Dina that's performing, and the blonde hair is the giveaway that it's certainly not Tearsten. I nod in the direction of the kitchen. Dharma turns her head, whereupon Blotto gives her a thumb's up directly. Blushing and giggling, Dharma turns back toward me. "Omigod!" she exclaims. *"They're certainly having a good time."*

"So are we, Dharma," I reply as I brush my fingers across her thigh.

"That's right," she replies in a whisper. *"We are."*

We immediately return to business. I'm sucking Dharma's tongue into my mouth as someone, a female, very deliberately clears her throat from somewhere very close to the couch. I look up to find the beautiful Jenna looking right through me as she stands in her pink bikini with her hands on her hips. "I guess I was completely wrong about you," she spits before storming angrily out onto the deck. My heart sinks to the fucking floor.

"Is Jenna your girlfriend?" Dharma asks curiously. "She's *beautiful.*"

"So are you, Dharma," I reply while trying to maintain my composure. "And Jenna's not my girlfriend."

Dharma nevertheless vacates the couch without comment and heads back outside on her shapely golden legs, leaving me both busted and now alone. Fuck! I exhale and try to again focus on changing my B string while keeping the events still unfolding in the kitchen in my peripheral vision. I finish changing my string and begin to re-tune. Now Tearsten enters the house through the side door. This is not good.

"How'd you get in here, Kirsten?" I ask loudly enough for Blotto to hear. His wide eyes now make him look like someone who was disloyal to Saddam Hussein must have looked when the Republican Guard suddenly showed up at the front door.

"The door was unlocked, dick," Tearsten replies not-so-pleasantly. "What's the big deal? Aren't we friends? Do you not like me for some reason?"

"No, but the doors are supposed to be locked. People are using the port-a-potties today."

"I don't have to pee, ass. I need some water." The angry, dark-haired doom machine heads toward the kitchen. I rise from the couch and halt her.

"We're fresh out up here. I'll run downstairs and get you a bottle."

"I checked the downstairs. I didn't see anything. You *have* to have something non-alcoholic in that fridge," she says, pushing me away and storming past. "I'm hot, I'm all sweaty, and if I have another drink I'll puke. Again."

I have failed yet another mission. I brace myself for the impending carnage. Three..two...one...

The initial scream from Tearsten could curdle the blood of the dead. She immediately launches a fierce attack at the Blotto-blowing blonde. I rush into the kitchen to separate the two bikini-clad beauties. Blotto, drunk, dazed, disappointed and naked with an erection still sticking straight up from his body, fumbles to get himself off the gas range. I hear the familiar 'whoof!' of gas alighting. He has somehow managed to light the burner directly under his ass as his tries to hop off the thing. The 6'4" former football star begins jumping up and down while yelping like dog that has just been struck by a Mustang speeding down the highway. Ditching the screaming, slapping, punching, hair-pulling, fighting girls, I grab Blotto's much larger (and still naked) body and push him toward the bathroom shower as quickly as I can in a very non-homosexual manner. I pull on the cold water and make sure he gets inside without cracking his head open. I lock the door behind me and return to the kitchen. The blonde is gone, and Kirsten is screaming and crying. "WHY DID HE FUCK ME ON TUESDAY NIGHT IF HE DIDN'T WANT TO GET BACK WITH ME!" she screams, followed by several Nancy Kerrigan-like moans of "*Whhhhhhhhhyyyyy...whhhhhhhhyyyyyyy...whhhhhhhhyyyyyy*" minus the sneak attack beating with a metal pipe and the crash of Olympic dreams.

"Kirsten!"

"WHAT!"

"Will you shut the fuck up!"

"NO! I don't have to shut the fuck up because..."

I tune her out like a dog being berated by an unreasonable master. She charges down the hallway toward the bathroom. She turns the doorknob. The lock holds. Frustrated, the full Tearsten is in effect as she screams and slams her fists on the door. I walk back out onto the deck and plug back in.

"What the *fuck* is going on in there?" asks Jake. "What took you so long?"

"Ask me later," I deadpan as we start 'Jack & Diane.' This one's just a people pleaser for drunks, and I find myself completely distracted. I'm finally able to concentrate and rid my mind of Jenna and her pink bikini when nearly the entire crowd of 1,000 people begins to sing along with the chorus, making me feel like a true rock star even though only about three dozen people are at the party to see Jake & The Pantydroppers specifically. Then, just as Jake bellows into the bridge and asks for his soul to be saved, the sliding door opens behind me. The still buck-naked Blotto bursts out onto the deck while trying to escape the nightmare known as Tearsten. "She carded open the bathroom door!" he exclaims. "She carded open the fucking door on me!" Kirsten, still giving chase, trips over the PA power cables and falls hard toward the deck, knocking down Danny's congas and two groupies in the process. The entire party starts booing like they're at an Eagles game and the offense just went three-and-out for the second possession in a row. Blotto, with a now-hairless red welt the size of a small plate on his right ass cheek, tries to run down the stairs and escape to the Board Room. Dizzy, who happens to be on the deck with camera in hand, is thrilled with this turn of events. "I won't be putting some of these on facebook," he says with a hearty laugh.

We hand things back over to DJ Buttfuck for the remainder of the day.

3:03 p.m.

Sharkey has entered one of the outside port-a-potties for some reason. This did not go unnoticed by Harry and Page. They promptly rush toward the portable toilet and push it to the ground with all of their might. About a minute later, the door opens and Sharkey arises from the john looking like the Creature from the Black Lagoon exiting a coffin. He is covered in toilet paper, piss, shit, and a strange purple dye that makes him look more horrific than he already does. He simply shakes his head, vomits, and heads for the nearest outside shower. A pretty blonde in a red bikini takes pity on him for some reason and enters the shower with him. Once he is completely cleared of the toxic mess, Sharkey has the last laugh when the woman inexplicably has sex with him.

3:57 p.m.

Harry and I are standing on the top deck with several others, observing the mayhem we have caused below. I've decided that it's best to avoid Jenna for now, as crushed as I am. God, I'm fucking stupid. People are starting to climb onto the pilings and dive into the water. Drunks are singing, dancing, splashing, and falling off their floats and boats everywhere. I spot Heather for the first time today. She looks sexy in a blue bikini (the same kind Stinky is wearing, which will surely be an issue to be discussed later) and has her long, blonde hair teased like she's attending an eighth-grade dance. I do hate her, mostly because I know how sweet her pussy tastes and she robbed it from me. Next to Heather is a rather large man who definitely is Dino Morelli from back in the neighborhood. If I punched him now, I don't think I'd survive the aftermath. He's huge, with a drunken sneer crossing his face as the pair begins to argue about something that is probably inconsequential. He is definitely one Hot Dude. Dharma has already moved on to making out with some guy who, for reasons unknown, is wearing a Speedo in public. I just lost-out to a dude in a fucking Speedo. It can't get any worse.

Suddenly, something looks wrong. Very wrong. Three cop cars pull up onto the bridge and clear it, followed by a hook 'n ladder. An ambulance arrives, along with a trailer of waverunners marked with the insignia of the Avalon Beach Patrol. The Coast Guard vessel begins issuing commands to clear the channel. I'm suddenly not very stoned. Harry asks me to go down to the bridge to talk to the authorities while he rushes into the house to check his police scanner. I tear down the outside steps toward the scene, pushing through the mass of drunken bodies in the back yard. I find myself face to face with Jenna.

"*Well, hello, Patrick,*" she says quite sarcastically with an evil look on her face that only a woman could deliver. "So who's your little blonde friend, huh?"

"I-"

"Fucking liar," Jenna says before I can even respond, striking me hard in the chest with a closed fist for emphasis. I note that her eyes are slightly bloodshot.

"You're drunk, Jenna."

"No shit, assssshole," she slurs. "I just worked the punch bar by myself for the past hour and we're out of bottled water."

She approaches a circle of Hot Dudes involved in a chugging contest, taps one on the shoulder, and immediately launches her tongue down his throat.

4:16 p.m.

I manage to find Chief Fitz on the bridge.

"What's goin' on, Chief?"

"Drowning," he replies casually. As if my stomach wasn't already twisted up enough.

"A what?"

"A drowning, supposedly. I talked to the person who called it in twice. Once, she described the guy as 5'9" with blonde hair and blue swim trunks. The second time she described the guy as 6'3" with dark hair and yellow swim trunks with flowers on them. So, believe it or not, I'm a bit skeptical that someone actually drowned, Mr. McShea. Still, we've got to take all of the necessary precautions. You'll assist me in clearing the property, I assume?"

"Of course. Do you know who called it in?"

"Probably a disgruntled neighbor, or something like that, who is now going to find themselves in a lot a trouble. I'm getting a skip trace done now. And congratulations, McShea. No arrests or fines today so far."

I walk back toward the house to report my findings to Harry as I dive team and a crew with a gaffe hook arrives on the scene to scrape the bottom of the channel for the 'body.'

5:45 p.m.

Page and I are sitting on the back deck before we start the clean-up effort with all available hands. Jenna is nowhere to be found, which disturbs me greatly. She's probably on her back with some Hot Dude somewhere while I'm empty-handed yet again. That kills me. It absolutely fucking kills me. There's a big chore ahead to distract me, though. There's thousands of plastic cups in the back yard along with hundreds of empty bottles of water, dozens of beer bottles, liquor bottles and deflated rafts. There's abandoned flip-flops. Empty packs of cigarettes. A sling. The remnants of a cast. Three funnels. A half-dozen t-shirts. Broken sunglasses. A bikini top or two or three. Page finishes a prolonged sip out of a large bottle of pinkish-colored Gatorade and looks out across the channel. "Remember when Gatorade only came as a powder?" he asks with a smile on his face.

"And there were only two flavors: Lemon Lime and Orange."

"I'm a big fan of the Ice variety, myself," Page says.

"I more of a Frost kind of guy. Riptide Rush."

"Did you ever drink that Tiger Woods shit? It comes on to strong, man. It's like drinking...medicine or something. Thank god he got busted and saved my taste buds. Mindy's been blowin' up my phone now."

"Sayin' what?"

"*I'm so sorry, I overreacted*, and all this other shit. What a disappointment, man. You can't judge a book by its cover. They all seem sweet and nice and cool, then they start using modern technology against you before you even know if you really like them or not. They check your 'friends' list on facebook and it's like, *"How do you know* this *girl? How do you know* that *girl?"* And it ain't because they're legitimately curious. They're picking out the girls who stole their last boyfriend or that they hate for some other reason or no reason at all. So, bottom line is that you've only kissed a girl once and they're already launched an investigation and are tryin' to hang you with all sorts of shit. The only positive- as disappointing as it is- is that you know within 24 hours that you've just hooked up with someone who is *totally* fucking insane. I've been into her for three summers, too. Damn!"

"Jenna caught me kissing Dharma on the upstairs couch."

"So?" Page asks with a knowing, shit-eating grin.

"I hooked-up with Jenna on Thursday."

"I figured sumthin' was up, man. Congrats, bro. That's awesome. Nail 'er?"

"No."

"Figured that," Page says before beginning to laugh his typically stoned laugh. "But the *one* time that Dharma actually performs an encore...and you *totally* got busted. I'm not laughing at you, just..."

"I understand."

"Now look. Don't try to patch things up with Jenna right now, though. She's a boiling pot of water at this point. You gotta let things start to steam over for a while before you have *that* conversation, and the fact that she still has a boyfriend gives you some kind of defense. Now...what the fuck do I do about Mindy?"

"It's trouble. You already know you're dealing with a CIA operative. And once you have those tan legs up on your shoulders and you're looking down at those bombs, you'll put up with her bullshit for absolutely as long as you can possibly take it."

"Exactly," Page laughs. "But I'm definitely going over to her place tonight, anyway. I mean, pussy is pussy. If I had better option, would I take it? Yes. Do I have a better option? Of course not." He laughs again as he looks out into the back yard before taking another sip of his Gatorade. "There's only one thing we need to clean-up this property efficiently," he says matter-of-factly after swallowing,

"What's that?"

"A match."

9:02 p.m.

The backyard has been cleaned by everyone at 728 and our associates, provided they were not passed out, at the ER, or fucking. A large board meeting was held to celebrate Blotto's return from the hospital. He has been fitted with a giant medicated patch onto his ass. During the meeting, I was absolutely relieved to receive a text from Jenna inquiring as to my whereabouts. Dizzy has taken Gina home and away from 728 per a request I made before the Dharma Affair. He had already fucked another girl in one of the port-a-potties at approximately 3:30 p.m., so he had no problem tapping into his Lazy List for Round 2. I'm too tired and sunburnt and stoned to even considering going to the Shipwreck, so I nervously head upstairs to face my new crush. I find Jenna passed out atop her bed, still in her mouth-watering pink bikini as Ray LaMontagne softly plays from her iPod dock. I crawl into her bed very gingerly. Princess waddles across the comforter to lick my face. "Hey," Jenna says very tired-ly as she stirs. "Where's Gina?"

"Dizzy's."

"Where's your little blonde friend?"

"She was last seen making out with a guy in a Speedo."

"I know," Jenna replies with a laugh. "Serves you right, you prick. I'm drunk."

"Where's your Hot Dude?"

"He was *such* a fucking jerk, Patrick. Ugh! He wouldn't stop following me around the party and has texted me, like, 47 times already. I finally shut my phone off. Like, get a fucking life, buddy."

"I can't blame him."

"I didn't really want to kiss that guy. You know that." Jenna follows this up with a prolonged kiss to my own lips. "The person I want to spend my night with is lying right next to me."

"Ditto."

"Ditto? Not very romantic, Patrick."

"Sorry. I'm a little uncomfortable."

"Why?"

"Because I kinda screwed up today."

"You did. And you can thank your friend Page for pulling me aside and explaining that you were suddenly attacked by a Ghost Kisser-er. Or something ridiculous like that. I'm cold." I pull the covers over us and Jenna immediately snuggles up to me. "So I guess we're even now, Mr. McShea?"

"I guess, yeah."

"No more Ghost Kisser-ers?"

"No more Ghost Kisser-ers. No more Hot Dudes?"

"There's one right here in my bed," Jenna replies.

"Should I leave, then?"

Jenna laughs sweetly, then begins kissing my cheek as the soft acoustic guitars of 'Shelter' drift out of the speakers. She kisses my neck next, giving me chills all over my body. I can smell the stale scent of alcohol on her breath. It doesn't bother me. I turn toward her lips and take Jenna's tongue into my mouth without hesitation. She grabs the front of my shorts and starts rubbing me. I push my hand into her bikini bottom. Our lips separate while she moans, so I attack her neck. She grabs my body and pulls me atop her.

"I wanna *fuck* you, Jenna."

"I wanna *fuck* you, too, baby," she replies with an excited sweetness. She reaches down the front of my shorts and takes me into her hand. *"I want you inside me, Patrick,"* she whispers. *"Right now."*

I untie Jenna's bikini bottom and remove it, burying my face into her magic. She pushes my head away from between her thighs. *"I want you to fuck me,"* she says in her sex voice. I grab the condom in my pocket of my shorts, fearing that I'll last no longer than seven seconds inside her. I toss both my shorts and boxers aside. I look down at Jenna. She suddenly looks seconds from death. It's seriously disconcerting.

"Are you okay, sweetheart?"

"No," she replies. "I haven't been drunk in 11 years and I suddenly have the spins and...I feel awful."

"Can I get you anything?"

"Just lie down next to me. Please."

I settle in next to Jenna, rubbing her smooth, tanned stomach.

"That feels nice, Patrick."

"Just relax. You'll be fine."

Jenna looks up at the ceiling for about a half-minute before speaking again. "Can I tell you something personal?" she asks.

"Sure. You have enough dirt on me already, don't you?"

"It's not dirt. It's your life."

"Whatever you want to call it..."

"Can this stay between us?"

"Of course."

I give Jenna a slow kiss. She settles herself onto my shoulder.

"I'm freaking out because the last time I was drunk, I got raped," she says softly. This isn't the kind of wasted banter that I was prepared to have with her. I figure it best to just be quiet and let Jenna speak. "I don't even remember it," she continues as I kiss her cheek. "I completely blacked out at my prom after-party. I didn't even realize it happened until a month later when I missed my period. And obviously, I'm not a mother, so..."

"No one would expect you to have a child conceived out of a crime, Jenna."

"It wasn't like a random guy jumped out of the bushes and grabbed me or something. It-"

"What's the difference?"

"Well, none, I guess. But my boyfriend was a fucking *asshole* and just kept feeding me drinks because I had made it clear that I still wasn't ready to lose my virginity. My brother had gotten his girlfriend pregnant his senior year of high school and it was chaos in the Love household for months. He was supposed to be roommates at college with Harry and never wound up going. But like a complete fucking idiot, I kept drinking because my boyfriend was on the football team and was popular so I wanted to impress him. I didn't even know what he was giving me. It could have been *anything*. And I weighed, like, 112 pounds at the time so-"

"And what do you weigh now? One-thirteen?"

"No, I'm usually like between 115 and 120."

Jenna must be fucking wasted if she's revealing her weight to a man. "Still have the spins?"

"Only if I close my eyes."

"Still think I'm handsome?"

"Of course, I do. Am I still gorgeous?"

"Without a fucking doubt."

"Even though I need a shower, I'm drunk, about to cry, and am only wearing a sweaty bikini top?"

"You'd be beautiful under any circumstances."

"I smell, Patrick."

"You do *not*. I'm lying right next to you."

"You showered, didn't you? You smell really good."

"You can finish your story if you want to."

"Omigod, it was awful," Jenna says, completely changing her tone. This may have been a mistake after I had rebounded her to being somewhat relaxed again. "First I lose my virginity by getting raped on my prom night, then I had to go to court behind my parents' back to get permission for the abortion because I was under 18. And I *completely* lied to the judge. I never disclosed it on my bar application, either, and I was sweating that there was some record of it somewhere. I mean, that was a total violation of Rule 3.3..."

"Omigod. Did you *really* just say that? Shut down the 'lawyer' switch, Jenna. *Fuck* Rule 3.3. It's none of the Supreme Court's business, even if you are required to disclose it on your bar application that you were untruthful with a court of law. You were fucking 17. Seventeen! And juvenile records are generally sealed, anyway."

"I felt like such a piece of white trash. I just wanted the whole thing over with didn't want the authorities involved, so I had to pretend that I wanted the abortion because the babies were just an unwanted inconvenience to my college plans."

"Babies?"

"I was carrying twins, Patrick."

I choose silence over any reply.

"And I had to let him get away with it because I was *terrified* that my boyfriend wasn't actually the father," she continues. "There was a rumor around school that all of his friends took their turn with me..."

Jenna buries herself in my chest and starts sobbing uncontrollably. As bad as my experience has been, it doesn't even come close to Jenna's. Graduating *magna cum laude* and landing a $145,000 job- after first obtaining a most prestigious clerkship with a judge of the United States Court of Appeals for Ninth Circuit in San Francisco- might afford you a nice lifestyle until your early retirement, but it will never take away the scars of rape, half of your high school class knowing about it, and having to abort a set of twins that Jenna had no choice in conceiving.

Selfishly, though, I am disappointed that The Slump will not meet its end tonight. It would have been a perfect ending to the greatest day of my life since college.

Sunday, August 8, 2010

12:23 p.m.

An arrest warrant is issued for one Kirsten K. Kramer. In addition to criminal charges, the Town of Angel Bay is seeking $69,026.42 in restitution for costs associated with the 'rescue' effort. Blotto is ordered by Harry to buy lunch for the entire house from Angel Bay's most exclusive restaurant and wash both his truck and boat.

7:26 p.m.

Jenna decided to spend some of her $346 in tip money from working the punch bar at Flotilla for a date with me in Stone Harbor. I was rendered speechless by her outfit tonight. She wore a short dress colored in a blue and white paint-brush type pattern that really brought out the color her eyes, as if that was even necessary. The outfit was completed by these sexy, ropey-looking wedge sandals on her feet. She implicated these very shoes as the reason for her 2-stroke loss on a rooftop miniature golf course prior to dinner. Dinner itself was awkward. The restaurant was nice and the food was great, but I never feel comfortable in a real restaurant. My irritable bowel always fears the menu. Fortunately, most of it was written in English and I went with the tilapia. I still don't know what fork and which spoon to use for which food item during which course, and that creates some discomfort. Jenna knew. They must teach those kinds of things at Ivy League schools. I was also a bit uncomfortable with some of the stares from the other patrons, especially the ones that were our age. That's what happens when a regular guy is seen out on the town with a beautiful woman. Everybody is wondering what I did or how much money I have in order to score a date with someone so stunning, while better-looking guys sit with miserable girls who are just starting to hit the stage where their bodies completely fall apart physically. I used to get those looks when I was out with Vanessa the Annoyer sometimes. I was a bit more confident then- sometimes cocky, I hesitate to report- and I used to relish the stares of envy and even downright hate from other men that Vanessa's tight ass was mine. They couldn't see all the bullshit, though. People never do.

We're currently cruising back to 728 from Stone Harbor in Jenna's $90,000 blue Mercedes and I'm behind the wheel. It's odd not seeing the Check Engine light glowing, worrying about a crack in the windshield, or hearing the many strange sounds my car tends to make if my stereo isn't playing loudly enough. And the ride is *so* smooth. It makes me feel much more relaxed, even though I'm still intimidated as hell by Jenna Rose. Getting the shorts off a beautiful woman for the first time is one thing, but it's actually the second legitimate hook-up that's the hardest.

"You have a really nice ride, Jenna."

"I don't even need a car this powerful," the brunette replies as she looks into the mirror in her sun visor while she re-applies her lip gloss. "I took over the payments from my brother after he had his third kid and finally had to buy a minivan. I'll only wind-up paying about $30,000 for it. I wouldn't ever spend $90,000 on a car myself. My conscience wouldn't ever allow it."

"What's your brother do?"

"Sells insurance. Never went to college. Makes six figures. No student loans to pay back. Can you imagine?" Jenna is now brushing something onto her cheeks for some reason.

"What time is your next date?"

"Maybe I want to keep myself looking good for *you* tonight, Patrick. Did you ever consider *that* possibility?"

"Don't bother. I think you look good the second you open your eyes."

"You must not have seen me this morning, then. I'm sorry about last night, by the way. I was a *total* trainwreck. I shouldn't have laid all of that stuff on you. I've never told anybody that story. *Especially* my brother. He'd be in jail for murder right now."

"No need to apologize, Jenna. We're both guilty of the same exact thing."

"Well, thank you for not taking complete advantage of me."

"You shouldn't have to thank me. I was a little disappointed this morning, though. I wanted to go down on you and all you kept worrying about was how puffy your eyes were and how many hairs were out of place."

"You wouldn't have wanted to go down on me this morning. *Trust* me."

"I could have managed."

"I'm sure you could have. I can't believe how many of my rules I'm breaking for you already."

"I think every woman that I've ever hooked-up with has said the same exact thing. And I'm not *that* much of a charmer and I don't look like Adonis."

"You know, I think you've actually complimented me tonight for the first time without being wasted. Congrats. It's very courageous of you."

"Screw you, Jenna."

"Oh, you'd *love* to..."

"Obviously. I get the feeling that not many people have."

"I can count the number of people I've slept with on my fingers," Jenna reveals. I'm not surprised given that she's had only four boyfriends and her introduction to the world of sex was under less than ideal circumstances. "It's funny, though," she continues. "I was on the beach today thinking about our sex potential."

"Really?"

"M'mm. I was, actually. What were you doing?"

"Kayaking down the channel with Page while cleaning all the stray cups and bottles out of the water. So what was your conclusion?"

"If our first wasted hook-up on Thursday night was any indication, I think that we could be something really special sexually."

"Me, too. I have a lot of repressed anger directed toward you."

"*That* wasn't very romantic...and I was going to ask you to kiss me at the next red light."

"You still can, Jenna."

"Hearing that you have repressed anger toward me doesn't exactly excite me."

"I was trying to be funny, Jenna."

"You failed."

"You're lucky you're so good-looking."

"Why?"

"It makes me want to put up with your shit."

Jenna laughs and smacks me in the chest. Then she begins giggling to herself as she continues to go through her small make-up bag.

"What's so funny, Jenna?" I ask as she begins to apply some additional dark blue eye shadow that makes her look much more slutty than she actually is.

"Nothing, Patrick."

"Just spill it."

"No. I'm *far* too shy."

"Come on."

"You'll see as soon as we get home. I promise."

8:17 p.m.

[*omigod jenna* ur mouth is so fucking wet 4 my stiff cock right now. it is fucking pathetic that i had forgotten how intense it feels 2 have 2 soft wet womanly lips wrapped around this throbbing piece of cursed flesh. ur so. fucking. beautiful. i dont have a care in the world right now because of u miss love. ur skin is golden and glowing from the soft light of the setting sun sneaking through the cracks in the blinds as u sit on the edge of ur bed in ur short white and ice blue eye-matching minidress and sexy strappy sandals with ur amazing brown legs crossed. ur sucking my cock like u mean it. up and down and up and down with those pink lips and pink-painted fingernails on your left hand working to make every serious fucking problem of mine slip far far far away into a heaven of jenna. every movement of your lips and hands over my swollen dickhead and down my shaft just past the place where i was cut is giving me the most incredible drug-like rush u gorgeous little slut u. but being in the mouth of the former big firm cunt who said she'd be sent to hell b4 sucking me off is priceless. *ur a fucking all star jenna.* u giggle with my cock still in ur mouth. then u moan because u know its true that ur driving me crazy. *hike up that dress for me sweetheart.* u lift the end of the blue cloth over your brown legs before uncrossing them to open them 4 me. no panties. no fucking panties. *ur such a bad girl for not wearing any panties miss love,* i say as i run my right hand through ur soft head of brown hair with golden highlights. i can see ur pussy baby and my excitement for you floods every pathway in whatever is left of my brain and the once-lifeless bloodstream of my entire body. i just want to get on my knees and fucking smell it jenna but i could never pull myself out of ur mouth right now. *touch urself baby.* u take me from ur mouth and smile at me. *im a shy girl patrick* u say with a hint of blush on ur pretty cheeks. *don't be shy jenna. im the luckiest guy in angel bay right now.* u smile at me before im put back into ur oral oasis. u place ur right hand between ur dark thighs and slowly start to circle ur hood. u moan on my cock. i groan in response. *thats so fucking hot jenna.* u suck harder faster longer stronger. *ur taking so much of my cock baby ur amazing.* u purr and moan and circle ur clit more quickly before using one finger to rub urself. that fucking clit of urs is going to be my plaything as soon as u suck every last drop of cum from my burdened miserable balls jenna. im going to lick it and suck it and bite it and push my tongue against it so hard and turn it in circles. my balls begin to stir and rise so all of my cum can be pumped into ur willing mouth jenna. *i know ur going 2 swallow 4 me baby.* u breathe the words *i am* for the single instant that my cock leaves ur mouth. its so incredibly sexy. *im so fucking horny for u beautiful.* i just want to push u over the bed 2 lick u clit 2 asshole 4 days jenna b4 i fuck u. i cant believe how sexy u are! every part of ur precious body makes me want to scream out like a rabid animal and tell u what ur mouth and ur feminine existence is doing to excite me. the way the ropes of ur wedge sandals cross your tanned feet and pink-painted toes in all of the right places is driving my balls crazy as u suck and suck and run your hand down every inch that u take into ur incredible mouth. u could never understand as a woman how sexy u are to a man jenna. my wasted eyes follow every curve of ur foot and ur calves and ur thighs as my balls begin to feel the overload brought on by ur mouth and ur hand and ur body and my hypersexual horny perverted masculine mind. *im so close baby!* i will never be as horny for u jenna as i am right now. *ur so fucking close to making me cum jenna!* and my balls! my fucking balls are raised so tightly against my stiff shaft that my own thighs are starting to quake. im *so* ready to give you my seed. and i need 2 more than anything else on earth right now. *omigod jenna ur so amazing baby.* i want to be ur bitch right now because i would do fucking anything u could ever ask me 2 do u sexy slut u. i want every inch of ur body in my mouth jenna. im not a man im a stiff-cocked raging animal on the edge of ecstasy that wants to get off on every part of your body from ur tongue to ur tits to ur legs to ur toes...and that tight little bump of an ass u have jenna. u own me right now. u always fucking did. *don't u dare fucking stop jenna! i am so fucking close.* i groan and keep repeating ur beautiful name. *jenna! jenna! jenna!* i feel that twist in my balls that comes when a man is at the point of no return and *must* cum. must! omigod its so fucking close to shooting out into ur mouth jenna i need the ultimate release and i need it right fucking now but u torture me by sucking slowly and more slowly to tease me u clever little bitch. ur smart enough to know that a man never gets this hard in ur mouth until he is seconds from release. u just want 2 hear ur name more jenna and only u can give me the relief i so desperately need right now. my knees are shaking for u in anticipation. *jenna! jenna! its right fucking there jenna!* suck it out! suck it out! *ur gonna make me cum! ur gonna make me cum u sexy little bitch u!* the most incredible indescribable rush leaves my balls and builds slowly up my rock hard shaft as it prepares for the ultimate natural release on planet earth. its so amazing that a man can be made to feel this way. i close my eyes while my cock twitches and flexes as the first shot leaves my body while the rush is still on. jenna inexplicably pauses at the start of my ecstasy. *keep sucking jenna! theres more! theres more!* omigod suck it out you whore! drain it! drain it! drain it u bitch! and suck she does until every blast of total ecstasy exits from my balls with a pronounced guttural moan and into her willing mouth. and ur fucking swallowing it all 4 me jenna. ur making me feel so fucking wanted. i cant fucking believe it. my balls are finally fully drained and at rest as jenna begins to choke]

"*Water,*" she gasps between coughs. "I need water." I walk out of the room with my penis still stiff and twitching as I head for the fridge and grab a cold bottle for her. She drinks the liquid like her life depends on it. "My *god,*" she says after removing her lips from the bottle. "I don't think I've ever swallowed so much sperm in my entire life. You almost *killed* me."

"Sorry. Not really."

"And what made you assume that I was going to swallow for you?"

"Because you're a perfectionist. With everything."

"You're going to turn me into a complete *whore* if we keep hanging out," Jenna says with more than a hint of disapproval toward her own actions.

"That's my goal, Jenna."

"What is? To keep hanging out with me? Or to turn me into a little slut for you?"

"Both."

"*You're very sexual,*" the brunette whispers as she runs one finger up and down my still-stiff shaft. "You're still twitching," she adds proudly.

"You did a spectacular job."

"That's because you make me feel *so* comfortable, Patrick, and pay so much attention to me. *And* you have *such* a nice dick. It feels *so* perfect in my mouth."

"So you're saying I'm small?"

"Small? Definitely not. I'm saying you're perfect. It didn't take you forever to cum, either."

"Why would it? You're sexy as hell."

"I am?"

"Now you're just fishing for compliments, Jenna."

"I know," she laughs. "I could *totally* be into giving you head all the time."

"Thank you. Looking forward to it."

"You're quite welcome, sweetie. Have I done enough to convince you that it's not worth having wandering eyes here in Angel Bay?"

"Duh."

"Now would you mind unzipping my dress for me, please?" Jenna asks as she stands and turns her back to me.

"Not at all."

"I'm just warning you," the brunette beauty says to me as she kicks off her shoes and her dress drops to the floor, "if you make me cum less than twice, I'm cutting you off."

"I'll take that challenge."

"I thought you would," Jenna says with another one of her stunningly white smiles as she crawls into her bed and begins to remove her bra. "And you'll meet it, I'm sure."

"You wouldn't have me here if I couldn't."

"That's very true," the brunette admits as the bra is tossed to the floor and her large, shapely breasts fall onto her chest. Jenna reclines and offers a bright smile accompanied by a sarcastic roll of her beautiful eyes. Her wonderful legs then open wide for me.

Monday, August 9, 2010

11:56 a.m.

I call my mother to wish her Happy Birthday. I fail to mention that I'm always able to remember it because August 9 also happens to be the same day that Jerry Garcia died.

8:01 p.m.

I begin my nightly ritual of smoking a phat jay while looking out onto the sound at sunset. No cops are in the vicinity, as is customary for a weeknight. Jenna came three times from my oral sex delivered in two different positions last night over the course of an hour. Time flies when you have a beautiful woman naked with a body that is a work of art. She refused to have actual sex with me both last night and this morning, but I ultimately didn't mind. I awoke at 6 a.m. to the wonderful surprise of having Jenna's soft lips wrapped tightly around me again. *'You're already starting to turn me into a whore,'* she whispered after swallowing. Then Jenna kissed my neck and put her head onto my chest before going back to sleep. She opted to return to Philly to do some errands rather than stay in Angel Bay for a few more days. I was very disappointed, of course. I'm already deeply in like with her. I never stood a chance against it. I'm dizzy with excitement over the prospect of sleeping with her, just like I'm in high school all over again. I'm trying to temper my feelings, because I know full well that the lingering Michael sprays this entire affair with the pungent odor of a fish story in the making.

It's been far too long since I've been able to fully enjoy the company and the body of a woman as great-looking and intelligent as Jenna is. In fact, it's been five long, pathetic fucking years. I recognize now that this wasn't some vast conspiracy perpetrated against me by the women of Philadelphia and the world at large. It was as much my fault as anyone else. Guys who are suicidal mental mindfucks like I was don't often attract many quality women. Now don't get me wrong: a lot women love to take on head cases and losers as projects. I would have loved to have been some hot chick's project boyfriend. It didn't happen. I just wasn't the right kind of head case or loser to be sympathetic enough. There was no drug problem or alcohol problem (besides 'lack of') or some kind of malady that made me look edgy or dangerous or rebellious, like an anger management issue or some other destructive, testosterone-fueled bent to my personality. I was miserable and fucked up and had a raging irritable bowel. There's nothing sexy or sympathetic about that at all.

Lori DiDominico remains the last all-star I had sex with. It wasn't just her Italian-American looks that caused such an atomic lust explosion during our only night together. Her performance was just as legendary. We had outstanding sexual chemistry despite the fact we slept with each other only once. I've had great sexual chemistry with only a handful of the people I've slept with. Part of the reason for this is, quite frankly, that most people I've had sex with weren't exactly my first or second or even my third choice and didn't excite me all that much. I wasn't always a first or second or third choice, either. Two people sleeping with each other's third choice doesn't often make for sexual fireworks. The other part of it is because I'm one of those people that loves eye contact during sex, and that's definitely not for all occasions. I'm not talking about 'I Love You' eyes. I'm talking about seeing the look of total confidence or attraction or just sheer pleasure on the face of a wide-eyed woman because she's getting fucked and it's *you* that's fucking her. Naturally, two people need to have a very tight emotional bond or some strong mutual lust that's boiling over for that kind of sex to work. Lori and I did. Otherwise, all of that eye contact is really fucking creepy and uncalled for.

Lori lived down the block from me for entire four years before I moved back in with my parents to save coin during law school. Unlike myself, she went to the gym four days a week religiously and it showed. She had the dark hair, the dark eyes, the olive skin, legs like a cheerleader, and was certifiably happy and sane. She always called me 'Peanut' and was hot enough to get away with it. I sometimes called her 'JB,' which was short for 'Jellybean,' her name when I was really stoned and no one else was around to overhear it. There was always a 'something' between us that was never discussed openly. She would *never* bring her boyfriend near me. That's usually a sign that a woman has placed you on standby in case the current beau really fucks up. It's too awkward for them to have worlds collide by both of you being in the same place. Lori had been on and off with Mark since college. I think I saw him three times and met him twice in four years. He was a former Ivy League quarterback who had a cup of coffee in the NFL as a clipboard holder. He didn't like me. He must have sensed that 'something,' too. Lori and I acted as each other's go-to person at parties or bars when significant others weren't around. There was never any awkwardness between us, even when we were just standing around and not saying a word. It was a comfortable silence. We were somehow on the same wavelength all of the time.

One night Lori spent two hours on my lap at a party where we were both totally fucked up and realized that we didn't even know anyone. It was a neighborhood thing, so everyone seemed real familiar when we had first arrived. Someone in the back yard was passing around a jay and we were invited to join for the sole reason that Lori was wearing a tight red sweater with tighter jeans and looked fucking hot. The two of us had already gotten totally toasted at my house beforehand. We eventually stumbled onto a living room couch together and sat for an hour before we finally had a stoned realization that we may not be at the right place. We kept trying to figure out who the fuck everyone was, whether these people also realized that we didn't know who the fuck they were, and which one of us had totally fucked up the address of where we were really supposed to be. Text message evidence showed that Lori had received the right address, later texted me the wrong address, and then we went by the address in my phone during our walk over. The real party was on the next block of the same street. The hosts of the gathering where we were actually supposed to be were only work friends of Lori's, so she decided it would be more fun to sit on my lap and play with my hair. I was wild about her. It was almost mutual, but 'almost' in an instance like that adds up to the space between New York City and the north pole of Mars. After nearly two hours of close talking and hair playing and brief, cheap nibbling and kisses on each other's cheeks and ears, Lori asked me to walk her home.

We both hesitated as we arrived at her front door. It was the first time that we ever had an awkward moment together. I demanded a kiss goodnight. I got a brief peck on my lips. That was unacceptable. I reiterated my demand. She held the next kiss just long enough to make me completely want all of her. I told Lori that it was in her best interest to come back to my place and stay the night. I was a straight shooter in those days when I sensed an opportunity. Now, I'm just a broken man despite my recent success with Jenna. Lori dismissed me with another cheap peck to the lips. I tried to follow her into her house and was rebuffed. I had no say in the matter. I retreated back to my place with my tail between my legs.

We were neighbors for another year. I always tried to kiss her and was always denied, so eventually I just stopped bothering and enjoyed her company like I always did. Her boyfriend was on the West Coast a lot for work, so we spent a good bit of time together. I was seeing Vanessa the Annoyer for a spell, so it wasn't costing me anything. Lori and Vanessa did not like each other. I could understand why my girlfriend was suspicious of her. Not only was Lori as hot as she was (much hotter in my eyes, actually) but Vanessa sensed the same 'something' between Lori and I that everyone else in the free world did. There was also a bit of jealousy on Lori's part that Peanut was no longer always available when she wanted to take a boyfriend vacation in my bedroom where we would get high and talk and flirt and snuggle for hours while listening to Van Morrison and Ryan Adams. There was no need for Lori to ever be jealous of Vanessa or anyone else in my life. I would have walked to the moon and split it in half if she asked me to. She knew it. There was just no way that she was ever going to make the bold move of giving up the familiarity, comfort, security and hotness of the former BMOC that she was off-and-on with for over five years already. That's always such a kick in the fucking teeth when you're probably somebody's #1 choice but they'll never take the risk of leaving #2. I could deal with losing to a former NFL quarterback, though. I'm *supposed* to. Lori made me dinner the night I left the neighborhood to move back home for law school. I think she wanted to sleep with me but just wasn't fucked up enough.

Two years later, my residence was my parents' basement and I was beginning to crack. One random October night, I was sitting in a brutally boring Professional Responsibility class with 75 other suckers. The lecture was delivered by a female professor whose vocal chords emitted such a high-frequency whine that I needed three Excedrin to get through each ninety-minute class. My lost crush, Megan McLaughlin, was seated but two rows away and she looked heartbreakingly adorable in her blue Pawtucket Red Sox hat. I was staring at the clock on my cell phone every thirteen seconds. There were 63 painful minutes remaining in the lecture. The phone suddenly started vibrating and I dropped it. The snotty fat girl sitting in front of me turned and shot me a very disapproving glance as she handed it back to me. The word 'Jellybean' was on my screen. My heart skipped instantly and I got that excited feeling in my gut and in my chest that only happens when some spectacular girl reaches out to you randomly. I crossed my brain fingers that this message might have some real worth to it. *'Meet me @ 17 & market peanut,'* it said. I gathered my things immediately and headed for the classroom door. Megan smiled goodbye. Thanks, Megan. It's so fucking awesome that you're my law school dream girl and dating someone else.

Lori was standing in the crisp Fall cold on the corner of 17th & Market when I pulled up in my familiar blue Civic, which looked a lot better in those days. I could see that she had on a pair of very tight jeans, black boots, and her favorite black leather jacket. I hadn't seen her in over a year. She looked spectacular, as always. I was greeted by a very excited wave from the corner before Lori rushed over to hop into my car. I got a very wet kiss on my cheek as soon as she was seated. She smelled like a distillery. There are few things as exciting as being in the company of a really hot, really drunk woman that has some sort of feelings for you on some level. Lori started a brief conversation, and it went like this:

"We're going to my friend Valerie's apartment. She's not going to be there."

"Where's it at?"

"18th & Pine. Is that okay with you?"

"Why wouldn't it be, Lor. You *own* me."

"I'm moving to Seattle tomorrow, Peanut."

"Seattle? *Tomorrow?*"

"M'mm."

"With Mark?"

"He's out there already."

[awkward silence]

"Are you seeing anybody, Patrick?"

"Like it *really* matters..."

"So how's law school?"

"It's great."

"Really?"

"No. It fucking blows."

"Do you have any pot?"

"In the console."

"I've had *such* a crush on you *forever*, Peanut."

"I know, Lor. You had a really funny way of showing it by always fucking Mark instead."

"We're there. Pull the car over."

I followed orders by pulling into an open space in front of a fire hydrant. Lori reached across to grab the back of my head and pull me toward her wet, red lips. She hesitated for a single breath before her mouth devoured mine. I thought that I was going to float out of my car seat. Even as a complete drunk, she was a great kisser. And a hot woman isn't just a hot woman. It's an experience that you'll never forget for the rest of your pathetic fucking life. I was taken up to her friend Valerie's apartment. I left my car parked in front of the hydrant. Sometimes you just have to do that. I sparked for the half-block walk to Valerie's place. There was no way that I was going to sleep with Lori straight, especially when she was totally fucking bombed. I needed to put the brakes on my brain cells before I started thinking too much or got freaked out by the profundity of this moment. We entered the apartment, which was already aglow with a dozen candles of all shapes and sizes. I was stunned. This entire thing was a plot concocted well in advance. Lori just had to go out and get bombed enough to execute the final and most critical phase. Contacting me beforehand wasn't necessary. We hadn't communicated in months other than a few other random texts and some e-mails, but there had been no doubt in Lori's mind that wherever I was and whatever I was doing couldn't possibly keep me away from her. She put Sade's 'By Your Side' on the stereo and slowly began to remove her clothes. It was the kind of scene that, if you saw it in a movie, you'd turn to your buddy and say, *'How come that shit never happens to me?'* But it *was* happening to me. And that very rarely happens.

"Do you want me to leave my boots on?" Lori asked with the naughty eyes that I'd always wanted to see from her.

"They can come off."

"How about my knee socks?"

"They can stay."

"I look cute in them, don't I, Peanut?"

"That's a bit of an understatement."

"I bet you were such a cute little Catholic school boy, weren't you?"

"Not really, Lor."

"What color was your uniform?"

"Blue and yellow. Plaid tie."

"How do you want me?"

"On the floor, on your back."

"Can I kiss you again first?"

"Sure, JB."

"I *love* when you call me that. It's *so* cute."

Lori and her beautiful body strutted toward me as 'By Your Side' continued to play smoothly through the nearby speakers. She was looking straight at me with her long, dark brown hair falling down around her perky breasts. Her nipples were perfect. I couldn't wait to touch her. She reached up to wrap her little arms around my neck. I slowly ran my hands along her soft skin until they finally settled in around her waist. She felt so warm and so naked in my arms.

"Do you think we're going to be able to handle this?" she whispered.

"Of course," I lied.

"Then why are your knees shaking, Patrick?"

This conversation needed to come to a quick end. I took Lori's wet mouth again for a minute before I pushed her onto the carpet. I went straight to the smooth skin of her flat stomach. I worked my way around her belly button ring that had three small beads hanging from it- one for every guy that had ever gotten below her navel, she always joked. I don't think she was kidding. It was very possible that I was only the fourth person to taste Lori in her 28 years on Earth. I moved my lips across the olive skin of her parted inner thighs. I could smell the slight but sweet scent of her flower, which put my shaking knees into overdrive. I knew Lori was going to taste fantastic, just like I always thought she would.

"Don't tease me, Peanut," she moaned.

"You teased me for six years, Lori."

"I'm so sorry, sweetie."

"You don't sound very sorry," I said after softly exhaling onto the small, pink folds of skin between her thighs.

"I'm so sorry I made you wait so long to fuck me, Patrick. I am so fucking sorry."

"I'm sorry, too."

I licked Lori like my life depended on it. I was so nervous about pleasing her that I couldn't even get hard until after I watched the muscles in her stomach convulse in waves as she came. "Sorry it took so long, Peanut," Lori said as she recovered. I have never understood why women offer these kinds of apologies to me. It's not exactly a chore to be between a beautiful woman's thighs. If I had to go down on Lori for three days to make her cum, I would have done it. I *have* to. Without a nice body for a woman to lust after, I have to give them a reason to want to call me again. Plus, I knew Lori would return the favor just as eagerly.

"Can I get you anything?" I offered.

"No," she replied. "Just take your clothes off and sit on the couch for me, please." I ditched my shoes, jeans, boxers and a long sleeve Polo that I got at Marshall's for $15 and took a seat on the couch. I kept my blue t-shirt on. I've always been insecure about my build. I'll never take my t-shirt off in front of a woman unless I'm swimming or someone simply rips it from my body. Lori returned from the kitchen with a glass of water. She put it on an end table and dropped to her knees without a word. She immediately wrapped her lips around me. Her mouth was so wet from the cool water, and she punctuated all of the work her hand and mouth was doing with enthusiastic moans. She was just as excited to be giving as receiving. That's the kind of woman Lori was. She suddenly slipped her lips from me and looked up.

"How am I doing, Patrick?" she asked with a deadly serious gaze as she slowly stroked me. There's nothing like eye contact during a great blowjob.

"You're an *amazing* little cocksucker, Lori."

"I know I am. You're going to fuck me, right?"

"Of course I'm going to fuck you."

"Even after I make you cum real hard in my mouth?"

"I *promise* I'm going to fuck you, Lor."

"You promise?"

"I definitely promise."

"You sure, Peanut?"

"You're killing me, Lor. I want to be back inside your mouth."

"Oh, really? So how badly do you want to be back inside my little mouth..."

"That's *so* not fair. I've never had someone so fucking beautiful sucking my cock for me."

"*Do you really think I'm beautiful?*" Lori replied with a wide smile because she already knew the answer.

"You're setting yourself up for a really rough time when I fuck you from behind, Lor."

"*I can't wait, Patrick. I can't fucking wait.*"

Lori *finally* placed me back between her lips. It wasn't long before she was swallowing everything my balls were giving her. I felt like I had run a marathon afterward.

"*Did I get everything?*" the Italian sexpot asked sweetly.

"Of course, you did."

"*I should make sure, Patrick.*"

Lori wrapped her lips around me again to top off her masterpiece. These are the kinds of things that separate a real woman from a pretender. Lori left me to walk into the kitchen. She put a small table next to me, then placed a glass of water and some snacks on it. "You'll need your energy," the brunette said as she took a seat on the couch and looked at me like I was some kind of all-star. She was still wearing her knee socks. Women look so incredibly sexy when they're undressed except for one or two articles of clothing. Lori was no exception. In fact, she was a poster child for looking totally hot without being totally naked.

"It was so hot when you kept saying my name right before you came," said the beauty.

"Why *wouldn't* I say your name? You're the entire reason why I'm excited."

"Mark doesn't do that..."

"Mark's a fag, Lor."

"He is, kinda," she confessed after a sip from her glass of water. "You know what?"

"What."

"I almost kissed you one time while we were snuggling in your room."

"Why 'almost?'"

"I was about to put my lips on your neck and you got up to pee. I even remember what song was playing. It was 'Caravan' so I wanted to make my move right before 'Into the Mystic' started. I thought that would be good music for our first kiss."

"Fucking polka would have been good music for our first kiss."

"I would *not* have kissed your sweet little lips if polka music was playing, Peanut. Mood and timing is everything."

"Why didn't you want to kiss me when I came back from peeing?"

"I still wanted to. But the Devil stopped whispering into my ear telling me to do bad things."

"Does...the Devil tell you to do bad things a lot?"

"All the time."

"Really."

"M'mm."

"What's he telling you to do right now?"

"He's still whispering. I think he's telling me to start kissing you again. And for you to take your blue t-shirt off."

"I don't think the Devil cares if I'm still wearing my t-shirt."

"I do. I want to see you completely naked."

"There's not much under there, Lor."

"And like I have such a massive chest myself? I'm a B-cup. Barely."

"That's *much* different. Your body is still perfect."

She smiled and rose from her reclined position on the couch next to me. *"The Devil stopped whispering,"* she said as she straddled my body and began to lift my t-shirt over my head.

"What'd he say?"

Lori put her lips so close to my opening in my ear that all of the hair on my arms immediately stood on end. *"He told me to suck on your dick again so you can get nice and hard to fuck me,"* she purred.

"You should always do what the Devil tells you to do, Lor."

"I am."

I was already stiff as a 2x4 before Lori even wrapped her lips back around me. It wasn't long before she was straddled across my lap. There were few things in my life as exciting as watching Lori lower her 115-pound body onto me until I completely disappeared inside the warm gap between her open thighs.

"There's nothing you need to worry about, Patrick," she whispered as her finger circled my lips. *"Nothing at all."* Her pretty brown eyes were set fully aglow by the catchlights from the burning candles. She looked right through me as Ryan Adams' 'She Wants to Play Hearts' started to slowly drip from the stereo. Neither of us uttered a single word as Lori started to take what was hers. She wrapped her arms around my neck. I ran my fingers down the smooth, olive skin of her thighs before cradling them like they were a priceless treasure. I wouldn't have relinquished them

under pain of death. The only negative was that my high was starting to wear off. I looked away from Lori's eyes for a split second because her drunken sex gaze was making me feel slightly self-conscious as the intoxicants left my brain and body. *"Don't you dare look away from me,"* she whispered as she grabbed my chin between her thumb and fist.

I was about to open my mouth to apologize but she covered it with a raised finger, which I immediately took into my mouth and bit down on. I released it. Lori started to perform in earnest. She took both of her hands and slowly ran them through her long, brown hair as she stared down the man who was deep inside her little body. Just as the tension seemed almost unbearable, she curled her lower lip underneath her teeth and looked away with the shame of an innocent girl being overcome with guilt and lust. I thought my heart was going to pound out of my chest and fall onto the fucking floor. I don't think I could have been this excited, nervous, or overwhelmed if I was strapped to a seat on some flight deck somewhere and about to launch for the moon. Lori knew that she was driving me tragically out of my mind and she was getting off on every bit of it. Her hands soon gripped the back of my head and I was pulled toward her slightly parted lips. She kept me at bay as she exhaled breath after warm breath onto my face. Her breathing became quicker. Her hips moved faster. Her breaths became sighs. Her sighs turned to moans. I gripped her tender thighs like my life depended on it. *"Patrick,"* she whispered repeatedly with increasing excitement. I didn't respond. This was Lori's moment, and I didn't need to coax anything out of her. The sound of her voice while she was cumming and the feeling of her body trembling inside my arms was surreal. I'd dreamt about it thousands upon thousands of times over the course of six years, and the reality totally eclipsed the fantasy. That rarely happens. After a long kiss to my lips, Lori got up to take another drink of water.

"How do you want me next?" she asked casually between sips. "God, my entire body is still shaking...nice job, Patrick."

"You're so welcome. I want you on the floor, on all fours."

"I knew you'd say that. You've already warned me."

"You know I need to get off on your crazy body, Lor."

"Of course, you do," she replied. "Just don't hurt me too much with that big stick of yours, Stud. I always assumed you had the Irish Curse."

"You assumed wrong. Is that what's held this up for so long?"

"Oh, shut up, Peanut."

This was going to be the dirty round. The beautiful brunette smiled at me and giggled before putting herself on the carpet with her back arched, her knees far apart and her tiny little ass up in the air. I took a moment to admire the view before I dropped to the floor. Usually there's a bar, a stage and several large bouncers separating me from a naked body like Lori's. I entered her so easily. I grabbed her waist, which was so slender that my thumbs were only inches apart on her back. Few things make me feel as powerful as taking a girl from behind. It's the only time where I'll ever enjoy such dominance and control over a beautiful woman. And I did assert my dominance. Lori was aggressively spanked for teasing me during my blowjob and making me wait so long for her pussy. As my right hand loudly slapped against her olive flesh, she apologized profusely for being such a fucking bitch and not getting straight on her back for me with her legs open as soon as we met like she wanted to. She begged me to pull her hair. She moaned that she wanted me to cum inside her. Hearing Lori beg for my sperm put me right up against the edge of ecstasy. I began scanning her wonderful body for the right curve or feature to get me off. I looked at the way her beautiful brown hair fell down the smooth skin on her back. I became preoccupied with the way the black-dyed cotton of her right sock gripped the curve of her arch. I admired the way her thighs looked so taut and tight when spread apart for me. I was entering her body in a frenzy of un-caged lust. I looked straight down and watched myself fucking Lori as I prepared to explode inside her. It was that tiny little ass of hers that finally threw me over the edge again. I pushed myself deeper inside her with every release as I moaned her name. I couldn't stop repeating it. I finally removed myself from her body and collapsed on the carpet. Lori immediately cuddled up to me and put her head on my chest. Her hair was pillow soft. I felt 'safe' for the first time since I dated Kim a half-decade ago. It was a crying fucking shame.

"Are you okay, sweetheart?" she asked with mock concern.

"I'm a little winded."

"That was amazing."

"You make me that way, Lori."

"You're already *such* a lawyer, Patrick."

She gave no thought to the fact that I may have been being sincere. She lifted her head from my chest to look at me and smile. I ran my fingers through her hair until she started kissing me again. It became a very, very lengthy goodbye kiss that turned into the goodbye round as soon as I was able again. Lori pulled my body on top of her and guided me back inside for some very passionate and very desperate sex. The only words we uttered were each other's names. Neither of us made any eye contact this time. I think it would have been too much. I pushing so deep inside of her, yet we both grasped and clawed and kissed each other like it wasn't satisfying enough to be simply having sex. I think we were both looking for something to hang onto because neither of us wanted to walk away from this. If there was any possible way to take more of each other, we wanted it. But that wasn't really possible. We both knew this was goodbye forever. I was able to last long and strong for her until I felt the warmth of her feet placed on the back of my legs. For some reason, that always excites me.

"*I can feel you getting harder,*" she whispered. "*Look at me, baby.*"

Seven seconds of looking into Lori's wide, excited eyes was all it took to put me over the edge again. Everything went blank. She took my head into her hands and kissed my entire face as I emptied myself into her for the last time. After my release, I collapsed onto her shoulder until I regained my breath. When I finally recovered, I found Lori's brown eyes already filled with tears. "*You need to go,*" she whispered. It felt like a punch to the center of my chest. My stomach twisted. My incredible high was all fucking over and I'd never have access to this blessed drug ever again. I'd be left to chase the dragon for years. I still am. I'm praying that Jenna's body provides the next fantastic high.

"Do you need a ride to the airport in the morning?" I asked.

She shook her head in the negative. I couldn't bear to leave and return to the real world, but my time was up. I took myself out of her, which was painful. I hate pulling myself out of a beautiful woman. The air around your dick always feels so fucking cold afterward. And in my post-college days, I can never be sure when I might find myself back inside someone so attractive again. I got dressed and gathered my things. I tossed Lori her black sweater, which landed on top of her as she continued to lie on the floor. I wasn't sure that she was going to walk me to the door, but she rose to her feet and did. I wanted those lips one last time. I always wanted them, but it wasn't my choice and it wasn't an option. We kissed briefly before Lori burst out sobbing and pushed me toward the door. I didn't resist. I didn't ask any questions. I exited the apartment building onto the street. It had just started drizzling and the urban air smelled like dust. My car had been towed, of course. I wandered the streets in an emotional and physical daze as I searched for an ATM to get cash for the trip back to the harsh reality of my parents' lonely basement. My legs were jelly. My knees were still shaking. I felt lost and was far from home.

I found a convenience store to withdraw $20 for a cab. My request was rejected for insufficient funds. The semester was almost over, so all of my student loan and work money was used up on tuition, books, car insurance, gas, maintenance, etc. I had $13.67 until my work paycheck was deposited on Thursday at midnight. My car would be spending a couple of days in the impoundment lot. I'd have to take the bus home. And to school. And to work. That would waste a ton of time I didn't have, and I'd need to bum my bus fare from my parents. After the $2.50 withdrawal fee and the $1.00 penalty taken by my own bank, my receipt showed a balance of seventeen cents. I actually smiled. I was still carrying a 3.45 GPA as a 2L at a good law school. In only 18 months, I'd be steeping into an $80,000 job and would never see such a low bank balance *ever* again. Or so I thought. Almost five years later, nothing has changed. My own blind arrogance was part of my problem. I never believed that my own mind was capable of controlling me. I always thought it was the other way around.

I walked up to the counter and politely asked the gentlemen behind the cash register to break my $10 since bus drivers don't provide change. He refused without a purchase. I was pissed, but comforted myself with the realization that this fat, miserable fuck would never in his life be inside a woman like Lori DiDominico without paying a hell of a lot of money for it. I bought a single cherry Now 'n Later for a nickel just to break his balls before searching for a bus stop. My best option would take me up Broad Street and through some of the city's worst neighborhoods. There were only three people on the bus that night: the driver, a man who appeared to be coming home from working at a restaurant and a dirty-looking drunk sitting in the back of the bus who had already pissed, shit and vomited all over himself. He may have been dead. The stench was unbearable and there was no escape. The next scheduled bus was in over an hour's time. I covered my nose with the blue t-shirt underneath my collared Polo, which smelled like Lori's perfume. That brought me a sense of longing and comfort at the same time. I hated it.

The Vomit Bus finally arrived in Northeast Philly and I got off at the first available stop even though the walk would be longer. I was exhausted after the 25 minute walk to my parents' back door. After finally taking a much needed post-sex piss, I walked to my dresser and opened the top drawer. I placed Lori's black lace thong into my collection of other relics from the women in my past: the half-pack of peppermint Life Savers that was in my pocket when I kissed Brigit O'Brien in eighth grade; a hair scrunchie that belonged to my first, Angel Brooks; one of Kim's Gamma Phi Beta t-shirts that was never washed and smelled like her favorite perfume for years; a hair clip that my pretty friend Natalie once left at my place in Manayunk after she got piss drunk and gave me a random blowjob; and Vanessa the Annoyer's med school ID card. I closed the drawer and crashed onto the couch. I couldn't think of anything but Lori. I tossed and turned for three hours and slept straight through class the next morning.

To this day, I still can't hear 'By Your Side' without my stomach twisting into the tightest of knots while my chest empties of any sense of contentment. One of my fraternity brothers used it as his wedding song three years later, and my dateless self wanted to crawl under my table and die as soon as I heard the track's first two seconds. It instantly sucked me back in time to Valerie's apartment. I haven't heard from Lori since that night. I don't even know if she arrived safely in Seattle. I'm sure she did. I could look her up on facebook, but I really don't want to see her picture appear on my monitor even after all these years. I just wish that Lori had never told me that she was going to kiss me while we were snuggling in my bed one night. I hate to think that my entire life may have changed if I didn't get up to take a fucking piss exactly when I did.

Thursday, August 12, 2010

   6:46 p.m.

   I enter the Board Room to find Sharkey sitting on a lower bunk and looking at the cell phone in his hand with a very perplexed stare. It's very uncharacteristic of him when sober.

   "Something wrong?" I ask.

   "I just had a conversation with my 15 year-old son," he replies.

   "I didn't know you had a son, Sharkey."

   "That's the thing here. Neither did I."

   He rises from the bunk and begins to pace around the room while running his hands through his mop of salt 'n pepper hair repeatedly. "I had this girlfriend Nicole my senior year at Miami," he begins. "Not the Miami that Page failed out of in only one year, but J. Crew U in Oxford, Ohio. She was hotter than hell. Blonde hair, blue eyes, waist in, tits out...a real Midwestern princess. Her parents were *loaded*. As in tens of millions of dollars loaded. Her dad invented the fuckin' post-it note or something really common that I can't even remember now. She had this really weird fixation with giving me blowjobs after wrestling practice when I was still in my trunks. Can you imagine how bad my *balls* musta smelled?"

   "Probably not, no."

   "Anyway, she wanted me to move to Indiana near her parents in some hick town that seemed hundreds of miles from any major city. I wasn't about to do that. College was great, but I wanted to move back to civilization here on the East Coast. I couldn't ever be in a state that was essentially landlocked, either. That would freak me the fuck out. So I move back home, and two weeks later Nicole calls me and says she's pregnant. I offered to fly her out to Philly and get an apartment together. She didn't want that. I offered to move back to the Midwest somewhere. She didn't want that, either. She told me to send her a check for a grand and she would 'take care of it.' I wasn't thrilled about it, but, hey, it's not really my choice, ya know? So here, Nicole started secretly seeing another dude the month before I left because she knew I was running out of Ohio and the rest of the Midwest as soon as I grabbed my diploma. She tells him that the baby is his, yadda, yadda, yadda and keeps it. She eventually marries this guy, and both me and this dude are totally in the dark that the kid's actually *mine*. So after her third kid, Nicole gets this major post-partum depression and has a complete and total meltdown. She tells the kid and her husband that I'm really the true father. So they hire a PI, she calls me, and...shit. I have no idea what to say or think. There's a kid running around out there that's 50% of my DNA, my *own* son, and I have no idea who the fuck this kid is. I mean, he seemed real cool on the phone. He plays baseball, plays the guitar, does well in school, wants to go to Michigan for college, all this shit. He wants to meet me, but...I dunno. I'm totally freaked the *fuck* out right now. Can you imagine when this kid meets me and realizes that *I'm* his dad? Shit. So I'll definitely fly out to meet him, I guess. He's in Noblesville right now, wherever the hell that is. I just...I mean, what the *fuck*. I feel like I should be involved now and shit. It's *my* son. And there's no doubt he's mine. He texted me a picture. I mean, look."

Sharkey hands his iPhone across to me. There's no doubt that the smiling kid in his high school baseball uniform is the offspring of one Peter Sharkey. The resemblance is striking, especially the eyes.

"And then on Wednesday, this past Wednesday," Sharkey continues, "I get a text from Mallory to meet her for happy hour because her boss at work made her real upset or some shit. I didn't think anything of it. Anyway, we both wind up getting piss drunk and take a cab home from Center City. Her place is like, twelve blocks away from my mine so it's not unusual for us to wind up in a cab together when we go out drinking in the city. She musta got changed before she left work, because she's wearing this light pink skirt that barely covered the tops of her thighs. I mean...I don't even want to think about that skirt anymore. I've done that enough over the past few days. So we get to her place first, and she pays the driver and pulls me out of the cab. So I'm like, '*Okay. This is unexpected.*' But I'm piss fucking drunk, and I somehow wind up fucking the shit out of her on her living room couch. I don't know how it happened. And her pussy- that pussy, man...holy shit. She tastes like water. She's 33 and it was like going down on a 20 year-old."

"That's what Jenna was like. She's 28 and tastes 16. I guess. I never tasted a 16 year-old."

"Well, it's a little late now. Sixteen will get you twenty."

"I think I'll get over it."

"That would be my suggestion. Unless you definitely think you can't get caught. But if you think Mallory's legs look long in her clothes, naked she's just...she's just amazing. *Amazing.* I was so pasted that I probably hit it from behind for a half hour. That body of hers...shit. So what the fuck do I tell Blotto?"

"Where's this thing with Mallory going?"

"I dunno. Nowhere, I think. This has been the best and worst week of my life. I wasn't one of the 27 people laid off at work, I fucked Mallory, I have a son...didn't see that last one coming, obviously. She says she's not into this dude she's been 'kinda sorta' seeing all summer, but women always mean the total opposite of whatever they say about a guy. Come to think of it, I bet the thing with her boss was a ruse. She probably got into another fight with *that* asshole. Where it's going is irrelevant, though. The question is, what do I tell my best friend from high school now that I've fucked his obsession, whether it's just this one time or it winds up happening again? Which I doubt."

"Why doubt it?"

"Just the vibe I got. Plus, I got other things on my mind right now. Shit. I gotta call 'im."

Sharkey suddenly vacates the room, phone in hand. If I found out I had a son, I might grab a gun again. How much deeper inside a financial and emotional hole could I find myself in? I grab my guitar and work through the intricate mysteries known as the Major 7th arpeggio and harmonic minor scale while Sharkey speaks with Blotto outside. He returns about 20 minutes later.

"Well?" I ask.

"We're kinda going to have to address it later, I think."

"Why's that?"

"Baxter died."

8:26 p.m.

From: jennajenna82@junkmail.com
To: PMcShea77@junkmail.com
Subject: (no subject)

Hello Patrick,

I won't be in Angel Bay for the final few weekends because I'll be going away to the Poconos with Michael. I want to thank you sincerely because I was contacted by the IP firm you suggested and I'm interviewing next week. You were so right- it meant nothing to work at the city's 'best' law firm if I'm miserable all of the time. It was affecting the relationships with my friends, family and my boyfriend- all relationships that I placed so much effort into building only to find them being torn down by the demands of unethical, sociopathic crooks. I'm crossing my fingers that my interview next week goes well.

I really admire the way you've tried to pull yourself together after all you have been through. It's given you a completely different perspective on life that will benefit you in the end. Good luck with your new job! Maybe we'll cross paths this winter sometime.

Jenna & Princess

1:14 a.m.

I am somehow awoken from my tranquilizer-induced sleep by a frenzied phone call from Fifty-One. Dizzy has apparently gone on a very destructive cocaine binge and has locked himself inside the cabin of his boat. Fifty asks for my intervention, unaware that he is asking the blind to lead the blind out of the Valley of Darkness. I rise from the couch and throw my shorts back on and place my favorite Iowa hat on my head backwards. Sharkey is nowhere to be found and is likely at the Crow's Nest drunk out of his mind with the woman he fucked after cleaning the remnants of the port-a-potty off his body during Flotilla. I take the short walk down St. Michael's Drive solo. I can't believe that I've already been cut-off by Jenna. Fuck! I'm crushed, but there is business at hand.

I walk through the front door of Dizzy's place and head upstairs to the main living area for a report. Molly is hiding under the living room table and won't come out to greet me, although I hear her wagging tail hitting the floor as I pass.

"Hi!" says Stinky as I enter the kitchen, catching me off-guard in my haze. I didn't expect to see the very pretty blonde here.

"No work tomorrow, Stinky?"

"Nope! I could hear you snoring when I dropped my stuff off at the house. How's things with Jenna, you little sneak..."

"Eh."

"That good, huh?"

"Yeah."

"I'm sorry."

"It's not your fault, Stinky."

The exasperated Fifty-One is looking around, holding a broom with no idea where to start the chore ahead of him. Several cabinets have had their doors ripped from their hinges and their contents emptied. The silverware drawer was launched across the room. The silverware is everywhere. The drawer itself is stuck inside the far wall. The floor is covered in a thick layer of broken glass, broken plates, broken bowls, broken mugs, and spilled alcohol. Fifty-One is able to provide no explanation for what triggered this destruction. I find Dizzy's cell phone on the floor in between a broken plate with blue flowers on it and a smashed bottle of Sambuca. The screen is cracked but is still readable, and the phone is still functional despite the licorice-scented liquor dripping from it. His last text was from a woman named Sharon that simply said, *#605 receipts for last week 7715.46*. The previous is from none other than Gina, which reads *thanks 4 texting me back asshole i guess ur other sluts r more important 2 u*. I guess I dodged a bullet with that whore. The next 16 messages are from Tearsten and say 'fuck you' in at least a dozen different ways and use the word 'dickbag' a lot. There's some propositions for sex from various women whose names I don't recognize. A few texts from his mom saying, 'Call me' or 'I love you.' Four texts from a girl named Shelly requesting both different work hours and Dizzy's penis. I don't see anything here that would constitute anything more than a total annoyance at worst. Then I check his phone log. The last call was placed to Magdalena Giordano over two hours ago. The conversation lasted less than three minutes.

I walk out onto the deck and down the steps toward Dizzy's boat. I don't hear anything as I approach the dock. The cabin light is off. I peer through the window and see only the flare from a lighter illuminating Dizzy's face as he smokes from a pipe. I knock. He sits still for a few seconds, then lights the flare toward the door. He rises to walk toward me and falls over instantly. After a minute or so, his hand finally reaches up to unlock the latch. I enter to find Dizzy kneeling on the floor while bleeding profusely from the head. He manages to get upright. I'm not sure if he's aware he's bleeding, because I toss him a nearby towel and he throws it right back at me before falling into the seat behind him. "*Magdalena*," he whispers with a hoarse voice. "I called Maggie."

"And?"

"She's engaged. And she's pregnant." He slumps forward and begins to cry like a motherless child, bringing a mixture of tears and blood to the cabin floor. Even having suffered my own experiences, I have no idea what to say to a totally broken man who has been freebasing cocaine. Except 'pass the pipe,' maybe. I feel only slightly less miserable than he does but desperately try to maintain a solid front. I decide that my silence is best until so much blood is flowing all over Dizzy's head and hands that I'm afraid he'll pass out from the huge gash opened over his right eye. He suddenly becomes alive, though, rising to punch his hand straight through the cabin paneling. I keep my cool, even though a punch like that to my head could kill me instantly. Blotto personally witnessed Dizzy put up 485 at the Angel Bay Gym just last week. Four times.

"We've got to get that cut closed, Dizzy."

"What cut?"

Oh, jesus. "The one above your eye, asshole."

"*I'm* an asshole?" Dizzy says with indignation and crazy, coked-out, wild eyes. "Let me tell you who's an asshole, Woodchuck. *You* are. You and all the other dickheads who think I'm some sort of hero for putting all of these fucking coke whores and all these other reject cunts like your friend Gina on their backs every weekend. I'm fucking tired of it, man. I'm fucking *sick* of it. I'm sick of their insanity. I'm sick of their insecurity. I'm sick and fucking tired of women that think they own me or I owe them something because we spend of few hours together and they *willingly* take their clothes off for me. Only *one* woman ever owned me, and she's engaged to a fucking doctor and having his kid. And what am I doing? Selling donuts and breakfast sandwiches and fucking Kirsten Kramer. Kristen *fucking* Kramer. I have money, I have a condo, I have a boat, I have my businesses, and *none* of it means shit, man. None of it! No one ever told me things would turn out like this. I want my Maggie back. I want my *fucking* Maggie back."

Another fist goes through the cabin wall before Dizzy slumps into a seat and continues to bawl his blue eyes out. I eventually convince him that he needs medical attention, but I'm not about to call the authorities to the house. I finally get him cleaned-up and into his Mercedes, using his condition as an excuse to do 135 down the Parkway to the nearest ER.

Thursday, August 19, 2010

> "Sometimes sex just isn't worth it. I never would have said that in my twenties." -Dizzy 5/28/10

> "Just because you can sleep with somebody, doesn't mean you should."
> -Blotto 5/28/10

> "So sometimes you take a bite at the worm, even though you know that there's a hook attached." -Dizzy 6/8/10

> "Sometimes the devil you know is better than the devil you don't know, you know?" -Dizzy 6/8/10

> "Anyone who brings that cunt into this house ever again is going to be tied-up in the side yard so I can run you over repeatedly with my truck. Back and forth, back and forth, forward and reverse until your guts spray out of your mouth like a seagull on Alka-Seltzer. How could any man on this green Earth be so fucking desperate to have sex with that thing?" -Harry 8/7/10

* * *

New Message: Tearsten
8/19/10 12:14 a.m.
So ur dick friend dizzy broke up w me by text message and went to san fran by himself prob 2 see some other slut. Dickbag!!

New Message: Tearsten
8/19/10 12:16 a.m.
So what ru doing? Is anyone at ur house?

New Message: Tearsten
8/19/10 12:21 a.m.
Want company?

12:22 a.m.

Just like the questions in her conversations, Tearsten's texts apparently come in threes when she's drunk and/or annoyed. I can't believe that she actually thinks she was somehow dating Dizzy. He last fucked her on two non-consecutive weekends. I guess this constitutes a long-term relationship in her warped mind. *But that body!* I stare at the screen on my phone as I contemplate a response. I pace around the room. *Those pretty eyes on that face of hers!* I smoke a bowl. I pull on my short head of hair. I apply deodorant. I change my t-shirt for no reason. *She has a pussy.* I open my laptop and check on my bank account. I have almost $400, am still collecting, and will be working in a matter of weeks. I can afford to buy a new windshield if necessary. I need a new one, anyway. I do what I must:

Message to: Tearsten
8/19/10 12:31 a.m.
No ones here. Stop by.

New Message: Tearsten
8/19/10 12:32 a.m.
K! Be there aft i finish my drink.

1:03 a.m.

I'm relaxing on the queen stoned out of my mind. I've resigned myself to the fact that I'm going to have sex with Tearsten the Terror and, like it or not, there's going to be hell to pay for it. She's going to text me 50 times a day. I'm certainly not going to respond to more than half of them. Her ever-paranoid and insecure 'mind' is going to dissect and examine my facebook daily like it's a potential key piece of forensic evidence in a high-profile murder investigation. She's going to get absolutely fucking loaded and show up yelling and screaming for me at 728 randomly, which will enrage Harry and Blotto and everyone else that paid damn good money to throw an incredible party that Kirsten's jealousy ended 2 hours early. She's going to constantly chew my ear off in trying to justify why it was all Blotto's fault that she filed a false police report, got arrested and now potentially owes the Town of Angel Bay almost $70,000. Nothing, I've noticed over the summer, is *ever* Kirsten's fault. She never looks in the mirror. And never will, until she kills her third husband and put his balls into a Ziploc bag before hiding it in the freezer. She's a *Lifetime* special waiting to happen. Maybe then she will admit she's not normal. But probably not. Our 'relationship' couldn't last more than a few weeks, anyway, though. I wouldn't even contemplate bringing her into my parents' house *sober*. *Ever*.

I hear the sliding glass door rip open in the living room. My heart is pounding. I hear footsteps on the carpet, then the sound of high heels clapping and stumbling against the tile on the bathroom floor. The bathroom door shuts. The toilet seat is placed into the down position. It flushes about a half-minute later. The heels are clapping again. They trip. Approximately 15 seconds later, Kirsten enters the Board Room. She looks breathtaking. She's wearing a way short denim skirt and a sexy black top with matching, busy-looking five-inch heels. She lets out an earth-shattering belch. "Hi," she says with nary a smile as she throws her purse to the floor. She seats herself on the edge of the queen. "I'm *ffff*fucking drunk," she offers as if I couldn't ascertain that for myself. Kirsten knows that I'm aware she's drunk. It's just code for, *'I'm angry and ready to fuck you to get revenge on your friends Blotto and Dizzy.'* But it's not like it's legitimate 'revenge.' Neither of them will care. Otherwise,

I wouldn't even *think* of doing this. "Could you take my sssshoes off for me?" the dark-haired beauty slurs somewhat sweetly. "My fucking *fffff*feet are *killing* me."

I make my way from the bed and kneel in front of Kirsten. There's one thing my brain has finally confirmed for me this summer: despite my general aversion to feet, I am absolutely obsessed with high heels. It's the fact they strike a balance between covered and exposed female flesh that makes them so sexy, just like lingerie does. And the 5'0" Kirsten always wears the most attention-grabbing and highest heels in order to out-do all of the other insecure girls running around the Shipwreck looking for permanent love in the most temporary of settings. Tonight is no exception. It's tough as straight male to even describe these shoes, so I won't even bother. "There's a buckle above my ankle," I'm informed, as Kirsten has become impatient with my stoned stare at her heels. I take the gold buckle on the left shoe into my hands and manage to undo it. I feel a stir in my balls. Kirsten's sexy as hell, and I'm going to fuck her. The shoe now off, I remove her other heel. "Could you rub my right foot for me?" Kirsten asks with an uncharacteristically pleasant tone. "I think I have, like, stress fractures or something in it from running."

"Is that how you stay so thin?" I ask as I take Kirsten's foot into my hand and begin to massage around her right arch. I'm hard as a fucking rock.

"Do you really think I'm thin?"

"Umm...you weight like, 100 pounds Kirsten."

"I *was* 100. Now I'm, like, 109. Almost 110. Too much [burp] drinking."

"I can't tell the difference, Tear-, er, Kirsten."

"Don't *fucking* call me that, okay?"

"Call you what?"

"You know exactly what I'm talking about. What you almost just said. You guys make it seem like I go around town all crying and acting crazy all the time. If guys weren't such fucking *assholes*, then we wouldn't have any of these problems in the first place. That feels really good, by the way. You're going to have to do my left one now." I take the opportunity while rubbing her left foot to kiss the tops of her tender tanned thighs. Her skin feels so smooth the way only sun-kissed skin can. Kirsten audibly exhales. "Stand up," she commands. As I rise to my feet, she grabs the back of my head and pulls me toward her lips. I have no idea what to expect from the drunken mess. I'm not disappointed. Her lips are soft, and Kirsten is somehow the smoothest kisser I have had the pleasure of experiencing this entire summer- even moreso than the much sexier Jenna. My cock is now in overdrive. I reach under Kirsten's tiny skirt. Lace panties. Moist. I push them aside. I can feel her soft flesh getting soaking wet onto my fingers as she moans. Kirsten then burps again, this time directly into my mouth. "Sssssssorry," she slurs awkwardly. I drop back to my knees to pull Kirsten's panties from underneath her skirt. Red lace. They're small and beautiful undergarments. Kirsten wastes no time in laying her on back. She pulls up her skirt and opens her little brown legs ridiculously wide. My chest is shaking with anticipation as I approach her cunt. It's a work of art. Completely shaved. Small, pink, glistening lips. I inhale deeply. Kirsten's scent is delicious. It occurs to me I've never had a 100-pound body from behind. My brain and cock are dizzy with excitement. As my tongue begins to move between Kirsten's moist lips, she issues her loudest burp yet. She rises from the queen and vomits all over my back.

1:57 a.m.

I threw my clothes and the rest of my laundry into the washing machine and took a shower outside as Kirsten continued vomiting in the bathroom. I stood under the hot water for a long time in order to rid myself of both the stench of vomit and the further disappointment associated with my latest spectacular sexual failure. When I returned to inside the house and got dressed, Kirsten was passed out on the cold tile of the bathroom floor. I somehow scooped her into my arms and back onto the queen. Though not gifted in the strength department, I can lift 100 pounds. The Fender amplifier I used to lug around to open blues mics and up and down and up and down countless flight of stairs weighed north of 60 pounds on its own. But this was the deadest 100 pounds I've ever felt in my life. A cinder block would have seemed more forgiving than Kirsten's body as I carried it to the Board Room. And now here I lie next to her clothed, tanned, skinny, sexy body as she snores loudly enough to wake the dead. *You can fuck this girl silly and she'll never know it happened.* That's not the way I operate, though. I never have. *If not now, when, McShea? It's been 15 fucking months! FIFTEEN FUCKING MONTHS!* By choice, really. I could have grabbed an overweight girl who is a 5 on a 10 scale at the Shipwreck any weekend. I didn't. *That's right. You didn't. But beggars can't be choosers. You ain't no frat guy no more. You're not a law student with all the potential for success in the world. You're a broke, mentally ill piece of shit that lives with mommy and daddy. That's why you need to fuck Kirsten Kramer right now. That's exactly why she's here, isn't it?* She was conscious when she showed up here. *What fucking difference does it make? Your cock is throbbing and twitching. If she was awake, one text message and she'd be gone in a flash like Heather or Amanda. This is a gift! Manna from Heaven! A blind drunk, completely passed out gorgeous whore who will never know, or probably even care, that you fucked her in her sleep!* Her phone starts buzzing and playing some annoying country music ringtone by Shania Twain. It's some dude Mitch calling. *And if Kirsten was awake, she'd stop you mid-fuck and run right out to see Mitch because he's definitely hotter than you. Even his name is hotter than yours! These Angel Bay girls are bitches. Whores! Do whatever the fuck you want to her! Now!* I grab the end of her denim skirt and lift it. My pounding heart is making my entire chest shake with sexual excitement. She has *such* a pretty pussy. I just want to smell it again. I need to smell the scent of that fucking cunt! *Then fucking do it! Smell it all you want before you fuck it! Then fuck it again. And again. Don't even wear a condom. Just fucking shoot it on the floor if you need to. And she'll never fucking know. Never!* God, I know that Kirsten's pussy must feel so fucking warm inside...and she must be virgin tight with that little waist and body of hers! Fifteen fucking months without the soft, warm, wet heaven between a woman's thighs. *Fuck her. Fuck her NOW!* I rise from the queen and lock the Board Room door. I shut it behind me and walk out into the living room, where I crash on the couch and take matters into my own pathetic hands before passing out.

New Message: Heather Ball
9/02/10 10:57 p.m.
hey. ru in ab this wknd? im down 2morrow morning.

New Message: Peter Sharkey
9/02/10 11:01 p.m.
My son is so cool. I cant believe he's half my dna.
I think he smokes weed too.

New Message: Dizzy
9/02/10 11:07 p.m.
Congrats!

Message to: Dizzy
9/02/10 11:08 p.m.
For what? The dump i just took?

New Message: Dizzy
9/02/10 11:10 p.m.
U dodged another bullet man! Tony gave Amanda
herpes. Thats the only reason why she stayed w that
dickhole. What a kick in SJPs balls! Frisco was awesome
man see u soon xoxo.

New Message: Dizzy
9/02/10 11:12 p.m.
And thanks bro for ur help.
Boarding now and i am fucking drunk.

Message to: Dizzy
9/02/10 11:13 p.m.
No prob. Have a safe flight.
Leave the coke where u found it. lol

Sunday, September 5, 2010
Labor Day Weekend

> *New Message: Heather Ball*
> *9/05/10 10:57 p.m.*
> *hey where ru*

> *New Message: Heather Ball*
> *9/05/10 11:42 p.m.*
> *hello?*

> *New Message: Heather Ball*
> *9/05/10 12:39 a.m.*
> *dick*

1:26 a.m.

The last two weeks of summer have blown by like the breezes across St. Michael's Sound. I realize now that I made a huge mistake in trying to keep up with the Joneses this summer. The plan was to clear my head, hopefully meet a nice girl or two, and reduce my stress levels to the point where I could function in an office setting again. There was one giant wrench in my plan: being out of the game for so long, I was caught totally unprepared by the quality, quantity, and severity of the trainwrecks disguised as women that I'd encounter this summer. I allowed myself to get so sidetracked by some women so horrendous that I only succeeded in destroying my fragile ego and mind even further. Reduced by my mental illness and my bank account to a boy in his thirties playing a man's game, I was both naïve and stupid in taking what I perceived as Gina's advances as anything that was serious or substantial. Amanda is but a professional flirt with an incurable STD. What a fucking disaster of a disappointment that would have turned out to be. Things sometimes *really* do happen for a reason.

And Heather- I shouldn't even address that thing. She's not worth the breath into my digital voice recorder or the motion of my fingers against the black keys on my old laptop. She receives no free pass from me, even though I've learned third-hand that she never finished college because of a severe case of bulimia. I can completely empathize with her because of it- her brutalization in the schoolyard by the mouths of bullies, the destruction of her academic career because of her eating disorder, and the lingering psychological scars that may haunt her for many years more. Though my empathy is real, I will never have time for her again. There are some occasions where you simply have to maintain respect for yourself and can't turn the other cheek or give forgiveness freely- and nor should you. Every minute I think about her is time I'll never get back. That's why even my gross desperation won't allow me to respond to her. I still have a smidgen of pride left, which I consider to be an encouraging sign even though I have no reason right now to take a stand against a 5'6" blonde with blue eyes, a killer tan and a body shape that could have been constructed by a teenage megageek behind a computer screen. I'm sure she got dumped by Dino and needs a shoulder to cry upon. But I'm not out to be anyone's shoulder to cry on right now. I'm here to fuck. I'm smart enough to recognize the experience of Jenna's soft lips and soft hands a few weeks ago will do nothing to shield my ego from the further frustration of yet another rejection. I've learned twice the hard way that nothing is *ever* guaranteed with a coke whore like Heather. Only an idiot would count on the third time being the charm.

Dizzy wasn't around for any of the last two weeks. He left Molly with his mother and hopped a flight to San Fran after the cabin incident to clear his head and avoid the crazy, insecure women that flock to him in Angel Bay like hungry feral cats looking for an unsuspecting mouse to sink their desperate claws into. His timing was unfortunate, because I twice spied the wayward drunken bird- which I have now identified as a vagrant reddish egret- during my own expeditions into the marsh. Dizzy wanted to report my finding to the State but I had no photographic proof. I feel sorry for him, in a small way. He's a successful, intelligent guy who is a victim of his own looks. There's a lot of shit masquerading as women out there, and they automatically prejudge Dizzy because of his looks the same way that I'm prejudged because of mine. That's why the loss of Magdalena is so devastating to him. They couldn't get along, but he knew she was loyal and smart and truly loved him for who he was. That's incredibly hard to find, especially when they come as beautiful as Maggie is. He finally got the heart to show me her picture when he came back from his two weeks photographing the city, Napa Valley, and Big Sur. She is simply a stunning woman who is the best of South Korea and the best of Italy rolled into one beautiful-looking human being. He'd certainly be willing to accede to her demands now. But it's far too late. And it's a damn shame.

The highlight of the past two weeks- or lowlight, if you're named Alexander Page- was Stinky getting so fed-up with getting ditched by Hot Dudes all summer that she hooked-up with the one man in Angel Bay who was guaranteed *not* to dump or cheat on her aside from Page himself: the 400-pound Fifty-One. I doubt she lets him get on top. She'd die. Fifty is grinning like a schoolboy looking up his second grade classmate's skirt as they drink together. I've been told that Fifty hasn't had sex without paying for it in at least three years, his last free episode being a threesome with two cows that was guaranteed to have destroyed whatever mattress and box spring that had the misfortune to handle the event. And now he's scored with one of the prettiest, skinniest girls that I've met in a long time. It's definitely a confidence buster when you discover that you're apparently less attractive than someone who is carrying 230 additional pounds of pure fat than you are. That's what Page has to contend with right now. We all do, really. I'm jealous myself. Stinky found me unattractive the second she laid eyes on me. As much as my lack of beef puts me at a disadvantage, I have learned one thing this summer, though: there is no rhyme or reason why anyone is ever attracted to anyone else. I never in a million years thought that Jenna would find me attractive when so many other girls destroyed any confidence I had in myself. She crushed me, too, though. Page, at least, is able to drown his sorrow by pounding Mindy Miller until her next impending, unnecessary meltdown.

Sharkey spent the past week in Indiana visiting his newly-discovered son. "Cool kid," he relayed to the Board after a few bong hits this afternoon. "I signed some papers, his other dad formally adopted him, and I'm welcome- and going to-stay involved somehow. Win-win, bitches." There was no storybook ending as far as his torrid Wednesday night Philadelphia love affair with Mallory. She finally decided that she's in love with the guy she is 'kinda sorta' seeing and intends to carry their relationship into the Fall, leaving both Sharkey and Blotto with broken hearts. It was so predictable. The more a woman attempts to trivialize her feelings about a man, the more she's actually in love with him. Why it is so difficult to simply state the truth rather than provide other men with false hope via these emotional equivocations remains unclear.

I'm crowded around Danny's bar with my 728 friends for the final time this summer. Harry had thrown $500 on the bar and it's been used up rather quickly. I can't say enough good things about these guys. As hellish as my summer has been, all of them provided a welcome distraction when they rolled into town each weekend with their weed and their stories. Harry and his crew were more generous to me than they ever had to be, and I'll never forget that. Just like I'll never forget the gorgeous sunsets, playing in a band in front of 1,000 people at 728, the lingerie party, learning to kayak, an attack by an osprey, learning to identify a dozen species of birds and their habits, my relationships with Molly, Princess, and the late Baxter, or my lone date with the spectacular Jenna Love. That still stings hard, though. Really fucking hard.

As I've noted, there's one final mission to be accomplished tonight. I've saddled up to the bar next to a redhead named Deborah who is no more than a 6 at best on a 10 scale but is laughing hysterically at every word I say. It's completely endearing her to me, even though I only find her physically attractive from the tits up and she's getting a bit sloppier with each drink. There's no point in ever arguing with a drunk that she's had too much to drink, so I've asked Danny to keep the next few light in order to keep Deborah upright, coherent and semi-attractive. I've finally made peace with my stubborn self and realized that I'm not exactly a catch right now. Just as my new friend polishes off her latest Malibu Baybreeze, a gaggle of gorgeous girls approaches her at the bar. "Watch out," mutters Sharkey in my ear. "The Twat Patrol is moving in to investigate your activities." Deborah introduces me to them, and the twisted expressions on their pretty faces and half-hearted 'hellos' indicate that none of them are the least bit impressed by me. Against her will, they quickly pull the redhead away from me and rush through the packed holiday crowd. Girls can get away with pushing guys aside and spilling their drinks while on the run. I can't. The chances of me wading through the mass of thousands of drunks and finding Deborah before last call are slim. "That's such fuckin' bullshit," says Sharkey. "At least you can look 'er up on facebook later, though. Not that it will do you much good tonight. I need another beer. Who's getting on that for me?"

I'm damn disappointed. Even when a woman appeared willing, I still failed the all-important 'approval of friends' test. Now Tearsten comes storming onto the scene, fruity drink in hand. She immediately moves in toward Stinky and Fifty-One, of all people. Fifty-One is soon wearing the drink. Stinky now has to deal with closed fisted blows headed in her direction. It appears that the extraordinary has happened: two women who are each an 8 on a 10 scale are fighting over a 400-pound community college dropout whose only income is disability insurance payments because both of his knees simply gave out under his own fat fucking weight and required extensive reconstruction. Now I've truly seen *everything*. As Tearsten and Stinky are separated by the bouncers, my phone begins to vibrate through the madness:

> *New Message: Jenna Love*
> *09/06/2010 1:29 a.m.*
> *where r u*

My heart literally skips a beat. This is totally unexpected. It could have been sent in error, though. I know Jenna's not at the Shipwreck, because she'd probably be here with the rest of us since her grade school buddy Gina is chasing the recently-returned Dizzy all over the bar like a new puppy after its master. He keeps rolling his eyes at me and laughing, even though the jet lagged Dizzy will wind up tapping into his Lazy List and bringing Gina and her amazing legs home solely out of convenience. I nod at Dizzy to let him know that I'm up to something, then pull an Irish Exit and silently slip out of the bar via the doors nearby.

1:36 a.m.

Jenna's Mercedes is not parked outside 728, but getting a spot at or near the house on a holiday weekend is impossible. I first walk downstairs into the Board Room so that my now-straight self can spark before I decide to respond to Jenna's text or possibly have a run-in with her. Or, in the alternative, find myself dealing with the miserable fact that I was on Jenna's mind for some reason but the text was really meant for Michael because he is late coming home with whatever snack Jenna demanded from the grocery store in some hick town near Mt. Pocono. There's the *Falcon* and plenty of weed, but no flare to be found anywhere in the Board Room. There's nothing in the Slut Room even though they constantly burn candles in there. I can't locate the grill lighter, either. I'm not about to even attempt to use a gas stove to light a bowl, although I'm sure some idiot at some frat house somewhere has tried. I'm forced to go upstairs to the Penthouse in search of flare. I climb the wooden stairway to the upper deck and enter. Jenna Love herself is seated at the dining room table in all of her miserable glory. It's such a relief. Her hair is up, she's wearing no make-up, and her outfit is a pair of black gym shorts and a red t-shirt with a white ringer and the number 87 on it. She still looks amazing, even if she'd never allow herself to be seen in public this way. An impressive collection of empty beer cans, liquor bottles, and an empty shot glass is in front of her on the dining room table. She's apparently had better days. "Have you seen a lighter up here?" I ask casually as I walk into the kitchen to search the drawers. I can hear Princess snoring in Jenna's bedroom nearby.

"Seriously, Patrick? *Seriously?*"

"I'm deadly serious. There's no lighters downstairs."

"And what am I? Chopped liver?"

"Maybe we'll cross paths this winter sometime, Jenna."

"Get the *fuck* out here," Jenna commands as I root through the kitchen drawers for a lighter like a fiend. "Right. Now. *Patrick McShea.*" She spits out my name like it's an epithet on par with the worst that modern language has to offer. I walk back into the dining room and look at Jenna, still seated at the table and looking adorable yet pathetic. And so drunk. Piss fucking drunk.

"What's the occasion, Jenna? New job? Successful colonoscopy?"

"As a matter of fact, asssshole, I did get the IP job," she slurs. "One-hundred and thirty thousand per year, plus bonus and a cut of whatever business I bring in, *fffff*for your information."

"Congrats. And you're welcome. That's a small pay cut, though, isn't it? What might the Women in the Law committee think? You just set your gender back another forty years."

"I really don't give a fuck, Patrick," Jenna sneers as she rises from her chair and stumbles toward me.

"And why not?"

Jenna launches her arms around my shoulders and pulls me toward her. *"Because right now I just want to be held by you,"* she sniffles. I put my hands on her slim waist and take in the scent of the skin on her neck, placing my lips on it. "I couldn't *wait* to see you," she says between my kisses, "but I didn't even have the guts to text you until I got myself *fffff*fucking wasted."

"Smells like you've been very successful at that..."

"I know," she quietly replies, her voice cracking and set with a noticeably nasal tone. "I told Michael the exact story that I told you, and..."

"And what?"

"He called me a fucking *baby killer*, Patrick. Three years I've dated him and was totally understanding of his issues and-"

"He doesn't deserve you, Jenna. I do."

"I am *so* sorry for the way I-"

"Shhhhh. It's over. I don't care. You're here now. That's all that matters to me, okay?"

"Okay. I'm still sorry, though."

"I know you are. Don't tell me again."

"I'll tell you whatever the fuck I want to tell you," the manic drunk says, separating herself from me while suddenly sporting a very playful smile. She pushes me with both of her hands. I don't move. She falls backward, flat onto the floor.

"You do your own stunts now, Jenna?"

"I think I hurt my back," she says. "Help me, please."

"You're a fucking mess."

"I know."

I walk over toward the prone brunette and extend my hand to assist her from the floor. She grabs my helping hand, then takes this opportunity to kick my own legs out from under me. I tumble onto the floor next to her. She's laughing hysterically.

"You are *such* a bitch, Jenna."

"Am I?" she asks in her sex voice after rolling herself atop me. Her body feels so warm. My knees are shaking, just like they did during my one night love affair with Lori DiDominico five long years before. "I think you *love* me, Patrick."

"I think you've confused love with lust."

"Then why couldn't you look me in the eye when you said that?"

"You talk too much."

Jenna looks straight through me with her bloodshot, ice blue eyes of hers as I run my hands down her back, over her museum piece of an ass and place them onto her trim thighs. *"You're going to fuck me tonight, Patrick,"* she whispers.

"Oh, I know I am."

Jenna stares at me a few seconds longer before starting an uncontrollable, drunken giggle.

"What the *fuck* is so funny, Jenna?"

"I don't know. I'm drunk."

"Come closer."

"I'd love to."

I completely lose myself in Jenna's soft lips and wet tongue for a few minutes until the upstairs door swings open, with Peter Sharkey entering first and singing verse about the immediate need to empty his bladder. "What the *fuck* are you two ambulance chasers doing?" he asks with a chuckle as Jenna struggles and fails to rise to her feet. "Bar just closed, quitters."

Gina, who is pulling Dizzy along behind her, is absolutely appalled at the events unfolding on the carpet in front of her. "Jenna!" the bitter bitch exclaims. "What the *fuck* are you doing here? You're supposed to be in the Poconos with your boyfriend."

"I came back to see Patrick," Jenna replies calmly.

"Eww!" Gina exclaims. "Why?"

"Why don't you just go into our room and let Dizzy give you gonorrhea or something," Jenna replies, straight-faced.

"Hey!" Dizzy replies, indignant. "I resent that remark. I got that drip cleared up at *least* three weeks ago."

"You had gonorrhea?" Gina asks with alarm.

"No, you stupid bitch. Your more intelligent roommate is fucking with you, dumbass."

"Hey! I have a right to know if..."

The sound of their argument trails off as they enter the bedroom and shut the door. Sharkey has now urinated and walks through the living room on his way back downstairs to the Board Room. "She needs it in the butt, Woodchuck," he says with a laugh while exiting. A twisted smile crosses Jenna's face and she grabs the front of my shirt.

"Umm...just give me a few minutes to put on some make-up and fix my hair. Do you need me to change?"

"You look adorable in that t-shirt, Jenna."

"That's very sweet, but I want to look good for you."

"You already do."

"Just give me a few minutes, okay?" Jenna asks sweetly before planting a prolonged, alcohol-flavored kiss on my lips and disappearing down the hallway on her incredible legs. If it was at all possible, I think they've gotten even darker over the past two weeks. She opens the door to her bedroom, and the sounds of Gina yelling at Dizzy about his phone blowing up are heard. Then Jenna's own Blackberry starts vibrating and making all kinds of noises on the dining room table. Jenna is fortunately oblivious and stumbles into the bathroom with a small make-up bag and some clothes, shutting the door behind her. I walk over to the table to investigate. It's a message from Michael: *i love u jenna. i always have and u know it. im so sorry i lost my cool.* And then another: *please forgive me french fry. ur the best thing 2 ever happen 2 me.* I fumble with the phone belonging to 'french fry' while trying to respond to him with a nice 'fuck off' from 'Jenna.' I can't figure out what the hell I'm doing and I'm not even stoned. I've never held a legal job that was so important that the firm required me to have a Blackberry. The bathroom door opens. I shove the phone into my pocket and pray it doesn't go off again. Jenna walks into the room in denim shorts with a black top and her hair down with some make-up applied. She looks spectacular for being so fucking drunk. She looks spectacular by any measure. I can't believe I'm going to have sex with her. Actually, I won't believe it until I'm deep inside her.

"I liked you in your t-shirt, Jenna."

"Seriously? I got it for seven dollars at Old Navy."

"You look hot in it. You have no fucking idea."

"Fine! I'll change it."

As Jenna returns to her bathroom, I rush onto the deck and throw her Blackberry clear into the channel. *Splash!* It's music to my ears. *That* potential complication has been completely eliminated. Her Blackberry now sits in a blob of muck under at least 12 feet of water surrounded by flounder scavenging along the bottom amongst the crabs and snails. And besides, I really did like the way Jenna looked in that t-shirt. In fact, I'm going to have Jenna keep it on when I go down on her tonight. I return to the living room and pace as I await Jenna to finish changing again. I'm fighting against time here. If she suddenly gets sick or passes out...

"I'm back," Jenna announces sweetly with a smile as she re-enters the room, now wearing her adorable t-shirt again. "Umm...are you sober?" she asks. "We could drive over to the beach in Avalon to be alone."

"I'm fine to drive."

"Have you seen my phone? I swear it was on the dining room table..."

"Haven't seen it."

"I won't need it," Jenna replies. *"So are you ready for me?"* she then asks with a sly smile as she hands me the keys to her Mercedes.

"Maybe," I reply coyly before I receive a generous smooch from the most beautiful woman that I'll probably ever sleep with.

3:26 a.m.

There is nothing like having sex on the beach with a woman that makes every ounce of desire and lust in your body burn with the destructive intensity of the tens of millions of stars in the sky above. I've fully and completely succumbed to Jenna's grievous bodily charms. *"Omigod,* you are *so* fucking deep inside me," she cries out in a voice set with awe and wonder as I *slowly* penetrate her beautiful body inch by soft, wet inch under the nearly-full moon. Her wonderful olive legs are exactly where they belong, which is firmly upon my shoulders as I look down to watch myself sink inside her. "I *love* watching you go inside me, Patrick," Jenna moans as the nearby surf crashes onto the sand. She's the most potent drug on this planet right now and the rush is like nothing that even the most fertile, perverted mind could ever imagine. I could never have visualized the way Jenna's eyes *really* look when a man is deep, deep inside of her. "I need you to *really* fuck me, sweetie," she suddenly commands in her confident bitch voice. I'm dizzy for her.

"Is that what you want, you little whore, you?"

"That's what your little whore wants. And you better fucking give it to her, Patrick. You better *fucking* give it to me. *Omigod, just like that. Don't fucking stop. Don't you dare stop, you fucking bastard!"*

"You've been such a fucking *bitch* this summer, Jenna."

"Then fuck me harder! My legs are open *so* wide for you, Patrick. This is your chance to take me like a man!"

"You're so *fucking* wet for me."

"Then just fucking *pound* me like you mean it."

I'm thrusting like a madman at this point. I close my eyes and silently thank Jenna for the amazing blowjob ten minutes ago that's allowing me to keep up this pace without shorting out or having to rely on thinking about baseball or wrinkled old ladies.

"I can feel your fucking *balls* slapping against me, Patrick," Jenna moans with delight and intoxicating feminine lust. "Omigod it feels like I'm cumming every time you thrust! I'm such a fucking *slut*, aren't I?"

"You *are* a slut, Jenna."

"*Look at me, Patrick.*"

I look up into Jenna's ice blue eyes and incredible smile. Her long hair is falling all over the blanket. She looks so fucking happy to be getting drilled by me. And she's so beautiful, to boot.

"You're *so* fucking handsome, Patrick."

"You're the hottest girl that's ever taken my cock, Jenna."

"Oh, am I?"

"Yeah, ya are."

"Prove it, baby! I want you to feel you cum inside me."

"Is that what you want, Jenna?"

"Yeah, that's what I want. I want you to fill me up with your cum and make my pussy even wetter for you."

"Omigod, Jenna. You dirty girl, you."

"I can feel you getting harder inside me. You want to cum inside this tight little pussy, don't you? I told you it was gonna be tight for you!"

"It's going right in your *cunt*, baby."

"Omigod! Just cum in my cunt, Patrick. Cum inside my fucking cunt for me."

"I'm *so* fucking close, Jenna."

"You fucking better be. That's why I have my legs spread so wide open for you, you bastard!"

"I *love* hearing you talk to me that way."

"Say my name, baby."

"*Jenna.*"

"Louder."

"Jenna!"

"Ugh! You can do *so* much better, sweetie."

"Jenna! Jenna! Jenna!"

"That's it! Who's giving you this pussy tonight, huh?"

"You are, Jenna! Omigod, I'm gonna cum!"

"That's it, honey. Cum inside your Jenna! Cum inside your Jenna *now*."

I close my eyes in ecstasy as the first release from my raised balls enters Jenna's body.

"Keep your eyes open, dammit!" Jenna commands. I look right into her wild eyes as the rest of my seed spills inside her. She echoes every masculine groan of release with a frenzied moan of her own while maintaining her wide, sexy, gorgeous smile. It's the most amazing, intense release and further words can only fail. Once finished, I push her legs from my shoulders and collapse onto her body to regain my breath.

"That was quite a workout for you, wasn't it, Patrick?" Jenna says with a laugh. I'm unable to respond. "I feel *so* comfortable with you," the brunette says as she runs her fingernails down my back. "I wonder why that is?"

"Because you're fucking wasted."

"Aside from that, genius. And you're not even stoned, are you?"

"Only by you, baby."

"That's kinda scary..."

"There's no reason for us to feel self-conscious or hold anything back from each other. There's absolutely no secrets between us. We've already spilled everything that we would ever want to hide from each other. "

"Hmmm...I never looked at it that way. You're probably right."

"I know I'm right. Did I hear you say the c-word?"

"I've *never* done that before," Jenna claims.

"Sure."

"Don't you *dare* question me, you little bastard. Especially after I let you cum inside me."

"Thank you, Jenna."

"You were *so* fucking excited for me. I couldn't be selfish and interrupt your ecstasy like that. I think I might have cum myself if you had lasted a bit longer."

"It wouldn't have been a problem if you weren't so good-looking."

"I'm not complaining. You have *no* idea how badly I need that. You would have been the first to get me off that way, anyway. I need to be on top, but I don't want you to take it out yet."

"I don't need to. Roll over toward your left."

"Okay," says the brunette before promptly rolling toward her right.

"Your *other* left, Jenna."

"Omigod, I'm so sorry."

"You're such a rookie."

"You should be *grateful* for that, Patrick."

"Eh."

"Oh, fuck you," the stunner giggles. She loves saying that to me. Jenna corrects her direction and she's now successfully on top without having me experience the disappointment of leaving her warm wetness for a single second. Jenna's soft, brown hair falls all over me while she pins my hands down atop the blanket, locking her fingers tightly into my own. *"I can already feel you getting harder inside me, Patrick,"* she whispers with her warm breath as she begins her slow, rhythmic ride that takes every inch of my manhood inside of her. I look down to watch my stiffened flesh enter Jenna's wonderfully dark body, sensitive as it is right now. *"You can't believe you're fucking me, can you?"* Jenna asks in her amazing sex voice,

"I wanted your pussy as soon as I met you."

"Well, you got it. And you can do whatever the fuck you want to it."

"You'll regret saying that, Beautiful."

"Never," Jenna whispers between moans. *"I wanted to suck your dick the second I saw you.* Until you opened your mouth..."

"We can't all be perfect, Jenna."

I brush aside the hair covering her left ear and whisper every dirty thought I have to her until Jenna orgasms fiercely. She takes a few minutes to recover in my arms while I look up at the thousands upon thousands of stars in the Avalon night sky. I don't feel insignificant, but it's an experience that's certainly surreal. Nothing in the entire universe above- every brilliant supernova, every planet, and every burning ball of fire in every spiral of every single galaxy- could be more important than having a post-orgasmic Jenna Love naked on this beach with me right now.

4:34 a.m.

[my god miss love u look so sexy on all fours like the whore that u want 2 be 4 me. im pounding that pussy jenna. ur in 4 a good long dirty fuck after u so expertly drained my balls three fucking times over the past two hours. i love hearing the *slap slap slap* of our bodies colliding with each other as i watch my ever-stiff cock penetrate your perfectly pretty pink cunt. even under the moonlight i can see the pinkish skin of your heavenly opening stretching as i slide in and out and in and out of your beautiful dizzying body. *pull my hair* u moan. i couldnt wait 2 pull ur hair u little bitch u. i just feel so fucking powerful right now watching my cock completely kill ur tight little cunt. i grab that beautiful brown hair of yours and yank it backward. *omigod* u scream for the thousandth time 2night. *i fucking love having my hair pulled. more! i want more!* u'll get more u dirty little cunt u. ur no longer *a* bitch. ur *my* bitch bent over on all fours and moaning my name. but that body jenna! u fucking own me with that body of urs and it would be the ultimate lie 4 me to think otherwise. those legs of urs jenna! those fucking thin toned ever-darkening legs are a grade school dream come to life. ur beautiful calves look so tight spread out alongside my knees as i pound u. i cant stop staring at them. my dirty balls quiver with excitement as i admire ur smooth dark olive flesh. *spank me!* is ur latest order. ive been *dying* to spank u jenna. im just afraid i might kill u. its not just jenna the bitch that im going to spank tonight. u will pay 4 donna and gina and all of the other italian secretaries and file clerks with amazing skin and bodies that refused to give me the pleasure of admiring them because they did not see me as a real man. *smack!* is the sound as my hand strikes the tanned flesh of ur right cheek. *omigod not so hard patrick! jesus christ!* i issue no apology. i take a little off the next blow. *oh just like that!* jenna says excitedly. *ive been such a bad girl all night patrick!* u *are* a bad girl jenna. and i love it. u know not the depth of the pure lust that resides in the balls and brain of a man nor the pain that comes with each unrequited advance to satisfy all of our dirty inner demons and desires. and ive desired a body like urs since the first hair appeared on my balls. kim? my god that was so long ago. but now i have u jenna. that back of urs is amazing. inch after inch of unblemished olive flesh with perfect proportions and the most wonderful feminine curves where it meets ur hips. thats where my hands firmly grab hold of ur body and grasp for my dear life. my balls were fucking dead jenna until you revived them this summer. and u have no fucking idea do u? *slap!* another spank to ur small target of an ass. a perfect ass. i wanted 2 attack ur body the second i saw u sunbathing in that crazy pink bikini of urs jenna love. but ur a woman. u could never understand the depths of the male sexual depravity and biological desire twisted into out dna without our consent. its a bitch to live as a regular guy until times like these which could never occur often enough. but right now i am in jenna overload. the way ur beautiful soft hair falls down ur back is driving me crazy. it makes u look so feminine and puts my balls into overdrive. ur 100% woman from the sand-covered arches of your feet up ur calves to ur thighs to ur ass and back and hair and neck and gorgeous face and eyes. u turn ur head and flash me those blue eyes as u watch me fucking u. my balls stir with unparalleled excitement. *ur pounding me baby* u squeal. that's right jenna. and im not stopping until i cum inside u again. *how does my pussy feel sweetie?* it feels amazing just like the rest of ur body feels in my hands and fingers and mouth. *oh god patrick pound me till u cum again.* i plan 2 jenna. ur mouth is making sounds that id never thought id hear from u as i fuck u with reckless abandon. *say the magic words jenna* i command with a *smack! cum in my cunt baby* u moan. *just fucking cum inside it patrick before u split me in half! my god!* my only desire is to cum in that wet pussy again. i look down at ur body as i destroy it. ive been *dying* 2 get off on u this way jenna. its ur legs and ur voice that will finally push me through to ecstasy. *cum in my cunt u* bastard u call out as i admire those incredible calves and feet of urs. the way ur arch curves right now is driving me wild. and ur tan is so deep and dark and sexy in ways that u could never appreciate. my balls are stirring jenna. whatever little of my seed that has not been drained into u is going to be there in less than a minute. *omigod jenna ur driving me fucking crazy.* her moans and squeals become louder and higher in pitch. *please cum in my cunt patrick! please! my pussy cant take it any longer!* i look down at those olive calves again. i can't take it any longer either jenna. ur 2 sexy for me to ever find the words to describe it. that smooth olive flesh on ur legs is going to make my balls explode like u could never appreciate. *jenna! jenna! jenna! JENNA! JENNA! its going right in ur cunt baby.* u beg for my cum jenna like u should. *omigod ur so fucking hard patrick.* thats because im completely fixated on ur perfect legs jenna. i cant last any fucking longer. my demon releases from my balls as i stare down ur left calf and its wonderful shape and fleshtones. i push deeper inside u with every groan. i am in awe of ur cunt and body jenna. no matter how confidently or manly i give u my throbbing stiff cock u will always fucking own me]

    5:47 a.m.

    Daybreak.

    The fiery pre-dawn sky awaits the final sunrise of the summer. The clouds are alight with yellows and oranges and purples pasted clear across the sky as far as the eye can see. Jenna and I sit silently on the blanket as I scratch her back through her red Old Navy t-shirt. The rest of her outfit right now consists only of a small pair of black lace panties. I still can't take my eyes from her legs. I decide that silence is best as we await the appearance of the sun. These endorphin-filled, post-sex, post-orgasmic moments are when the most damning admissions are made and the sweetest lies are told. My guard is up. I'm not making any admissions to Jenna about the depth of my lust or the fact that I'm now completely hooked on her. I don't want to hear any lies or promises from Jenna. I just want to enjoy a moment in my life that simply does not happen often enough. I wish I could put the perfection of this episode into a bottle and save it, but I know that is impossible. I will feel a pang of longing in the pit of my stomach for years when I think back to this very time, when Jenna will probably be just another in a long line of failed memories with no one to adequately replace her intelligence and beauty and our off-the-charts sexual chemistry. Jenna turns to face me, then her eyes turn back toward the water and sky without saying a word. I guess neither of us is comfortable breaking the silence in this delicate moment.

    "I'm cold," Jenna finally says before retrieving her denim shorts. Now fully dressed again, she sits herself in front of me. I wrap my arms around her body and softly kiss her neck. "You're *so* affectionate, Patrick," she says with an approving tone. "It's so nice to be with someone who is equal parts manly and sweet."

"By 'manly,' do you mean dirty?"

"Yes, that's *exactly* what I mean," she replies with a laugh. "It's so peaceful right now. But I'm going to be sore for days after the way you treated me like a whore tonight."

"I'm not offering any apologies."

"Don't. It's a *good* sore. Tonight was amazing. And you should know that." She leans back to kiss my lips again. And again. And again. The sun finally rises over the horizon. We gather our blanket as the joggers appear on the shoreline and the fishermen begin to line the nearby jetty. "You're driving," Jenna informs me, which makes me happy because I feel like a rock star driving that machine. We walk across the sand onto Eighth Street and begin a quiet ride back to Angel Bay.

6:34 a.m.

Dizzy is exiting 728 as we arrive home. "Perfect conditions," he says as he sneaks off the property. "Low tide is 6:36. I'm already running late! Man, is Gina gonna be *pissed*. I guess you're sitting this one out?"

"Yes," Jenna replies on my behalf. "Patrick has snuggle duty right now."

"Congratulations to you two. What are you going to name the kids?"

"Hopefully we made one tonight," I reply. "Then I can divorce 'er in five years and take half."

"*Please*, Patrick," Jenna responds with a roll of her eyes.

"By the way," says Dizzy, "some redhead stopped by looking for you, Woodchuck. I forget the name."

"It doesn't matter," I reply.

"So there's a redhead now, huh?" Jenna says in her bitch voice. Before I can even stammer a reply, she starts laughing and plants a kiss on my cheek while grabbing my hands into hers. It's such a rush. Jenna already knows *exactly* where she stands with me. We separate so that Dizzy can give her a hug and bid her goodbye for the summer. "I'm sure you'll see us in the city," Jenna says to him. Dizzy almost smothers me to death with a bearhug before bidding 'us' farewell. Jenna and I make the climb up the steps toward the Penthouse. I allow her to go first just so I can view the body that I just fucked silly. She must know this, because she turns and shoots me a disapproving glance before she starts to giggle. We raid the fridge and counters for water and munchies before retiring to bed. Gina is livid that Dizzy has fucked her and left her bed already. She is rushing around packing her bags in a huff. "Go back to bed, Gina," Jenna suggests. "Dizzy will be back in a couple of hours."

"I going to stick that fucking camera of his up his *ass* the next time I see that fucking dick. Snowy egrets? You've *got* to be fucking *kidding* me."

Jenna shakes her head and removes her shorts before we jump into bed together. Gina gathers more of her shit and makes a trip to the bathroom. "You have *no* idea how badly I needed you tonight," Jenna says as she cuddles up to me and places her head on my chest.

"It was mutual."

"I don't know about that..."

"You can believe whatever you want to believe, Jenna."

"Well, I guess there's only one thing left for me to say to you, Patrick."

"What's that?"

"*Goodnight*," she whispers with a kiss.

Epilogue

Jenna and I remained hot 'n heavy after Labor Day. Her typical work week dropped from 70-80 hours to 55 overnight with her new job, and she had so much free time that she didn't even know what to do with herself. I was always kicked out of work by 6 p.m. to avoid federal overtime rules for contract employees, so Jenna gave me a key to her modern, spacious Center City condo that she stole for $285,000 at auction once the economy really tanked. It was only a few blocks from where I was working, so I would walk over to her place 2-3 nights a week to get dinner and a hot bath ready for her before she arrived home around 7:45 each night. She was always so warm, affectionate and appreciative once we were dating. She complimented me endlessly. We couldn't keep our hands off each other. Spending time with Jenna was the best therapy I could have asked for. Her company aside, it was so relaxing being at her place with the giant panoramic windows overlooking the Philadelphia skyline instead of being in my parents' cold, cramped basement. On Saturday afternoons, we would go to an early dinner or a movie before spending hours and hours having the most intense, passionate, and dirty sex that I had experienced since college. There was *nothing* that I found unattractive about Jenna physically, and we became very close very quickly both in and out of her bedroom. We would wake up on some mornings and couldn't believe what we had done to each other the night before. With only the lights from the nearby skyscrapers cutting through the darkness, Jenna would sometimes have me chase her around the place naked until I caught her for an episode of very rough sex on the couch, on the floor, or up against the windows looking out onto Center City. She only weighed 119 pounds, and to my own surprise I did begin lifting weights in the privacy of my parents' basement once the summer ended. I could push Jenna around like a ragdoll when I really wanted to.

By the beginning of October, I got the elusive 'safe' feeling whenever Jenna and I would be snuggling on the couch with Princess while watching a movie or the Phillies' latest run toward the World Series. We would talk for hours and hours about absolutely anything and everything when I wasn't inside her. I didn't even mind talking about her job and I'd review her motions and briefs with my neutral eye when she asked, even though I admit to some pains of jealousy ripping through my gut when I realized how interesting and sophisticated some of the litigation with which she was involved actually was. There was a time when I really *wanted* to be a lawyer, even if that desire has finally and fully begun to pass. Seeing Jenna's direct deposit stubs lying around her room didn't help things, either, but I was a good soldier. Jenna earned the right to that job and that paycheck. And after all, I had fallen stone in love with her. I was powerless to stop it. I first realized this when we went food shopping together one Saturday night because she was cooking dinner at her place for her family on Sunday. I normally hate food shopping. It's up there with going to the dentist and getting my car inspected. But I walked and laughed and pranced around those supermarket aisles like I didn't have a care in the world. Because I didn't. I was with Jenna. That alone made me happier than anything on Earth. It was scary, though, to fall for a woman so far out of your league. The countdown is always on until your eventual demise. Her parents and brother loved me that Sunday night. Jenna's bro, a massive tattoo-covered man, might be one of the coolest guys I've ever met. He referred to Michael as 'Maggot' the two times he was mentioned during dinner. Jenna was exhausted after cooking all day, so I loaded the dishwasher and gave her a massage before we passed out for work the next morning.

The following Wednesday night while I was sitting on the couch eating take out with Jenna, she unexpectedly said while chewing a mouthful of lo mien that she loved me. That struck me as particularly powerful. We weren't in the heat of passion or having any kind of moment together when she made her declaration. It made it all the more sincere. I calmly responded in kind and was able to resist the urge to dance around her condo in celebration like a complete idiot.

Though my mother has filled my head with all kinds of misinformation through the years, she was correct when she maintained that, *'When things seem too good to be true, they always are.'* Only three weeks later, Jenna suddenly became very cold and distant. She wasn't returning my calls or texts promptly like she always would, and our conversations were unusually terse. She was "working" quite late every night. I finally got the call which I had been dreading. We needed to talk, she said. I had a gigantic lump in my throat as I drove down I-95 on a cold December night to be formally kicked to the curb. Jenna answered the door looking smashing with Princess eagerly sniffing around next to her. My knees buckled when I saw the massive engagement ring on her left hand.

"Michael finally came to his senses, huh?" was the only thing I could say.

"M'mm," was Jenna's only reply. Her eyes started to fill with tears. I have no idea why. I'm the one that should have been crying. I wanted to tell her that I loved her one last time, but Jenna started sobbing. I declined to address her cruelty by making things even more dramatic. I handed over the key to her condo, pet the panting Princess for the final time and walked away. My only memento of Jenna, aside from some candid photographs taken by Dizzy during the course of the summer, is her red ringer t-shirt that I quietly stole from her drawer one night and added to my collection of relics from fish stories past.

The following day, a senior and junior associate at the firm for which I was reviewing documents called a meeting with the team for an update on the status of the litigation. The junior associate at the meeting was my law school nemesis Pear Butt. Within 30 minutes of the meeting's close, I received a call from the staffing agency informing me I was terminated effective immediately due to an unspecified "attorney complaint." No further services would be provided on my behalf. I drove straight to Dr. Karlis' office because I knew that my next step was off the Ben Franklin Bridge. Medication can do wonders for your mind, but it can't pay your bills, find you a good job, or bring back the top-shelf pussy you just lost to a man that won't even have sex with it. The good doctor managed to calm me somewhat and prescribed me more powerful anti-anxiety medication so that I could focus on my fifth job search in three years. It was important that I stayed focused. I would be completely out of funds within 60 days. When I returned to my parents' house with the news, my Irish Catholic father gave me a hug and cried.

Dizzy called me that weekend and managed to completely turn my life around. He introduced me to an incredible woman named Shannon that had suddenly become available and desperately needed someone. It was truly love at first sight all over again. She had these big, incredibly soulful brown eyes that made my heart melt instantly. Her coat was a shaggy gray and white tuxedo, her paws were furry, her ears were floppy, and she was incredibly obedient and affectionate. Like Molly, she was a herding dog. The particular breed was a bearded collie, and she was very low maintenance.

My father was a dog person, but my mother had always forbid having a dog in the house. She thought that they were dirty, wild creatures and there was no debating the issue. Dad suggested that I bring the non-drooling, non-shedding dog home to see if we could persuade my mother to make Shannon a part of our family. My mother leapt out of her chair in horror as soon as the shaggy thing entered the house with her tail a-wagging. She said that the dog looked like a walking bathroom rug. Shannon approached to sniff her, and Mom was instantly smitten by her human-looking eyes. Now that I have this wonderful presence in my life, I have no idea how I ever lived without my own canine companion. Shannon loves listening to my guitar playing. Whenever I have the instrument in my hand, she'll lie on the floor near my feet and look up at me as I strum and pick through whatever song or scale exercise that strikes me at the moment. But like most women, Shannon has little tolerance for my cell phone going off in her presence. Whenever I interrupt my petting to return a text, she immediately uses a paw to knock the phone out of my hand so that I may resume my duty. It's a small price to pay for the company. When she climbs onto the couch with me at night and puts her big head on my chest or gives me kisses each morning, I don't have a care in the world. If only the company of a woman could be as wonderful and certain as life with a loyal dog. There's nothing like true love to fill a desperate, wayward soul with hope.

ABOUT THE AUTHOR

Kenner R. McQuaid was born in Abington, Pennsylvania to Irish Catholic parents and raised in Philadelphia from the age of three days. He earned a B.A. from Rutgers University in New Brunswick, NJ and attended law school in Philadelphia. He practiced there for six years, losing two jobs due to major clinical depression. No longer practicing law full-time, Mr. McQuaid divides his time between Philadelphia and Cape May County, NJ.

Made in the USA
Lexington, KY
02 May 2011